SEEING
A LARGE CAT

SEEING
A LARGE CAT

ELIZABETH PETERS

G.K. Hall & Co. • **Chivers Press**
Thorndike, Maine USA   Bath, England

This Large Print edition is published by G.K. Hall & Co., USA and by Chivers Press, England.

Published in 1997 in the U.S. by arrangement with Warner Books, Inc.

Published in 1998 in the U.K. by arrangement with the author's agent.

U.S.   Hardcover   0-7838-8211-4   (Mystery Collection Edition)
U.K.   Hardcover   0-7540-1058-9   (Windsor Large Print)
U.K.   Softcover   0-7540-2045-2   (Paragon Large Print)

The text of this Large Print edition is unabridged.
Other aspects of the book may vary from the original edition.

Set in 16 pt. Plantin by Al Chase.

Printed in the United States on permanent paper.

British Library Cataloguing in Publication Data available

Library of Congress Cataloging in Publication Data
Peters, Elizabeth.
    Seeing a large cat : volume nine of the journals of Amelia
Peabody / Elizabeth Peters.
       p. cm.
    ISBN 0-7838-8211-4 (lg. print : hc : alk. paper)
    1. Large type books. I. Title.
[PS3563.E747S43   1997b]
813'.54—dc21   97-14525

To the M.C. and his chief lieutenant,
wherever they (or he?) may be

Acknowledgments

Those readers who are planning to visit the Valley of the Kings in the near future should not bother looking for tomb Twenty-A. Its location has been lost, and I have been unable to persuade any of my Egyptological colleagues to search for it. Even Dr. Donald Ryan, who recently re-excavated numbers Twenty-one and Sixty, among other neglected tombs in the Valley, was strangely resistant to the idea. However, I would like to express my appreciation for his advice and assistance in innumerable other matters.

Dennis Forbes, editor of *KMT*, graciously allowed me to read the galleys of his forthcoming book, *Tombs, Treasures, Mummies*, which will deal with seven of the most exciting finds made in the Valley of the Kings. George Johnson supplied innumerable photographs and hard-to-find reference books. I am indebted to the Wilbour Library of the Brooklyn Museum for copies of other out-of-print books, and to Dr. Raymond Johnson, Director of the Epigraphic Survey of the Oriental Institute, for suggestions as to how to commit deadly assault in the Luxor Temple. I have coolly ignored all this excellent advice when it didn't fit the plot.

Foreword

The Editor is pleased to announce to the world of literary scholarship that there has recently come to light a new collection of Emerson Papers. Unlike Mrs. Emerson's journals, they do not present a connected narrative, but are a motley lot, including letters, fragments of journal entries by persons as yet unidentified, and bits and pieces of manuscript ditto.

It is hoped (by some) that a further search of the mouldering old mansion from which this collection derived may yield additional material, including the missing volumes of Mrs. Emerson's journals. Be that as it may, the present Editor expects to be fully occupied for years to come in sorting, collating, attributing, and producing the definitive commentary on these intriguing fragments. The relevance of many to Mrs. Emerson's journals is at present questionable; it will require intensive textual analysis and travel to faraway places to determine their chronological place in the saga. However, certain sections of what the Editor has designated "Manuscript H" seem to fit into the sequence of the present volume. She is pleased to offer them here.

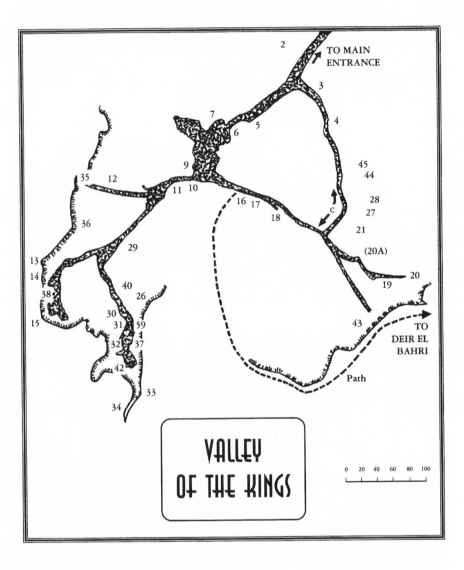

2

TO MAIN
ENTRANCE

3

7

4

6   5

45
44

9

35   12

28
27

11   10

16   17

18

C

36

21

29

(20A)

13

14

40

26

20

38

19

30

15

31   59

43

TO
DEIR EL
BAHRI

32

37

42

Path

34

33

VALLEY
OF THE KINGS

0   20   40   60   80   100

CHAPTER ONE

Husbands do not care to be contradicted.
Indeed, I do not know anyone who does.

"Really," I said, "Cairo is becoming overrun with tourists these days — and many of them no better than they should be! I am sorry to see so fine a hotel as Shepheard's allowing those male persons to hang about the entrance making eyes at the lady guests. Their behavior is absolutely scandalous."

My husband removed his pipe from his mouth. "The behavior of the dragomen or that of the lady guests? After all, Amelia, this is the twentieth century, and I have often heard you disparage the rigid code of morality insisted upon by Her late Majesty."

"The century is only three years old, Emerson. I have always been a firm believer in equal rights of all kinds, but some of them are of the sort that should only be pursued in private."

We were having tea on the famous terrace of Shepheard's Hotel. The bright November sunlight was only slightly dimmed by the clouds of dust thrown up by the wheels of vehicles and the hooves of donkeys and camels passing along Shari'a Kamel. A pair of giant Montenegrin doormen uniformed in scarlet and white, with pistols thrust through their sashes, were only moderately successful in protecting approaching guests from the importunities of the sellers of flywhisks, fake scarabs, postal cards, flowers, and figs — and from the dragomen.

Independent tourists often hired one of these individuals to make their travel arrangements and supervise their servants. All of them spoke one or more European languages — after a fashion — and they took great pride in their appearance. Elegant galabeeyahs and intricately wound turbans, or becoming headcloths of the sort worn by the Beduin, gave them a romantic look that could not but appeal to foreign visitors — especially, from what I had heard, female visitors.

I watched a couple descend from their carriage and approach the stairs. They could only be English; the gentleman sported a monocle and a gold-headed cane, with which he swiped irritably at the ragged merchants crowding around him. The lady's lips were pursed and her nose was high in the air, but as she passed one of the dragomen she gave him a quick glance from under the brim of her flower-trimmed hat and nodded emphatically. He raised his fingers to his bearded lips and smiled at her. It was clear to me, if not to the lady's oblivious husband, that an assignation had been made or confirmed.

"One can hardly blame the ladies for preferring

a muscular, well-set-up chap like that one to your average English husband," said Emerson, who had also observed this exchange. "That fellow has all the animation of a walking obelisk. Imagine what he is like in —"

"Emerson!" I exclaimed.

Emerson gave me a broad, unrepentant grin and a look that reminded me — if any reminder had been required — that he is not an average English husband in that or in any other way. Emerson excels in his chosen profession of Egyptology as in his role of devoted spouse. To my fond eyes he looked exactly as he had looked on that long past day when I encountered him in a tomb at Amarna — thick dark hair, blazing blue eyes, a frame as muscular and imposing as that of the dragoman — except for the beard he had eschewed at my request. Its removal had revealed Emerson's strong chin and the dimple or cleft in that chin: a feature that gives his handsome countenance additional distinction. His smile and his intense azure gaze softened me as they always do; but the subject was not one I wished him to pursue in the presence of our adopted daughter (even if I had introduced it myself).

"She has good taste, Aunt Amelia," Nefret said. "He is the best looking of the lot, don't you think?"

When I looked at her I found myself in some sympathy with the horrid Muslim custom of swathing females from head to toe in black veils. She was a remarkably beautiful girl, with red-gold hair and eyes the color of forget-me-nots. I could have dealt with the inevitable consequences of her looks if she had been a properly brought up young English girl, but she had spent the first thirteen years of her life in a remote oasis in the Nubian desert, where she had, not surprisingly, acquired some peculiar notions. We had rescued her and restored her to her inheritance,* and she was dear to us as any daughter. I would not have objected to her peculiar notions quite so much if she had not expressed them so publicly!

"Yes," she went on musingly, "one can understand the appeal of those fellows, so dashing and romantic in their robes and turbans — especially to proper, well-behaved ladies who have led proper, boring lives."

Emerson seldom listens to anything unconnected with Egyptology, his profession and his major passion. However, certain experiences of the past few years had taught him he had better take notice of what Nefret said.

"Romantic be damned," he grunted, taking the pipe from his mouth. "They are only interested in the money and — er — other favors given them by those fool females. You have better sense than to be interested in such people, Nefret. I trust you have not found your life proper and boring?"

"With you and Aunt Amelia?" She laughed, throwing up her arms and lifting her face to the

*The Last Camel Died at Noon

sun in a burst of exuberance. "It has been won-derful! Excavating in Egypt every winter, learning new things, always in the company of those dear-est to me — you and Aunt Amelia, Ramses and David, and the cat Bastet and —"

"Where the devil is he?" Emerson took out his watch and examined it, scowling. "He ought to have been here two hours ago."

He was referring, not to the cat Bastet, but to our son, Ramses, whom we had not seen for six months. At the end of the previous year's exca-vation season, I had finally yielded to the entreat-ies of our friend Sheikh Mohammed. "Let him come to me," the innocent old man had insisted. "I will teach him to ride and shoot and become a leader of men."

The agenda struck me as somewhat unusual, and in the case of Ramses, alarming. Ramses would reach his sixteenth birthday that summer and was, by Muslim standards, a grown man. Those standards, I hardly need say, were not mine. Raising Ramses had converted me to a belief in guardian angels; only supernatural in-tervention could explain how he had got to his present age without killing himself or being mur-dered by one of the innumerable people he had offended. In my opinion what he required was to be civilized, not encouraged to develop un-civilized skills at which he was already only too adept. As for the idea of Ramses leading others to follow in his footsteps . . . My mind reeled.

However, my objections were overruled by

Ramses and his father. My only consolation was that Ramses's friend David was to accompany him. I hoped that this Egyptian lad, who had been virtually adopted by Emerson's younger brother and his wife, would be able to prevent Ramses from killing himself or wrecking the camp.

The most surprising thing of all was that I rather missed the little chap. At first I enjoyed the peace and quiet, but after a while it became boring. No muffled explosions from Ramses's room, no screams from new housemaids who had happened upon one of his mummified mice, no visits from enraged neighbors complaining that Ramses had ruined their hunting by making off with the fox, no arguments with Nefret. . . .

Two men pushed through the crowd and approached the terrace. They were both tall and broad-shouldered, but there the resemblance ended. One was a nice-looking young gentleman wearing a well-cut tweed suit and carrying a walking stick. He had obviously been in Egypt for some time, since his face was tanned to a handsome walnut brown. His companion wore robes of snowy white and a Beduin headdress that shadowed features of typical Arab form — heavy dark brows, a prominent hawklike nose, and thin lips framed by a rakish black mustache.

One of the giant guards stepped forward as if to question them. A gesture from the Arab made him step back, staring, and the two men proceeded to mount the stairs.

14

"Well!" I exclaimed. "I don't know what Shepheard's is coming to. They ought not let the dragomen —"

But my sentence was never completed. With a scream of delight Nefret jumped up from her chair and ran, her hat flying from her head, to throw herself at the Beduin. For a few moments the only visible part of her was her red-gold head, as his flowing sleeves wrapped round her slim body.

Emerson, close on Nefret's heels, pulled her away from the Beduin and began vigorously wringing the latter's hand. Nefret turned to the other young man. He held out his hand. Laughing, she pushed it away and hugged him as she had done Ramses.

Ramses? Little chap? Ramses had never been a normal little boy, but there had been times (usually when he was asleep) when he had *appeared* normal. The sleeping cherub with his mop of sable curls and his little bare feet protruding innocently from under the hem of his white nightgown had become this — this male person with a mustache! I supposed the transformation could not have occurred overnight. In fact, now that I thought about it, I recalled that he had been growing taller year by year, in the usual way. He was almost as tall as his father now, a good six feet in height. I could have dealt with that. But the mustache . . .

Trusting that my paralysis would be taken for dignified reticence, I remained in my chair.

15

Emerson had so forgot his usual British reserve as to put an arm round his son's shoulders in order to lead him to me. Ramses's naturally swarthy complexion had been darkened by sun and wind to a shade even browner than that of his young Egyptian friend, and his countenance was as unexpressive as it always was. He bent over me and gave me a dutiful kiss on the cheek.

"Good afternoon, Mother. You are looking well."

"I can't say the same for you," I replied. "That mustache —"

"Not now, Peabody," Emerson interrupted. "Good Gad, this is supposed to be a celebration. The important thing is that they are both back, safe and sound."

"And cursed late," said Nefret, settling herself in the chair David held for her. One of the waiters handed her her hat; she clapped it carelessly onto her head and went on, "Did you miss the early train?"

"No, not at all," David replied. His English was now almost as pure as my own; only when he was excited did a trace of his native Arabic creep in. "The Professor and Aunt Amelia may be getting complaints from some of the passengers, though; the tribe gave us a proper send-off, galloping alongside the train shooting off their rifles. The other people in our compartment fell cowering to the floor and one lady went into hysterics."

Nefret's eyes shone with laughter. "I wish I

could have been there. It is so damned — excuse me, Aunt Amelia — it is so unfair! If I had been a boy I could have gone with you. I suppose I wouldn't have enjoyed spending six months as a Beduin female, though."

"You would not have found it as confining as you may think," David said. "I was surprised at how much freedom the women of the tribe are allowed; in their own camp they do not veil themselves, and they express their opinions with a candor that Aunt Amelia would approve. Though she might not approve of the way in which young unmarried girls express their interest in —" He broke off abruptly, with a sheepish glance at Ramses. The latter's countenance was as imperturbable as ever, but it was not difficult to deduce that he had signaled David — perhaps by kicking him under the table — to refrain from finishing the sentence.

"Well, well," said Emerson. "So why were you so late?"

"We stopped at Meyer and Company, on the Muski," Ramses explained. "David wanted a new suit."

David smiled self-consciously. "Honestly, Aunt Amelia, neither of us has a respectable garment left to our names. I didn't want to embarrass you by appearing improperly dressed."

"Hmph," I said, looking at my son, who looked blandly back at me.

"As if any of us would care!" Nefret exclaimed. "To keep us waiting, fidgeting and worrying for hours, over something so silly!"

"Were you?" Ramses asked.

"Fidgeting and worrying? Not I! It was the Professor and Aunt Amelia. . . ." But her scowl metamorphosed into a dazzling smile; with the graceful, impulsive friendliness that was so integral a part of her nature she held out her hands, one to each lad. "If you must know, I have missed you desperately. And now I see I will have to play chaperone; you are both grown so tall and handsome all the little girls will be making eyes at you."

Ramses, who had enclosed her hand in his, dropped it as if it had become red-hot. "*Little girls?*"

How often, dear Reader, is a small, seemingly insignificant incident the start of a train of events that builds inexorably to a tragic climax! If Ramses had not chosen to appear in that dashing costume; if Nefret's impulsive welcome had not drawn all eyes to them; if Ramses had not raised his voice in indignant baritone outcry . . . The consequences would draw us into one of the most baffling and bizarre criminal cases we had ever investigated.

On the other hand, it is possible that the same thing would have happened anyhow.

Ramses got himself under control and Nefret wisely refrained from further provocation. She and Ramses were really the best of chums — when they were not squabbling like spoiled infants — and a request from her soothed his temper.

"Can you persuade M. Maspero to let me examine some of the mummies in the museum?" she demanded. "He has been putting me off for days. One would think I had proposed something illegal or shocking."

"He probably was shocked," said David, smiling. "You can't blame him, Nefret; he thinks of ladies as delicate and squeamish."

"I will blame him if I like. He lets Aunt Amelia do anything she wants."

"He's used to her," said Ramses. "We will go there together, you and I and David. He can't resist all three of us. What particular mummies have you in mind?"

"Most particularly, the one we found in Tetisheri's tomb three years ago."

"Good heavens," David said, appearing a trifle shocked himself. "I can see why Maspero . . . Er, that is, you must admit, Nefret, it was a particularly disgusting mummy. Unwrapped, unnamed, bound hand and foot —"

"Buried alive," Nefret finished. She planted both elbows on the table and leaned forward. A lock of gold-red hair had escaped from her upswept coiffure and curled distractingly across her temple; her cheeks were flushed with excitement and her blue eyes shone. An observer might have supposed she was discussing fashions or flirtations. "Or so we assumed. I want to have another look. You see, while you were gadding about in the desert, I was improving my education. I took a course in anatomy last summer."

"At the London School of Medicine for Women?" Ramses asked interestedly.

"Where else?" Nefret's blue eyes flashed. "It is the only institution in our enlightened nation where a mere female may receive medical training."

"But is that still strictly true?" Ramses persisted. "I was under the impression that Edinburgh, Glasgow, and even the University of London —"

"Confound you, Ramses, you are always destroying my fiery rhetoric with your pedantic insistence on detail!"

"I apologize," Ramses said meekly. "Your point — the unfair discrimination against females in all fields of higher education — is unaltered by the few exceptions I have mentioned, and the difficulties of actually qualifying to practice medicine are almost as great, I believe, as they were fifty years ago. I admire you, Nefret, for persisting under such adverse conditions. Let me assure you I am one hundred percent on your side and that of the other ladies."

She laughed at him and squeezed his hand. "I know you are, Ramses, dear. I was only teasing. Dr. Aldrich-Blake herself allowed me to attend her lectures! She feels I have an aptitude . . ."

Pleased to see them in amicable accord, I was following the conversation so intently I was unaware of the young lady's approach until she spoke — not to any of us but to her companion.

20

It was impossible to avoid hearing her; they had stopped next to our table and her voice was piercingly shrill.

"I told you to leave me alone!"

I had not observed her approach, but Ramses must have done. He was instantly on his feet. Removing his khafiya — a courtesy he had not extended to the female members of his family — he said, "May I be of assistance?"

Hands fluttering in appeal, the girl turned to him. "Oh, thank you," she breathed. "Please — can you make him go away?"

Her companion gaped at her. A long jaw and crooked nose marred an otherwise pleasant face. He was clean-shaven, with gray eyes and hair of an indeterminate tannish color. "See here, Dolly," he began, and put out his hand.

I don't believe he meant to take hold of her, but I was not to find out. Ramses caught his wrist. The movement was apparently effortless, the grip without apparent pressure, but the young fellow squawked and buckled at the knees.

"Good Gad, Ramses," I exclaimed. "Let him go at once."

"Certainly," said Ramses. He released his hold, but he must have done something else I did not see, for the unfortunate youth sat down with a thump.

Humiliation is a more effective weapon against the young than physical pain. The youth got to his feet and retreated — but not before he had given Ramses a threatening look.

He held Ramses accountable, of course. Being a man, he was too obtuse to realize, as did I, that the girl had deliberately provoked the incident. Her little hands now rested on Ramses's arm and she had tipped her head back in order that she might gaze admiringly into his eyes. A mass of curls so fair as to be almost white framed her face, and she was dressed in the height of fashion. I guessed her to be no more than twenty, possibly less. The young ladies of America — for her accent had betrayed her nationality — are much more sophisticated and more indulged than their English counterparts. That this young lady had a wealthy parent I did not doubt. She positively glittered with diamonds — most inappropriate for the time of day and her apparent age.

I said, "Allow me to present my son, Miss Bellingham. Ramses, if Miss Bellingham is feeling faint after her terrible ordeal, I suggest you offer her a chair."

"Thank you, ma'am, I'm just fine now." She turned her dimpled smile on me. Hers was a pretty face, with no distinctive characteristics except a pair of very big, very melting brown eyes that formed a striking contrast to her silvery-fair hair. "I know you, of course, Mrs. Emerson. You and your husband are the talk of Cairo. But how do you know the name of an insignificant little person like myself?"

"We met your father last week," I replied. Emerson growled, but did not comment. "He mentioned his daughter and referred to her as 'Dolly.' A nickname, I presume?"

"Like 'Ramses,'" said the insignificant little person, offering him a gloved hand. "It is a pleasure to meet you, Mr. Emerson. I had heard of you, too, but I had no idea you were so . . . Thank you. I sure appreciate your gallantry."

"Won't you join us?" I asked, as courtesy demanded. "And allow me to introduce Miss Forth and Mr. Todros."

Her eyes passed over David as if he had been invisible and rested, briefly, on Nefret's stony countenance.

"How do you do. I am afraid I cannot stay. There is Daddy now — late as always, the dreadful man! He will fuss at me if I keep him waiting."

After giving Ramses a last languishing look she tripped away.

The man who awaited her near the top of the stairs wore an old-fashioned frock coat and snowy stock. Since his military title, as I had been informed, derived from service in the Southern forces during the American Civil War, he must be at least sixty years of age, but one would have supposed him to be younger. He had the erect carriage and lean limbs of a cavalryman, and his white hair, worn rather longer than was the fashion, shone like a silver helmet. His neatly trimmed beard and mustache recalled photographs I had seen of General Lee, and I supposed he had deliberately cultivated the resemblance.

However, the benevolence that beamed from

the countenance of that hero of the Confederacy was not apparent on the face of the Colonel. He must have observed the encounter, or part of it; he shot us a long look before drawing the girl's arm through his and leading her away.

"Interesting," said Ramses, resuming his chair. "From your reaction to the mention of his name I gather your earlier meeting with Colonel Bellingham was not altogether friendly, Father. What precisely did he do to provoke your ire?"

Emerson said forcibly, "The fellow had the audacity to offer me a position as his hired lackey. He is another of those wealthy dilettantes who are amusing themselves by pretending to be archaeologists."

"Now, Emerson, you know that was not his real object," I said. "His offer to finance our work — an error on his part, I confess — was in the nature of a bribe. What really concerned him was —"

"Amelia," said Emerson, breathing heavily through his nose. "I told you I refuse to discuss the subject. Certainly not in front of the children."

Pas devant les enfants?" Nefret inquired ironically. "Professor, darling, we are no longer 'enfants,' and I'll wager I can guess what the Colonel wanted. A chaperone, or governess, or nursery maid for that doll-faced girl! She certainly needs one."

"According to the Colonel, it is a bodyguard she needs," I said.

"Peabody!" Emerson roared.

One of the waiters dropped the tea tray he was carrying, and everyone within earshot stopped talking and turned to stare.

"It's no use, Emerson," I said calmly. "Nefret is not guessing; she knows what the Colonel was after, though how she knows I am reluctant to consider. Eavesdropping —"

"Is cursed useful at times," said Nefret. She gave Ramses a comradely grin, and he responded with the slight curl of the lips that was his version of a smile. "Don't scold me, Aunt Amelia, I was not eavesdropping. I happened to be passing the saloon while you were talking with the Colonel, and I could not help overhearing the Professor's comments. It was not difficult to deduce from them what the subject of the conversation must be. But I cannot believe that little ninny is in danger."

"From whom?" Ramses asked. "Surely not the fellow who was with her?"

"I shouldn't think so," said Nefret. "Colonel Bellingham said he could not keep a female attendant for her; three of them have fallen ill or been injured under mysterious circumstances. In the last case, he claimed, a carriage driver tried to seize Dolly, and would have dragged her into the vehicle if her maid had not prevented it. He denied knowing who might have been responsible, or why anyone would want to make off with darling little Dolly."

"Ransom?" David suggested. "They must be

25

wealthy; she was wearing a fortune in jewels."

"Revenge," said Ramses. "The Colonel may have enemies."

"Frustrated love," murmured Nefret, in a saccharine voice.

Emerson's fist came down on the table. Since I had expected this would happen I was able to catch the teapot as it tottered.

"Enough," Emerson exclaimed. "This is precisely the kind of idle, irrelevant speculation in which this family is fond of engaging — with the sole exception of myself! I don't give a curse whether the entire criminal population of Charleston, South Carolina, and Cairo, Egypt, are after the girl. Even if it were not stuff and nonsense, it is none of our affair! Bodyguard, indeed. Change the subject."

"Of course," Nefret said. "Ramses — how did you do that?"

"Do what?" He glanced at the slim hand she had extended. "Oh. That."

"Show me."

"Nefret!" I exclaimed. "A young lady should not —"

"I am surprised that you should take that attitude, Mother," Ramses said. "I will show you too, if you like; the trick might come in useful, in view of your habit of rushing headlong . . . Er, hmm. Well, it is simply a matter of pressure on certain nerves."

He took hold of Nefret's wrist, raising it so we could see where his fingers rested. "Your wrist is too narrow for me to get a good grip, as I would with a man," Ramses said. "The thumb presses here, the index finger here; and . . ."

A little squeak escaped Nefret's lips, and Ramses immediately released his grip and cradled her hand in his. "I beg your pardon, Nefret. I was endeavoring to exert the least possible pressure."

"Ha," said Nefret. "Let me try it on you."

Before long she was laughing and — I regret to say — swearing, as she tried, unsuccessfully, to duplicate his hold.

"Your hands, as I suspected, are too small," Ramses said, submitting equably to her pinches and squeezes. "I would be the last to deny that a woman can equal a man in everything except physical size and strength, but you must admit — Damn it!"

She took his hand in hers and raised it to her lips. "There, I have kissed it and made it well."

David burst out laughing. "Bravo, Nefret. What did you do?"

"It is simply a matter of pressure on certain nerves," Nefret said demurely, as Ramses ruefully examined his wrist. Even from where I sat I could see the impressions of Nefret's nails.

"Enough of that," I said severely — reminding myself that I must ask Nefret later to show me how she had located the vulnerable points. It would have taken more than a random jab of the fingernails to wring a cry of pain out of Ramses. "We should return to the dahabeeyah."

"Yes, let's go home, where we can be comfortable together," Nefret said, jumping to her feet. "How rude these people are! They are all staring. I want to get out of this ridiculous frock and into my trousers."

"It is very becoming to you," David said gallantly.

"It is very uncomfortable," Nefret grumbled, inserting a slim finger into the high net collar.

"You aren't wearing corsets," Ramses remarked, looking her up and down.

"Ramses," I said wearily.

"Yes, Mother. We'll go ahead, shall we, and hire a cab."

They went off arm in arm, Nefret between the two lads. I could not blame people for staring; they made a handsome and unusual trio. The boys were almost of a height; their crops of curly black hair might have belonged to brothers. Both had turned to look down at Nefret, the crown of whose golden-red head barely reached the level of their ears. Shaking my head but smiling, I retrieved her hat from the floor where she had left it and took the arm Emerson offered me.

There was something of a little bustle when we caught the others up. A carriage was waiting; Nefret and David had already taken their seats, but Ramses was deep in conversation with the driver, who had turned out to be an old acquaintance of his. He and his father had old acquaintances, many of them the sort of individuals a respectable person would not care to know, all over Egypt. The driver was exclaiming, in the exaggerated way Arabs have, over Ramses's changed appearance. "Tall and handsome and fearless, like your admired father! Strong of arm when you strike with the clenched hand! Pleasing the women with your —"

At this point Emerson, rather red in the face, cut the compliments short with a curt phrase. Quite a little crowd had assembled; he had to shove a number of other old acquaintances out of the way before he could lead me to the cab. I had just put my foot on the step when Emerson suddenly let go my arm and whirled, clapping his hand to his pocket. "Who did that?" he barked, and repeated the question in Arabic.

David's hand steadied me and drew me into the carriage, depositing me neatly on the seat between him and Nefret. Looking back, I saw that the audience of beggars, vendors, and gaping tourists had hastily retreated. The power of Emerson's voice, as well as his command of invective, had earned him the title of "Father of Curses," and his infuriated demand could have been heard forty yards away.

There was no response, however, and after a moment Emerson said, "Oh, the devil with it!" and climbed into the cab. He was followed by Ramses, who had lingered to complete a financial transaction — or so I believed — with one of the flower vendors. Seating himself next his father, he handed a pretty little nosegay to me and another to Nefret, and then proceeded to destroy the nice effect of the gesture by ignoring our thanks.

"What did the fellow do?" he asked his father.

Emerson drew a crumpled sheet of paper from his pocket. Scanning it in a glance, he said, "Bah!" and would have tossed it away had I not snatched it from him.

The message was written in a crabbed hand — obviously disguised. It read: "Stay away from tomb Twenty-A."

"What is the meaning of this, Emerson?" I demanded.

Emerson ignored the question. "Ramses, did Yussuf see the man who shoved the paper into my pocket? For I suppose your primary reason for buying flowers from him was to question him."

"Why, no, sir," Ramses said righteously. "My primary reason was to please my mother and sister. However, during the transaction I did inquire of Yussuf, since he was nearest to you, and from your startled exclamation and gesture I thought perhaps some individual had attempted to pick your pocket or —"

Over the past years Ramses had been trying to overcome his unfortunate tendency to verbosity, but he had occasional relapses. I said automatically, "Be quiet, Ramses."

"Yes, Mother. May I see the note?"

I passed it round. "How strange," Nefret murmured. "What does it mean, sir?"

"Cursed if I know," Emerson said.

He took out his pipe and began to fill it. I leaned forward. "Emerson, you are being deliberately enigmatic and provoking, not to say mysterious. Your habit of keeping things from us — particularly from me — has got entirely out of hand. You know perfectly well —"

"It is a threat," Nefret exclaimed. "Or a warning. Oh — do forgive me for interrupting, Aunt Amelia; I was carried away by excitement. Which tomb is meant, Professor? Is it one of those you mean to excavate this year?"

We all waited, with pent breath, for Emerson's answer. One of his annoying little habits was to keep the site of our future excavations a secret until the last possible moment. He had not confided even in me.

He did not confide in me now. "Let us wait until this evening to discuss the matter," he said coolly. "I don't want to get into a loud, embarrassing argument in public."

Indignation momentarily robbed me of breath. Emerson's voice is the loudest of anyone's, and Emerson is the quickest of anyone to enter into an argument. His sanctimonious expression was maddening.

David, always the peacemaker, heard me draw in my breath and put an affectionate arm round my shoulders. "Yes, let us save business until later. Tell me about Aunt Evelyn, and Uncle Walter, and the children — it has been too long since I saw or heard from them."

"They sent their fondest love, of course," I

replied. "Evelyn wrote every week, but I don't suppose you received many of her letters."

"The post is not regular in the desert," David said with a smile. "I have missed them very much. They haven't changed their minds about coming out this season?"

"Someone had to stay in London to supervise the preparation of the final volume of the Tetisheri tomb publication," I said. "It is the volume of plates, you know, and since Evelyn was responsible for the paintings she wanted to make certain they were properly reproduced. Walter is working on the index of objects and inscriptions."

David demanded more information about his foster family. He was the grandson of our reis, Abdullah, but he had been virtually adopted by Emerson's brother, Walter, and spent the summers with the younger Emersons learning English and Egyptology, and heaven knows what else; he was an extremely intelligent young fellow and absorbed information as a sponge soaks up water. He was also a talented artist; when we first ran into him he was making fake antiquities for one of the greatest villains in Luxor, from whose baleful influence we had been instrumental in freeing him.* His parents were both dead, and his feelings for Evelyn and Walter were those of a devoted and grateful son.

As he had no doubt hoped, the subject occu-

*The Hippopotamus Pool

32

pied us for the remainder of the drive, though Ramses was uncharacteristically silent and Nefret contributed less than was her wont and Emerson fidgeted, tugging irritably at the cravat I had insisted on his wearing. When the dahabeeyah came into view he let out a gusty sigh, removed the offending article of dress altogether, and undid his collar button.

"It is uncommonly warm for November," he declared. "I am in full agreement with Nefret; I want to get out of these uncomfortable garments. Hurry up, Peabody."

I deduced, from the affectionate employment of my maiden name, and the meaningful glance he shot me, that he might want something else as well. But I lingered for a moment after he had helped me down from the carriage, to bestow a proud, fond look upon the boat, our floating home, as I termed it.

Emerson had purchased the dahabeeyah several years earlier. It was one of his most romantic and touching demonstrations of affection, for he dislikes traveling by water; he had made the sacrifice for me, and whenever I beheld the *Amelia*, as he had named the boat, my heart swelled. The graceful sailing vessels that had once been the favored method of Nile travel had now been largely replaced by steamers and by the railroad, but I would never lose my allegiance to them, or forget that first wonderful voyage, during which Emerson had asked me to be his.

The crew and domestic staff, headed by Captain Hassan, awaited us at the top of the gang-plank. After they had greeted the returning wan-derers and David and Ramses had returned the compliment, the latter's eyes moved round the deck.

"Where is the cat Bastet?" he asked.

I looked at Nefret. She bit her lip and bowed her head. Neither of us had looked forward to this moment. Nefret had had a close relationship with the matriarch of our large pride of felines, but not so close as that of Ramses; Bastet had been his companion and, according to some of the more superstitious Egyptians, his feline fa-miliar, for many years. She would certainly have been foremost among those waiting to greet him.

Realizing that Nefret had not the courage to break the news, I cleared my throat.

"I am sorry, Ramses," I said. "Very sorry in-deed. Nefret wrote you, but obviously the letter never reached you."

"No," said Ramses in a cool, expressionless voice. "When did it happen?"

"Last month. She had lived a long life for a cat, Ramses; she was full grown when we first found her, you know, and that was a good many years ago."

Ramses nodded. Not a muscle in his face had moved. "I dreamed of her one night last month. I don't know the date." I started to speak; he stopped me with a shake of his head. "One doesn't keep accurate count of time in a Beduin encampment. Odd, that. For the ancient Egyp-

34

tians, to dream of a large cat meant good luck."

"It was quick and painless." Nefret put a gentle hand on his arm. "We found her curled up as if she were sleeping, on the foot of your bed."

Ramses turned abruptly. "I feel certain Mother would prefer to see me in civilized attire. I will change at once. Excuse me."

He strode away, his full skirts billowing out behind him.

"I told you he wouldn't make a fuss, Nefret," I said. "He is not a sentimental person. I did think, though, that just before he turned away I saw a glimmer of moisture in his eyes."

"You imagined it," Emerson said gruffly. "You women are the sentimental ones. Men don't shed tears over a cat." He fumbled in his pocket, drew out a handkerchief, stared at it in mild surprise — his handkerchief is hardly ever where it is supposed to be — and blew his nose vigorously. "It was — hrmph — only a cat, you know."

Emerson must have been right, for when Ramses joined us in the saloon a little later he greeted our other Egyptian cat, Anubis, with perfect composure. Anubis returned the salutation with matching composure; larger and darker in color than the late lamented Bastet, he had not her amiable nature. He tolerated the rest of us, but saved his affection, what there was of it, for Emerson.

"My clothes are all too small, Mother," Ramses began.

35

"Those garments fit you well enough," I said. He was wearing flannels and a collarless shirt like the ones his father wore on the dig — an ensemble that was, in my opinion, quite unsuitable for a famous archaeologist. None of my arguments had ever persuaded Emerson to assume more dignified attire, and of course both boys insisted on imitating him.

"These are David's," Ramses said.

"You are entirely welcome," said David with a grin. When we first met the lad, mistreatment and semistarvation had made him appear to be younger than Ramses, but he was in fact two years older, and proper food and loving care had made him shoot up like a weed. He had been several inches taller than Ramses the previous season; I now noted, with a somewhat ambiguous mixture of emotions, that his last year's garments were a trifle too small for my son.

"That mustache," I began.

"Confound it, Peabody," Emerson shouted. "What is this obsession of yours with facial hair? First my beard, and now Ramses's mustache! Drink your whiskey like a lady and leave off badgering the boy — er — lad — er — chap."

Ramses fell like a vulture on this noble attempt to defend his mustache. "Since I am no longer a boy," he began, eyeing my whiskey and soda.

"Not on any account," I said firmly. "Spirits are bad for young people. Whiskey will — er — stunt your growth."

Ramses looked down at me — quite a long

way down. The corners of his mouth turned up just a trifle. He was wise enough to leave it at that, however, and was about to take a chair when Nefret came in. I had expected she would have assumed her working costume, modeled on mine — trousers and shirtwaist with, of course, a long loose jacket — but the garment she wore was a glittering robe of peacock green silk embroidered with gold and gemstones. It had been a gift from an admirer, but I had never seen her wear it, or the elaborate jewel-encrusted earrings. She curled up on the divan, tucking her slippered feet under her and settling the cat she was carrying comfortably on her lap.

"I dressed up in your honor," she announced, smiling at the boys.

Visibly dazzled, David stared openmouthed. Ramses's eyes passed over her and focused on the cat.

"Which one is that?" he asked.

Over the years Bastet had had quite a lot of kittens, but since the sires were local felines the offspring had displayed a bewildering variety of colors and shapes. Her last litter, produced in cooperation with Anubis, resembled their parents to a striking degree — long and well muscled, with sleek coats of brindled brown and fawn. They tended to have rather large ears.

"This is Sekhmet," Nefret replied. "She was only a tiny kitten when you last saw her, but now she —"

"Quite," said Ramses. "Father, will you now

tell us about your plans? I presume that you mean, for your next project, to investigate the lesser-known, uninscribed, nonroyal tombs in the Valley of the Kings. Some might consider this an unusual choice for a scholar of your eminence, but familiar as I am with your views on excavation I am not surprised you should take this course."

Emerson fixed him with a suspicious glare. "How did you arrive at that conclusion?"

Ramses opened his mouth. I said hastily, "Don't ask him, Emerson, or he will tell us. You tell us. For I confess I am unable to understand why you should concentrate your formidable talents on work that cannot possibly produce meaningful results, either in historical terms or in terms of valuable artifacts. . . ."

My voice trailed off. Emerson had turned the glare on me.

The only people who are not in awe of Emerson's powerful voice and well-nigh superhuman strength are the members of his own family. He is aware of this, and often complains about it; so from time to time I like to put on a little show of being intimidated. "Proceed, my dear," I said apologetically.

"Hmph," said Emerson. "I don't know why you should be surprised, Peabody. You know my views on scientific excavation. From the first, archaeology in Egypt has been a haphazard, slipshod business. There has been some improvement in recent years; however, much of the work that is being done is still scandalously inadequate, and nowhere is this more evident than in the Valley of the Kings. Everybody wants to find royal tombs. They go dashing from place to place, poking and probing, abandoning an excavation as soon as they become bored with it, ignoring the broken scraps of debris unless they find a royal cartouche. None of the smaller, uninscribed tombs has been properly cleared, measured, and recorded. This is what I propose doing. It will be hard, tedious work — unexciting and possibly unproductive. But one never knows. And at worst we will have a definitive record."

Crimson and purple streaked the sky, and from a mosque in a nearby district the high, pure voice of the muezzin began the sunset call to prayer. "God is great! God is great! There is no God but God." As if responding, the cat rose and stretched and left Nefret's lap for that of David, who began stroking it.

Ramses said, "So Maspero would not give you permission to look for unknown tombs in the Valley?"

I had expected Emerson would be annoyed at this cynical and — I did not doubt — accurate guess. Instead he chuckled and splashed more whiskey into his glass. "Right on the mark, my boy. After Vandergelt decided to give up his concession in the Valley, Maspero handed it over to that arrogant ignoramus from New York, Theodore Davis. Our distinguished director of antiquities is infatuated with wealthy dilettantes.

He would not have considered my application in any case; he is a trifle put out with me these days."

"Small wonder," I said, holding out my own glass. "After you locked up Tetisheri's tomb, tore down the stairs to the entrance, and refused to hand over the key."

"I misplaced it," said Emerson.

"No, you didn't."

"No, I didn't," Emerson said, showing his teeth. "But I am damned if I will allow the Service des Antiquités to open the tomb to hordes of tourists. Candle smoke and magnesium flares, idiots rubbing up against the paintings and prying at the plaster with their fingernails. . . ." A shudder of genuine horror ran through his body. "We worked too hard to conserve and restore those paintings. What the devil, we handed over the entire contents of the tomb to the museum. Why won't Maspero be content with that?"

"I agree with you, sir, of course," David said. "There is an additional danger; for if the tomb is opened, it won't be long before some of the men of Gurneh get into the place and start cutting out sections of the plastered walls to sell to tourists."

"Not while I draw breath," Emerson muttered. "That is one of the reasons why I have decided to work in Thebes for the indefinite future, so I can keep an eye on *my* tomb. We will get under way tomorrow."

A general outcry followed this statement. Even the cat let out a mournful wail.

"Impossible, my dear," I said calmly.

"Why?" Emerson demanded. "We are all here, ready for —"

"We are not ready, Emerson. Good gracious, the boys have just now arrived after six months in the desert; Ramses has outgrown all his clothes and both lads undoubtedly require to have toilet articles and boots and heaven knows what else replaced. If you mean to stay in Luxor indefinitely, the house we built two years ago will have to be enlarged, and that means more furniture, more supplies, more of — er — everything. And furthermore —"

I ran out of breath and Emerson said, "And furthermore, you have planned one of your confounded social affairs. Curse it, Peabody, you know how I hate them! When?"

I had indeed arranged one of my popular dinner parties, at which we renewed old acquaintances with archaeological friends and got caught up on the news. They had become an annual custom and were, I had been assured, greatly enjoyed by all who participated. Emerson enjoyed them too; he only complained because he had got in the habit of complaining.

My principal reasons for delaying our departure were, however, precisely the ones I have mentioned. We were busy all next day laying in supplies and buying new clothes for the boys. At least

41

I was busy. Ramses grudgingly agreed to have his measurements taken by boot makers and tailors; after that he and David went off together, ostensibly to finish their shopping. When they returned to the dahabeeyah that evening the dusty, wrinkled condition of their garments strongly suggested they had been prowling the narrow alleys of the old town. Both reeked of tobacco.

They got away from me before I could deliver the lecture I intended, with the disingenuous excuse that it was late and they wanted to wash up and change before dinner. I turned in exasperation to Emerson, who was placidly sipping his whiskey and stroking the cat. The cat in question was Sekhmet, who had coolly pushed her father, Anubis, off Emerson's knee in order to take his place. Anubis, growling under his breath, had gone off to a corner to sulk.

"Emerson, you must talk to them. Heaven only knows where they went today, and I suspect they were smoking cigarettes."

"We can count ourselves fortunate if that is all they were smoking," Emerson said. "I don't approve of young people indulging in tobacco either." He paused to fill his pipe. "But it is not so harmful as hashish."

"I didn't smell that on their clothes," I admitted.

"Or — er — anything else?" Emerson inquired.

"I don't know what you mean, Emerson. That is . . . Good gracious! You are not suggesting they may have gone to . . . To be with . . .

42

They are only boys, they aren't old enough to . . ."

"Now, Peabody, calm yourself and listen. I know it is difficult for a fond mother to admit that her little boy is growing up, but you cannot go on treating Ramses like a child. He has led an unusual life. One might say he stands astride two worlds. In one of them he is still a schoolboy — but let me assure you, Peabody, lads of his age even in England are old enough to — er — well, you understand me. In Egypt, where Ramses has spent most of his life, some of his contemporaries are already husbands and fathers. The experiences of this past summer have surely strengthened the influence of that second world. You may be certain the sheikh gave him the full responsibilities and privileges of an adult."

"Heavens!" I exclaimed. "I cannot believe you mean . . . What do you mean?"

Emerson patted my hand. "I mean that Ramses — and David — are now of an age where they are more likely to heed my advice than yours. I am convinced they are not so lacking in good sense or moral fortitude as to consort with those poor, wretched women in El Was'a, but you may be sure I will raise the subject with both of them. Suppose you leave the lectures to me, eh? That goes for you, too, Nefret."

"Oh, good Gad," I exclaimed. She had been so quiet I had forgot she was there — curled up in her favorite place on the divan, reading — or

I would never have allowed Emerson to refer, however obliquely, to such a shocking subject.

Nefret said coldly, "If I believed either of them would so degrade himself, I would do more than lecture."

"They wouldn't," Emerson said, sounding a little rattled. "So don't. Enough of this. I cannot imagine how we get onto such subjects."

The arrival of the steward with the daily post ended the discussion, though it certainly did not stop me thinking about it. Emerson sorted through the letters and messages and passed on the ones directed to me or to Nefret. "Two for you, Ramses," he said as the boys came in. "And one for David."

The aura of attar of roses, which I had not, thank heaven, detected on Ramses's clothes, now wafted strongly to me from the dainty pink envelope he held in his hand. "Whom is that from?" I demanded.

"Have another whiskey, Peabody," Emerson said loudly.

I took the hint, and the whiskey, and looked through my own messages. Several were invitations. I reported these to Emerson, who told me to decline all of them, including the last, which was from Colonel Bellingham.

"I've no intention of wasting an entire evening with him and his silly daughter," Emerson grumbled.

"This note is from her," Ramses said. "Repeating her father's invitation."

Instead of handing me the paper, he folded it and tucked it into his pocket. Sekhmet, making the rounds of various laps, had moved from Emerson's to David's; now she settled herself onto Ramses's knee. He ignored her and opened his second letter.

"Nothing of interest," Nefret announced, tossing her messages aside. "Invitations I shan't accept and a particularly silly effusion from Monsieur le Comte de la Roche which I shan't answer."

"Another of the victims?" David inquired — for so he and Ramses called Nefret's admirers.

"He has been sending her flowers and gifts since they met at a party last week," I said with a frown. "You haven't encouraged him, have you, Nefret?"

"Good heavens, no, Aunt Amelia. His chin is positively concave."

"Perhaps you had better write him a stiff note, Emerson. Tell him his attentions are unwanted."

"Mmmm," said Emerson, who was reading the letter from Evelyn that David had passed on to him.

"I am going to the museum tomorrow," Nefret announced. "Ramses, you said you would . . . Ramses? What is wrong?"

"Nothing is wrong," Ramses said slowly. His eyes were fixed on the letter. "Only unexpected. Mother, do you remember Mrs. Fraser — Miss Debenham, as she was before she married?"

"Certainly, though it has been years since we

were in communication with her. Is that —"

"From her, yes. She is in Egypt — in Cairo, to be precise."

"Why would she write to you instead of to me?"

"I don't know. She says . . . But perhaps you had better see for yourself."

"Who is Mrs. Fraser?" Nefret demanded.

Ramses handed me the letter and answered his sister. "A young lady we — Mother, that is — saved from an accusation of murder some years ago.* She married one of the other suspects, a fellow named Donald Fraser."

"And lived happily ever after?"

"Apparently not," I said. Emerson was watching me curiously, for the name had, of course, aroused his interest. "What an odd letter! It is very rambling — almost incoherent. She says she saw us yesterday, on the terrace at Shepheard's, but does not explain why she did not greet us at that time, or why she requests a meeting with us in terms of some urgency."

Ramses said softly, "Us?"

"Why, yes. She says . . ." I read the relevant sentences aloud. " 'Seeing you again recalled memories of bygone days, and a promise you once made. I wonder if you also remember it? Please, may I see you and speak with you? My husband and I are at the Hotel Continental . . .' Hmph."

"Quite," said Ramses. "The pronoun 'you' can

*Lion in the Valley

46

be singular or plural, but does not the context suggest that it is I she means?"

"It does," Emerson agreed. "Did you make her a promise, Ramses?"

Ramses let out an exclamation and pulled his hand away from the cat. She had wrapped her front paws around his wrist and was enthusiastically licking his fingers.

"Disgusting," he muttered, wiping his hand on his trousers.

"It is a sign of affection," Nefret said. "Bastet often —"

"This creature is slobbering, not licking." Sekhmet rolled over and gazed with idiotic admiration at Ramses, who went on irritably, "Whatever prompted you to name her after the goddess of war? She is hopelessly affectionate and completely without discrimination."

He scooped up the cat and put her on the floor. "Is it time for dinner? I am hungry."

We took our places at the table, for dinner was indeed ready, and Mahmud had been waiting to serve. I caught Nefret's eye; she shrugged and shook her head. Our little scheme for finding a new feline companion for Ramses had obviously been unsuccessful.

And complaining about Sekhmet had enabled him to avoid answering Emerson's question.

I could not remember that he had made a promise to Enid. I was surprised that *she* had remembered. Ramses had been only seven or eight years old at the time. She had had a wholly unaccountable fondness for him, though, and he had been quite attached to her, probably because she had listened with a well-bred pretense of interest to his interminable lectures on Egyptology.

Matters were becoming interesting. Threats, or warnings, from some unknown party, an unspecified peril awaiting us in tomb Twenty-A, and an old friend in distress. Naturally I intended to deal with Enid's little trouble myself. A child's promise, however well meant, was of no importance. There was nothing Ramses could do for Enid that *I* could not do better.

CHAPTER TWO

*There is nothing like continued proximity
to strip away the veils of romance.*

At breakfast the following morning I informed Ramses I had written Enid inviting her, and of course her husband, to take tea with us at Shepheard's that day.

His dark brows drew together. "Why not here? I had intended —"

"That is just why I took it upon myself to respond," I explained in a kindly manner. "You have a great deal to learn about the subtleties of social intercourse, Ramses. Inviting them here would indicate a degree of intimacy we may not wish to encourage."

"But —"

"We have not seen them for years, Ramses, and the initial acquaintanceship was based on circumstances of an extraordinary nature which are not likely to recur."

"I should hope not," Emerson grunted. "See here, Amelia, if you allow this young woman to drag you into another criminal investigation — or, even worse, romantic entanglement —"

49

"My dear, that is precisely what I am trying to avoid," I said soothingly. "Not that I have any reason to suppose either of those difficulties has arisen."

"Hmph," said Emerson.

"No doubt you are right, Mother," Ramses said. "You always are."

After we had crossed the Kasr en Nil Bridge we separated in order to pursue our various errands. The shopping was of course left to me. Having permitted themselves to be measured for various articles of attire, neither of the lads saw any reason to return to the establishments in question, and when I mentioned items such as handkerchiefs and stockings they informed me that they had got everything they needed, and that if I felt anything else were necessary, I was at liberty to supply it. Emerson's vigorous nod indicated that he was in complete agreement with this statement.

This suited me quite well, for I do not particularly enjoy being accompanied into shops by bored male persons who keep looking at their watches and inquiring how much longer I will be. Emerson and the boys went on to the museum, where we were all to meet later, and Nefret and I proceeded to the Shari'a Kamel and the Muski, where many of the establishments carrying European goods are located. I had found a shop that would make parasols to my specifications, with a strong steel shaft and a somewhat pointed tip, and had ordered two new ones. Stout as they were, my parasols tended to wear out rather quickly; I had to purchase at least one every year.

I was pleased to find the parasols ready, and after brandishing them experimentally in order to test the weight, I told the shopkeeper (after he had come out from under the counter) to send them to the dahabeeyah. Nefret had declined a parasol; while admitting its all-round usefulness, she preferred to carry a knife. We selected a new one of good Sheffield steel, and after completing the remainder of our shopping, we proceeded to the museum.

The previous year the antiquities collections had been moved from the old palace of Gizeh to a new building in the Isma'iliyeh district. It was a handsome structure of yellow stucco in the Graeco-Roman style, with a pillared porch in front and in front of that a bare space that would one day be a garden. At the moment it was adorned with a few spindly palm trees and a large marble sarcophagus — no ancient relic, but a modern monument in which rested the remains of Gaston Mariette, the revered founder of the Service des Antiquités.

The boys were waiting for us next to the bronze statue of Mariette. David swept off his hat; Ramses raised a hand to his brow and looked surprised to discover he was not wearing a hat. He had had one on when we left the boat. I did not bother asking what he had done with it. Hats and Ramses were not compatible. I had come to believe it was a hereditary trait.

"Where is your father?" I asked.

"He went off on some errand or other," Ramses replied. "Since he chose not to volunteer information concerning his destination or his intentions, I did not inquire. He said he would meet us here at the agreed-upon hour."

I was pleased to hear this. Emerson always loses his temper when he visits the museum, and it is necessary for me to be with him in order to prevent him from storming into the office of the director and calling him rude names. "Have you paid your respects to M. Maspero?" I inquired.

"He was not in his office," Ramses said. "We spoke with Herr Brugsch. I — er — happened to mention to him that Father would be along shortly."

Emerson does not get on well with very many Egyptologists, but he had a set of special curses reserved for Emile Brugsch, Maspero's assistant, whom he considered both incompetent and dishonest.

"Ah," I said. "So Brugsch will take care not to be in his office either. Well done, Ramses."

"Well done?" Nefret exclaimed. "If Brugsch and Maspero have both left, how am I to get permission to see my mummy? Curse it, Ramses, you promised —"

"I asked about it," Ramses said. "Unfortunately, the mummy in question appears to have been misplaced."

"What?" It was my turn to be outraged. "Our

mummy? Lost, do you mean?"

"Brugsch assured me it was not lost, only — er — temporarily misplaced. They are still moving objects from the old museum. He is certain it will turn up."

"Turn up, indeed. Emerson is absolutely right to criticize Maspero's methods; there is no excuse for such slipshod measures now that the new museum has been built. But I see Emerson coming; for pity's sake don't mention this to him or he will explode."

After an affectionate exchange of greetings we entered the museum and went up the handsome staircase to the Galerie d'Honneur on the first floor, where the materials from Tetisheri's tomb were prominently displayed. As Maspero had been gracious enough to admit, they were one of the treasures of the museum, even though they did not include the mummy and coffins of the queen. What had become of them no one knew, not even ourselves; but there had been enough of the queen's funerary goods remaining to make a breathtaking display — ushabtis and statues, inlaid chests and alabaster jars, a throne-chair completely covered in gold leaf chased with delicate designs — and the pièce de résistance, a chariot. When we found it in the queen's tomb it was in pieces, but all the parts were there, including the spoked wheels. The body, of wood covered with gesso and linen, had been carved and gilded, and we had had the devil of a job stabilizing the fragile materials so that they would not deteriorate any further than they already had. Emerson had himself supervised the removal of the chariot to Cairo and seen it reassembled in a large glass case. Every time we visited the museum he walked round and round the case, examining every inch of the precious thing to make certain no more bits had fallen off.

Unfortunately, they usually had. This put Emerson in a bad humor, and he began grumbling about everything he could think of. "Maspero ought to have kept everything together, curse it. The jewelry —"

"Is, as is proper, in the Jewel Room," I replied. "Where it can be more easily protected."

"Hmm," said Ramses. He was studying the padlocks on the wooden cases with a degree of interest that made me somewhat uncomfortable. But no, I assured myself. Ramses was older and more responsible now, and not even in his younger days would he have tried to rob the Cairo Museum. Not without an excellent reason, anyhow.

So we went next to the Jewel Room, where Ramses gravitated to the cases containing the Treasure of Dahshur, as the guidebooks called it — the jewels of the Twelfth Dynasty princesses discovered in 1894 and '95. The labels on those cases attributed the discovery to M. de Morgan, who had been Director of the Service des Antiquités. I had my doubts about the accuracy of that attribution and, to judge by his expression, so had Ramses. Since he had never actually admitted finding the jewelry before M. de Morgan — which would have been tantamount to admitting he had been guilty of illicit excavation — I had never asked him.

Nefret and Emerson stood before the case containing the Cushite royal scepters. Here again the official label was not entirely inaccurate. The scepters, magnificent examples of their kind, *had* been found in a remote wadi near the Valley of the Kings, by Professor and Mrs. Radcliffe Emerson; but they had been found in that location because we had put them there. Nefret had brought them away with her from the Lost Oasis, and since the very existence of that spot must never be disclosed to the world, we had been forced to engage in a small spot of misdirection in order to make the scepters accessible to the scholarly world.

Baedeker had given the Dahshur Treasure two stars. Tetisheri's jewelry awaited a new edition of that invaluable book for its evaluation, but I did not doubt it would rate at least as high. The queen's parure had included several massive gold bracelets, even finer than the ones that had belonged to her daughter, Queen Aahhotep, which rested in a nearby case. My favorite pieces were the beaded collars and bracelets, multiple strands of carnelian and turquoise, lapis lazuli and gold. They had been only a jumble of color when I first set eyes on them, lying on the floor of the burial chamber where they had fallen from the collapsed wooden case.

Standing beside me, David studied them with the same pride and interest. It was due to our joint efforts that the exquisite things had survived in their present form. We had spent hours studying the patterns of the fragments that had not fallen apart and restringing hundred of tiny beads in the same order. I had had considerable experience with such work, but I daresay I could not have done it so well without David. He had been trained by one of the finest forgers of antiquities in Luxor, and he had an artist's eye.

I gave his arm a little squeeze and he looked down at me with a reminiscent smile. "There will never be anything like it again," he said softly. "What an experience that was!"

"You have hardly reached the peak of your career at eighteen," I assured him. "The best is certainly yet to come, David."

"Quite right," said Emerson. Jewelry is not one of his principal interests, and he had become bored. "Well, my dears, what shall we see next?"

"The royal mummies," Nefret said promptly.

Emerson was agreeable. Mummies *are* one of his interests, and he was certain he could find something in the exhibit to complain about.

The royal mummies had come for the most part from two caches, one in the cliffs above Deir el Bahri, the other in the tomb of Amenhotep II. In the old museum they had been dispersed in different rooms. Maspero had brought them together here, at the end of the same vestibule off which the Jewel Room was located. It was a very popular exhibit, and as we approached Emerson burst out, "Only look at those ghouls! The whole business is so unseemly it makes me wild with rage! I told Maspero he had no right to put those poor cadavers on display, as if they were artifacts; how would you like, I asked him, to be exposed naked to the stares of the vulgar?"

"That is certainly a grisly thought," said Ramses.

Nefret raised her hand to her mouth to hide her smile and I frowned reproachfully at Ramses, who pretended not to see. M. Maspero was quite stout, but that was no excuse for making fun of him.

David had missed the vulgar reference to poor M. Maspero. He was a serious, sensitive lad, who could probably claim a closer relationship with the remains than could any of the tourists who proposed to gape at them. Looking troubled, he said earnestly, "You are in the right, Professor. Perhaps we should express our repugnance by refusing to view the mummies."

"That is a different matter altogether," Emerson declared. "We are scholars. We are not moved by idle curiosity."

Ramses, in the lead as usual, was suddenly thrust aside by a figure that rushed precipitately through the crowd. It ran full tilt into Emerson, who is not easily thrust aside. Since the figure was that of a woman, my gallant husband did not push it away. Supporting her as she recoiled — for running into Emerson is rather like running into a large boulder — he said mildly, "Watch where you are going, madam. You are presently standing on my foot."

Rubbing her forehead, the lady looked up at him. Her incoherent apologies had barely begun before she interrupted them to exclaim, "Can it be you, Professor Emerson? But — but I believe we are engaged to have tea with you in an hour's time. What a strange coincidence!"

"Not at all," I said. "We frequently visit the museum and so, I fancy, do most serious-minded visitors to Cairo. It is good to see you again, Mrs. Fraser. Shall we just step aside, out of the way of the people who are waiting?"

Emerson, who had been staring fixedly at her, remembered his manners and introduced the rest of our party. I believe he was as shocked as I at how she had changed. She had been a handsome young creature, as vigorous and graceful as a tigress. Now her thick dark hair was streaked with silver and her shoulders slumped like those of an old woman. The alteration of her features was less easy to define; it was not so much a matter of pallor and wrinkles, but of expression — a haunted look in the fine dark eyes, a tight set to her mouth. To be sure, she was eight years older than she had been when we first met her, but that span of time should not have had such a devastating effect.

Conquering my amazement, I inquired, "Where is Mr. Fraser? Will he meet us at the hotel?"

Enid appeared not to hear the question. After acknowledging the introductions to Nefret and David, whom she had not met before, she had returned her gaze to Ramses. Offering her hand, she exclaimed, "Ramses! Forgive the familiarity, but it is difficult for me to think of you by any other name. I would scarcely have recognized you. You have grown up!"

"The passage of time does have that effect," said Ramses. "Did something unpleasant occur in the Mummy Room, to prompt your precipitate departure from it?"

Enid laughed rather hollowly and raised her hand to her brow. "You have not changed so much after all. Direct as ever! No, don't apologize. . . ."

(I cannot imagine why she supposed he was about to.)

"Nothing at all occurred," Enid went on. "It was just . . . They are so horrid, you know. One hideous, grinning face after another — suddenly I couldn't endure it."

From what I had heard it would not be the first time a foolish female had fainted or fled screaming from the room — though why the silly things would go there in the first place if they were so squeamish I could not imagine. Enid had never struck me as of a nervous temperament, however, and she at least ought to have known real mummies were not so pretty as the poetic descriptions in works of fiction.

"So here you are," said a voice behind me. "I

wondered where you had got to. And I see you have found friends!"

I knew the voice, and recognized the speaker. Donald Fraser's hair was as bright and his face as youthful as ever. Exclaiming with pleasure, he shook hands all round.

"It lacks but a quarter of an hour to the time we were to meet at Shepheard's," he went on. "How fortunate we should find you here instead! It gives me the opportunity to present a dear friend. She had declined to join us for tea, since she had not been included in the invitation, but I was determined to make her known to you sooner or later, for she too is a distinguished Egyptologist. Mrs. Whitney-Jones, Professor and Mrs. Emerson."

The lady had been standing modestly to one side. At Donald's beckoning gesture she came toward us.

I have been accused of being superficial when I judge people, especially females, by their attire. It is a laughably inaccurate appraisal. There is no single feature so important as costume; it indicates the artistic tastes and economic means of the wearer, among other significant characteristics.

This individual was obviously well-to-do. Her costume was brand-new and of the latest mode, with an umbrella skirt and short jacket over a chiffon blouse and (to judge by her rigid posture) a straight-fronted corset. Hats were a trifle smaller that year; hers was of fine tan straw

60

trimmed with ostrich feathers. I had seen the exact same model at Harrods the past summer. She was approximately my height, though (despite the corset) somewhat stouter.

"Pleasure, I'm sure," said Emerson. "Egyptologist, are you? I have never heard of you. What sites have you excavated?"

I had long since given up apologizing for Emerson's manners. In this case it was not necessary. The lady laughed in the friendliest manner imaginable and shook her finger playfully at my husband.

"But I have heard of you, Professor, and of your forthright character. How I do appreciate honesty and candor! It is so rare in this sad world."

She had not answered his question, nor was he given the opportunity to repeat it. "Well, but why are we standing here?" Donald demanded. "Let us go on to the hotel."

"An excellent suggestion," I said. "You will join us, of course, Mrs. Whitney-Jones? Naturally I would have included you in the invitation had I known you were not only a friend of Enid and Donald's, but a fellow scholar."

In fact, I doubted that either designation was correct. As the others turned away, Donald offering the lady his arm, Enid's stiff social smile slipped for a moment. The expression that distorted her face was not simple dislike. Loathing would be more accurate — and mingled with it, something strangely like fear.

Yet no one could have appeared less likely to inspire either emotion than Mrs. Whitney-Jones. I had ample opportunity to learn more about her while we were taking tea; in fact, uncharitable persons might have said she rather monopolized the conversation.

Mr. Fraser had exaggerated her expertise, she explained with charming modesty. She had studied hieroglyphs and Egyptian history at University College in London, but she was only the humblest student, and this was her first trip to Egypt. How she had looked forward to it! How thrilled she was to meet in person the individuals for whose work she had such admiration! In fact, she seemed quite familiar with it — not the sensational stories that had too often filled the English newspapers, but our scholarly productions. She was particularly effusive in her praise of Emerson's monumental *History of Egypt.*

Emerson, who had anticipated "a tedious hour of idle chit-chat with those boring young people," was delighted to lecture instead about Egyptology, and not at all inclined to let anyone else get a word in.

I wondered if Mrs. Whitney-Jones was going to fall in love with Emerson. Women did. Compared with some of the others she did not present much of a threat, I thought. It was difficult to estimate her age. Her face was smooth and unlined, but her abundant hair was streaked with gray in oddly regular stripes like the coat of a tabby cat. In fact, she reminded me of a cat, especially when she smiled; her lips turned up in exaggerated curves and her eyes were an unusual shade of greenish gold. Even more suggestive of the feline was her expression. Nothing looks as self-satisfied as a contented cat.

Now that I was able to get a closer look at Donald Fraser, I realized he had changed, and not for the better. He had gained some flesh and looked flabby and out of condition. He seemed in excellent spirits, however, and followed the conversation between Emerson and his admirer with considerable interest — another change, since Donald had never been intellectually in-clined.

The young people had the blank, patient look of children who have been forced to attend a grown-up social function and are counting the seconds until it is over. Ramses kept glancing at Enid. His imperturbable countenance gave me no clue to his thoughts, but I wondered if he was struck, as I was, by her altered looks.

Not until we were about to take leave of one another did anything out of the way occur. It was Donald who introduced the subject.

"Will you be looking for tombs in the Valley of the Kings this season, Professor?"

"Not precisely," said Emerson.

"The Valley of the Queens, then?"

I found his persistence peculiar. Even odder was the way Enid watched him, like a cat at a mousehole.

"I don't know why you give a curse," Emerson said, amiably enough for him. "We will be working in the Royal Valley, but if you are hoping to be on the spot when a sensational discovery is made, Mr. Fraser, you will have to follow after some other Egyptologist. The tombs I mean to investigate are all known, and none is of interest except to scholars."

"Then why bother with them?" Donald demanded. "Surely you would be better employed looking for a new, unknown tomb — the tomb of a queen or princess."

"Now, Donald, you musn't lecture the Professor," Mrs. Whitney-Jones exclaimed. "He is an authority, you know."

"Yes, of course. But —"

"Gracious, how late it is," said Mrs. Whitney-Jones. "We mustn't keep you any longer. What a rare treat it has been!"

Enid had said very little. Now she murmured, "But this is not good-bye, is it? Surely we will meet again — in Luxor, if not here in Cairo?"

I said, not altogether truthfully, that I hoped that would be the case, and after a further exchange of courtesies Mrs. Whitney-Jones took Donald firmly by the arm and led him away.

Enid lingered, drawing on her gloves. "We leave for Luxor in a few days," she said in a low voice. "Will there be an opportunity for me to see you — speak with you alone — before —"

Emerson took *me* firmly by the arm. "We leave tomorrow," he declared.

It was the first I had heard of it, and since I took the statement to be not a declaration of fact, but one of Emerson's futile attempts to prevent me from "meddling in other people's affairs," as he is pleased to term it, I ignored the statement.

"Are you coming, Enid?" It was Donald's voice that called her, Donald who had stopped and looked back; but my intuitive intelligence, which seldom fails me, told me that the summons had come not from him, but from the pleasant, harmless-looking woman who clung demurely to his arm.

Again a look of revulsion and despair darkened Enid's face. "In Luxor, then," she whispered. "Please! Please, Amelia."

"Enid!" Donald called.

"Go," I said in the same low voice. "We will see you in Luxor."

"No, we won't," said Emerson, as Enid went with dragging steps to join her companions.

"She is in deep distress, Emerson. We owe it to an old friend —"

"No, we don't." He took his watch from his pocket. "What time is that confounded dinner party of yours? We are going to be late if you don't stop arguing and hurry."

We would not have been in such a rush if Emerson had agreed to my suggestion that we take rooms at a hotel for a few days. He hated fashionable hotels and had bought the dahabeeyah, as he often reminded me, in order to

65

avoid the necessity of staying at Shepheard's or the Continental. I had selected the latter establishment for our dinner that evening. Though Shepheard's will always be my favorite hotel, for sentimental as well as practical reasons, the Continental was newer and had recently acquired a Swiss chef whose reputation was of the highest.

Nefret had cast her vote for the dahabeeyah too. "You always make me wear a hat and tight shoes when we are at the hotel," she had declared. "And the place is full of boring people who want to talk to me about boring things, and you won't let me be rude to them."

"Certainly not," I said, pretending to look shocked.

In fact, I was secretly pleased that Nefret found most of the young men she met boring. She was a very wealthy young woman as well as a very beautiful young woman, so it was no wonder she always had a string of admirers trailing after her. Most were well-bred idlers, interested only in sport and frivolity and attracted to Nefret for the wrong reasons — her fortune or her beauty. She had much more to offer than that, and I was determined she should not marry until she found a man worthy of her — a man who shared her interests and respected her character, who loved her for her intelligence and independence, her sensitive nature and quick wit; a man of honor and intellectual understanding, but one who was not devoid of the physical characteristics that attract a handsome young woman. A man, in short, like Emerson!

Thanks to the recalcitrance of that admirable but aggravating man, we had to return to the dahabeeyah to dress. When our party assembled on deck, Emerson was looking fairly affable, since I had relaxed my rule about wearing evening kit, which he detests. After Ramses had got himself as far into his last year's evening suit as was possible (muttering indignantly all the while), I had been forced to agree that it was indeed too small for him. A new wardrobe had been ordered and was in process of construction, but the only thing we had been able to find ready-made was a tweed suit similar to David's. Nefret's golden-tan skin was set off by her white chiffon gown lavishly trimmed with Cluny lace and crystal beads, and I believe my own frock of crimson satin did not detract from the generally impressive appearance of the group.

Certainly the admiring looks of our friends supported this assumption, and when I took my place at the foot of the table in the dining salon, I saw that Howard Carter, on my right, could hardly take his eyes off Nefret. I did hope he was not going to fall in love with her. No one, I believe, could ever accuse me of snobbishness, and I was genuinely fond of Howard; but his origins were humble, he had no independent means, and his lack of formal education would prevent him from rising much further in his profession than his present position of inspector over the antiquities of Upper Egypt.

My eyes moved speculatively over the faces of the men who were present. Mr. Reisner, the brilliant young American excavator; our old friend Percy Newberry; Mr. Quibell, Howard's counterpart as inspector in Lower Egypt; Mr. Lucas, the chemist; M. Lacau, who was copying the coffin texts in the Cairo Museum. . . . No, none of them would do. If they were not already married, they were too old or too poor or too dull. Yet it would be a pity if she did not marry an archaeologist; all her interests and her tastes inclined her toward that profession.

Howard jogged my elbow. "Excuse me, Mrs. E., but you seem to be in quite a brown study. What is on your mind? Another villain pursuing you, another lost treasure to be found?"

"What a tease you are, Howard," I said with a little laugh. "I was thinking of something else altogether — a subject so frivolous I refuse to confess it. But now that you mention it . . ." I motioned him to lean closer and lowered my voice to a thrilling whisper. *"What is in tomb Twenty-A?"*

Howard stared. "Not a bloody — Oh, good heavens, Mrs. Emerson, do forgive me! I cannot imagine why I so forgot myself."

Emerson had not failed to observe our whispers and exclamations. The dear fellow suffers from the (flattering, I confess) delusion that every man I meet has romantic designs upon me. He broke off his conversation with Mr. Quibell and demanded loudly, "What is it you and Carter find so absorbing, Peabody? Share it with us — unless it is of a private nature."

Poor Howard started convulsively. He had once been the victim of Emerson's suspicions — the innocent victim, I hardly need say — and was still nervous about it.* "Not at all sir," he exclaimed. "I mean — er — Mrs. Emerson was asking about one of the tombs, and I was about to tell her there is not a bloo— not a blooming thing there worth the attention of an excavator of her — of your — skill. Er — that is —"

"Hmph," said Emerson. "So what are your plans for this season, Carter? Still plugging away at that elongated tomb of Hatshepsut's?"

Conversation became general, to Howard's obvious relief. When we parted at last it was with the expectation of seeing many of our friends, including Howard, at a later time. I was chatting with Mr. Reisner, who had very politely invited me to visit him at Gizeh — "The third pyramid is part of our concession, Mrs. Emerson, and it is always at your disposal" — when another gentleman joined us.

"Forgive the interruption," he said with a courtly bow. "May I beg the favor of a word with you, Mrs. Emerson, when you have finished your conversation with Mr. Reisner?"

It was Colonel Bellingham. Mr. Reisner excused himself and somehow I was not surprised to find Emerson suddenly at my side. For so very

*This incident may be described in one of Mrs. Emerson's missing journals. Or it may not.

large a man he can move as quickly and silently as a cat when he chooses.

"Come, Amelia," he said brusquely. "The cab is waiting."

"If I may have a moment of your time —" the Colonel began.

"It is late. We are leaving Cairo early in the morning."

"Indeed? Then," said the Colonel with perfect aplomb, "it is all the more necessary that I speak with you this evening. Won't you take a chair, Mrs. Emerson? I promise I won't keep you long." He added with a smile, "It will give the young people a chance to improve their acquaintance."

One of them, at least, was already improving it. Dolly, in pink silk and lace embroidered with pearls, had Ramses firmly by the arm.

"Good evening, sir," she said. "Good evening, Mrs. Emerson, ma'am. I am so glad Daddy was able to catch you. I think he wants to talk with you about boring old tombs, so we will just wait on the terrace."

"Without a chaperone?" I exclaimed.

Dolly tossed her head and glanced over her shoulder at Nefret and David. "Why, sure 'nuf, Miss Forth will be a perfect chaperone. And — David? Hurry along now, Mr. Emerson."

Ramses allowed himself to be removed. Nefret took David's arm. "May I lean on you, David?" she inquired with a dazzling smile and eyes as hard as lapis beads. "At my age one tires so easily."

"They make a handsome pair, don't they?" Bellingham said. He was not speaking of Nefret and David, though the description would have been accurate.

"What is it you want?" Emerson demanded.

"Why, sir, first of all to thank your son for coming to Dolly's assistance the other day. But I expect she is doing that now, and much more prettily than I could."

I had not found the young lady's manners especially pretty. She had been sweetly rude to Nefret, and by using his first name, she had relegated David to the status of a servant.

Emerson had not missed the slight to his protégé. "Miss Bellingham was not in need of assistance. The young man may have annoyed her, but she was in no danger from him or anyone else in such a public place. If that was your sole motive for detaining us —"

"I have not yet mentioned my principal reason for wishing to speak with you."

"Do so, then."

"Certainly. I heard today, from M. Maspero, that your excavations this season will be restricted to the more obscure and least interesting tombs in the Valley of the Kings." He looked inquiringly at Emerson, who nodded brusquely. "I made so bold as to tell M. Maspero that it would be a pity to hand over such an important site to less competent archaeologists, when he has available in you the most skilled excavator in Egypt."

"Oh, you did, did you?" Emerson, who had

71

been shifting restlessly from one foot to the other, suddenly sat down and fixed the other man with a steady stare. "And what did Maspero say?"

"He did not commit himself," was the smooth reply. "But I have reason to believe he would be receptive to your application should you approach him again."

"Indeed? Well, I am obliged to you for your interest."

Colonel Bellingham had sense enough to leave it at that. He bade us good evening, and we watched him walk away.

"Well?" I said.

"Well. You don't suppose I am going to follow up that interesting suggestion, do you?"

"I know you too well to suppose any such thing," I replied. "You have taken a dislike to Colonel Bellingham, though I am at a loss to understand why."

"I do not need a reason to take a dislike to a man," Emerson declared.

"That is true," I admitted.

Emerson gave me an amused look. After knocking out his pipe, he pocketed it and rose to his feet. "I don't know what Bellingham was up to, but his implied promise was pure poppycock. Davis has the firman for the Valley of the Kings, and Maspero would have no reason to revoke it. Come along, my dear, the children will be waiting for us."

One of them was. Nefret stood at the entrance to the hotel, looking out toward the street.

"Where are the others?" I asked.

"David went to hire a cab. Ramses . . ." She swung round to face me and burst out, "They have gone into the gardens. They were standing together at the top of the steps — Miss Dolly having made it clear to me and David that our company was not welcome — when she suddenly darted off across the street. Ramses went after her."

The Ezbekieh Gardens cover an area of over twenty acres. They afford a popular promenade at all times of day; the attractions include cafés and restaurants, as well as a variety of rare plants and trees. After dark, in the limited glow of gaslight, they are even more romantic than the Moorish Hall at Shepheard's, and not at all the sort of place into which a young unmarried lady should venture even with an escort.

Colonel Bellingham — having, as I assumed, sought in vain within — hurried up to us. "Into the gardens, did you say?" he exclaimed. "Good heavens! Why didn't you stop them?"

Without waiting for a reply, he rushed down the steps.

"It was not your responsibility," I assured Nefret. "I am certain there is not the slightest cause for alarm, but perhaps we had better go in search of them."

Emerson caught hold of Nefret as she started impulsively down the stairs. "Ramses will find her and bring her back," he said. "I see David has a cab waiting; come along, my dears."

Nefret would not get into the cab. "Please, sir, let go my arm," she pleaded. "You are hurting me."

"You are hurting yourself, child," Emerson said in increasing exasperation. "Stop trying to pull away from me. Do you suppose I will allow you to enter that dark den of iniquity alone? Oh, very well, we will go as far as the entrance, but not a step farther. Damnation!"

"What is wrong?" David asked in alarm.

"Nothing is wrong," I said. "Miss Bellingham went into the garden and Ramses followed her, that is all. I can't think what has come over Nefret. She is usually more sensible."

"Perhaps we should go with them." David offered me his arm.

Fending off beggars and pedlars of dubious goods, avoiding carriages and camels and strolling tourists, we made our way across the busy thoroughfare. There was a little crowd gathered around the entrance to the gardens; as we hurried toward it I heard Nefret's voice raised in appeal and Emerson's loud response. It was, I am sorry to say, a swear word.

I had to use my parasol to get through the ring of staring spectators, and I believe our arrival saved Emerson from assault by the gentlemen who were present. He had both arms round Nefret, who was pounding on his chest and demanding he let her go on into the gardens.

"Shameful!" exclaimed one of the watchers. "Someone call a constable."

74

"No need for that, I reckon," said another man, clenching his fists. "Unhand the lady, mister."

"Damned if I will," said Emerson. "Oh, there you are, Peabody. See if you can talk some sense into . . . Nefret! Good Gad, girl, don't faint."

For her hands now lay quiet against his breast and she had stopped struggling. "I have not the least intention of fainting," she said, and turned her head to glare at her champions. "What the devil are you staring at?" she demanded.

The Englishman and the American exchanged glances. "Appears to be a family fight," said the latter.

"Righto. None of our affair, eh?"

"You can let me go, sir," said Nefret to Emerson. "I won't run away."

"Your word on it?"

"Yes, sir."

Cautiously Emerson relaxed his grip. Nefret smoothed her hair and took a mirror from her evening bag.

I lifted my parasol and addressed the gaping watchers. "Some people, I am sorry to see, take an impertinent interest in the affairs of others. Disperse, if you please. The performance is ended."

However, it was not.

Movement along the shadow-shrouded path leading into the gardens drew all eyes in that direction. The spectators fell back as a form emerged and advanced into the glow of the gaslight.

Ramses had lost his hat. That was not unusual. What was a trifle unusual, even for Ramses, was the blood that covered one side of his face and stained the pink silk skirt of the girl he carried in his arms. She appeared to be unconscious, though I was beginning to suspect that Dolly Bellingham was not always what she appeared. Her head rested against his shoulder and her loosened hair fell like silver rain over his arm.

"I beg your pardon for being so long," Ramses said. "I assure you the delay was unavoidable."

"Apparently the Colonel's concern for his daughter was not without foundation," I remarked.

Over an hour had passed, and we were all together in the saloon on the *Amelia*. We had handed the young lady over to her father, who had been summoned from the garden by Emerson's stentorian shouts, and had bundled Ramses and ourselves into the waiting cab. Ramses had stubbornly refused to answer any questions; that is, he had pretended, not nearly so convincingly as Miss Bellingham, to feel faint. She had taken no injury; the blood on her frock had come from a cut on Ramses's forearm. His brand-new coat was damaged beyond repair.

As soon as we reached the dahabeeyah he declared he was perfectly well and would not go with me to have his injuries attended to. So I fetched my medical supplies to the saloon and had the satisfaction of seeing Ramses struck momentarily dumb with embarrassment and fury when we overpowered him and forced him to remove his coat and shirt.

He must have gone about half-clothed the whole summer, since the upper part of his body was as brown as his face. After he had simmered down he allowed me to bandage his arm, but refused to let me put a few neat stitches into the cut, remarking, with what I supposed to be an attempt at humor, that scars were regarded among the Beduin as marks of manhood. He had acquired several new ones over the summer, together with a fine collection of fading bruises. Ramses was always falling off of or into natural objects, but some of the marks strongly suggested, to the suspicious mind of a mother, that he had been fighting. Another indication of manhood, I assumed — and not only among the Beduin. I forbore comment at that time and concentrated on cleaning the bits of gravel and other debris from the abrasions on his face.

"You fell onto the path, did you?" I asked, probing one of the deeper gashes.

"Are you enjoying this?" Ramses inquired.

"Don't speak to your dear mama in that way," said Emerson, who was holding his head so he wouldn't squirm.

The sound Ramses made might have been a groan or a laugh — except that he hardly ever laughed. "I apologize, Mother."

"I know you didn't mean it," I assured him, flicking out a largish bit of gravel.

I do not know how he had managed it, but the skin around his mustache was relatively unscathed. I was tempted to cut off just a bit of it — it was quite long and hung down at the ends — but Emerson was watching me with an expression that assured me he had not forgot the time I had deprived him of his cherished beard after he had been wounded on the cheek. Shaving the cheek had been absolutely necessary, but Emerson still bore a grudge.

"There, that should do the job," I said. "Nefret, would you just get me . . . Never mind, my dear; sit down and take a little wine, you are still rather pale."

"With fury," said Nefret. She had been inspecting Ramses with the cool appraisal of a surgeon trying to decide where to insert the scalpel. Now she turned the same frigid stare on David. "Do you look like that too?"

David clutched at his collar, as if fearing she would have the shirt off him. "Like what?" he asked warily.

"Never mind. You probably do. Men!" Nefret took the glass I handed her and passed it on to Ramses.

"I don't suppose," he began.

"No whiskey," I said.

Ramses shrugged and tossed the wine down. It was a rather nice little Spätlese, which deserved more respectful treatment, but I did not comment — or object, when Emerson, after a questioning look at me, refilled the glass.

Having cleaned my medical instruments and tidied myself, I accepted the whiskey and soda Emerson had ready for me and took a chair. "It appears," I repeated, "that Colonel Bellingham's concern for his daughter was not without foundation. You had better tell us precisely what happened, Ramses, so we can assess the situation accurately."

"Oh, curse it," said Emerson. "I refuse to assess the situation or be drawn into it."

"Please, Emerson. Allow Ramses to proceed with his statement."

Sekhmet crawled onto Ramses's lap and began to purr. "The creature oozes like a furry slug," said Ramses, eyeing it without favor. "Very well, Mother. The tale is quickly told."

I did not suppose it would be, since brevity was not one of Ramses's strong points. To my surprise, he was as good as his word.

"Miss Bellingham and I were standing midway down the stairs, talking," Ramses began. "All at once she turned and pointed toward the gardens. 'Look there,' she cried. 'Isn't that just too sweet!' Or something to that effect. I did not see anything or anyone I would describe as — er — 'sweet,' but naturally when she ran off I went after her. She is very quick. I didn't catch her up until after she had gone quite a distance into the gardens. It was dark. The gaslights in that area appeared to have gone out —"

"Or been broken," I interrupted. "There were bits of glass in those cuts."

79

Ramses gave me a sidelong look. "I thought you would notice that. To resume. She was standing still, peering into the shadows under a large specimen of *Euphorbia pulcherrima,* when I found her. She started to tell me someone was following her, but I cut her short; I was a trifle exasperated by her reckless behavior. I was trying to convince her to return at once when someone rushed out from the shrubbery and tripped me up. No, Mother, I did not get a good look at him, then or later; he wore a mask, naturally, and it was, as I have said, very dark. I fell rather hard, but not as hard as he had hoped, I fancy, for I was back on my feet almost at once. I managed to block his first attack, with minimal damage to myself. He fell back a step or two, and then Miss Bellingham began to scream — somewhat belatedly, in my opinion. He ran. She fainted. I picked her up and came back."

He finished his wine and I said in disbelief, "Is that all?"

"Yes."

EDITOR'S NOTE: The Reader may find it illuminating to compare Ramses's version of the incident with another account that occurs in one of the manuscripts in the newly discovered collection of Emerson family papers. The authorship of the fragment is as yet undetermined, but one may reasonably conclude that it was written either by Mr. Ramses Emerson himself, under the guise

of fiction (in emulation of his mother), or by someone more in his confidence than his parents were likely to have been in such cases as this. Excerpts from this manuscript will be designated henceforth as "from Manuscript H."

They stood at the top of the stairs from the terrace, looking out at the Shari'a Kamel, filled even at that hour with cabs and carts, donkeys and camels, and an occasional motorcar. Across the busy street the gaslights of the Ezbekieh Gardens twinkled through the dark foliage like fallen stars. Dolly Bellingham was prattling on about something or other; he paid scant attention to what she was saying, but he rather enjoyed the sound of her soft voice, with its quaint foreign accent. Intelligent conversation was not one of Dolly's strong points. It was the voice and the big brown eyes and the soft little hands. . . .

Then he realized that the little hands were plucking at his sleeve and that the soft voice was saying something that startled him into giving her his full attention.

"Let's run away and make them look for us. Wouldn't that be fun?"

"Run away? Where?"

"We could take a walk in those pretty gardens. They must be just plain gorgeous at night."

"Well, yes, but it's hardly the sort of place for —"

"I'd be perfectly safe with you," she murmured, clinging to his arm and looking up into his face.

"Er — yes, of course," said Ramses, in some

confusion. "But your father —"

"Oh, he'll fuss at me. I don't mind him, I can always talk him around. You aren't afraid of him, are you?"

"No. But my mother wouldn't approve either, and I'm absolutely terrified of her."

"Scaredy cat!"

"I beg your pardon?"

He had expected she would go on pleading, and he was beginning to enjoy the game. (He was, you must remember, rather new to it.) She caught him completely off guard when she exclaimed, "Oh, look!" and ran down the stairs, laughing at him over her shoulder. By the time he got his wits back she was threading a perilous path through the traffic that filled the street.

He thought he had her once, but she twisted gracefully away from the hand he had put on her shoulder and darted straight into the shadowy entrance. The gatekeeper intercepted him when he tried to follow; cursing with almost as much eloquence as his father, he fumbled in his pocket for a coin. The delay had given her ample time to elude him, but that was not what she wanted; glimpses of fluttering pink silk and silvery tinkles of laughter led him on, from one winding path into another. At first the walkways were well populated, but people made way for them, with smiles and laughing comments. One woman — an American, by her voice — exclaimed, "Aren't they cute?"

Ramses was not feeling at all cute, if he understood the word correctly. He could only hope to get the

82

spoiled little creature back to the hotel before anyone noticed they were missing, and pray none of the amused spectators were friends of his parents or her father. There were not so many strollers now. She was heading away from the cafés and the restaurant, back into the darker, less populated areas.

For a few long seconds he lost sight of her. Then the glow of a lamp ahead shone on pink silk, and he turned into the side path, swearing with relief and renewed anger. She was there, only a few feet ahead of him — not running now, walking slowly, and looking from side to side. No one else was in sight. Breaking into a run, he caught her up, took her by the shoulders, and spun her round to face him.

"Of all the silly, stupid stunts —" he began.

She caught hold of his lapels and leaned against him. "There's someone there," she whispered. "In the bushes. He was following me."

"Oh, right," said Ramses.

"I'm frightened. Hold me."

The tremulous pink mouth was close to his. She must be standing on tiptoe, Ramses thought.

That was his last coherent thought for some time. She fit snugly if stiffly into his arms — he had never been in such close contact with a girl wearing corsets before — and the soft pink mouth was a good deal more experienced than it had appeared.

The interval might have lasted even longer had he not been distracted by the crash of shattering glass. The flame of the nearest lamp — the only one along that stretch of the path — popped and hissed and went out.

Though he could see nothing he heard the sounds from the shrubbery and knew what they meant. He tried to pull away from Dolly's clinging arms, but she tightened her stranglehold round his neck and buried her face against his chest. His hands were raised, trying to loosen hers, when an indistinct form emerged from the shrubbery, snatched the girl away, and kicked his feet out from under him. He heard a strangled squawk from Dolly and managed to twist in midair, so that it was the side of his face instead of his nose and forehead that came into jarring contact with the gritty ground. When he scrambled up his eyes had begun to adjust to the darkness. He could see the glimmer of Dolly's light-colored frock and the pale oval of her face. He wondered why she wasn't screaming.

The fellow let her go and darted at Ramses. He blocked the blow but was somewhat disconcerted to feel a sharp pain run along his forearm. He had not seen the knife. Simultaneously he landed a blow of his own, a hard backhanded swing that struck the man across the side of the head and sent him staggering back.

Then Dolly screamed. The sound startled both men; it was, as Ramses later remarked, rather like having a shell explode right next to your ear. The other man turned and plunged into the shrubbery.

Instinctively Ramses started in pursuit. It was perhaps just as well Dolly stopped him, stepping out into his path and fainting gracefully but decisively against him.

Her screams had attracted attention. A few belated

84

strollers were coming their way, calling out questions. There was no chance of catching up with the attacker now, even if he had not been encumbered with a swooning maiden.

Ramses hoisted the girl unceremoniously into his arms and began to retrace his steps, politely declining offers of assistance from the curious people he encountered. "Thank you — our friends are waiting — she is unhurt — frightened by the dark — you know how women are. . . ."

Thank God, he thought piously, his mother had not heard him say that. What his mother would say to him he dared not think. "Another shirt ruined?" Not to mention his new suit, which he had owned less than forty-eight hours. He had got blood all over Dolly's dress, too. It looked very expensive.

His family was waiting at the entrance to the gardens. He was not surprised; his mother had an uncanny instinct for being in the wrong place at the right time. They were all staring at him — all except Nefret, who was examining her face in a small hand mirror. She glanced in his direction and shook her head, smiling as if at the antics of a naughty little boy.

Which was, of course, precisely how she thought of him.

Since it seemed clear that God was not going to do him the favor of striking him dead on the spot, he tried desperately to think of something to say that would not make him appear more of an idiot than he already felt. "Er — I beg your pardon for being so long. I assure you the delay was unavoidable."

85

"The would-be abductor must have done something to attract her attention and draw her away, into the gardens," I said thoughtfully. "Hence her exclamation. Didn't she tell you what she saw?"

"There was not time," said Ramses, staring intently at his empty glass.

"What was he wearing?"

"Amelia," said my husband. "May I interrupt for a moment?"

"Certainly, my dear. Have you thought of something you want to ask Ramses?"

"I do not want to ask him anything. I do not want *you* to ask him anything. I do not want anyone to ask him anything."

"But, Emerson —"

"I don't care who is after Bellingham's daughter, Peabody — if anyone is. She is not our responsibility. Neither," Emerson went on, smiling at me in a fashion that would have made some women run whimpering from the room, "is Mrs. Fraser our responsibility. Our responsibility, Peabody, is to our children — I include David, of course — and to one another, and to our work! So firmly convinced of this truth am I that I have determined to leave Cairo at once. We will sail tomorrow."

I was not at all put out, since I had expected something of the sort from Emerson. He is always complaining about interruptions to our work, and interfering in other people's affairs, and so on. I knew perfectly well that we would end up being involved no matter what he said or did to prevent it, so I said only:

"We cannot leave so soon, Emerson. The tailor has not finished with Ramses's clothes, and if he goes on as he has begun, he will certainly require a quantity of them. That coat is ruined, and he has had it less than —"

"Very well, my dear," said Emerson in the same mild voice. "We will go round to the tailor tomorrow morning — you and I together, Peabody, since I don't intend to let you out of my sight until we are under way. We will collect what is finished and have the rest sent on."

"I think that is a very sensible suggestion," said Nefret. "Our leaving as soon as possible, I mean. It would also be sensible for us to go to bed. Good night."

She swept out of the room.

"What is she so angry about?" David asked.

"Whom is she angry at, would be more accurate." Ramses removed the cat from his lap and deposited it on a chair. "I expect it's me. Good night, Mother. Good night, Father. Are you coming, David?"

David was, of course. He had said very little — he seldom got the chance to say anything when we were all together — but I knew he was blaming himself for not being at Ramses's side when danger threatened. They were the closest of friends and David took his self-assumed responsibilities far too seriously. No one, as I had good cause to know, could keep Ramses out of trouble for long.

"Now that is odd," I remarked after they had gone.

"What?"

"I would have expected Ramses to stay, speculating and theorizing and talking and arguing. He must be feeling more ill than he admitted. I had better go and —"

"No, you hadn't." Emerson put his arms around me and held me fast.

"Now, Emerson, don't do that. At least don't do that here in the saloon where people can —"

"Elsewhere, then."

"Gladly, my dear." As we strolled — or to be more accurate, hastened — toward our room, I said, "I am in complete agreement with your decision to leave tomorrow, Emerson. It will be good to be back at work again. You will begin, I assume, with tomb Twenty-A?"

Emerson drew me into the room, kicked the door shut, and swung round to face me. "Why should you assume anything of the sort?"

"It seems evident that quite a number of people want you to investigate it."

"What the devil are you talking about, Peabody?" Emerson demanded. He shook his head. "One would think that after all these years I would have become accustomed to your mental gyrations, but it really is deuced hard to keep up with them. The messages demanded I stay out of the place. And besides —"

"Emerson, you know perfectly well that the surest way of getting you to do something is to forbid you to do it. Colonel Bellingham's offer this evening was a subtler variation of the same method. He offered you the chance to look for unknown tombs, knowing full well that the suggestion of patronage on his part would make you even more determined to go on with what you had originally planned — that is, investigate the known tombs, including Twenty-A."

Emerson opened his mouth as if to speak.

"Furthermore," I went on, "Donald Fraser also endeavored — clumsily, I admit, but he is not a subtle person — to turn your attention away from the lesser-known tombs in the Valley — which includes, I hardly need point out, tomb Twenty-A! Can all these seemingly unrelated incidents be part of a single sinister plan? There can be no doubt of it, Emerson. Someone is trying to get you into that tomb. The only question is — why?"

Emerson's mouth was still open. He began mumbling. "It's getting worse. Or is it that my wits are failing? I used to be able to follow . . . Well, more or less . . . But this is . . ."

I deemed it advisable to change the subject. Turning, I said, "May I request your assistance with the buttons, my dear?"

CHAPTER THREE

Cats cannot be held accountable for their actions, because they have no morals to speak of.

Emerson was as good as his word. He followed close on my heels next morning while I made the rounds of boot makers, tailors, and haberdashers. Not even the hour I spent at the linen drapers got him off the trail, though he had never willingly entered that establishment before; arms folded, brow thunderous, he stood behind me while I selected handkerchiefs, serviettes, and sheets. It was well on toward midday before I finished, and when we returned to our hired carriage (Emerson holding my arm in a hard grip the whole time), I suggested that since the day was half gone we should postpone our departure till the following morning.

"No," said Emerson.

So we got off that same day, and I confess I was not unwilling to enjoy again the pleasures of Nile travel — to sit on the upper deck under the shade of an awning, watching glide past the fields upon which the water of the inundation lay in glimmering sheets, the mud-brick villages shaded by palm and tamarisk, the naked children splashing in the shallows. It was a scene that had not changed in thousands of years; the majestic shapes of the pyramids of Giza and Sakkara, their scarred slopes smoothed by distance, might have been just completed by the same half-naked men who tilled the muddy fields.

Emerson at once retired to the saloon, which we used as a sitting room and library. I knew better than to disturb him; he was accustomed to use this period of time to work out his plans for the winter, and he did not like to be questioned about them until he had things clear in his mind. At least that was what he always claimed. The truth is he took a childish pleasure in keeping the rest of us in suspense.

It was not until late afternoon that I was able to get Ramses alone. He and David were with Nefret on the upper deck, engaged in an animated discussion about mummies and examining some very nasty photographs. Averting my eyes from the face of an unfortunate queen whose cheeks had burst because of an excess of packing material under the skin, I requested that he try on his new clothes. He objected, of course, but only as a matter of form, since he knew it would have no effect.

The parcels I had fetched that morning were piled on the bed and the floor, unwrapped and uninspected. I removed a bundle of shirts from the chair and seated myself. Ramses eyed me warily.

"I want to be certain the trousers and shirts

are a proper fit," I explained. "Go behind the screen to change if you like."

Ramses assured me he did like. When he emerged he looked quite respectable except for the rolled-up bottoms of his trouser legs. I seated myself on the floor and took my sewing kit from my pocket.

"What are you doing?" Ramses asked in surprise.

"Measuring your trouser legs. They will have to be hemmed."

"But, Mother! Never in your entire life have you willingly —"

"Your father left me little choice," I replied, putting in pins. "The tailor would have done it properly if you had returned for the final fitting. Oh, dear, I am sorry. Did I prick you?"

"Yes. Why not spare yourself and me and tell me what it is you want to talk to me about?"

I looked up. Like the Egyptians he resembles in so many ways, Ramses has very long, thick lashes. They give his dark eyes quite a penetrating expression, but I knew that impassive countenance well, and I detected an underlying look of uneasiness.

"I suppose we can find a tailor in Luxor," I admitted, taking the hand he offered and allowing him to raise me to my feet. "Just tuck them into your boot tops until then."

"That temporary solution had occurred to me. Will this take long? I promised Father —"

"Let him wait. It is his own fault, for refusing

to allow me to discuss the matter earlier." I seated myself and arranged my skirts.

Ramses remained standing, arms folded and feet apart. Thanks to my study of psychology I recognized the posture as one of defensiveness and attempted domination, but of course I did not allow it to affect me. I had determined to follow Emerson's advice and treat Ramses like a responsible adult, confiding in him and asking his opinion. It was an effort, but one I felt obliged to make.

"What do you suppose is worrying Enid?" I inquired.

Ramses sat down rather suddenly on the bed. It might have been surprise that made him relax his aggressive posture. However, I thought I detected a flicker of relief in his hooded eyes. He had expected me to interrogate him about something else.

After a moment he shook his head. "I have no more information on the matter than you, Mother. If I might be allowed to theorize . . ."

"Pray do," I said with an encouraging smile.

"Hmmm. Well, then, I would guess the lady whom we met yesterday is somehow involved. She appears to be travelling with them, but in what capacity? It seemed strange to me, as it must have done to you, that her precise relationship was never explained or defined, as is ordinarily the case when introductions are made. She is not an Egyptologist, or we would know her name; if she were a kinswoman, however distant, that fact would surely have been mentioned. One possible relationship does come to mind. . . ."

He hesitated, looking at me from under lowered lids, and I reminded myself again of what Emerson had said. One small consolation was that Ramses could have learned of *that* relationship only secondhand. He had not the means to support a mistress.

Assuming a neutral expression, I said, "Unlikely in the extreme. Not only is she too old and too plain, but Donald would never be ungentlemanly enough to force his wife to accept his — er — to accept her as a travelling companion."

To my astonishment I saw that Ramses was blushing. I had never supposed he could. "That was not what I had in mind, Mother."

"What other possible relationships are there?" I demanded, hoping *I* was not blushing. "If she is not a hired guide or a relative or an old friend?"

"Companion," said Ramses. The blush had been no more than a slight darkening of his brown cheeks; it faded and his expression became grave. "Mrs. Fraser did not look well. People often come to Egypt for their health, yet if she had been ill and required the services of a nurse, why was this harmless fact not mentioned? Her behavior was erratic, and she obviously fears and dislikes Mrs. Whitney-Jones."

"A nervous disorder," I breathed. "Good heavens."

"You had thought of it, of course," said Ramses, watching me.

"Of course," I said automatically.

I had not thought of it, in fact, and the idea was so distressing that when Ramses pointed out it was almost teatime, and that Emerson would be looking for me, I did not pursue the subject. After tucking his trousers into his boot tops, Ramses politely escorted me to the saloon, where, as he had predicted, we found Emerson irritably demanding his tea.

Over the next few days I gave more thought to Ramses's theory and found it hideously convincing. It explained Enid's strange behavior and Mrs. Whitney-Jones's anomalous position. Mental disorders were viewed by the unenlightened as something shameful. Donald might hesitate to confide his wife's true condition even to such old friends as we.

After careful consideration, I decided not to confront Ramses with the other matter concerning which I had intended to interrogate him. I did not believe for a moment in his account of the incident in the Ezbekieh. My well-developed maternal instincts assured me he had told the truth, but not the whole truth. However, Emerson was right on two counts: the Bellinghams had nothing to do with us, and Ramses's relationships with persons of the female sex were best left to his father — for the present, at any rate.

I had enough to occupy my mind during the remainder of the trip — the usual domestic crises, woman-to-woman talks with Nefret, discussions of our plans for the winter — and, when Emerson was not in the saloon, refreshing my memory of the topography of the Valley of the Kings. Emerson had admitted the correctness of our surmises; it was the smaller, insignificant tombs he meant to investigate that season. I would have found the prospect depressing had it not been for the mystery of tomb Twenty-A. To my annoyance I was unable to find any reference to this tomb, nor was it marked on the only map I had been able to locate. The map was an old one that had appeared in Lepsius's monumental work circa 1850, so I decided Lepsius had probably overlooked it.

Ramses was no more enthusiastic about small uninscribed tombs than I. Being Ramses, he found a specious excuse for avoiding the task.

"If the tombs are uninscribed, there will be nothing for me to do, Father. You have Nefret to take photographs, and David to make plans and sketches, and the men, especially Abdullah, to assist in excavating. And," he added quickly, "Mother, who can turn her hand to anything. Would there be any objection to my continuing the project I began last year? I have worked out a new method of copying I am anxious to try."

The project had, in fact, originated several years earlier, but our clearance of Tetisheri's tomb had not given Ramses much time to work at it before the preceding winter. Though Ramses was a reasonably skilled excavator and surveyor, he had an extraordinary talent for languages, and it was in this realm that his primary interests lay. A remark of his father's had inspired this latest project — copying the inscriptions that covered the walls of Theban temples and monuments.

Every year, every month (said Emerson, in passionate commentary), more of these irreplaceable texts were lost. The infrequent but violent rainstorms, the slow, insidious attack of sun and sand, had caused the stone to crumble over the centuries, and now the new dam at Aswan had raised the water table so that the monuments were being eaten away from below. Some of the texts had been copied by earlier visitors, but Ramses had a method involving a combination of photography and hand copying that he hoped would produce more accurate reproductions than any heretofore. His knowledge of the language gave him an additional advantage. When the hieroglyphic signs are badly weathered only a trained linguist can tell what they must have been.

I am, in fact, somewhat unjust to Ramses when I claim his sole motive was to get out of work he found tedious. The cause was a worthy one, and since it required him to stand for long hours on flimsy ladders, examining the marks on sun-baked walls, it was not a task for the faint of heart.

Sailing has a soothing effect on even the most restless personalities. We had one of the most idyllic voyages I can recall. The river was high and the north wind swelled the white sails. We moored one night near the beloved site of

Amarna, where in the days of our youth Emerson and I had first learned to appreciate one another. Whether by design or accident the children went early to bed, and Emerson and I stood long at the rail, holding one another's hands like young lovers and watching the slender silver sickle of the new moon swing low above the cliffs. It seemed as if 'twere only yesterday; and when Emerson led me to our cabin I felt like a bride again.

In the enjoyment of such pleasures my concern about Enid diminished. Dr. Willoughby, in Luxor, was a specialist in nervous disorders; he would be able to help her. The only minor flaw in our arrangements was Ramses's steadfast refusal to take up with Sekhmet. Not that he was unkind; one of Ramses's few virtues was his fondness for animals, and he would not have mistreated any creature. Firmly, gently, and in silence, he simply removed her when she tried to crawl onto his knee. I thought Sekhmet felt it a great deal, but when I taxed Ramses with it he gave me one of his peculiar half-smiles and asked how I could tell.

Ramses and I were getting on quite well; I reflected, with pardonable complacency, on how neatly I had handled the conversation about Enid and how appreciatively he had responded to my courtesy.

Which only goes to show that even I can be deceived, and that Ramses had indeed matured. He was even more duplicitous, and better at concealing it, than he had been in his youth.

Though I am British to the core and proud of it, Egypt holds a place in my heart that is un-equalled even by the green meadows of Kent. It would be hard to say which of Egypt's many antique sites is dearest to me: I have a particular weakness for pyramids, but Amarna has senti-mental as well as professional associations and Thebes had been our home for the past several years. As the *Amelia* maneuvered in toward shore my heart beat fast with anticipation and a sense of homecoming. It was always the same, yet it was always different — the light on the western cliffs a softer gold, the shadows a more subtle shade of lilac. Evening was drawing in; for the past few miles we had glided through water stained crimson and gold with reflected sunset. Across the river the monumental ruins of the temples of Karnak and Luxor shone pale in the dusk, with the lights of the modern town twin-kling between them.

When the gangplank went down I held the others back so that David might be the first to disembark. Prominent among the group of friends who awaited us was the tall, dignified form of Abdullah, our reis, and I knew he yearned to clasp his grandson in his arms.

"What the devil are you doing, Peabody?" Emerson demanded, trying to detach himself from my grip.

"Abdullah yearns to clasp David in his arms,"

I explained. "Allow them a few moments alone to enjoy the bliss of their reunion."

"Hmph," said Emerson.

Other arms were waiting to clasp him and Ramses: Daoud, Abdullah's nephew and second in command; Selim, Abdullah's youngest son; Yussuf and Ibrahim and Ali and the other men who had been faithful friends and workers for many years. Abdullah came at once to offer me a hand as I stepped onto the bank. His dark, dignified face was stern and unsmiling, but affection warmed his eyes.

Emerson cut short the embraces and cries of welcome. He greeted Abdullah in characteristic fashion, with a hearty handclasp and a loud complaint. "Curse it, Abdullah, where are the horses?"

"Horses?" Abdullah's eyes shifted.

"Large, four-footed animals. People ride on them," said Emerson with awful sarcasm. "The horses we hire every season. How are we supposed to get to the house?"

"Oh. Those horses."

"The house is ready, I trust?" Emerson demanded. "I telegraphed you when to expect us."

"Ready? Oh, yes, Emerson."

I took pity on Abdullah — and myself. Emerson ought to have recognized the familiar evasive maneuvers that indicated the individual being questioned had not, in fact, done the job he had been asked to do.

The difficulty was not that Abdullah was lazy

or inefficient. The difficulty was that he was a man. He honestly could not understand why I made such a fuss about dust and cobwebs and spiders and sheets that had not been aired since the previous spring. He anticipated a fuss, though, and he was — manlike — hoping to put it off as long as possible.

"It is too late to move all our belongings now, Emerson," I said — and heard an exhalation of relief from Abdullah, so soft I would have missed it if I had not expected it. "We will stay on board overnight."

So we had a pleasant little celebration in the saloon with our friends. It was very lively at first, with everyone talking at once. Daoud wanted to know about Evelyn and Walter, for whom he had conceived a great admiration; Selim bragged of the health, beauty, and intelligence of his children (in my opinion he had far too many of them for a man not yet twenty, but that is the Arab way); David gave his grandfather an (expurgated, I did not doubt) account of his experiences that summer with Sheikh Mohammed; Emerson asked about the tomb and the latest activities of the industrious tomb robbers of Gurneh.

Then the groups broke up and re-formed. I observed that Selim had gone off into a corner with David and Ramses, and deduced, from the smothered laughter and low voices, that he was getting another, unexpurgated version of the summer's adventures.

Abdullah had come to join me on the divan.

We sat in companionable silence for a time. As the darkness deepened, the mellow light of a nearby lamp softened his stern features, and I thought how strange it was that I could feel so at ease with an individual so different from myself in every way — in gender, age, religion, nationality, and culture. How well I remembered his contemptuous question that first season in Egypt: "What is a woman, that she should cause such trouble for us?" He had gone to considerable trouble for me in the intervening years, risking his life not once but several times; and my initial suspicion of him had been transformed into profound respect and affection.

I did not know how old Abdullah was. The beard that had been grizzled when first we met was now snowy white, and his tall frame was not so straight as it once had been. Emerson had tried on several occasions to persuade him to retire, but he had not the heart to insist. Abdullah was proud of his position, and with good cause. He was the most skilled reis in Egypt and I did not doubt he could have conducted an archaeological excavation more competently than many of the self-proclaimed Egyptologists who bumbled around the sites.

Abdullah was watching the young people. Nefret had joined them, her coppery gold head the focus of the circle.

"He has become a fine man," Abdullah said softly. "They will be well mated, he and Nur Misur."

"Light of Egypt" was the name the men had given Nefret. For one shocked moment I thought the masculine pronoun referred to David. When I realized whom he did mean, I was almost as shocked.

"Ramses and Nefret? Where on earth did you get such an idea, Abdullah?"

Abdullah gave me a sidelong look. "It was not in your mind, Sitt Hakim, or in that of the Father of Curses? Well, well, it will be as Allah decrees."

"No doubt," I said dryly. "David is a fine young man too, Abdullah. We are all very proud of him."

"Yes. It comforts me to think he will stand in my place when I am too old to work for the Father of Curses."

There was another shock! We meant to educate David as an Egyptologist; he was a talented artist and his intelligence was of a high order — too high to be wasted on the position of foreman. Had Emerson discussed our plans with Abdullah? Surely he must have done. However, Emerson did have a way of assuming there was no need to tell people what he meant to do, since they would have to do it anyhow.

"But," I began, "that would not be fair to Daoud and Selim and the others — to put over them a boy so much younger, without their experience —"

"They will obey my command. David has learned of things they do not know. He will be . . ." Abdullah paused and then said grudgingly,

103

"He will be almost as good as I, one day."

The party went on for quite some time. I had known we would not go ashore that night, so I had ordered the cook to prepare food for a large group. After the men had returned to Gurneh and we had retired to our rooms, I told Emerson what Abdullah had said about David.

"Curse it," Emerson said, throwing the boot he had just removed at the wall.

"Swearing won't help, Emerson. You must talk with him. Surely he would be pleased to see his grandson advance in the world."

"You don't understand." Emerson pitched the other boot after the first. "In Abdullah's world his position is the proudest a man can achieve. How can he admit that a beardless boy, his own grandson, will be his superior?"

"That is very clever of you, Emerson," I said in surprise. "In psychological terms —"

"Don't say that word, Amelia. You know how I hate that word! It is not psychology, it is simple common sense. I will talk to him again, I promise." Emerson rose and stretched and yawned. Golden fingers of lamplight caressed the rippling muscles of his chest. "Er — do you need any help with your —"

"I would not like to trouble you, my dear."

"It is no trouble at all, Peabody."

I did not intend to mention Abdullah's other astonishing assumption, but it preyed on my mind, to such an extent that I found myself becoming angry. Not with dear old Abdullah, of course; arranged marriages are customary in Egypt, and financial factors count for more than the feelings of the young people involved. A cynic might claim that similar considerations prevail in our own society, and the cynic would probably be right. Few doting mamas would consider any subterfuge immoral if it helped their sons to "good" marriages. Was that what the world thought of me — that I was keeping Nefret, Lord Blacktower's heiress, for my son?

Fortunately my well-known sense of humor came to my rescue before I lost my temper completely. "They say — who says? Let them say!" Never would such a contemptible scheme find a place in the bosom of Amelia P. Emerson! Nor, I felt certain, had any such idea entered the children's heads. They had been raised as brother and sister. There is nothing so destructive of romance than proximity, as someone — possibly I — has said.

Besides, they were both far too young. A responsible young man does not even consider marriage before he reaches his mid-twenties.

I do not know what peculiar psychological quirk prompted me to ask, "What do the men call Ramses, Emerson?"

Emerson chuckled. "Quite a lot of things, Peabody."

"You know what I mean. Nefret is Nur Misur, I am the Sitt Hakim, and you Abu Shita'im. Don't they have a similar nickname for Ramses?"

But I did not get an answer at that time, since

105

Emerson had something else on his mind.

We were up before daybreak, eager to get to the house and begin work. As usual, we breakfasted on the upper deck, watching the stars fade out and the eastern cliffs brighten and shift through the spectrum of reflected dawn colors, from smoke-gray to amethyst and rose to pale silver-gold.

As usual, the day began with an argument.

Ramses and David (i.e., Ramses) had decided they would prefer to live on board the dahabeeyah during the season. They (I did not doubt David had been well coached by Ramses) presented a series of specious arguments. The house was rather small for four people and the necessary offices. There would be no need for additional servants, since they could take their meals with us and clean their own rooms, and Hassan and the crew would be on the dahabeeyah much of the time, and . . .

And so on. It was all true and it had nothing to do with their real reasons for proposing the scheme.

As I might have expected, Emerson took their side. Men always stick together. Nefret further complicated the situation by proclaiming that if Ramses and David were allowed to stay on board, she should be given the same privilege. Needless to say, I gave that idea short shrift.

"Really!" I said after she had stormed off to her room to finish packing and the boys had discreetly removed themselves. "I begin to wonder if that girl will ever learn proper civilized behavior. Can you imagine the gossip if I permitted her to stay here with them unchaperoned? *At night?*"

"They are often together, unchaperoned, during working hours," Emerson said mildly. "I have never understood the obsessiveness of the prurient with the hours of darkness. As you are well aware, Peabody, the activity of which they disapprove is not only entirely possible in broad daylight, it can be even more interesting when —"

"Yes, my dear, I am well aware of that," I said, laughing. "You need not demonstrate."

Emerson removed his arm and returned to his chair. "As for Nefret becoming civilized, I hope to heaven she never does, if by civilized you mean behaving like a prim English girl. She is another of those who walk in two worlds," said Emerson, obviously pleased with this poetic metaphor. "The formative years of her life were spent in a society with different, and in some ways much more sensible, standards of conduct. Besides, my dear, your own behavior is not exactly conventional. Nefret is bound to imitate you because she admires you so much."

"Hmmm," I said.

Most of our packing had been completed the day before. We had been waiting for some time before we saw the little caravan approaching — donkeys and carts and the horses Emerson had hired. The men began carrying boxes and bundles to the carts, and Abdullah hurried to me.

"Everything is ready, as you see, Sitt."

"Good," I said. "Selim, just make certain that box of cleaning rags is on top of the pile."

"You will not need them, Sitt," Abdullah assured me.

We had the same little discussion every year, so I simply smiled and nodded — and made certain the cleaning materials were easily accessible. Then I went to join Emerson, who was inspecting the horses.

"They have been washed, Sitt Hakim," said Selim, grinning. "And the donkeys."

I smiled and nodded at *him*. I meant to look the animals over myself, of course, at a more convenient moment. Donkeys and camels and even some of the cherished horses are not well cared for; when I first began washing and doctoring the animals in my charge I was regarded as wildly eccentric. I was still regarded as eccentric, but I was obeyed.

"Quite a good lot of animals," Emerson said approvingly. "Especially those two. Where did you find them, Abdullah?"

The horses he indicated merited a more enthusiastic description. One was a bay mare, the other a silver-gray stallion. Both were obviously of pure Arab stock, for they had the hard, clean limbs and small well-shaped feet of that superb breed. They were unusually large, however — over fifteen hands — and their saddles, of fine leather ornamented with silver, had never been rented in Luxor.

I had one of my famous premonitions. It may have been prompted by Abdullah's failure to answer Emerson, or by the sight of Ramses stroking the neck of the gray and murmuring in its pricked ear.

"Ramses!" I exclaimed.

"Yes, Mother?"

I moderated my voice. "Whose horse is that?"

Ramses came toward me. The stallion followed him, stepping as daintily as a cat.

"His name is Risha. He and Asfur" — he indicated the mare — "were gifts to us from Sheikh Mohammed. Naturally he is at your disposal, Mother — or Father."

"He's not up to my weight," Emerson said tactfully. "And a little large for you, Peabody, don't you think? Magnificent creatures, both of them! I trust you thanked the sheikh properly."

"Yes, sir." Ramses was not looking at him. "Er — Nefret?"

"Are you offering him to me?" Nefret held out her hand; the splendid creature nuzzled it and then bowed its head as she ran caressing fingers along its jaw and into its mane.

"He is yours if you want him." Ramses spoke without hesitation. I saw him swallow, though.

The smile she gave him would have recompensed many a young man for a gift as great. "You really would? Thank you, Ramses, dear, but you cannot dispose of an animal like this one as you would a piece of furniture."

Gravely, and with a good deal more courtesy than she often displayed to human beings, she introduced herself to Asfur as she had to Risha. "Try her," David urged.

"You are not as gallant as Ramses," Nefret said, laughing. "Aren't you going to offer to give her to me?"

"Oh, yes, of course," David exclaimed in confusion. "I thought you said —"

"Don't tease him, Nefret," I said. "She is only teasing, David."

Nefret patted him on the shoulder. "Help me up."

The stirrup was too high for her to reach. David cupped his hands under her little boot and lifted her into the saddle. The animals were so splendidly proportioned, one did not immediately realize how large they were; she looked like a child perched there on the high saddle. She laughed aloud and gathered the reins into her hands.

"She wants to run! Hurry, or I will be the first to the house. You don't mind, do you, David?"

"No — yes — wait!" David caught at the bridle.

Emerson began to mutter uneasily. He believes in the equality of the sexes, except where his daughter is concerned. "See here, Nefret . . . I don't think . . . Peabody, tell her . . ." He grabbed me round the waist and tossed me onto a randomly selected horse.

"At least wait until David shortens the stirrups," said Ramses. He was standing by Risha, his hand lightly resting on the saddle. . . . And then he was in the saddle.

He may have done it to distract Nefret, though the desire to show off was certainly an element. It certainly distracted me. I had not seen his foot touch his own stirrup; it was as if he had flowed, in a single movement, from the ground to the horse's back.

Nefret stared. "How did you do that?"

"He's been practicing all summer," David said innocently.

Ramses gave his best friend a less than friendly look. "It is not that difficult."

"Then you can teach me," Nefret said.

"Er — yes. Don't let her run, Nefret. There are too many irrigation ditches and soft spots here. Can you hold her?"

"Ha!"

"Hmmm," I said, watching the pair ride off side by side. "He managed that rather well. I hope —"

But I was speaking to myself. Emerson had gone in pursuit, and David was mounting one of the hired animals. Leaving Abdullah to finish the loading, I followed the others across the green fields of the cultivation into the desert.

We had had the house built the year after our discovery of Tetisheri's tomb, when it became evident that we would be working in western Thebes for several seasons. It had always been

111

Emerson's intention to build a permanent expedition house, with the *Amelia* serving as a residence only until we had made up our minds where we wanted to settle down. Pleasant as the boat was, it was not really commodious enough for five people, their books and papers, and a great many antiquities. In my opinion the house was not commodious enough either, and I intended, that season, to add a wing. I had always dreamed of a house with ample office and storage space.

Not that we were likely, in the near future, to require much storage space. I had not openly objected to Emerson's plans, for that never does any good. Subtle persuasion is the only way to get him to come round to my way of thinking.

The small tombs Emerson meant to investigate held no interest for me. Most of them had been visited by earlier archaeologists and were known to contain nothing of interest. Thanks to M. Maspero's petty-mindedness the rest of the Valley of the Kings was closed to us, but there were other sites in western Thebes — Drah Abu'l Naga, where we had discovered the tomb of Tetisheri, the cemetery of the nobles at Gurneh, and quite a number of nice temples — that would give my husband's talents greater scope. Once we had solved the mystery of tomb Twenty-A — which should not take long — I would tactfully persuade Emerson to work elsewhere.

We spent the rest of the morning unpacking and cleaning the house. Driven out of the sitting room by the strong stench of carbolic and Keating's powder, we retreated to the verandah and waited for luncheon to be served.

The verandah ran along the front of the house, which faced east; it offered a beautiful view, clear down the desert slope to the green fields and the river beyond. Comfortable chairs and sofas, small tables and bright rugs scattered across the tiled floor, gave the place a cozy look. The low wall bounding the terrace supported columns along which I had caused trellises to be built, in the hope of training pretty flowering vines that would frame the open arches. By the time we left Egypt at the end of the season, the vines were doing splendidly. By the time we arrived at the start of the next season, the vines were only withered stalks. Horticulture was not one of Abdullah's interests.

"I hope you did not leave any arsenic lying about," said Emerson, poking tobacco into his pipe.

"Now, Emerson, you know I do not employ arsenic to kill rats when the cats are with us, for fear of their being poisoned. They will rid us of resident rodents."

Anubis had already presented us with two unlucky mice and was presumbly still at it, since he had not joined us on the verandah. Stretched out on the ledge next to Nefret, her head on the girl's lap, Sekhmet appeared to be smirking in her sleep.

"Not that one," said Ramses. "Does she ever

113

do anything but sleep and eat and shed on people?"

Abdullah, who had appeared in the doorway, remarked, "Let us hope not. One demon cat is enough. Will you have the food brought here, Sitt Hakim?"

I said we would and invited him to join us. Abdullah looked down his nose at me. "I must make sure the men finish sweeping the desert, Sitt," he said. "How far from the house should they go?"

"Now, Abdullah, don't sulk," I said. "And don't try to be sarcastic."

"It is a waste of time," Emerson agreed. "You did well, Abdullah. I forgot to ask you last night: Were there any messages waiting for us?"

"Selim brought them here from Luxor," Abdullah said. "I will ask him where he put them." Then he reached into the breast of his robe. "There was also this, Emerson. I found it pinned to the door this morning when I came to clean — to finish cleaning the house."

He held it up so we could all read it. The lettering was large and clear.

"The curse of the gods fills tomb Twenty-A. Enter it at your peril!"

Emerson's eyes narrowed. "Hell and damnation!" he cried. "The bastard has followed us to Luxor!"

I have almost given up trying to keep Emerson from using bad language. I have not entirely given up trying to keep the children from doing it, but there are times when I fear I am losing the battle. It is natural that they should imitate one they admire so much, and since I am a firm believer in women's rights I can hardly single out Nefret for scoldings. Whatever is permitted to a man should be permitted to a woman — even swearing.

Our house was near the small village of Gurneh, conveniently close to the quarters of Abdullah and our other men and a mere twenty-minute walk from the Valley of the Kings. The location had another advantage in that it enabled us to keep an eye on the goings and comings of the Gurnawis. Some of them were among the most expert tomb robbers in Egypt.

When Emerson announced that we would go over to the Valley immediately after luncheon I did not demur. There was still a great deal to be done around the house, but how could I content myself with dull domestic duties when archaeological fever burned all the brighter after a six months' absence?

The direct path to the Valley leads up and over the cliffs behind the temple of Deir el Bahri. We were all in excellent spirits as we mounted the steep slope; Emerson's handsome countenance wore an anticipatory smile, and he considerately slowed his steps to match mine, allowing the children to precede us. Below lay the beautiful temple of Queen Hatshepsut, its colonnades shining in the sunlight. The air was very warm and very still. The only color was the blue of the sky overhead; white dust and sun-bleached rock stretched out ahead.

When we reached the top of the plateau Emerson stopped and drew me to his side. I was not sorry to rest for a minute; after a summer in damp rainy England it always takes me a few days to become accustomed to the dry Egyptian climate.

After a moment Emerson looked down at me and smiled. "Well, Peabody?"

It was not difficult to find a way of summarizing my sentiments. With considerable emotion I said, "I am the most fortunate of women, my dear Emerson."

"Damn right," said Emerson. "Hurry along now, we are wasting time. Oh — by the by, Peabody —"

"Yes?"

"You are the light of my life and the joy of my existence."

"Damn right," I said.

Emerson burst out laughing and took my arm.

The path we followed curved across the surface of the plateau, skirting the southwestern end of the deep canyon, or wadi, in which the kings of the empire were buried. There are two Valleys of the Kings, but the eastern valley contains the greater number of royal tombs, and it is the one tourists and guidebooks refer to when they speak of it without a qualifying adjective. From above,

116

the Valley resembles a complex leaf like that of an oak or maple, with branches extending in all directions. The cliffs that enclose it are almost vertical; even the nimble-footed Egyptians cannot scale them except in a few areas where paths as ancient as the tombs themselves descend in sinuous curves into the Valley.

The young people were waiting for us at the top of one such path, and we paused to admire the view. Some individuals might have found it stark and forbidding; no flow of water to refresh the eye, no tree nor flower nor blade of grass. Groups of tourists, foreshortened into limbless lumps from above, moved lethargically along the Valley floor. Most had already left for the East Bank and the comfort of their hotels, but there were enough of them to inspire a mutter of "Cursed tourists!" from Emerson.

"Where are we going first?" Nefret asked.

Hands on his hips, Emerson surveyed the scene. I suspected he was up to something, and my suspicions were confirmed when he said casually, "Carter is still working at the Hatshepsut tomb, isn't he?"

"So he said at dinner the other evening," Ramses replied. "The passage appears to be endless; he had dug down almost two hundred meters last season, with no end in sight. He hopes to reach the burial chamber this month, but I doubt he will; the fill is almost as hard as cement. The men were using pickaxes, and the heat was intense."

I did not ask how he knew. He might have got the information from Howard, but it was more likely he had been into the confounded place himself. I had neglected to forbid him to do so since it had not occurred to me that he might.

"Suppose we have a look," Emerson said. "The tomb is so remote and undistinguished that none of the cursed tourists will be there."

He was the first to begin the descent, but Nefret was close on his heels. Ramses had learned through painful experience that Nefret would haughtily reject any offer of assistance from him, so he let her go on and offered me his hand. I did not need it, but I took it anyhow.

"What is the number of Hatshepsut's tomb?" I asked.

"Twenty."

"Aha," I exclaimed. "I knew it! Your father is not interested in Hatshepsut's tomb; he is looking for tomb Twenty-A, which must be in the same area. Good Gad, Ramses, watch what you are doing."

His foot must have slipped. He caught himself at once and steadied me with a hand almost as hard as that of his father. "I beg your pardon, Mother. You took me by surprise. I thought you knew. There is no such tomb."

"What? But the tombs are numbered."

"Yes, in numerical sequence. Mr. Wilkinson, later Sir Gardiner, numbered the tombs known to him eighty years ago; the last of his were numbers Twenty and Twenty-one. M. Lefebure added to the list —"

"Ramses," I said, trying not to grind my teeth. "Please get to the point."

"I am endeavoring to do so, Mother. Er — to summarize, then. Other tombs have been located and numbered since, in the order of their discovery. I believe the latest one is Forty-five, found last year by Mr. Carter. There are no A's or B's or other sub-categories."

I dug in my heels. "Stop a moment. Are you telling me there is no tomb with the number Twenty-A?"

"No, Mother. Er — yes, Mother, that is what I am telling you. I assumed you and Father had discussed the matter. He is certainly aware of the fact."

"Is he indeed?" I pondered the underhanded behavior of Emerson. Had he deliberately refrained from setting me straight so that I could dig myself even deeper into the pit of ignorance? Well! Thanks to Ramses I could now avoid that embarrassment — if I could think how to wriggle out of it. I wondered why Howard Carter had not corrected me when I mentioned the number to him.

A more urgent question found utterance. "Why should anyone warn us away from an imaginary tomb? If it does not exist, we cannot investigate it."

"Quite true," said Ramses. "However, it is possible that the individual in question meant to indicate —"

"Peabody!" Emerson was far below, but his voice would have been audible on the other side of the Valley. "What are you stopping for?"

"Coming, my dear," I called, and hastened to do so. Ramses kept trying to catch hold of me as I scrambled down the slope, but I managed to elude him. In fact, I was feeling rather kindly toward the lad just then. Not only had he warned me about the pitfall ahead, but he had given me a clue as to how I could avoid it.

The descent ends near tomb Sixteen, which is that of Ramses I. Mr. Wilkinson had numbered them in the simplest and most straightforward manner possible; with a pot of paint in one hand and a brush in the other, he had walked from one end of the Valley to the other, stopping at each entrance long enough to paint the numeral on the rock above or beside it. I had seen the numbers so often that I had not taken particular notice of them.

When I reached the Valley floor I found Emerson conversing with Ahmed Girigar, the reis of the Egyptian watchmen, or *gaffirs*. In theory their duties were to guard the tombs from vandals, thieves, and unauthorized visitors. In practice their primary activity consisted of squeezing baksheesh out of the tourists whom they admitted to the tombs. Since Howard had assumed his post as inspector for Upper Egypt, he had done a great deal to improve conditions in the Valley, erecting iron gates in front of the more important tombs, clearing a few paths through the sharp stones and heavy boulders that litter the Valley floor, and hiring watchmen. How useful the *gaffirs* were was questionable; they were local men and, like all the locals, very poor. Few of them, I suppose, would have refused a visitor anything if the price were high enough, and some peddled stolen antiquities on the side.

However, Reis Ahmed was well regarded by Howard and by Emerson. "He is honest if you make it worth his while," was Emerson's assessment, which was no more cynical than his assessments of most people.

Ramses lingered to exchange compliments with Reis Ahmed ("Tall and handsome like your honored father, pleasing the women . . ."), and the rest of us went on. I was grateful for my stout boots, but I envied, even as I deplored, Emerson's unprofessionally comfortable attire. Heat beat down from above and rose from below, reflected from a surface that shimmered so white it dazzled the eyes. Rivulets of perspiration trickled down my face, and my hand, enclosed from wrist to fingertips in Emerson's very large, very warm grasp, felt like a soggy wool mitten. On the rough rocky wall to our right I saw one of Mr. Wilkinson's numbers. It was the number Nineteen; as I recalled from my reading, it marked the tomb of a Ramesside prince with a polysyllabic name. Belzoni had discovered the tomb in 1817, but the entrance was now almost entirely blocked with debris.

"Stop," I ordered, drawing Emerson aside into

a patch of shade. "I want to talk to you."

"What about?"

"For one thing, your failure to confide to me your true purpose. You have no intention of visiting Howard. He won't be there; like all sensible excavators, he stops work during the hottest part of the day, and it is extremely rude to explore other people's tombs without their —"

"Yes, yes," said Emerson. He studied me with mild curiosity. "A trifle warm, are you? Small wonder. Why do you insist on wearing a coat and buttoning your shirt clean up to your chin? Nefret has better sense; she has removed hers."

I spun round with a gasp and was relieved to see I had mistaken his reference. It had not been to Nefret's shirt, but to her coat, which David was carrying.

Her working uniform, like mine, consisted of boots and trousers below, shirtwaist and coat above. Now her costume resembled that of Ramses and David, for she had pushed her sleeves up and unfastened the top buttons of the shirt, and she walked with a lad's easy stride. No one would have taken her for a boy, though, not even with her hair hidden under her pith helmet. It was not only the delicate, flower-fair face that defined her gender. The trousers must have shrunk in the wash.

"Put your jacket on at once, Nefret," I exclaimed.

"Oh, Aunt Amelia, must I? It is so cursed hot!"

"And don't swear."

"That was not swearing," said Ramses. "You ought to hear her when she is really angry."

He ducked the playful blow she aimed at him and continued, "Hatshepsut's tomb is just ahead. I don't hear any sounds of activity; perhaps Mr. Carter has stopped for the day."

"Hmph," said Emerson, thereby indicating his contempt for excavators who curtailed their activities because of a mere one hundred degrees of heat.

"All the same, I would like to have a look," Nefret said.

Ramses and David immediately declared their intention of doing the same, and the trio started off. The path was steep and quite rough; this part of the Valley was seldom visited by tourists, so the Antiquities Service had not gone to the trouble of making access easy.

As in all parts of the Theban mountains, the opposite wall of the wadi was pocked with holes and crevices. The place was deserted, except for a motionless bundle of cloth at the base of the cliff — one of the guards, taking his midday nap. His dusty robe blended so well with the rock I had not noticed him until then. The only parts of his person visible to me were the soles of his bare feet, and he appeared to be sleeping as soundly as an Englishman would rest on a soft feather bed. Nevertheless, I lowered my voice when I addressed my husband.

"As I was saying, Emerson, I know your true

purpose in coming here. You hope to locate the mysterious tomb mentioned by our anonymous correspondent."

Emerson leaned against a boulder and began filling his pipe. "Your habit of jumping to conclusions has served you badly this time, Peabody. I regret having to inform you —"

"That there is no tomb numbered Twenty-A. I knew that, of course."

"You did? Then why the devil didn't you say so?"

"For the same reason you didn't say so." I smiled at him in a kindly fashion and he had the grace to look embarrassed. "Our minds were following along the same track. The number indicates a tomb that has not been discovered — except by our mysterious informant. In so designating it, he has given us a clue as to its location. It lies somewhere between Twenty and Twenty-one. Hatshepsut's tomb, number Twenty, is at the end of that small finger of the wadi, so Mr. Wilkinson must have started back toward the main Valley after numbering it. If we begin at the tomb of Hatshepsut, and follow the cliff toward tomb Twenty-one —"

Emerson drew a breath so deep it strained the buttons of his shirt. "I do not propose to waste time on such nonsense, Peabody."

So we went to join the children, who were, as I had expected, arguing. Nefret was taunting Ramses because he had refused to enter Hatshepsut's tomb or allow her to do so, and David was trying unsuccessfully to make peace between them.

The prospect was certainly not enticing. Above the sloping, tunnel-like entrance the cliffs soared sheer toward the sky. Mounds of loose scree, washed down to the Valley floor by rainstorms and weathering, rose on either side. Some of the mounds had been formed by the debris removed from the tomb; they were darker than the pale limestone visible elsewhere, and the bits of stone had the jagged look of shale or some other soft rock.

It was a forbidding place. One look inside the dark hole tucked under the cliff convinced me I did not want to enter it either, at least not that afternoon. If a pyramid is not available, I will settle for crawling into a nice deep tomb, but from what I had heard of this one it had nothing to offer except bat guano, a temperature like that of a blast furnace, and the possibility of being brained by a chunk of falling rock. Besides, I was anxious to begin the search for the lost tomb.

This suggestion delighted Nefret and made her forget her annoyance with her brother. Turning to him with a sunny smile, she said, "Shake hands, Ramses, and let us be friends. I am sure your intentions were good, and I did not mean to imply you were afraid."

"I am pleased to hear it," said Ramses, folding his arms and frowning at the little hand she had offered. "Ordinarily the word 'coward' does carry that implication, especially when it is shouted at

125

the top of one's lungs."

Nefret only laughed and threw her arms around him in an affectionate hug. Instead of softening, his face became even gloomier.

The distance involved was less than a hundred and fifty meters, in a straight line. But there were no straight lines in that ravine; the cliff face was as uneven as broken teeth and the foot of it was deep in loose scree and fallen rock, with piles of debris on every hand. We began at the opening that marked the entrance to Hatshepsut's tomb and followed the base of the cliff back toward the main wadi, scrambling, climbing up and down, poking at interesting depressions — all of us except Emerson, who had flatly refused to participate. He stalked along parallel to our erratic path with his nose in the air. He was obliged to walk quite slowly in order to keep level with us, and his progress rather resembled that of a military funeral, with pauses between each step. I called out a jocund comment to this effect; Emerson responded with a growl and a grimace, and David, who had kept close by me, looked anxious.

"Is he angry? Have I done something?"

I paused to wipe my wet forehead and gave him a reassuring smile. David took life very seriously. Small wonder, some might say, after the distressing time he had had before he joined our family; but I sometimes wondered whether the lad lacked a sense of humor. Some individuals do. It is necessary to make allowances for cultural differences, of course; it had taken Abdullah a good many years to understand some of my little jokes.

"The Professor is pretending to be annoyed with me," I explained. "Pay no attention to him, David."

However, it was necessary to pay attention to him, for he let out a roar. "Nefret! How many times have I told you not to put your bare hand into a crevice like that one? Ramses, what are you thinking of to let her do such a thing?"

Nefret began, "I was only —"

"Come here." Emerson had halted near the entrance of tomb Nineteen. Scowling blackly, he waited until we had gathered round him before speaking. "Snakes and scorpions live in holes in the rock. They are not aggressive creatures, but they cannot be blamed for attacking when their nests are invaded." He transferred his frown to Ramses, who was shifting his weight from one foot to the other, and inquired gently, "Am I boring you, Ramses?"

"Yes, sir," said Ramses. "All of us, I believe, are aware of the facts you have mentioned. Nefret was only —"

"You are supposed to be looking after her."

Ramses's lips parted in indignant rebuttal, but Nefret, equally offended, anticipated him. "Don't blame him! He is not responsible for me. I knew better. I forgot. I will not forget again."

Emerson glanced at his son. I thought I detected the suspicion of a twinkle in his keen blue eyes. "Hmmm, yes. I was unjust. It was entirely Nefret's fault, and she ought to have known better, and if I catch her doing such a foolish thing again, I will confine her to the house. To which," he continued, "we will now return. It is late and we have a long walk ahead of us."

No one felt inclined to argue with him, but at my insistence we all had a refreshing drink of water before we started back. Except for Emerson, whose capacity for going without water resembles that of a camel, we all carried canteens.

"Where is the *gaffir?*" Emerson asked suddenly.

"What *gaffir?* Oh, that fellow." I glanced around. The dusty bundle was not in evidence. "He has gone about his business, I suppose, whatever that may be."

"I didn't see anyone," Nefret said.

Inevitably, Ramses said that he had. "Was he doing something to arouse your suspicions, Father? For when I observed him he was, or appeared to be, sound asleep."

"So he did," Emerson agreed.

He had not answered Ramses's question. I concluded he was being deliberately vague and mysterious in the hope of getting me off on a false trail. He does that sort of thing when we are engaged in one of our friendly little competitions in crime.

To be sure, there was no indication as yet that a crime had been committed. Perhaps Emerson knew something I did not. Cheered by this thought, I allowed him to lead me away.

CHAPTER FOUR

*If someone lies down and invites you
to trample upon him, you are a remarkable
individual if you decline the invitation.*

By the time we reached the house, thoughts of crime had been replaced by thoughts of water — not of drinking it, but of immersing myself completely in it. The usual arrangement for bathing consisted of having pots of water poured over one's person by a servant. Obviously this is not appropriate when the person is of the female gender, so I had had a bath chamber built and equipped it with an elegant tin tub. The tub had to be filled by hand, of course, but a drain led from it into my little flower garden, so the precious water was not wasted. (The tub had not been used all winter, so the flower garden, like the vines, now survived only as a fond memory.)

When I emerged from the bath, refreshed in mind and body, I found that Emerson had availed himself of the primitive arrangement heretofore mentioned. He was in our room, vigorously toweling his person and his wet black hair. By the time we adjourned to the verandah the sun had dropped below the western mountains and stars shone in the darkening eastern sky.

Nefret had lit a lamp and was reading, with Sekhmet draped across her lap. A soft breeze drifted in through the open arches, stirring her loosened hair so that it shimmered in the light like golden threads. I asked after the boys and was informed that they had decided to dine on board the dahabeeyah.

"Dine? What are they going to eat?" I demanded.

"Whatever the crew is eating, I presume." Emerson had gone to the table. He handed me a brimming glass of whiskey and soda. "Put your feet up and rest, Peabody, you appear to be a trifle — er — stiff. I hope the exertion I put you through today was not excessive?"

Emerson was obviously in one of his humorous moods, so I deemed it advisable to ignore the query. I began looking through the pile of letters and messages that had arrived that morning, for I had not had an opportunity to do so earlier. The European community of Luxor was growing, thanks in part to the Cook's tours and in part to the growing reputation of the area as a health resort. Visitors and residents exchanged calls and invitations, gave dinner parties at the hotels and on their dahabeeyahs, played tennis, and gossiped about one another. As the Reader may suppose, Emerson detested this community, which he referred to contemptuously as "the dahabeeyah dining society."

Among the messages was one from our wealthy

American friend Cyrus Vandergelt, who had arrived several weeks before us and taken up residence in his magnificent home, "the Castle,"
near the entrance to the Valley of the Kings.
Cyrus had financed expeditions in the Valley for
many years before finally giving up his concession
and turning to what he hoped would be more a
productive area — the cliffs of Drah Abu'l Naga,
where we had found the tomb of Tetisheri. Poor
Cyrus had had no luck at all in the Valley, and
the immediate success of Mr. Theodore Davis,
who had taken over his concession, had galled
him a great deal. During the past winter a new
royal tomb, that of Thutmose IV, had been
found. Though robbed and vandalized, it still
contained fragments of the funerary equipment,
including a magnificent chariot. (Our chariot had
been the first, of course.)

Mr. Davis was not a person I much admired,
and it did seem unfair he should have had the
luck Cyrus had not. Davis had something else
Cyrus had not had, however: to wit, the active
participation of Howard Carter. Howard did the
work, Davis financed it; Howard carried on the
hard, dirty job of excavating, Davis dropped by
whenever he was so inclined, accompanied by a
horde of friends and relations. He also received
a generous share of the objects Howard found.

"Cyrus asks us to dine," I said to Emerson.

"Too late," said Emerson, with satisfaction.

"Not tonight. At our convenience, any time we
choose."

131

"Curse it," said Emerson.

"Don't grumble. You know you are fond of Cyrus."

"He has his good qualities," Emerson admitted. "But he is altogether too fond of company. Who else wants to waste our time?"

I sorted through the messages. "Mr. Davis is having a soiree on his dahabeeyah —"

"No."

"I admit he can be annoying, but he is Howard's patron and a fellow enthusiast."

"I am surprised you should countenance him, Peabody." Emerson fixed me with a stern stare. "The man is a pompous, arrogant ignoramus, and that Andrews woman who travels with him —"

"That is just idle gossip, Emerson. She is his cousin."

"Ha," said Emerson. "Who else?"

I concealed the message from Enid Fraser behind the others. It said that they were staying at the Luxor Hotel and that she hoped for a meeting soon.

"The others are only greetings and messages of welcome, Emerson. Dr. Willoughby, M. Legrain, Mr. de Peyster Tytus — he is digging at Malkata with Newberry —"

"An interesting site," said Emerson, diverted. "We must go round one day and . . . Confound it! We haven't been here twenty-four hours, and already people are dropping in. Oh, it is you, Carter. Is this a social call, or have you come in your official capacity?"

132

"The former, of course." Howard accepted the chair I indicated. "None of your activities, Professor, could inspire a visit from the inspector for Upper Egypt. At least I hope you have not been engaging in illicit digging, or selling stolen antiquities?"

I acknowledged his little joke with a smile, Emerson with a grunt. Howard went on, "I hear you paid me a visit this afternoon. I am sorry I was not at the tomb to greet you."

"Any sign of a burial chamber?" Emerson inquired.

"The passage appears to be endless," Howard said with a sigh.

"It is Hatshepsut's tomb, though, isn't it?" Nefret asked eagerly.

Howard turned to her. "The foundation deposit we discovered last season makes the identification certain."

"The great Queen Hatshepsut herself," Nefret said dreamily. "How astonishing it is to think that the tomb has been known since Greek times, and yet no one thought of excavating it before. It was clever of you, Mr. Carter!"

I honestly do not believe she realized what a devastating effect those wide, admiring blue eyes had on persons of the opposite gender. Howard blushed and coughed and tried to look modest.

"Well, you know, some of my predecessors did make the attempt. One can hardly blame them for giving up, however. It has been a deuced difficult job; the corridor is almost entirely filled with rubble."

"That only makes your achievement more impressive," Nefret declared. "Do you think you will find Hatshepsut's mummy?"

As any woman would be, she was fascinated by this remarkable female, who had assumed the title of pharaoh and ruled Egypt in peace and prosperity for over twenty years. Dazzled by cornflower blue eyes and sweet smiles, Howard would have promised her Hatshepsut and twenty other pharaohs if Emerson had not thrown cold water on the idea.

"Few royal mummies have been found in their own tombs. It is much more likely hers was removed and hidden by the priests, like the mummies found in the Royal Cache. Hers may even be one of them; there are several unidentified females in that group."

All three of them were enjoying their archaeological argument, and I was anxious to hear the latest news, so I invited Howard to stay for dinner. Not until later in the evening, when Nefret had retired to her room and Emerson was in his study looking for something he wanted to show Howard, did I have an opportunity to ask the young man a question that had nagged me for days.

"Why didn't you tell me the other evening, when I asked about tomb Twenty-A, that there was no such place?"

"What?" Howard stared at me. "Tomb Twenty . . . Oh! Yes, I recall. I thought you said 'Twenty-eight.' It is only a pit, Mrs. Emerson, uninscribed and empty of all but insignificant fragments."

"As simple as that, then," I said with a rueful smile. "I owe you an apology, Howard. I had wondered . . . Curse it, Emerson, how long have you been standing there in the doorway?"

"Not long," said my husband. "So you claim you misunderstood Mrs. Emerson, Carter? I wonder if you are speaking the truth."

Howard's long chin quivered nervously. "Sir, believe me! I would never, ever, be guilty of lying to you or Mrs. Emerson."

"Of course not," I exclaimed. "Emerson, stop bullying him."

The archaeological discussion resumed, to Howard's obvious relief, and the evening ended with Howard begging us to come round to the tomb again next morning. "If you are in the neighborhood, that is," he added.

"I doubt we will," Emerson said with a sniff. "I have not yet determined where I mean to begin. Logic would suggest I start with number Five, which is the first of the anonymous tombs, but it is close to the entrance to the Valley and I would prefer to work in an area where the cursed tourists won't bother me. I want to have another look round before I decide."

After Howard had gone, I turned with some exasperation on my spouse. "You are becoming too cryptic for words, Emerson. What did you mean to imply when you accused Howard of lying?"

135

"I did not say he lied. I said he had not spoken the truth."

"Curse it, Emerson —"

Emerson grinned. "Peabody, if you told Howard Carter in that firm, let-us-hear-no-argument voice of yours that you were looking for the tombs of the rulers of lost Atlantis, he would not have the courage to tell you they don't exist. The truth is, my dear, that I am the only man alive who dares disagree with you. That is why you have remained passionately attached to me for so many years."

"One of the reasons," I said, unable to resist his smile or the hand that had taken mine in a firm, warm clasp.

"Quite so," said Emerson, and blew out the lamp.

The boys returned to the house bright and early next morning. They knew Emerson would put an end to their scheme of independence if it delayed his work, and both of them preferred a good hearty English breakfast to the peculiar kinds of food Egyptians consume at that meal.

I asked how they had got on the night before and was assured the arrangement had worked admirably. The assurance came, I hardly need say, from Ramses. David usually let him do the talking — since it would have been difficult to stop him — but my infallible instincts informed me that Ramses's interminable description of their activities was incomplete. I felt certain they had done something of which I would not approve.

I did not pursue the matter at that time. Emerson was impatient to get to the Valley. When I asked where he meant to work that day, he changed the subject.

The temperature was cool and pleasant, and although certain of my muscles were still stiff, I strove to conceal discomfort — all the more so because Abdullah accompanied us, along with several of the men. Abdullah was not as nimble as he once had been either, though he would rather have died than admit it. In my case a few days of exercise would restore me to my old form. In his case the passage of time would only worsen his condition. So I let him help me on the steeper parts of the path and insisted on stopping at intervals to catch my breath.

During one of these pauses he said, "It is good to be at work again, Sitt. But I do not understand why the Father of Curses is not searching for another royal tomb."

"You know his methods, Abdullah," I replied. "He cares more for truth and knowledge than for treasure."

"Huh," said Abdullah.

I smiled affectionately at him. "I could not agree more, old friend. It will be a dull season, I fear."

Abdullah's bearded lips twitched. "I do not think so, Sitt. Not while you are here."

I was touched and flattered and I said as much.

"As a matter of fact, Abdullah, something has come up that offers a possibility of interesting activities. You recall the message about tomb Twenty-A?"

"There is no such tomb, Sitt."

I informed him I was well aware of that fact and told him about the earlier messages, or threats, we had received while in Cairo. "It must be as obvious to you as it is to me," I concluded, "that this mysterious individual is trying to get Emerson to search for the tomb, which must lie between numbers Twenty and Twenty-one."

"Must?" Abdullah repeated blankly.

"You are not paying attention, Abdullah. Listen and I will go over my reasoning again."

"No, Sitt, you do not have to do that. I heard your words. They took me unawares. So, then, you want to look for this tomb?"

"I am depending on you for help, Abdullah. You know the signs of hidden tombs."

"*Aywa*. Yes, Sitt. We will look." Abdullah's face brightened. "It will be better than digging in empty holes."

Early as it was, some of the Cook's people had arrived. Our descent, which was unavoidably slow owing to the steepness of the path, was observed by one enterprising tour leader, and when we reached the Valley floor a group of tourists had gathered to gape at us. The young man had already identified us to his followers and was in the middle of a highly exaggerated account of our history. Emerson put an end to this with his usual decisiveness and the tourists dispersed, squawking and swearing. The young man did not appear to be much hurt, for he limped only a little.

"I suppose we will be getting another complaint from Mr. Cook," I remarked.

"He will be getting another complaint from *me*," Emerson grumbled. "How dare those fellows lecture about us as if we were an ancient monument!"

The incident had put him in a surly mood, so none of us ventured to ask him where he was going. My hopes began to rise when Emerson headed toward the small side valley we had visited the previous day, with the tomb of Hatshepsut — number Twenty, as I hardly need remind the Reader — at its end. Instead of entering it, the exasperating man turned in the other direction, studying his list and mumbling to himself.

I exchanged glances with Nefret, who was walking beside me. She grinned and raised her eyebrows inquiringly. I shook my head and shrugged.

It turned out to be tomb Twenty-one Emerson was after that morning. While Nefret and David set up the cameras I tried to remember what I knew about it. There was not much to remember. The tomb had been entered once or twice before, in the early days of excavation. Belzoni, that ubiquitous Italian, had mentioned seeing a pair of anonymous mummies. Since that time flood debris had filled part of the entrance, but the upper portion of it was still visible. Emerson put the men to work removing the rubble. It was Selim who found the first artifact, if I may use that term loosely; grinning, he handed it up to Emerson.

"A champagne cork," said Emerson. "Curse it!"

I had taken the time, as I always do, to prepare a shady nook in the shadow of the cliff, where we could rest from our labors. Nefret came to join me on the blanket. "A champagne cork?" she repeated. "That means, surely, that someone has been inside the tomb quite recently."

"It means that a party of frivolous tourists has been poking around," I replied. "Let us hope they have not done too much damage."

Emerson called her back. I remained where I was. I ought to have been sifting the debris, but to be honest I was feeling a trifle surly myself. We were maddeningly close to the area where I felt sure tomb Twenty-A must be located. So near, and yet so far away! I felt certain Emerson was deliberately tantalizing me.

From time to time tourists passed by, in pairs or in groups. Few had the temerity to pause, and I was beginning to think of opening the picnic basket and summoning my family to luncheon when I recognized a familiar form. I had to look twice, in fact, before I recognized it. The Colonel had exchanged his formal black for a tweed suit and sturdy boots, and his face wore a benevolent smile. The face of his daughter, who clung tightly to his arm, was flushed with exercise and heat. Unlike her father, she had not had the good sense to select suitable attire; her trailing skirts were white with dust and her corsets were clearly too tight.

"Good morning, Mrs. Emerson," the Colonel said, removing his hat. "One of the *gaffirs* told us you were here; I hope we are not intruding?"

Courtesy demanded that I tell an untruth. "Not at all. Will you sit down and rest for a moment?"

"We were about to pause for a bite of lunch," the Colonel said. "Perhaps you will join us."

Turning, he beckoned the servant who had followed them. The poor man was loaded down, not only with a heavy basket but with a folding stool and several cushions. After he had arranged these he immediately retreated, and Dolly lowered herself onto the cushions and assumed a graceful pose.

"Where are the others?" she asked.

"Working," I said.

The Colonel had remained standing. "I will go and have a look, if I may. As I told your husband in Cairo, I have an interest in the subject. I had thought of sponsoring some excavations myself."

"There are areas other than the Valley of the Kings that would repay investigation," I said.

"It is one of the questions I had hoped to consult Professor Emerson about," was the courteous reply. "If you will excuse me, ladies?"

I did not bother trying to carry on a conver-

141

sation with Dolly. It was not my company she wanted. Her face fell when the first person to join us was Nefret.

"Are the others coming?" I asked, before Dolly could do so.

"Shortly," Nefret answered. "Colonel Bellingham began asking questions, and you know how the Professor is when someone gives him the opportunity to lecture."

A rattle of pebbles nearby brought a little squeal from Dolly. "Is the cliff going to fall on us? Oh, heavens, what a horrid place this is!"

"Nothing is going to fall on you," Nefret said with a contemptuous curl of her lip. She turned and looked up, shading her eyes with her hand. "There is something on the path."

There was a path of sorts, though few creatures other than goats would have ventured on it. The way we had come that morning, over the *gebel* from Deir el Bahri, was frequently used — a virtual highway compared with this steep and hazardous ascent. I was about to comment when I heard a small, faint sound from above. Nefret stiffened.

"It is a goat — a kid, rather. It must be in trouble, it is not moving."

The sound came again. There was no question about it, the creature was frightened or in pain — and young, to judge by the pitch of its voice.

"Nefret," I exclaimed. "Wait. I will call —"

I knew it was in vain. That tender heart could not resist the cry of a creature in need of help.

By the time I got to my feet she had started up.

"Curse it," I said, and hastened, not toward her, but toward the tomb entrance. "Ramses! Emerson! David!"

The peremptory note in my voice brought them running. She was a good twenty feet up by the time they arrived on the scene, moving carefully but quickly on her hands and knees.

Emerson swore and started forward.

"Wait, Father," Ramses said. "She's gone after something — a goat, I think. You know Nefret, she won't come down without it. We will need a rope."

His cool voice stopped Emerson in his tracks. "Rope," he repeated in extreme agitation. "Yes. Damn the girl! No! No, I didn't mean that —"

"Good heavens," Bellingham exclaimed. "Stop her. Go after her!"

"I intend to," Ramses replied. "No, Father, please remain here. The rock is friable, your weight may bring more of it down." I observed that he had removed his boots and stockings. Now he took the coil of rope David handed him and slung it over his shoulder.

Ramses had always been able to climb like a monkey. On this occasion he ascended almost as rapidly as I could have walked, pulling himself from one handhold to another. Nefret, perilously spread-eagled across a stretch of sheer cliff, stopped and looked back. Then — I was tempted to say, "Damn the girl!" myself — she crept on. The ledge where the goat lay was not easily accessible from the path; she had to cross that sheer stretch to reach it. The goat must have been encouraged, or possibly it was irritated, by her approach. It began bleating loudly and tried to scramble up. Pebbles rained down.

Ramses had reached a point just below her booted feet — foot, I should say, since the other one was stretched out, feeling for an invisible foothold. Up to that moment I had been praying only that he would get to her before she fell. Now I began to wonder how the devil he was going to get her back down.

He did not pause. Instead of trying to catch hold of her he went to one side, passed her, and stopped, slightly above and to her left. After uncoiling the rope, he tossed a loop of it over some projection — I assumed that was what it was, though I could not see it from below — grasped the dangling end, and swung himself down until he was within a foot of her and on the same level. Finding a purchase for his bare toes, he leaned over and seized her round the waist.

Emerson's breath came out in an explosive whoop. He had not dared to speak before. Now he bellowed at the top of his lungs, "Come down this instant!"

Neither of them moved. They were arguing. I could hear raised voices, but could not make out the words, which was probably just as well.

"I had better go and fetch the goat," David said cheerfully. "She won't come without it, and Ramses cannot manage both of them."

With a smile at Emerson and a pat on my shoulder, he started up. He too was barefooted. It was the safest way, of course; that was how the Egyptians managed such climbs, but their feet were more hardened than those of the boys. At least I had assumed that was the case. It was obvious that both David and Ramses had been up and/or down that path before, unbeknownst to me.

The goat had decided it would rather stay where it was. Ramses had to unhand Nefret and drag the creature, kicking and bleating, off the ledge before he could drop it into David's up-stretched hands. Fortunately it was not a very large goat. Tucking it under one arm, David started down, and Nefret allowed Ramses to draw her back onto the path — such as it was. They went on arguing, probably because he had taken hold of her again. At least she had sense enough not to struggle to free herself. Though one of his hands still gripped the rope, their position was far from stable.

They had reached a point less than twenty feet from the ground when the inevitable happened; one of her boots slipped, the other lost its tenuous hold, and for one awful second she hung suspended by her hands before Ramses's arm slammed her against his side with a force that made her yelp with pain. He completed the descent in a rush, dropping the last six feet onto the slope of scree at the base of the cliff and clinging to the rope to stop himself from falling.

Emerson, cursing quietly and monotonously, mopped his perspiring face with his sleeve. He stopped swearing and said curtly, "Put her down."

Nefret took one look at his infuriated countenance and tightened her grip on Ramses. He was still holding her with her feet dangling several inches off the ground, and she was extremely short of breath, but the unevenness of her voice was primarily due to laughter. "No — please! Not while he is so angry! Protect me!"

Some part of this affecting performance was aimed, I felt sure, at Dolly Bellingham. She had risen to her feet and was staring raptly at Ramses, her hands at her throat. I wondered if she had any idea how silly she looked. "You were wonderful," she breathed.

Ramses returned Nefret to solid earth with a thump that made her knees buckle. "Do your worst, Father. I cannot in conscience stand between her and your righteous wrath." Turning to Dolly, he added, "I had no idea you were an animal lover, Miss Bellingham. It is good of you to share your luncheon with the goat."

And indeed, the intelligent creature had taken advantage of our distraction to invade the luncheon basket. It was probably the best meal it had ever enjoyed, and it had made the most of its opportunity. Dolly screamed and flapped at it with her parasol, and Emerson did his worst with his daughter — i.e., he seized her in a tight embrace and kissed her on the top of her golden head.

After the Bellinghams had gone and Nefret had examined the goat — it had suffered a broken leg, which she splinted quite neatly — we tied the protesting animal to a large rock and opened our own picnic basket.

"What a pity the Bellinghams lost their lunch," Nefret said, her eyes dancing.

"The Colonel took it with more grace than one might have expected," I said. "He actually laughed."

"He appears to have a genuine interest in Egptology," Emerson admitted grudgingly. "He asked some intelligent questions. I told him he might come by another time if he liked."

"Here?" I inquired.

"Where else?" Emerson replied. "We will probably be here for another day or two. Longer, if we dawdle. Come along, my dears."

Ramses lingered. "We may as well give the rest of the food to the goat," he suggested, as I began to pack the luncheon things. "What shall we call it?"

"Why should we call it anything?"

"You know Nefret will want to adopt it." He tossed the creature a large chunk of cheese. "We will be lucky if she doesn't insist one of us sit with it until its leg is healed."

"That was well done, Ramses," I said.

"What?" He turned, dusting breadcrumbs off his hands, and looked at me in surprise.

"Don't say 'What?' It sounds ill-bred. You

understood my meaning, I am sure. Wait a moment, I want to talk to you."

"Father will expect me to —"

"It will not take long. How did you find Mrs. Fraser last night?"

The slight start he gave would have been imperceptible to anyone but me. He said resignedly, "Who told you?"

"No one. Your early departure from the house yesterday afternoon suggested that you had plans for the evening. The fact that you did not see fit to mention them to me further suggests that they were of a nature I might not approve. The amusements available to young men in Luxor immediately come to mind. I do you the credit to assume your motives were not entirely frivolous or — er — improper, so I conclude you went to call upon an acquaintance. You knew Mrs. Fraser was in Luxor —"

"Your reasoning is, as always, irrefutable," said Ramses.

"You did see her."

"Yes. I — er — had intended to tell you about it."

"Of course," I said dryly.

"It is difficult to find an opportunity of speaking privately with you. You know Father's views about matters that interfere with his excavations."

"Better than you, I fancy. Never mind your father, I will deal with him. Don't beat around the bush, Ramses."

"In a nutshell," said Ramses, "it appears my original theory was completely in error. It is not Mrs. Fraser who is suffering from a mental disorder. Her husband has received messages from an ancient Egyptian princess named Tasherit. She wants him to find her tomb and . . ." He placed his hand respectfully but firmly over my mouth. "I beg you will not shout, Mother. Take a seat on this rock. Compose yourself before you speak."

I sat on the rock. It would have been difficult not to, for he put me on it by pressing down on my shoulder.

After he had removed the hand that covered my mouth, I remarked, "If you had wished to avoid an involuntary exclamation from me, Ramses, you would have chosen your words more carefully. I have had occasion, in the past, to suggest that brevity is to be cultivated in the course of narration, but I did not intend you should take it quite that far. However. The messages to Mr. Fraser came, I assume, through Mrs. Whitney-Jones?"

He nodded, and I went on, "And the princess — the young, beautiful princess — died an untimely death? Murdered by her cruel father, perhaps, because she had dared to love a commoner? Or did she waste away after seeing her lover murdered by the aforementioned cruel father?"

The ends of Ramses's mustache quivered. I deduced this indicated an expression of amusement. "The princess and her lover were both murdered by Papa — entombed alive, to perish in one another's arms."

"Good Gad, the woman has no imagination whatever," I said in disgust. "She can't even invent an original scenario. I suppose she has been extracting large sums of money from Donald. I am not surprised at his gullibility — more intelligent men than he have fallen victim to charlatans — but I would not have supposed him to be susceptible to such flagrant romanticism. So that is why he was trying to persuade Emerson to dig in the Valley of the Queens!"

"You observed how quickly Mrs. Whitney-Jones got him off the subject," said Ramses. "Skepticism, especially of the variety Father expresses, might weaken Mr. Fraser's belief. The longer the lady has him under her influence, the more money she can extract from him."

"The money is, or was, Enid's," I said. "No wonder she is so distraught. And yet my intuition tells me that there is something else amiss, something darker and more dangerous than simple extortion! I wonder what . . ."

I paused invitingly, but this time Ramses did not take advantage of my tolerance to propose another theory. I supposed he was embarrassed at being so wide of the mark the first time.

"It is, after all, a commonplace story," he said with a shrug of his shoulders. "Any stranger who asks for money should be immediately suspect, and yet people go on contributing to causes as questionable as their sponsors are corrupt."

"We must think of a way of exposing the woman."

"It will be difficult. Mr. Fraser is stubborn and uncommonly stupid."

The statement was unkind, but probably correct. After a moment he added, as if to himself, "Mrs. Fraser does not deserve such bad luck. I would like to be of service to her if I can."

"You don't fancy yourself still romantically attached to her, I hope."

Ramses's brows drew together. Like his father's, his eyebrows are thick and black. Unlike Emerson's, his tilt up at the outer corners. The resultant shape was a mirror image of the shape of his ridiculous mustache, and for some unaccountable reason I found myself becoming vexed.

"Don't glower at me," I said sharply. "I have no recollection of any promise you made Mrs. Fraser, but the promise of a little boy in the throes of puppy love has no significance. You are no longer a little boy —"

"Thank you," said Ramses.

"And don't interrupt. You are no longer a little boy, and I hope you have sense enough to refrain from making some childish, romantic gesture that would do more harm than good. If an idea occurs to you, discuss it with me before you act."

"Father wants us," Ramses said, and walked away.

He did, but that was only an excuse. I felt certain Ramses had not told me everything.

Ramses had *not* told his mother everything, as the following excerpt from Manuscript H demonstrates:

The dahabeeyah rocked gently at its moorings. From the crewmen, relaxing after their evening meal of bread and beans, mutton and lentils, came the sounds of laughter and idle conversation. The men who worked for the Father of Curses were the envy of others because they were extravagantly well fed — meat at least once a day! — and paid their wages even when the boat was docked. The lectures of the Sitt Hakim on diet, cleanliness, and other superstitions were a small price to pay. She meant well, they assured one another tolerantly.

"Should we?" David asked, glancing apprehensively at the open window of Ramses's room, as if he expected to see his adopted aunt staring in at them. "We haven't permission."

Ramses gave himself a final inspection in the small mirror and tossed his brushes into the drawer. Trying to flatten his hair was an impossible job; it was not as rampantly curly as it had been when he was younger, but it persisted in waving no matter what he did to it.

"We are not children," he said stoutly. "A man does not ask his mama's permission every time he takes a step. What's the harm in running across to Luxor for a few hours?"

David shrugged. "Shall we take the cat?" he asked, trying to detach Sekhmet from his trouser leg.

"That furry blob? Good God, no. Why did you bring her with you?"

"She wanted to come," David said.

"You mean she stuck to you, and you couldn't get her off."

"She likes to ride horses." David rubbed the cat under its chin. "Why not bring her along? She will never learn unless you train her."

"Cats cannot be trained."

"The cat Bastet —"

"Pry the creature loose and come," Ramses said shortly.

The sunset colors were particularly vivid that night; ribbons of fiery rose and purple shimmered in the wake of the small boat. When it reached the East Bank the rowers settled back to smoke and fahddle (gossip), and Ramses and David climbed the steps to the street. The hotel was a short distance from the riverbank, and their progress was slowed by encounters with friends and acquaintances, all of whom wanted them to stop and talk. By the time they reached the Luxor darkness had fallen. Ramses went to the desk and spoke with the clerk, and the two young men seated themselves in the lobby to wait for a reply to the message he had sent.

"I still cannot understand why you didn't tell your mother you intended to call on Mrs. Fraser," David said. "She is a friend of the family, is she not?"

Ramses's lips set in an expression his friend had come to know well. "It was I whom Mrs. Fraser addressed in that first letter. She reminded me of a promise I once made. A gentleman responds in person

153

to a lady's request; he does not allow his 'mama' to do it for him."

"Ah," said David.

Ramses's haughty pose relaxed and he went on in the rapid idiomatic Arabic that came as easily to him as to David, whose first language it had been. "You of all people should understand. How is it for you, to be treated like a child by my mother and my aunt — you, who have done a man's work and borne a man's responsibilities?"

"They care for me," David said simply. "No one had cared before."

Ramses was not unmoved, but exasperation won out over sentimentality. "I care for them too. I love my mother, but if she had known of my intentions, she would have insisted I allow her to deal with the matter. You know how she is, David; there is no woman on earth I admire more, but she can be an extremely . . ."

The Arabic word that followed made David stiffen with shocked reproach until he realized it had not referred to Ramses's mother.

Ramses made an abortive movement toward a large potted plant, but stopped himself. It was too late. The Bellinghams, on their way from the lift to the dining salon, had seen them.

Dolly was dressed as if for a grand ball, in a pale blue satin frock and ornaments of sapphires and diamonds. Blue ribbons twined through the silvery masses of her hair. Her gloved hand rested on the arm of her father, who wore evening dress and carried a gold-headed stick. The third member of the group was unfamiliar — a woman, gray-haired and plainly dressed. She had, Ramses thought sympathetically, a rather hunted expression.

Leaving the unknown woman standing alone in the middle of the lobby, the Colonel led his daughter toward Ramses and David.

"Good evening," he said, bowing to the former.

"Good evening," Ramses said, frowning.

Bellingham glanced at the girl who clung to his arm. "Dolly told me what happened that night in Cairo. I confess I was angry with you for persuading her to go into the gardens with you, but she made me realize that your unusual upbringing was largely responsible for your failure to understand the reverence with which a flower of Southern womanhood should be treated."

Ramses turned an outraged stare on Dolly. She had opened her lace-trimmed fan; raising it so that it hid her mouth, she met his gaze with wide, innocent eyes.

"And," the Colonel continued, "the courage with which you fought in her defense must go far to excuse your unwitting offense."

"Thank you," said Ramses in a strangled voice.

"Not at all. We are about to go in to dinner. Perhaps you will do us the honor of joining us?"

"I fear we must plead a previous engagement," said Ramses.

The Colonel nodded and withdrew his arm from his daughter's. "Go along with Mrs. Maplethorpe, child. I will join you in a moment."

"Yes, Papa. Good night, Mr. Emerson. I hope I

may have the opportunity to express my appreciation more eloquently on a future occasion." She offered her gloved hand — to be kissed, he supposed, to judge from its position. He was spared that exercise; her fan fell to the floor, and he bent to pick it up. When he handed it to her, he got something in return. Automatically his fingers closed over the small square of folded paper, and Dolly turned away.

The woman moved timidly to meet her. Dolly did not pause or acknowledge her existence by a word or a glance; head high, she glided gracefully toward the dining salon, with the other woman trailing after her like a well-trained dog.

"Is she a governess or a guard?" Ramses inquired. "Or a slave?"

Irony was wasted on Colonel Bellingham. "She is not an effective guard, but she was the best I could find — an Englishwoman who teaches in a girls' school in Cairo. She is a lady, at least, and she knows she must never let Dolly out of her sight. Your father did not believe me when I told him Dolly was in danger. Perhaps now he has had cause to alter his opinion."

"No doubt he has." Ramses's hand went to his cheek. Most of the abrasions had healed, but the marks were still visible. "However, sir, his opinion as to his responsibility in the matter remains unaltered. To put it as bluntly as he would — what the devil has your daughter to do with us?"

"One would have supposed the safety of a young lady would concern any gentleman."

"If I happen to be in the vicinity when next she

156

is attacked, I will do the proper thing," Ramses said. "You are not suggesting, I hope, that I take on the role of bodyguard? Even an upbringing as — er — unusual as mine would view that arrangement as improper."

The Colonel's gloved hand tightened on his stick. "You are impertinent, sir!"

"My mother would be distressed to hear it," said Ramses. "Now, if you will excuse us — that previous appointment I mentioned."

Bellingham turned on his heel and marched off.

"You were very rude," David said admiringly.

"I hope so." Ramses let out his breath. "He ignored you as if you were a piece of furniture and had the effrontery to criticize my mother for bringing me up badly! As for his daughter . . ."

"She is very pretty."

"Like a poisonous flower. The little witch lied to her father, put the blame on me, and expected me to back her up!" He unfolded the slip of paper.

"What is that?" David asked.

"A request, I suppose you might call it. 'Meet me in the garden at midnight.' She has a penchant for dark gardens, doesn't she?"

"Are you going to meet her?"

"Good God, no!" He crumpled the note and put it in his pocket. "She's got me in enough trouble already. I wonder how she plans to elude her watchdog? I don't doubt she can manage it, though."

"How did she manage the note, do you suppose?" David asked interestedly. "She could not have anticipated you would be here."

157

"No doubt she carries one with her all the time, on the chance of running into a victim. Any victim." Ramses took out his watch. "I wonder what is keeping Mrs. Fraser? I want to be out of here before —"

She came so quickly and silently that he did not observe her until she put her hand on his. "Is that the same watch I gave you all those years ago?" she asked softly. "I am flattered, Ramses, dear, that you carry it in preference to any another."

He had composed a dignified little speech in response to the greeting he had expected from her. This was not the one he had expected. She didn't look the way he had expected either. Her frock of rosy pink framed her white shoulders and fell in soft folds to the floor, and her face was becomingly flushed.

"Er — yes. I mean to say — a gift from a friend, however undeserved, is of course . . ." He gave up the attempt to frame a graceful compliment and returned to his prepared speech. "I hope I was not mistaken when I believed you wished to speak with me?"

"You were not mistaken." She gestured toward a table half hidden by potted plants. "Will you sit down? I have much to tell you."

"You don't mind David, do you?" Ramses said, holding a chair for her. "He is my best friend and completely trustworthy."

He rather thought she did mind, but she had better manners than Bellingham; forcing a smile, she shook hands with David and motioned him to join them. Glancing frequently over her shoulder as if she feared interruption, she told him the story

158

he later related to his mother.

"What am I to do?" she asked despairingly. "He is completely in her power; he listens only to her and obeys her every whim. I fear for his sanity, Ramses. They are at it every night —" Her voice broke. She raised a handkerchief to her face.

"At it?" Ramses repeated involuntarily.

"Table turning," Enid said. "Communicating with that — that damned dead woman!"

Ramses blinked. "But, Mrs. Fraser —"

"Please call me Enid. It is impossible for me to think of you as Mr. Emerson, and I can't address you as Ramses unless you use my first name."

"Well, er — thank you. What I was about to say was that — if you will forgive me — you sound almost as if you had come to believe in her yourself."

"I suppose it did sound that way," Enid admitted. "One doesn't curse a fantasy, does one? She is real enough to him, though; so real she has stolen him from me, heart, soul, and . . ." She covered her face with her hands, but not before he had seen a rush of hot blood stain her cheeks.

He had a horrible feeling he was blushing too. Could she possibly mean . . . Surely not. No lady would mention such a delicate subject. Thoroughly ashamed of his evil thoughts — which had, regrettably, increased of late — he cleared his throat.

"Mrs. Fraser — Enid, then, if you permit — you ought to discuss this with my parents. My mother has little patience with spiritualists and my father has none at all; they have had considerable experience with such cases and can influence Mr. Fraser more

effectively than I. Though of course I would like to help in any possible . . . er."

Enid bent her head and fumbled in her embroidered evening bag. "That is excellent advice, Ramses. I had intended to do just that. Now I must return, before I am missed. Thank you so much."

She rose and offered him her hand. "I have done nothing," he began.

"You have listened," she murmured. "The relief of confiding in a sympathetic hearer is greater than you can imagine. We will meet again soon, I hope."

She glided away, leaving Ramses staring at the folded paper she had pressed into his hand.

David did have a sense of humor, though it was probably not of the variety his adopted aunt would approve. Ramses turned a savage glare on him. "What are you laughing at?"

"I'm not laughing," David protested. "At any rate, I'm trying not to. How do you do it? Two in one evening!"

Ramses turned and strode toward the door. By the time they reached the boat landing David deemed it safe to speak.

"I apologize," he said in English. "I should not have made a joke about the lady."

"It is not a joking matter," Ramses said repressively. "The confounded woman is draining Mr. Fraser — of his fortune, I mean. Damn it! I had not supposed the English language was so susceptible to double meanings. Mrs. Fraser is lonely and afraid, and she thinks of me as the child who once admired her. It is easier to open one's heart to a child, I

suppose, but Mother will know better than I how to help her."

They climbed into the boat. The night was still; the men bent to the oars.

"*You are going to tell your mother?*" *David inquired.*

"*I must.*" *He read the note again, shook his head, and returned it to his pocket. "The account will require some revision.*"

"*I know I ought not ask, but . . . What does it say?*"

Ramses sighed. "She asked me to meet her in the garden at midnight."

David tried to control himself, but he was only human. He was grateful that it was too dark for him to see Ramses's face.

Emerson spent the entire day on his wretched tomb. At the end of the afternoon he had a set of illegible notes and I had a sick headache.

Dusty and — in my case, at least — disgruntled, we returned to the house. I took pleasure in informing Emerson that I had asked Cyrus to dinner, but he did not respond with the acrimony I had expected.

"Supper, you mean. This is *my* castle and I shall be as informal as I like."

"You mean you won't change?"

"Not into evening kit. It is a courtesy to Ramses," he added with a maddening grin. "His new clothes have not arrived from Cairo."

"Thank you, Father," said Ramses. "With your

permission, Mother, David and I will take the horses out before supper. They have been in the stable all day and need to be exercised."

Nefret went with them. I supposed she would be after Ramses to teach her that spectacular mount and could only hope the boys would not let her do anything dangerous.

When Cyrus arrived he was riding his favorite steed, a mild-mannered mare he called Queenie. Dismounting, he tossed the reins to the grinning houseboy — who anticipated Cyrus's usual generous baksheesh — clasped our hands, and told us it was sure good to have us back.

"I ran into the kiddies on my way over here," he said, accepting a chair and a glass of whiskey. "Though I guess that's not what I should call 'em now. That boy of yours has sure shot up this past summer, and he rides like a centaur. Where'd you find those magnificent horses?"

We brought one another up-to-date on our experiences of the past months and assured one another that we had not aged a particle. Cyrus really did look well. Winters in Egypt had given his fair skin a leathery look, but the wrinkles in his face lent it character, and he had hair of the sandy shade that changes very little as it lightens to silver. Before long Emerson, who has little patience with amiable and inconsequential conversation (and who did not appreciate fulsome compliments directed at his wife), tried to turn the subject to archaeology. The attempt was a failure, for I wanted to hear about our other friends. Cyrus knew everyone in Luxor and was, as Emerson had implied, socially inclined.

"The Davis entourage is here," he said, "but I don't suppose you want to hear about them. The usual tourist crowd, including a few of your lords and ladies and honorables — you don't want to hear about them, either," he added with a knowing look at Emerson. "Oh — I did run into someone today who asked to be remembered to you. Fellow name of Bellingham."

In silence Emerson got up and refilled our glasses. "He came by to see us this afternoon," I said. "Did you meet his daughter, then?"

"Miss Dolly?" Cyrus grinned and shook his head. "Pretty as a picture and mean as a sidewinder, that little gal."

"Why, Cyrus, how cynical," I exclaimed.

"I know her type, Mrs. Amelia. Fell for a few of 'em myself, when I was younger and not so suspicious-minded. There's a certain look —" He broke off with an embarrassed cough and rose to his feet as Nefret and the boys came out of the house. They had washed and changed. Nefret wore one of the long Egyptian robes she favored for casual wear; she curled up on the sofa and the boys seated themselves on the ledge.

"Did Bellingham talk to you about finding a maid or a companion for Miss Dolly?" Cyrus asked. "He wants an English or American female, and I told him I didn't know of anybody like that."

"What happened to the —" David broke off with a grunt.

"Did you speak, David?" I asked.

"No, ma'am. Yes, ma'am. I was thinking of something else."

"Oh." I turned my attention back to the question of Dolly Bellingham. "No, he did not mention the subject today. However, there were a few — er — distractions. Has the girl travelled all this distance without a female attendant?"

"Impossible," said Nefret scornfully. "She couldn't lace her own boots."

"She's never had to," Cyrus said. "The old plantation is still overrun with former slaves and their children. One of 'em came with the Bellinghams, but she took sick in Cairo and had to be sent home — steerage, I suppose. The girl's had a streak of bad luck with her servants; lost three altogether, from accidents or illness. The latest one took sick last night, so bad she had to be moved to the hospital. That's why her daddy wants — Well, hello there!"

The surprised greeting was addressed to Sekhmet, who had jumped from the floor to his knee. Cyrus put a gingerly hand on the cat's head; she squirmed appreciatively and began to purr.

"Just push her off, Cyrus," I said. "Gently, of course."

"No, that's all right. To tell you the truth, I'm kind of flattered. She never favored me before; she was always following Ramses around."

164

A rather uncomfortable pause followed. Darkness hid the faces of the others, including that of Ramses. He was perched on the low wall, his back against one of the pillars. The light from the doorway fell across his raised knees and the thin, steady brown hands that clasped them.

It was Nefret who broke the silence. "That is not the cat Bastet, but Sekhmet, one of her kittens. Bastet died last month."

"Well, I'm sorry to hear that," Cyrus said politely. "Sekhmet, is it?" He chuckled as the cat rubbed against his shirt in an ecstasy of purring. "You should have named her Hathor. She's sure a loving little lady. Maybe I should put in a bid for one of the kittens myself. Always fancied cats; don't know why I didn't think of getting one before."

We had to shut Sekhmet in Nefret's room when we went in to supper. Even the most dedicated of cat fanciers does not appreciate having a long tail dragged through his soup while he is sipping it. Emerson managed to keep the conversation on professional matters during the meal, but when coffee was served Cyrus reverted again to the subject of the Bellinghams' need for a companion.

"So you can't think of anyone that would suit?" he asked me.

"I can think of several Egyptian ladies," I replied. "David's aunt Fatima took excellent care of me one winter, when I suffered a minor accident, and —"

165

"Out of the question," Emerson said. "The position of maid or companion, or whatever you choose to call it, appears to be unlucky. I wouldn't be surprised to learn that the others feigned illness; the young woman is a spoiled, tyrannical little brat who probably treats servants like the slaves her father once owned. I do not object to encouraging Bellingham on a professional level — the Department of Antiquities needs all the funds it can get — but I will not allow our children or our friends to become intimate with him. He has had too many wives for my taste."

"Why, Emerson, what an extraordinary statement!" I exclaimed. "Are you implying that he murdered them?"

Having allowed rising anger to provoke him into an indiscretion, Emerson became even angrier — with me. "Confound it, Peabody, I implied nothing of the sort. That imagination of yours has got entirely out of hand."

"Now, now, folks, just take it easy," Cyrus said, without attempting to conceal his amusement. "The Colonel's no Bluebeard. He's suffered several tragic losses, but they were all — er — in the course of nature, so to speak. Except . . ."

He looked self-consciously at Nefret, who was leaning forward, her elbows on the table and her blue eyes fixed on his face.

"Do you mean his wives died in childbirth?" she asked. "How many of them?"

"Two. Just two of 'em." Cyrus took out his handkerchief and wiped his forehead. "Look here, I didn't mean to bring up a subject like this in front of you ladies."

"Women are not too fragile to experience childbirth," I said dryly. "Why should they not speak and hear of it? Nefret has been raised by modern methods, Cyrus, and I daresay she knows more about the subject than you do. Anyhow, you cannot leave us with the dangling, evocative word 'except.' Except what?"

"Well, if you're sure it's all right." He gave Nefret another doubtful look. She grinned cheerfully back at him. "I thought you'd heard about it," Cyrus went on. "It was the talk of Cairo for weeks. But maybe — yep, that's right; you were in the Sudan that year. By the time you got back there was something new to talk about. There usually is."

"Go on," I urged.

Cyrus shrugged and abandoned himself to the gossip he so enjoyed. "They were here on their wedding trip — the Colonel and his new bride. Number four, she was, and a good many years younger than he. Well, ma'am, she up and eloped with his secretary! That's what the fellow called himself, at any rate; never saw him write any letters, but he was at the Colonel's beck and call all day and all night, for everything."

"An Egyptian, was he?" I asked.

"An American, to judge by his accent. Name of . . . just let me think a minute . . . that's right,

167

name of Dutton Scudder. Don't know where Bellingham picked him up. He hadn't been with them long, I believe. Mild-looking young fellow, not the sort you'd think would sweep a lady off her feet."

"A sudden, unaccountable passion," I murmured.

"Not so unaccountable, perhaps." Ramses broke a long silence — long for him, that is.

"No." Nefret had been counting on her fingers. "That was five years ago, but the Colonel was an old man even then. How old was she?"

"Enough!" Emerson's fist came down on the table. "Amelia, I am astonished that you should allow a discussion like this to go on at my table — and with Nefret present! By Gad, I ought to insist you follow the custom of having the ladies retire to the drawing room after dinner!"

"So that you men can smoke and drink port and tell vulgar stories?" I rose. "Come, Nefret, we have been dismissed."

David hastened to hold her chair. Side by side, with great dignity, we swept from the room — followed, somewhat sheepishly, by the men. Nefret's cheeks were rounded with suppressed laughter.

"Well done, Aunt Amelia," she whispered.

However, she was quick to agree to Emerson's request that she sing for us, and she gave him a forgiving pat on the cheek as she passed his chair. We had had the pianoforte brought down by dahabeeyah the year before; all of us enjoy music and it was pleasant at the end of a hard day's work to sit at ease and listen to her sweet, untrained voice — all the sweeter, I felt, because it was so natural.

"Well, now, I call this just about perfect," Cyrus declared, cheroot in one hand, glass of brandy in the other, long legs stretched out, cat across his lap. I had put out all the lamps except the ones on the piano, and the soft, dusky night of Egypt wrapped round us. "How about some of the old favorites, Miss Nefret, my dear?"

So she gave us "Drink to Me Only" and "Londonderry Air," singing as unselfconsciously as any bird. Emerson's face had the gentle look he kept especially for her, and even Ramses put aside his book in order to listen.

He had learned to read music because it was "an interesting notational form," but Nefret refused to let him turn the pages for her because, she said, he did not pay attention. That honored role had gone to David, who sat beside her on the piano bench. He could not follow the notes, but his eyes never left her face, and he responded instantly when she nodded.

"How beautiful she is," Cyrus said softly. "And as good and true and fine as she is beautiful, I reckon."

"And as intelligent, I reckon," I remarked.

Cyrus's soft, sentimental smile widened into a grin. "Right you are, Mrs. Amelia, my dear. Envy is an emotion I try to avoid, but I opine I am just a little jealous of you and your husband right now. Seeing those handsome young faces and bright eyes makes me wish I were not a sorry old bachelor. You don't happen to know of a kind female, not too young but — er — still young enough, who would take me on?"

"Don't encourage her," Emerson growled around the stem of his pipe. "Women are inveterate matchmakers, Vandergelt, and she is the worst of the lot. She'll have you — what is that expressive American word? — yes, she'll have you hogtied and handed over to someone like Mrs. Whitney-Jones before you can say Jack Robinson."

"Well, now, Emerson, you never know, she might be just the lady for me. Who is she?"

I hesitated, but only briefly. Nefret was trying to teach David the words to "Annie Laurie," and they were both laughing over his attempt at a Scottish accent. I had the utmost confidence in Cyrus's discretion and the greatest respect for his unusual American brand of intelligence. (And Cyrus's presence might keep Emerson from bellowing when I told him Enid's story.)

He did not bellow. He sputtered, swore, and snorted, but when I had, despite these obstacles, completed my narrative, he said resignedly, "I suppose we must do something. Can't have people taken in by charlatans. I will just go round there tomorrow and get rid of the woman."

"Emerson, you are hopeless!" I exclaimed. "What do you intend to do, take her by the collar, drag her to the train station, and shove her into a compartment?"

"I reckon the situation is too complicated for that," Cyrus said thoughtfully. "We could get rid of the lady, but that wouldn't cure your afflicted friend. Sounds as if he's too far gone for a common-sense talk."

"I intend to talk with him, of course," I said. "But he is extremely stubborn and not very —"

I broke off. We were speaking softly, but Ramses was seated not far away, and he has ears like a cat's. I knew he was listening. I had not yet determined whether I wanted the children to become involved in Enid's problem. Ramses already was involved, through no fault of my own, but I had no intention of allowing him to take charge of the affair.

"I'll just strike up an acquaintance with them," Cyrus offered. "Mutual friends, and all that. Mebbe I'll get an idea once I've met the fellow."

I thanked him; and the evening ended with all of us gathered round the piano, blending our voices in song. Nefret had learned "Dixie" as a compliment to Cyrus. To my surprise, he did not seem to know the words.

Because of the late hour the boys decided to remain at the house. After Cyrus had bade us good night and the children had gone to their rooms, I left Emerson at his desk and went out onto the terrace. The cool, clear air was refreshing after the atmosphere of the drawing room, filled with the smoke from Emerson's pipe and

Cyrus's cigars; the stars, never so bright as in Egypt, emblazoned the dark sky. The only romantic element missing was the scent of jasmine, which would have been there if Abdullah had remembered to water my vines.

I wanted this time alone for serious reflection. Something had been on my mind, not only that day, but for many days. It was not of the Bellinghams I thought, nor of poor Enid. It was of tomb Twenty-A.

Emerson believed someone was playing a joke on him. Some of his rivals might well enjoy watching him dig fruitlessly and endlessly for a tomb that did not exist, but I did not believe that any of our archaeological acquaintances would stoop to such a childish trick. (Except for Mr. Budge of the British Museum. He was certainly malicious enough, but I doubted he had the imagination to think of it.)

No, it was no trick. There was such a tomb, and it must contain something our mysterious correspondent wanted us to find. Who — what — and why? The why and what must wait; there were too many possibilities. As for who . . . One name — one soubriquet, rather — came immediately to mind.

An arm, hard with muscle, encircled my waist.

"Curse it, Emerson, I wish you wouldn't creep up on me like that," I said.

"No, you don't. What are you thinking about, out here all by yourself?"

I remained silent. After a moment Emerson

said, "Shall I tell you what you are thinking about?"

"Guess, you mean."

"No, my dear. I know you too well for that."

"Mystery is your meat and drink," Emerson went on. "You can no more resist hints of hidden tombs than another woman can resist a new hat. Those messages were directed to me, but the sender must have known you would read them, for I have never yet succeeded in concealing anything from you. One name comes immediately to mind — or, to be more accurate, a confounded set of cursed aliases. The Master Criminal, the Genius of Crime —"

"Sethos is dead."

"He is not dead." Emerson spun me round and took me by the shoulders. "You know he is not dead. How long have you known, Peabody?"

I met his gaze unfalteringly. "Emerson, you swore we would never mention that man again."

"I swore no such thing! What I swore was . . ." He groaned loudly and pulled me into his arms. "My darling, I swore I would never doubt your affection. I will never doubt it! But I will not get over being jealous of that bastard until I see him buried ten feet deep! No, not unless I shovel the dirt over him myself. Peabody, say something. Tell me you forgive me."

I let out a squeak. Emerson immediately relaxed his grip.

"I beg your pardon, my dear. Did I hurt you?"

"Yes. But I don't mind." I laid my head on

his breast and he held me close, with careful consideration for my bruised ribs.

"I'll make it up to you," he murmured, his lips brushing my temple.

"Emerson, if you believe your romantic attentions are sufficient compensation for —"

"My romantic attentions, Peabody, are your due and my pleasure. Supposing I find the damned tomb for you. Will that compensate for my unreasonable suspicions and for bruising your ribs?"

If you, dear Reader, are of the female gender, you will be fully cognizant of the motive behind this generous offer. (If you are of the other gender, you will also know, but you will not admit it.) Emerson was bored to death with his tedious tombs, but he was too stubborn to admit he yearned to respond to those mysterious messages. Pretending to do it as a favor to me gave him an excuse to do what *he* wanted to do.

"You are so good to me, Emerson," I murmured, nestling into his arms.

CHAPTER FIVE

*There is a layer of primitive savagery
in most of us.*

In fact, I did not believe our old adversary, the Master Criminal, was behind the mystery of tomb Twenty-A; it lacked his panache, his imaginative daring, his flair. I knew Sethos well. Only too well, Emerson would say; my strange rapport with that brilliant, tormented man was the source of my husband's jealousy. Love did not enter into it, at least not on my part. My heart was, and is, and always will be Emerson's. However, I could not suppose that mentioning these facts would reassure Emerson, and I was not anxious to discuss Sethos's current whereabouts or potential activities with Emerson — or anyone else.

He — Emerson, I mean — was in an excellent mood next morning. So he should have been, for he was about to get his own way and the credit for appearing to give me mine.

He had not announced his intentions at breakfast, but I happened to overhear him talking confidentially with Ramses as they waited on the verandah for Nefret to get her hat. "Your mama will not be able to concentrate on meaningful work until we have exploded her little fancy, so we will spend a day looking for her imaginary tomb Twenty-A."

"That is good of you, Father," said Ramses in his even, uninflected voice.

"Well, my boy, that is how one gets on with the ladies, you know. A small concession to their whims now and then does no harm and promotes good feeling. It is the least a fellow can do."

Ramses inquired, "Will not M. Maspero object to your looking for this — er — imaginary tomb, Father? The terms of your concession limit you to known tombs."

"This tomb, if it exists, *is* known — to someone." This bit of sophistry, worthy of Ramses himself, produced a murmur of admiring agreement from my son, and Emerson, who had never had the least intention of conforming to the terms of his concession anyhow, continued, "The most important thing is to please your dear mama. Mutual consideration is the only possible basis for a successful marriage."

"I will bear that in mind, Father."

I announced my presence with a little cough. Emerson snatched up his notebook and hurried away. Ramses glanced at me and waited politely for me to speak if I so chose. I did not. As Emerson had said, mutual consideration is the only possible basis for a successful marriage.

A group of our men had come from Gurneh to join us, and as we made our way across the plateau toward the Valley, Emerson gave Abdullah his instructions. Abdullah knew better than to express surprise when Emerson told him to send Selim and a few of the others to close tomb Twenty-one, but he gave me a quick glance and raised his eyebrows when Emerson looked away for a moment. I nodded. Abdullah nodded. He seemed to be enjoying himself.

We trailed obediently after Emerson as he led the way, into the side valley we had visited the first day. This time we were not alone; voices and sounds of activity could be heard from the far end where Hatshepsut's tomb lay, and as we proceeded we encountered one of his workmen carrying a loaded basket on his shoulder. Emerson, who treats Egyptians more courteously than he does his fellow Englishmen, greeted him with a stentorian shout of *"Salaam aleikhum"*; the fellow mumbled something in return and hurried past us toward the mouth of the wadi.

"Mr. Carter must be driving his men hard today," Nefret remarked. "They are usually ready to stop and chat."

Emerson stopped. "Hmph," he said.

"What is it?" I asked.

"Nefret was correct. That fellow was in too much of a hurry. And why would he go so far to empty his basket?"

He went on more slowly, looking keenly from side to side, but it was Ramses who first observed the object that stood up from the rubble at the base of the cliff.

"It is only a stick or a broken branch," I said.

"A broken branch, here?" Emerson inquired.

But that was what it was, protruding at an angle from the loose scree. It had been neatly trimmed of twigs and leaves so that it resembled a stout walking stick. We stood staring at the harmless thing as warily as if it had been a coiled snake.

Emerson was the first to speak. "This is too much. Curse it! Is the fellow trying to insult me?"

"Do you think it is a marker, then?" I asked.

"What else can it be? Hell and damnation," Emerson added with considerable feeling.

Nefret's face was flushed with excitement. "Let's begin digging!"

"Damned if I will," said Emerson.

"Now, Emerson, don't be childish," I said. "What do you think, Abdullah?"

The old man studied the terrain. Then he said slowly, "There is something. The stone is different here; it has been disturbed."

"Go ahead, then," I said, glancing at Emerson. He turned his back and folded his arms, but he did not countermand the order.

The men began digging where Abdullah indicated. It soon became obvious that this area had been recently disturbed; the rock fill was loose and easy to move. Before long I saw the top of an opening below.

"Good morning!" called a cheery voice. I turned to see Howard Carter approaching. "One of the men told me you were here," he went on. "I might have known you would find something

I missed when I was investigating this wadi last season. But . . ." He leaned over the excavation and looked down. "But I'm afraid it is only another uninscribed pit tomb. You have found no stairs?"

"Not yet," said Ramses. "However . . ." He lowered himself into the hole, which was by then approximately as deep as he was tall. "However, there is an interesting feature. A wooden door."

"Impossible," Howard exclaimed. "The Egyptians did use wooden doors in some tombs, but this —"

"Is not ancient," Ramses interrupted. "It appears to have been cobbled together from smaller scraps. I believe I can remove one of them, if you, Mr. Carter, sir, will hand me that chisel next your foot."

"Just a moment," Emerson said. "Are you certain the door is modern?"

Ramses straightened. "Yes, sir. Modern tools were employed. The marks are quite clear."

"Take care, all the same." Emerson handed him the chisel with one hand and placed the other hand firmly on Nefret's shoulder. "There is not room for you down there, Nefret. You will have to wait, like the rest of us."

We did not have to wait long. The section of wood came away with a screech and a comment from Ramses — "Iron nails, Father" — and after lighting one of the candles he carried in his pocket, Ramses put it and his head through the opening.

"Well?" Nefret demanded.

Ramses did not answer immediately. After a long pause he remarked, "Curious. Very curious indeed."

"What is curious?" Nefret demanded. "Curse you, Ramses!"

Ramses withdrew his head. "There is a mummy."

"What is curious about that?" I inquired. "Mummies are often found in tombs. That is the function of a tomb, to contain one or more mummies."

"Quite right," said Howard with a laugh. "I found two of them last season, in that pit tomb across the way."

"Did they have long golden hair?" Ramses asked.

If he hoped for a sensation, he did not get it — this time. Howard laughed again. "Yes, as a matter of fact. The golden shade was, of course, the result of the embalming materials on hair that was white with age."

Ramses took the hand Emerson offered and climbed back up the rocky slope. He was looking particularly enigmatic. "I fear, Mr. Carter, that the two cases are not analogous. This female was not elderly. Nor are her wrappings ancient."

Emerson gave him a long look, but did not speak. Howard smiled in a patronizing fashion. "Come now, Ramses. How could you tell the age of the wrappings by the light of a single candle?"

"Because," said Ramses, "they were covered

with silk embroidered flowers."

Howard let out a whoop of laughter. "Jolly good, young fellow! You have developed quite a sense of humor."

"Ridiculous," I exclaimed. "Your eyes played you false, Ramses."

Nefret, squirming in Emerson's grasp, said, "How would a man recognize silk embroidery? Let me look."

Emerson said, "Not without my permission, young lady."

Ramses's eyes met those of his father. "You will want photographs before we have it out, sir. It is a rather . . . extraordinary sight."

"Ah," said Emerson. "You recommend excavating, then?"

"I believe," said Ramses with a strange emphasis, "we have no choice but to do so."

He refused to describe what he had seen, remarking that none of us would take his word for it anyhow. Though this statement was unquestionably designed to provoke Nefret (and me), it was correct; we all wanted to see for ourselves. So Emerson lowered himself into the hole and lifted me down beside him.

His candle cast a limited light, but it was sufficient. The shrouded form lay near the entrance, its feet toward the door. Emerson drew in his breath and let it out in a whispered invocation.

Ramses had been right about the silk flowers. The fabric covered the body like the sheet of linen employed by the ancient embalmers as the final, outermost wrapping. The ancients had used strips of bandage to bind the shroud at ankles, knees, shoulders, and neck. Here the ties appeared to be faded satin ribbon — once blue, now sickly gray. The face was shrouded by gauze so fine that the outline of the features could be seen, and the hair had been carefully arranged to frame the head in long curling locks of pale gold.

As I stared, mesmerized, I was visited by a haunting sense of déjà vu. It did not take me long to identify the memory that prompted it. I had never seen a mummy like this one. There had never been a mummy like it — except in works of fiction. The heroes of romantic novels were always running across the perfectly preserved bodies of ancient Egyptians or, in some cases, the people of a lost civilization. These remains were always female, astonishingly beautiful, and wrapped in gauzy fabric that barely concealed their charms. The unfortunate young gentleman who found one was instantly stricken with hopeless passion.

"Oh, dear," I murmured.

"Always the mot juste, Peabody." Emerson withdrew his arm and handed me the candle. Picking up the bit of board Ramses had removed, he fitted it over the hole and pounded it firmly into place with his fist. This produced an indignant outcry from Nefret, who was at the edge of the excavation, looking down.

"You will see it soon enough," said Emerson, lifting me out of the hole and climbing up to join me. "Abdullah, get the men started. . . . No. Don't move so much as a pebble until I return. Peabody, stay here with him and make certain no one disturbs the area. The rest of you come with me."

He was on his way even as he spoke, his long strides covering the broken ground as rapidly as another man might run. The others trotted after him. Nefret had Ramses by the arm and was peppering him with questions.

I dusted off a rock and sat down. "He didn't mean you to go with him," I explained to Howard, who had taken an uncertain step after Emerson. "Would you care for a sip of cold tea?"

"No, thank you." Howard looked from me to Abdullah, who had settled himself on the ground, knees raised and arms folded, and was watching me with an unblinking stare. "Where has he gone? What is in there? Why did he —"

"You had better have some tea," I said, investigating the basket of food I had caused to be brought along. "Orange? Sandwich? Boiled egg?"

I tossed him an egg and passed the basket to Abdullah. He took it, without removing his eyes from my face, and I looked away, dreading the moment of disappointment that was to come. Poor man! He knew Emerson would not have reacted as he did if the find had not been truly extraordinary, but to Abdullah that word implied an archaeological find. He had dismissed Ramses's description of silk embroidered wrappings, which meant nothing to him; he hoped for an undisturbed burial even finer than that of Tetisheri, a mummy glittering with gold, a tomb filled with wonderful things.

"Emerson has gone to fetch certain materials," I explained, wondering how best to break the bad news to Abdullah. "He ought also to notify the police, but if I know Emerson —"

Abdullah let out a grunt, like a man who has been struck in the stomach. Howard exclaimed, "Why the dev— Why should he notify the police?"

"You will prolong my narrative unnecessarily if you continue to interrupt me, Howard. The authorities will have to be called in because . . ." I could not bear to look at Abdullah. "Because Ramses's description of long golden hair and silken wrappings was unfortunately accurate. The mummy in that tomb is not that of an ancient Egyptian. It is that of an individual who met her end within the past few years; certainly within the last decade."

Silently and slowly, dignified as a tragic Muse, Abdullah lowered his head onto his folded arms.

"But — but," Howard stuttered. "It can hardly be a mummy if it is as — er — fresh as that. Do you mean a corpse — a cadaver — a skeleton?"

"Well, as to that, I cannot say without a closer examination," I replied, smacking an egg against the rock and starting to peel away the shell. "However, the remains appear to be in a state of preservation that renders the last word, at least, inaccurate. I distinctly saw the outline of a nose under the gauze that concealed the face. Skeletons, as you know, lack a nasal appendage. It consists of cartilage, which —"

"Mrs. Emerson!" Howard cried loudly. I stopped speaking and gave him a reproachful look. "I beg your pardon," he continued more temperately. "I should not have shouted at you, but this is the strangest thing I have ever heard."

"No," said a muffled voice. "It is not strange. She finds them often. Fresh dead people."

"I don't do it on purpose, Abdullah. Anyhow, I didn't find this one. Ramses did. Have a boiled egg, it will do you good. In point of fact, this is one of the more unusual cadavers I have come across. Except for the hair, which has been left unbound, it is wrapped in the ancient style. More or less," I amended, and paused to take a bite of my egg. "The outermost covering is fashioned of silk brocade and tied with satin ribbons. As you are both aware, silk was unknown to the ancient Egyptians. This fabric is somewhat faded, but the original colors are still discernible, and it is obviously of modern manufacture."

My companions had recovered themselves. Abdullah was morosely peeling an orange, and bright-eyed interest had replaced Howard's initial astonishment.

"Was it the condition of the fabric that led you

to suggest a date of less than ten years?" he asked respectfully.

"No. I recognized the pattern. Mr. Worth, the famous couturier, used it in a ball gown he designed for . . . I believe it was Lady Burton-Leigh . . . eight years ago. He was — for he is now deceased — a leader of the world of fashion, so it cannot have been procurable much before that time."

"Incredible!" Carter exclaimed.

"My dear Howard, that is only one of the deductions a trained observer may make. I know, for instance, that the owner of that garment was well-to-do. Even if it was not purchased from Mr. Worth, but at a later time from one of the lesser designers who imitate him, the fabric itself is costly. That does not mean that the body is necessarily that of the woman who owned the frock. It might have been stolen from her. However, the remains are those of a female with fair hair, and since the color of the garment was azure, one may provisionally conclude that it belonged to her." Observing his bewildered expression, I explained, "Blue is a shade favored by blond ladies."

"You amaze me, Mrs. Emerson!"

The long walk and the excitement of the discovery had given me quite an appetite. I unwrapped a tomato sandwich.

"The trouble with you men is that you dismiss 'women's things' as frivolous and unimportant. Fewer crimes would remain unsolved if we had a female at the head of Scotland Yard!"

When Emerson returned he was accompanied by more of our loyal men and by a number of extraneous individuals, several of whom appeared to be tourists. Driven back by his eloquent curses, some of them wandered off, but the majority settled down some distance away and prepared to watch. Luncheon baskets were unpacked, and one of the dragomen began lecturing his group in atrocious German. *"Meine Dame und Herren, hier sind die Archaeologer sehr ausgezeichnet, Herr Professor Emerson, sogennant Vater des Fluchen, und ihre Frau. . . ."*

"Ignore them, Emerson," I said to my seething spouse. "The more you fuss, the more convinced they will be that we have made an important discovery. Let us all have a spot of lunch. If we do nothing but eat, the cursed tourists will become bored and go away."

The others had gathered round, awaiting orders. After a moment of cogitation, Emerson nodded grudgingly. "Right as always, Peabody. We will take twenty minutes. But we must have the cursed — er — the poor thing out of there today. By evening false rumors of a rich find will have reached every tomb robber on the West Bank." He turned to glare at one of the robbers — a younger member of the notorious Abd er Rassul family, who smiled guilelessly back at him — and then transferred the glare to Howard Carter.

187

"Why are you hanging about? Don't you have an excavation of your own?"

"He only wants to help," I explained. "After all, Emerson, he is chief inspector for Upper Egypt. He has a responsibility to be here, especially considering the unusual circumstances."

"Hmph," said Emerson, accepting a cup of tea.

Howard shot me a grateful look. "Unusual is hardly the word. Mrs. Emerson tells me the remains are modern — less than ten years dead, according to her."

"Lower your voice," Emerson growled.

"How did you arrive at that conclusion, Mother?" asked Ramses.

I remained modestly silent while Howard repeated what I had told him. It gave me great satisfaction to see the expression on Emerson's face. He was always teasing me about my interest in fashion. Of course he felt bound to express doubts about my theory.

"Jumping to conclusions again, Peabody. The fabric may be modern, but —"

"I believe, Father, that we must accept her conclusions," said Ramses. "Provisionally, at least."

"I appreciate your condescension, Ramses," I said.

"How can you discuss this so coolly?" Nefret demanded, rising impetuously to her feet. Her cheeks had lost some of their color, and her eyes flashed. "It is horrible! Let us get her out of there at once."

"If she has been there for ten years, a few more hours won't matter," said Emerson. "You must cultivate detachment, Nefret, or you will never make an archaeologist."

"I should emulate Ramses, I suppose," the girl said scornfully. "He is impervious to sentiment."

One would certainly have supposed so. Seated cross-legged on the ground, devouring bread and cheese, Ramses only raised one eyebrow and went on eating.

The audience did not go away. If anything, the number of gaping watchers increased, and Emerson declared there was no sense in further delay. Ibrahim the carpenter began nailing together the boards he had carried with him, and the men returned to removing the rubble.

There were steps under the loose stone — twelve of them, rock cut and regular. The men could have cleared them in short order had it not been for Emerson's insistence that we examine every square inch of the fill for extraneous objects. It was his invariable rule, but in this case he had an additional reason. The murderer might have left a clue.

"What murderer?" Emerson demanded after I had commended him. "We have no evidence that a crime has been committed."

"Ah, so that is to be your excuse for not notifying the authorities immediately."

"Excuse be damned," said Emerson. "At this moment we know only that there is what appears to be a mummified body in that pit. It may or

189

may not be ancient; it may or may not be human. It may even be a perverse joke perpetrated by a modern tourist or by one of my professional enemies. Some of those fellows — I name no names, Peabody, but you know to whom I refer — would like nothing better than to see me make a fool of myself over a bundle of sticks or a dead sheep. Wallis Budge —"

"Yes, my dear," I said soothingly. When Emerson gets on the subject of his professional rivals, especially Wallis Budge, the keeper of Egyptian antiquities at the British Museum, it is necessary to cut him short. "You are right. We must not jump to conclusions."

"Ha," said Emerson.

He appeared to be in a state of some exasperation, so I went to join Nefret, who was inspecting the objects found in the rubble. It was an unimpressive collection — brittle bones and fragments of coarse pottery.

"Animal?" I asked, picking up a piece of bone.

Nefret wrinkled her pretty brow over the bone and put it aside. "Certainly not human. Goat, perhaps."

It was the hottest, drowsiest time of the day. The dry air was utterly still. The sky was bleached to a pale blue. I found it hard to keep my eyes open, especially since there was not a single object of interest in the collection, not even a collar button.

After a time I was roused from a half doze by Emerson. Dropping down beside me, he drew his sleeve across his wet forehead and asked if there was any tea. I did not tell him to use his handkerchief or ask what had become of his hat. I make certain Emerson always begins the day with his pith helmet on his head and a nice clean white handkerchief in his pocket. By afternoon he has usually lost both of them.

"Are you stopping work, then?" I asked, for Ramses had joined us and the men had laid aside their shovels and baskets.

"For the moment only," Emerson said. "Something odd is going on."

Looking in the direction he indicated, I understood what he meant. By midafternoon most of the tourists had retreated to their hotels, and even archaeologists and Egyptians knocked off work. Yet the crowd of watchers, held at bay by our men, seemed to have increased, and not one but two lecturers were competing.

". . . the famed Mister Professor Emerson and his family . . . *un sépulcher nouveau* . . . what will be unclosed when the door flies open . . . *trésor d'or magnifique* . . ."

The last phrase was too much for Emerson, who bounded to his feet, fists clenched. I caught hold of his booted ankle.

"Sit down, Emerson, for pity's sake. It is the fault of your reputation," I added as Emerson, grumbling like a thunderstorm, resumed his seat. I handed him a glass of tea. "Our last discovery made headlines in every newspaper in the Western world. The poor credulous creatures are expecting something equally sensational. But how did the news spread so fast, I wonder?"

"Daoud, most probably," said Ramses. "You know how he loves to tell tall tales. But it could have been any of the others, or one of Mr. Carter's chaps. I only hope . . ." He checked himself, but the look he gave me made his meaning only too clear.

An involuntary gasp of dismay escaped my lips. I knew — who better? — how fact can be distorted and embroidered by gossip, and I did not doubt our men had overheard Ramses's description of what lay within the tomb. No wonder the curious crowd lingered! Long golden hair, silken wrappings — by this time the description probably included golden diadems and jewel-encrusted ornaments. If Donald Fraser got wind of this, he would be certain we had found his imaginary princess. I must speak to him and to Enid before word reached them.

"Emerson," I said, "would it not be better to delay in removing the mummy so that we can contradict the rumors and reduce public interest? The mere sight of it, as it now appears —"

Emerson shook his unruly black head. "Delay will only whet curiosity, and wild rumor will increase the expectations of our neighbors from Gurneh, curse the tomb-robbing swine."

"Then let us get at it," I agreed.

Nefret, assisted by David, was taking photographs of the closed door and its surroundings. Long exposures were necessary since Emerson refused to employ magnesium flares or black powder for lighting. Reflectors of polished metal had served us well in the past and would continue to do so until the entire Valley was electrified. The generator Howard had installed lighted only a few of the tombs.

While Nefret and David completed their work I studied the wooden door, now fully visible. It is difficult to find large pieces of wood in Egypt, since the native trees are small and spindly. The door had been pieced together, but it was a neat bit of carpentry, and it fitted snugly into the aperture. There was no visible bolt or bar; plaster filled the uneven joins between the wood and the stone.

Emerson inserted the end of a crowbar. Abdullah cleared his throat.

"Emerson."

"What is it?" Emerson heaved on the crowbar.

"The curse."

"The what?" Emerson turned to glare at his foreman.

"I know there is no such thing," Abdullah said self-consciously. "But Daoud, and these other fools . . ."

"Hmph. Abdullah, we are rather short on time. Supposing I perform the exorcism first thing tomorrow?"

Abdullah looked doubtful. Ramses cleared his throat. "I will be happy to say a few words, Father."

"You?" Emerson turned the glare on Ramses.

He enjoys performing exorcisms, for which he is famous in Egypt, and did not appreciate being supplanted.

Nefret, who had been looking very solemn, could not repress a giggle. "They call him 'Akhu el-Afareet,' you know. Have at it, Ramses, and I will add a word or two of my own."

I had wondered what affectionate nickname the Egyptians had given Ramses. I started to expostulate, but Emerson spoke first.

"Make it quick," he grunted, turning back to the door.

So my son, also known as the Brother of Demons, began waving his arms and chanting in a mixture of languages from medieval French to classical Arabic. He kept one eye on Emerson, however, and when the portal showed signs of yielding he brought his incantation to a sudden end. Turning to Nefret, he grasped her hands and raised them high.

"Hear the blessing of the daughter of the Father of Curses, the sister of the Brother of Demons, the Light of Egypt," he intoned, adding in English and under his breath, "Speak up, my girl, don't stand there gaping."

Nefret's first word was hardly more than a gurgle, but she was quick to recover, reciting the sonorous testimonial of the call to prayer and "May the Lord bless thee and keep thee." The performance would have been more impressive, however, if she had not concluded with, "How did you like that, my boy?"

"Perhaps Father and I should leave it to you from now on," was the reply.

All our faces were grave and unsmiling, however, when we gathered round the opened portal. At that very moment, with an uncanny suggestion of celestial stagecraft, a ray of sunlight reflected off the sheet of tin one of the men was holding and fell full upon the head of the shrouded form.

It woke no spark from the long strands of curling hair.

Jewelry made of intricately braided human hair had been popular in the recent past. Even more common was the custom of placing a lock of a loved one's hair under crystal or glass, in a brooch or ring or bracelet. Father had given me a brooch enclosing a raven curl of my mother's. I cherished it as a sacred relic, but I never wore it. The hair was dry and dull and dead.

As was this hair. The shrouded face was no less disturbing. I could now make out details that had been obscured by the shadows cast by candlelight — the curving cheekbones, the shape of full lips. Impossible, I thought. The silken fabric had faded and begun to shatter; it had covered the quiet breast and slender limbs for years. The soft flesh of the face could not have endured unmarred.

I heard a smothered sob from Nefret. Emerson, whose formidable facade conceals an extremely tender heart, sniffed loudly. Rude and unfinished, empty and barren though it was, none of us wished to take the first step into that final resting place of the dead.

Except, of course, Ramses. Slipping past his father, he approached the recumbent form. "Note the arms, Father. They appear to be placed vertically, alongside the — er — hips."

"Hmph," said Emerson, discarding sentiment in favor of scholarship. "That position became general in the Twenty-first Dynasty. However, this individual is decidedly later in date. Come back here, Ramses, you may be treading on important clues — er — artifacts. David, how long will it take you to make a sketch?"

"I will be as quick as I can, sir," was the quiet response.

By the time he had finished the drawing, and Nefret had taken several exposures, Emerson and I had explored the small room. It was a curious place, scarcely two meters wide and four meters long. The surface underfoot was not smoothed stone, but a layer of smaller pebbles packed hard to form a level surface. The ceiling sloped sharply down from the entrance till it met the floor. The side walls were of dressed stone, with no trace of carving or inscription.

"That will have to do," Emerson said at last, gesturing to David to put his pencils away. "You can make a detailed watercolor tonight, at the house, before I unwrap . . ." He hesitated for a moment and then said gruffly, "it."

"How are you going to get her — it — there?" I asked.

"Carry it, of course," was the reply. "The jolting of a carriage or wagon might damage it."

"Past all those staring tourists?"

"If you can think of an alternative, I will be happy to consider it."

I remained silent, and Emerson said, "They won't see anything except a wooden box, Peabody. I brought blankets to cushion and cover it."

I had seen the pile of blankets and wondered what *we* were going to use for coverings that night. If Emerson thought he was going to put them straight back on the beds, he was mistaken.

However, the decision had been made, and indeed he had had little choice. There was no way of knowing how fragile the remains might be until we attempted to lift them.

Watching me, Emerson said, "Get up there and do what you can to disperse the mob, Peabody. Nefret, go with your aunt Amelia and tell Ibrahim to bring the coffin — box, I should say."

I knew why he was sending me away, and I did not envy him the task that lay ahead — gathering the dull dead hair in his hands, lifting the slight form — and hoping it would hold together. Thus far none of us had ventured to touch that still shape; for all we knew, the slightest touch might cause it to crumble. Moving it might be as dangerous, but it could not be examined properly under those conditions, and to leave it there was impossible. Emerson had taken all the precautions he could.

Nefret followed me without comment, although ordinarily she would have objected to being dismissed. She was accustomed to mummies and corpses — our family seems to encounter a good many of them — but there was something about this set of remains that affected her painfully, as it did me. She was a little pale, but the color rushed back into her face when she saw the people crowded behind the makeshift barrier the men had constructed from sticks and rope.

"Ghouls," she muttered.

"Be fair," I replied. "They don't know what is there, and this is not private property. I am going to tell them to take themselves off, but I will do it courteously and —"

"Hell and damnation!" Nefret exclaimed.

I could hardly scold her for bad language when I had been on the verge of employing it myself. The news had spread more rapidly than I had hoped it would, but it was pure bad luck — or so I supposed — that the Frasers were among those whom it had reached. Why the devil couldn't they have been visiting some remote temple that day?

Donald had bared his head. He was a tall man; his flaming red hair stood high above the crowd. Enid and Mrs. Whitney-Jones flanked him on either side. Both women gripped his arms like prison warders. Mrs. Whitney-Jones's fashionable bronze hat was tipped over one eye, and Enid appeared to be tugging at Donald. His face flushed, his eyes fixed on vacancy, he paid no heed to either.

I ought to have known that Nefret's profane comment had not been prompted by the Frasers, whom she barely knew and with whose strange situation she was then unacquainted. I was still trying to decide what to do about Donald when another voice drew my attention to an additional distraction.

"Will you do me the courtesy, Mrs. Emerson, of telling this native to let me pass?"

The Colonel held Dolly within the protective circle of his arm, as if the girl had been threatened by the native in question — Abdullah's nephew Daoud. Poor Daoud glanced at me in appeal. "Sitt Hakim," he began.

I reassured him with a few phrases in Arabic and addressed Bellingham. "Daoud was obeying orders, Colonel — my orders. What are you doing here?"

"Responding to your invitation, Mrs. Emerson."

"Invitation?" I repeated in astonishment. "I sent no invitation."

The Colonel glanced at the tourists crowding round, with the look a mastiff might bestow upon a pack of alley cats, and tightened his grasp on Dolly. "Perhaps we might discuss the situation in greater privacy. My daughter, Mrs. Emerson, is not accustomed to being jostled."

I was not feeling as kindly toward the Colonel as I had the previous day, but his surprising statement had aroused my curiosity. "Daoud, you may let them pass."

Dolly slid out of her father's grasp. Raising her parasol — a frivolous piece of frippery quivering with lace — she made me a little curtsey and then sidled up to Nefret. "Good afternoon, Miss Forth. What a fetching costume!"

And what a little cat you are, I thought. In my opinion she had committed a strategic error in emphasizing the contrast in their appearances. Her elaborate attire, from flower-trimmed hat to trailing skirts, made her look like a wax doll. Nefret's boyish garments were dusty and damp with perspiration, but they clung only too becomingly to her slim body, and aggravation gave her cheeks a pretty color.

"Good afternoon," she said shortly. "Excuse me, I must also obey orders."

She put a friendly hand on Daoud's shoulder and addressed him in Arabic. A broad grin spread across his face. With a nod he raised the stick he was holding and assumed a pugilistic posture, side by side with Nefret. In a pungent mixture of Arabic and English she told the audience to go about its business.

Not all the watchers moved away, so I felt obliged to add a few comments of my own. My voice was emphatic, for I was beginning to feel somewhat rattled. There was too much to attend to and very little time. Emerson had taken longer than I had expected to move the body — I hoped it had not disintegrated into bits when he touched it — but he would soon emerge from the tomb, and what he would say when he saw the Bellinghams, not to mention the Frasers, I did not like to think.

The Colonel, hat in hand, awaited my attention, but first I had to deal with the Frasers and Mrs. Whitney-Jones. The lady, wearing a fashionable costume of yellow flannel, appeared less composed than upon the occasion of our first meeting. She continued to tug at Donald, to no avail; he was as immobile as the pharaonic statue he rather resembled, his eyes straight ahead, his arms at his sides. Enid was looking desperately around, as if searching for someone or something. I assumed, naturally, that it was I, so I hastened to approach her.

"I am sorry, Amelia," Enid said in tremulous tones. "I cannot get him to come away."

"No apologies are necessary. I know the whole story, and I am ready and able to deal with the situation."

She had been very pale. Now her cheeks took on color — with relief, I supposed, at finding me willing to help. "You — you know?"

"Yes, my dear, Ramses told me this afternoon about Donald's delusion. I suppose you heard the rumors about our discovery? But never mind that, time is of the essence. You must take him away from here at once. Donald? Donald!" He made not the slightest response, even when I prodded him with my parasol. I shot Mrs. Whitney-Jones a hard look. "This is your doing. Persuade him to go back to the hotel."

The woman was not so easily intimidated. Her

chin lifted, and her eyes looked unflinchingly into mine. "Unfounded accusations may render an individual liable to legal action, Mrs. Emerson. I forgive you because you are concerned about your friend, but let me assure you I did not bring him here; I tried to persuade him not to come here; I would like very much to take him away from here. If you can tell me how to accomplish that, I will cooperate to the fullest."

"She did try," Enid said reluctantly. "Amelia, what are we to do?"

I glanced over my shoulder. The Colonel was pacing back and forth, Nefret and Dolly were smiling fixedly at one another, and there were signs of movement around the opening of the tomb. Immediate action was imperative. I seized Donald by the collar and shook him vigorously.

This had the desired effect.

"Mrs. Emerson," he gurgled (for I had a fairly tight hold on his collar). "What — what has happened? Have I done something to annoy you?"

"Yes," I replied. "Go away, Donald. Go away this instant."

But I had delayed too long. Emerson emerged from the tomb, followed by Ramses and David.

The long wooden box had been suspended in a cradle of ropes supported by carrying poles. Some of the blankets must have been used to pad the interior of the box; others had been laid over it, concealing the contents. The very shape of the container was suggestive, however, and a murmur of ghoulish interest arose from the audience.

Emerson stopped. The boys, behind him, also paused. The sight of my husband's majestic form, dominating the scene as he always does, did not on this occasion produce the customary thrill of admiration in me. I knew what was about to transpire and could only curse helplessly (under my breath, of course) and shove at Donald, who was staring, white-faced, at the wooden box.

Then the ambient air was shattered by a mighty cry.

"Peabody!"

I abandoned my ineffectual attempt to budge Donald and hastened to my husband.

"What the devil is going on here?" he demanded. His eyes, blazing with sapphirine fury, moved from Bellingham to Donald, and to the audience, which had surged forward. "Where have these — these people come from? Did you send out invitations?"

"No, my dear. At least I don't think so. Emerson, please calm yourself. The situation has got a little out of hand."

"So I see."

"I did my best, Emerson."

The hard blue eyes softened, and he clasped my shoulders in a brief, comradely embrace. "All right, Peabody. It is a pleasant change to hear you admit incompetence for once. Just keep them back, will you? The sooner we get away from here the better. Come ahead, boys."

I always say no one can clear a path better than Emerson. His emphatic gestures and even more emphatic expressions sent the onlookers scuttling for safety. The boys took a firmer grip on the carrying poles and proceeded, with our men following.

I turned back to Colonel Bellingham.

"I cannot speak with you at the present time, Colonel, I must get on. There is some mystery about this business that will have to be cleared up, but it must wait. You will hear from me in due course."

Instead of answering me he emitted a horrible choking cry. Turning, I saw that Donald had sprung forward. Emerson's mighty arms were quick to seize and hold him fast, but not before he had snatched the covering off the coffin and set it swinging between the suspending ropes. The tourists, held at bay, could not have seen what lay within, but the rest of us were treated to an excellent view of blue silk wrapping and coils of flaxen hair.

Gripped tightly by my enraged and swearing husband, Donald raised an ecstatic face to heaven. "At last!" he cried. "At last! It is she!"

Another, deeper voice echoed his. White to the lips, Bellingham repeated, "It is she! Oh, God — it is she!"

Clutching at his heaving breast, he toppled forward and crashed to the ground.

It was a pleasure to observe the prompt efficiency with which my family responded to this latest emergency. Emerson's reaction was, naturally, the quickest and most effective. He delivered a sharp blow to Donald's jaw, caught the sagging body, and handed it over to two of our men.

"Mahmud, Hassan, take him to his carriage," he ordered. "Any carriage. Commandeer one, if necessary. Mrs. Fraser, remove your husband. Ramses, David —"

The boys had already continued on their way, escorted by Abdullah and Selim, and Nefret was kneeling beside the Colonel, knife in hand. Dolly stood staring down at him; as Nefret's glittering blade touched her father's throat, she emitted a piercing scream.

The knife slid neatly through the layers of the Colonel's shirt, stiff collar, and silk cravat, and Nefret said without looking up, "Keep the damned girl quiet, Aunt Amelia, can you? I almost cut the poor man's throat when she let out that howl."

"Certainly," I said. "Dolly, if you scream again, I will slap you. Is it a seizure, Nefret?"

She had bared his chest and pressed her ear against it. "He is pale, not flushed. His heart, perhaps."

Emerson stood beside me, hands on his hips, brow furrowed. "Curse it," he said. "Why does this sort of thing always happen to me? One would suppose people might have the decency to die somewhere else."

I knew Emerson's good heart too well to take this callous speech literally. Like myself, he had seen that the color was returning to the Colonel's face and that his eyes had opened. They gazed, not at us, but at the golden head that rested on his breast.

"The beat is steadier," Nefret said.

She sat back on her heels. The Colonel's hand moved in a feeble attempt to adjust his clothing. She drew the cloth back into place and smiled at him.

"You are better, sir, aren't you? I am sorry to have spoiled your nice cravat, but it was necessary."

"You are . . . a physician?" he asked weakly.

"Oh, no. We should take him to a doctor as soon as possible, don't you think, Aunt Amelia?"

I was beginning to share Emerson's vexation at people who were constantly collapsing on the premises. However, common decency as well as the duty of a Christian woman made me keep this opinion to myself.

I administered a medicinal sip of brandy from the flask I carry with me, and the Colonel, supported by Emerson's brawny arms, rose shakily to his feet. "Where is your carriage?" Emerson asked. "And your dragoman?"

A man who had been standing quietly among the watchers came forward. He had the dark skin of a Nubian and the prominent aquiline nose of an Arab. His other features were concealed by a grizzled beard and mustache. "I am the servant of the Howadji, Father of Curses."

"Then why the devil aren't you looking out for him?" Emerson demanded.

"He told me to stay at a distance from him and the young Sitt unless he called to me."

"Hmph," said Emerson. "Well — what is your name?"

"Mohammed."

"I have not seen you before. Are you a Luxor man?"

"No, Father of Curses. I come from Aswan."

"Well, Mohammed, take the Howadji to his carriage."

"Wait," the Colonel said faintly. "Dolly . . ."

Nefret drew me aside. Her face was troubled. "Aunt Amelia, we cannot let them go back to the hotel alone," she whispered. "Unless they have found someone since last night, she has not even a maid to help her. She isn't fit to look after him, and if he is right about her being in danger, he isn't fit to watch over her. I could accompany them —"

"Not under any circumstances!" I exclaimed.

Her little chin stiffened. "Something must be done."

"I agree." I turned back to Emerson, who was beginning to look somewhat uneasy. He claims to despise all religions, but his moral standards are superior to those of most people who call themselves Christians — if he takes the time to think about them. He had taken the time; he scowled but did not even swear under his breath

207

when I ordered the dragoman Mohammed to take his employer to our house.

"Ibrahim will go with you to show you the way," I finished. "And I will send someone to Luxor directly to fetch Dr. Willoughby."

Dolly had not uttered a word nor moved an inch, even when her father called her. She looked more than ever like a wax doll; her brown eyes were as expressionless as glass. I poked her with my parasol. "Go along with your father."

"Yes, ma'am," Dolly said in a faraway voice. "Your house, ma'am?"

"We will be there before you," I assured her. "Now hurry, can't you see he is waiting for you? The sooner we get medical attention for him the better."

Emerson attended them to their carriage. I would like to believe he was moved by Christian charity and gentlemanly manners, but I think it was rather that he was anxious to be rid of them as quickly as possible. Nefret and I started back along the path over the plateau. Briskly though we climbed, it was not long before Emerson caught us up. He was, of course, swearing.

"That is just a waste of breath, Emerson," I said. "I don't like the situation any better than you, but we had no choice."

"Yes, we did. However," Emerson said grudgingly, "the choice was forced upon us by our confounded sense of duty. There is a limit to mine, Amelia. I depend on you to get them out of my house as soon as possible."

"Dr. Willoughby may wish to take the Colonel to his clinic," Nefret suggested.

"Precisely what I was about to suggest," I said. "It is obviously the best place for the Colonel, and there are female nurses and attendants to look after the girl. Have no fear, Emerson, they will be out of your house by nightfall."

"They had damned well better be. We still have a mummy to contend with, Peabody — or have you forgotten? I want to examine it tonight."

I murmured reassurances. I too was anxious to examine the mummy, though I was no longer in any doubt as to its identity.

CHAPTER SIX

I have never been particularly fond of mummies.

When I saw the familiar walls of our house ahead I felt as if we had been gone for days instead of hours. It would have been a pleasure to relax on the shaded verandah with a cool drink in my hand, but I knew that indulgence was still some hours away. Girding up my loins and stiffening my spine, I went into action. The carriage arrived shortly after we did, and I saw the Colonel helped to bed in Ramses's room, his dragoman and coachman sent to the kitchen for food and drink, and Dolly supplied with the means of refreshing herself.

Nefret had been right, the girl was absolutely hopeless; she could not take care of herself, much less her father. She sat at my dressing table with her hands folded on her lap, staring at her reflection in the mirror; it was I who drew out the hat pins, removed her hat, and smoothed her wet, tangled hair. When I offered her a damp cloth she only looked blankly at it, so I began to wipe the dust and perspiration from her face, noting that there were no signs of tears.

The cool water roused her — or perhaps it was my assault on her porcelain-fair complexion. She took the cloth from my hand and dabbed delicately at her lips. (I had suspected their pretty pink color was not entirely natural.) Then she asked for her handbag.

Smoothing rice powder on her cheeks, she inquired, "How is poor dear Daddy?"

"Resting easily, I am happy to say. Miss Forth is sitting with him."

"Miss Forth?" I watched the pretty, composed face reflected in the mirror and saw her eyes narrow. "Why is she with him?"

"Because she is a kind, compassionate individual. She has had some medical training. Since I was busy with you, there was no one else to send."

"Where is Mr. Emerson?"

I was about to reply when I realized she might not mean my husband. I supposed I would have to get used to that, too.

"If you are referring to my son, he and David have taken the horses to be exercised. Are you feeling better now? No doubt you will wish to go to your father."

Dolly put a hand over her eyes and shook her head. "I just can't face it, Mrs. Emerson. It breaks my heart to see him looking so poorly."

So I led her to the verandah and told Ali to serve tea. Dolly responded only with abstracted murmurs to my attempts at polite conversation. She had taken a chair next to one of the open arches that offered an excellent view of the sandy

211

path that led toward the riverbank, and her eyes remained fixed on that scene. I assumed she was watching for the doctor, and my annoyance with her subsided a trifle.

Dr. Willoughby made as much haste as he could. It was not long before the carriage drew up. The doctor's calm face, his quiet, soothing voice, his very presence, made me feel that a burden had been lifted from my shoulders. We had known him for many years and had complete confidence in him.

I was about to lead him to the chamber where the sick man lay when Emerson emerged from the house. I had assumed he was skulking in his study, avoiding both Dolly and her father, but his first words assured me that I had misjudged him. Admirable man! He had neglected neither his duties as a father nor his obligations as an English gentleman.

"Nefret and I have been with the Colonel," he explained. "I believe he is resting more easily. Come along, Willoughby."

When Emerson returned, Nefret was with him. She was still wearing her dusty boots and trousers; arms bared to the elbows, shirt open at the throat, she pushed the loosened locks of red-gold hair back from her face and dropped wearily into a chair. The cat Sekhmet instantly crawled from my lap to that of Nefret.

"Forgive my appearance," she said formally, stroking the cat. "I really would like a cup of tea before I change."

There was no response from Dolly, who continued to scan the terrain. She might have been admiring the late afternoon light on the golden sand. However, I was beginning to suspect that was not the case. She had barely spoken to the doctor.

Dolly was the first to see the riders approaching. Why they had not gone round to the stables I did not know, but I supposed it was because Ramses had some notion of showing off. He made a good job of it, I must say, bringing the beautiful, obedient creature he bestrode to a spectacular rearing stop in front of the verandah. Even I caught my breath in a gasp of admiration. I knew my son well enough to be sure he had not employed force; his hands were light on the reins and when he leaned forward to pat the horse's neck, it tossed its head like a pretty girl who has received a compliment.

Dolly clapped her hands and ran to the entrance. "Oh, lovely!" she cried. "What a beautiful creature! And how beautifully you ride!"

Ramses gave the dainty, posed little figure a blank look, and I revised my earlier opinion. If he had meant to show off, it had not been Dolly he wanted to impress. I realized then that he had not even known she was there; the decision to bring the Colonel to the house had not been taken until after he and David had left with the mummy.

The boys dismounted and I explained the situation. "Miss Bellingham is waiting to hear from

Dr. Willoughby, who is examining her father now. We felt it was best to bring the Colonel here."

"I'll take the horses to the stable," David began.

"No, wait." Dolly gathered her skirts in one graceful hand and approached Risha, who studied her with polite disinterest. "What a beauty! Is she yours, Mr. Emerson?"

Ramses, no more accustomed to that form of address than was I, glanced involuntarily at his father before replying. "Er — yes."

"You will let me try her out, won't you?"

"Now?"

She gave a tinkling laugh. "Silly boy! How could I ride dressed like this?"

Ramses, obviously at a loss, was saved by the return of Dr. Willoughby. He declined my offer of a cup of tea, saying, "I want to get the Colonel to my clinic at once. Not that there is any need for concern," he added with a reassuring smile at Dolly — at her back, rather, for she had not even bothered to face him. "But I would like to keep him under observation for a few days. You will be quite comfortable with us, Miss Bellingham, and I am sure more at ease about your father."

That got Dolly's attention. A frown wrinkled the porcelain surface of her brow. "You want me to stay at the hospital with him? You said there was no need for concern. Why must I go there?"

I knew what the selfish little creature was think-

214

ing. The quiet ambience of a clinic, with responsible persons watching over her, was not at all to her taste. She was hoping I would propose that she come to us, and I felt certain that if I did not, she would propose it herself.

"You cannot stay alone at the hotel," I said in a voice that brooked no argument. "This is a very suitable arrangement. Thank you, Dr. Willoughby."

Dolly gave me a cool, measuring look. Realizing she had met her match, she bowed her head and murmured submissively, "Yes, thank you, Doctor."

She must have been watching Ramses out of the corner of her eye. As soon as he started to move away she pounced like a playful kitten. "Thank you so much for your kindness, Mr. Emerson. You won't forget your promise?"

"I haven't done anything," Ramses said. "Er — what promise?"

"To let me ride your beautiful horse."

I was beginning to be very tired of Miss Dolly. "Out of the question, Miss Bellingham. Risha has not been trained to a sidesaddle. You ought not be thinking of pleasure with your father so ill. Emerson, take her to Dr. Willoughby's carriage and put her into it."

Dolly had not been trained either, but few people disobey me when I speak in that tone, and my dear Emerson was quick to follow my suggestion. While he led Dolly away I went with Dr. Willoughby to assist the Colonel, who was sitting up and who did indeed look almost himself again. After assuring me of his gratitude, he added meaningfully, "We have much to discuss, Mrs. Emerson. May I beg the favor of an interview at your earliest —"

"It must be at your convenience, Colonel," I interrupted. "We will have that discussion, to which I look forward as eagerly as you, as soon as Dr. Willoughby feels you are well enough."

"To endure another shock? Have no fear of that, Mrs. Emerson. Nothing could affect me more painfully than what I have seen this day. Whatever comes of it —"

"I understand," I said, for Dr. Willoughby, behind him, was shaking his head and making motions toward the door. "It will all come right in the end, I daresay."

He was not so easily got rid of, though; he insisted on shaking my hand and Emerson's and thanking us again. The boys had made their escape, with the horses. They did not appear until after the carriage had driven away.

Seeing my critical eye upon him, Ramses said, "Do you mind if we don't change for dinner, Mother? It is late, and Father means us to work on the . . . to work this evening."

"Yes, quite all right," said Emerson. "Sit down, my dear Peabody. Put your feet up, and I will get you your whiskey and soda. You have had a trying day, but I must tell you, my dear, that — except for one or two forgivable lapses — I have never seen you perform better. You got rid of the Bellinghams quite neatly."

I accepted the whiskey, but I could only shake my head at his naiveté. We were not rid of the Bellinghams — far from it! Dolly seemed to have taken an unaccountable fancy to Ramses, and I had not at all liked the way the Colonel had looked at Nefret when he said good-bye. He had presumed to kiss her hand. The Colonel was old enough to be her grandfather, but he was probably vain enough to consider that unimportant. Most men are. And he was now a widower.

"It is Mrs. Bellingham," I said.

The words fell into a solemn silence. I did not doubt they were all thinking the same thing, for no one asked what I meant. Ramses, in his favorite position atop the low wall, was the first to speak.

"If it is — and we have yet to make a positive identification — how did she get from Cairo to a tomb in the Theban hills?"

"That is only one of many unanswered questions," I replied.

Nefret drew her feet up and clasped her hands around her bent knees. "It cannot have been the Colonel who put her there."

"An unproven assumption," Ramses said coldly.

"A reasonable assumption, however," I said. "This is his first trip to Egypt since his wife disappeared. His movements during that earlier visit must have been a matter of public knowledge. Preparing the body, transporting it, locating and excavating a suitable tomb, concealing the location — those activities would have required weeks, possibly months."

"Anyhow, why would a man do such a thing?" David asked, his sensitive lips quivering.

"Well," I began.

"Don't say it, Peabody!" Emerson shouted.

"I see there is no need. You have all thought of it too. But speculation is fruitless at this point; an examination of the body may indicate how she died." Watching Emerson's apoplectic countenance with some concern, I added, "Or it may not. Have more whiskey, Emerson, I beg. There is another possible explanation for the presence of those remains. In criminal investigations one must always ask the question *'Cui bono?'* " I translated for David, whose Latin was not very good. "Who profits? Now I put it to you that one person does stand to profit from the discovery of the body of a woman, young and beautiful, wrapped in silken garments. . . ."

A hissing, spurting noise and a gurgled expletive from Emerson stopped me. He had been at the table adding soda to his glass. He turned. Liquid dripped from his chin and the end of his nose.

"Do be careful, my dear," I exclaimed. "Is there something wrong with the gasogene?"

"No," said Emerson. "No, Peabody. There seems to be something wrong with me — with my hearing, or possibly my brain. Are you seriously suggesting that Mrs. Whitney-Jones put

that body into that tomb so that she could produce it at the appropriate moment in order to
convince Donald Fraser —" His voice broke. "To
convince him . . ." He could not continue. Leaning helplessly against the table, he laughed till he
choked.

I went to him and pounded him on the back.
"I am so pleased to have given you a hearty laugh,
my dear. Let us dine, and then — then we will
be one step nearer the truth."

It was a salutary reminder of the unhappy task
that lay before us. No one had his usual appetite
for dinner; Nefret only picked at her food. I had
almost come to hope that the mummy might be
a tasteless joke after all — a bundle of sticks and
padding, designed to deceive — but I knew that
there was little chance of such a harmless out-
come. The Colonel had recognized something
about the body — the hair, or more probably the
fabric. As a fond bridegroom he may have selected that gown as part of his bride's trousseau.

After dinner we gathered round the long table
in the room Nefret used for developing her photographs. The windows could be, and now were,
tightly shuttered. Emerson was taking no chances
on our activities being overlooked.

The temperature was high and the faces of the
watchers shone with perspiration. In addition to
ourselves, Howard Carter and Cyrus Vandergelt
were present. It was I who had suggested to
Emerson that we ought to have impartial witnesses present, but the promptness with which

he had agreed assured me that he had had the same sensible thought. I had explained the situation to Cyrus and Howard over a postprandial glass of brandy. There is nothing like brandy (unless it is whiskey and soda) to soften the impact of shocking news.

Why is it, I wonder, that we are more affected by contemporary cadavers than by the remains of someone long dead? There is no real difference; the physical shell has been abandoned, it is only a husk, a crumpled chrysalis. We were all on familiar terms with mummies. But Nefret's rounded cheeks were paler than usual, and the faces of the men were lined and grave. (Except, of course, for the face of Ramses, which seldom showed emotion of any kind.)

The anonymous bundle lay on the table before us, the dry, pale hair framing the muffled face. My eyes went involuntarily from it to David's watercolor sketch, which was propped on a shelf to finish drying.

He had reproduced the faded blue of the wrappings and the strawlike hair quite accurately, but he had done more than that. All good copyists — Howard Carter and my dear sister, Evelyn, for instance — have the ability to capture the spirit as well as the form of an object. David's drawing might have served as an illustration for a romantic novel about ancient Egypt. Unless Ramses had introduced him to that deplorable variety of fiction, David could not be familiar with it; yet without departing from an accurate representation, he had caught the same aspect I had noticed earlier.

I believe Emerson was the only one of us who anticipated what we were about to see. He was the only one who had handled the body — who had been, one might say, face-to-face with it. Now he selected a pair of sharp scissors from the implements he had laid ready and with a steady hand inserted one of the blades under the edge of the gauzy fabric that covered the face.

"Observe," he said in the dispassionate tones of a lecturer on anatomy, "that the mask is held in place by strips of cloth passed round the head and knotted behind it. We will preserve the knots; they may be significant. Now then —"

He had cut round the entire oval of the face. Putting the scissors down, he took hold of the fabric with his fingertips, one hand on either side of the face, and with the utmost care, he lifted it up.

It *was* a mask, stiffened and shaped. The delicate features were fabric, not flesh.

If I had seen a face like that one in a painted coffin or stone sarcophagus, I would have thought it quite well preserved — much more sightly than many a mummy I have beheld. The nose had not been flattened by tight bandages, the cheeks were sunken but undistorted, the color of the skin was yellow, not brown. The withered eyelids were closed. But the dried skin had drawn up into thousands of tiny wrinkles, and the lips had shrunk and pulled back over the front teeth.

That dry, dead face in its nest of fair hair was one of the most horrible sights I have ever beheld.

"I wonder what Mr. Fraser would say if he saw this."

Ramses's cool, clinical voice broke the spell. Drawing a deep breath, I concealed my unprofessional feelings with an equally cool response. "Are you suggesting we invite him for a viewing?"

"Good Gad, no!" Emerson exclaimed. "How can you think of Fraser at such a time? We have a much more serious problem to contend with. What do you say, Vandergelt? Do you recognize her?"

Cyrus, who had been staring at the dreadful face, raised horrified eyes. "Holy Jehosaphat, Emerson, how could anybody recognize *that*? I only met the lady a couple of times. Good gracious to goodness, her own husband wouldn't know her!"

"Let us hope it won't come to that," Howard said earnestly. He was standing next to Nefret, and he must have put a steadying arm round her waist — as any gentleman might do — for she glanced at him with a faint smile.

"Thank you, Mr. Carter, but I am not in the least danger of swooning."

Howard flushed, and Ramses, arms folded and brows raised, said, "There are other, more accurate methods of identification. What do you think of the teeth, Nefret?"

"I am trying not to think of them." But professional interest overcame girlish qualms; she moved closer to the table and bent forward. "The incisors appear to be unworn, with no signs of decay, but as you know perfectly well, Ramses, only a full dental examination could give any indication of her age."

"There are no scars or visible wounds, and no broken bones," I said. "Not in the face. Unless the skull —"

"I regret having to inform you," said Emerson, "that the skull is intact. I made certain of that when I lifted her — it."

"That appears to be all we can learn from the head, then," I said briskly. "Proceed, Emerson."

Emerson picked up the scissors. Cyrus said uneasily, "It don't seem right for us men to look at the poor creature."

"Turn your back, then," said Emerson, cutting delicately. "But I think the outer wrapping is only one of several. In deference to your sensibilities, Vandergelt, and in accordance with proper methodology, I will try to remove them layer by layer. Ah, yes. As I suspected. . . ."

Emerson's big brown hands can, when the situation requires it, exhibit a delicacy of touch equal to or exceeding mine. Not a crack or a tear marred the pale blue silk when he folded it back. Under it was not the layer of bandages one finds on an ancient mummy, but a shroudlike wrapping, yellowed and spotted with ugly brown stains.

"Rust," I said.

"Not blood?" my son inquired.

"No. Such stains result when damp fabric is in prolonged contact with metal — hooks and eyes and other fasteners, for example. This wrapping, gentlemen, was a lady's petticoat."

"But it covers all of her, from neck to heels," Cyrus objected.

"There may be as many as eight yards of cloth in a petticoat," I explained. "Gathered to a waistband which has, in this case, been cut off. You can still see the gathering threads" — I pointed — "here and again here. It has been opened up and wrapped round her like a shroud. The material is the finest cambric — cotton to you, gentlemen — and it shows no signs of wear."

"He used her own clothing," Howard muttered. He passed his handkerchief over his wet forehead. "I don't know why that should be so horrible, but . . ."

"Come, come, Carter, get a grip on yourself," Emerson said with a scornful look at the young man. "Peabody, is it not customary for ladies to sew a nametag or inscribe their initials on a garment before it is sent to the laundry?"

"I don't know how you would know that, since it is I who take the responsibility for doing the same for your shirts and underclothing," I replied. "You are correct, however. In this case the name would probably have been on the waistband. Could it have been removed in order to conceal her identity?"

"We will see," said Emerson.

Layer after layer of cloth was cut through and

folded back. There were ten of them in all, each finer than the last, trimmed with filmy lace and broderie anglaise. The final wrapping was of muslin almost as thin as silk; that it was the last was evident to all of us, for it veiled but did not hide the angular shapes beneath it. Emerson reached again for the scissors. His long, large, but sensitive fingers rested for a moment on the bony shoulder.

"If you believe you ought to cover your eyes, Vandergelt, now is the time," he said, and began to cut.

It was not a naked corpse that lay exposed when he drew the last wrapping aside. It was worse — a caricature of coquetry and beauty, a vicious commentary on woman's vanity. These garments had been designed not to conceal, but to suggest and invite. Of the sheerest shell-pink silk, they showed every ugly outline of bone and rope-thin muscle. Frills of transparent lace framed the shoulders, once white and sweetly rounded, now hard as old leather. The arms had been arranged in a position familiar to me from ancient examples, drawn down and across the abdomen, with the hands modestly covering the juncture of thighs and body.

Cyrus turned away with a muffled oath, and Nefret's eyes were wide with pity and horror. Even Emerson hesitated, the scissors in his hand motionless over the body.

It was the hand of Ramses that drew the flimsy fabric carefully aside. Between the withered breasts the skin was marked by a deep, dark scar.

"This is how she died," he said. "A sharp blade made this incision; it must have penetrated her heart. The wound has been sewn together with ordinary thread. Could it have come from her own sewing kit?"

His dispassionate voice challenged me to match it. I leaned over the body for a closer examination. "A wealthy lady does not mend her own clothing. This appears to be white cotton thread, too coarse for delicate fabrics like silk and muslin."

"Enough," Emerson broke in. He drew a sheet over the body. "We have learned all we need to know. You were right, Peabody, confound you. No accident could have produced such a wound. It was made by a large, heavy knife in the hand of a man familiar with such weapons. Now what the devil do we do?"

We restored Cyrus with several stiff whiskeys, which he took neat, American style. We had retreated to the verandah, as far from the poor remains as we could get; the more air the better, was how I felt. The brilliant stars of Egypt, serene and remote, were salutary reminders of the brevity of human life and the promise of immortality.

Sipping my own whiskey, I remarked, "It is in your hands now, Howard. As inspector for Upper Egypt —"

"No, ma'am, Mrs. Emerson," Howard protested. "This is out of my jurisdiction, and that of the local police. It is a matter for the British authorities. Whoever that poor woman may have been, she was not Egyptian."

"Oh, it is Mrs. Bellingham," I said. "There can be no doubt of it. I don't know her first name, but the initials embroidered on the hem of her — er — lower garment were LB."

David cleared his throat. "Those garments — were they the usual . . . Are they the sort of thing ladies . . . But perhaps I should not ask."

"That is quite all right, David," I said, gratified to discover that he was ignorant of such matters. "Without going into improper and irrelevant detail, I should explain that well-bred ladies ordinarily prefer to wear undergarments that — er — offer more protection against the elements, and require less effort in laundering."

"Oh," said David in a voice that indicated bewilderment rather than comprehension.

"She means," said Ramses, a dark silhouette against the moonlit sand, "that those particular articles of clothing are thinner and less practical than cotton or woollen undergarments, as well as much more expensive. They belonged to a young, wealthy woman who followed the latest fashions. Older ladies are more conservative."

"And how do you know that?" I demanded.

"It is an accurate analysis, is it not, Mother?"

"Yes, but how —"

Ramses continued without pausing. "The point, David, is that he — whoever he was —

227

must have removed her clothing and then dressed her again after the process of desiccation was complete. The liquids that drain from the body during the process of mummification would have left stains —"

Nefret interrupted him with a sound that can only be reproduced, and that inadequately, as "Ugh."

"We are all familiar with the process, my boy," Emerson said.

"Yes, but how was it done?" Howard asked. "We know how the Egyptians mummified their dead, but I did not observe an incision."

"Neither did I," said Emerson. "The ancient procedures were not followed in this case. The body was wrapped, not bandaged, and apparently the internal organs and the brain were not removed. A closer examination would certainly tell us more, but even if I were inclined to make such an examination, I cannot in conscience do so. I will telegraph Cairo in the morning. Good night, Vandergelt. Good night, Carter."

Our friends were accustomed to Emerson's little ways. Cyrus drained his glass and rose. "I'll go with you to Luxor. What time?"

They settled on an hour and our friends took their departure, Howard apologizing for his inability to take any further part in the proceedings. There had been an outbreak of tomb robbing at Kom Ombo, which was part of his jurisdiction, and he was obliged to leave at dawn.

"You are not going to the dahabeeyah tonight,

I hope," I said to Ramses. "It is very late, and you should go to bed."

"I am not going to the dahabeeyah tonight," Ramses said. "But I am not going to bed just yet."

"What are you —" I began.

Emerson took me by the arm. "Come along, Peabody."

So the rest of us retired, leaving Ramses perched on the ledge like a brooding vulture.

Emerson tried to creep out of the house without me next morning, but since I had anticipated he would, I was ready for him. He stumbles over things quite a lot in the process of coming fully awake.

"It is Friday," I reminded him, when he informed me I could not go to Luxor with him. "The men won't be working today, so what is the point of going to the Valley?"

"There is plenty to do here," Emerson grunted, lacing his boots.

"What?"

"Er — cleaning. You are always wanting to clean things." My expression warned him this argument was not going to carry any weight. "Photographs," he said wildly. "The plates we took yesterday —"

"Developing the photographic plates is Nefret's job, as you know perfectly well. She can't do it today, though, not with that body in the darkroom."

"Oh, curse it," said Emerson. "I suppose no one can do anything, can they? How do I get into these situations? I have always considered myself a reasonable sort of fellow — harmless, on the whole — inoffensive — kindly, even. What have I done to deserve this? Why in heaven's name am I not allowed one season, one single season of uninterrupted . . ."

I left him muttering and went to see about breakfast. Anubis was in the kitchen, threatening the cook. Anubis did not scratch or bite. He did not have to. He had a stare that could be felt across the width of a room, and he was known to have commerce with evil spirits. I picked him up from the table where he was perched with his green eyes fixed on Mahmud and persuaded the latter to come out from behind the cupboard. As I carried Anubis into the parlor I heard the encouraging clatter of pots and pans and the mumbled curses of Mahmud.

"I have seen very little of you lately," I remarked, putting Anubis on the sofa and taking a seat next to him. He did not as a rule care to sit on people's laps. Ramses, who was already there, looked up from the notebook in which he was writing. "I was speaking to Anubis," I explained.

"He is avoiding Sekhmet," said Ramses. "He finds her as annoying as I do."

"How do you know?"

Ramses shrugged and returned to his scribbling.

I tried another question. "What are you writing?"

"My observations on the condition of Mrs. Bellingham's mummy. It is as close as I will ever come, I suppose, to learning what a recently preserved body looks like. We know the precise date she died, and once an autopsy has been performed —"

"Ramses, you are absolutely disgusting."

The sentiments were mine, but the voice was that of Nefret, who came in with Sekhmet draped over her shoulder like a furry scarf, and David at her heels.

"Some might consider the subject disgusting," Ramses admitted. "But if you plan to take up the study of cadavers, you ought to be more dispassionate."

"That is entirely different," Nefret said. She put the cat down on the floor. Sekhmet wandered toward Anubis, who spat at her and left the room via the open window.

"I will be back in a minute, Aunt Amelia," Nefret went on. "I want to have a look at Tetisheri."

"I suppose you are referring to the goat," I said with an involuntary glance at Ramses. "If you will forgive me for saying so, the name does not seem particularly appropriate."

"I have already been to see her," said my son without looking up. "If appetite is any indication of a successful convalescence, she is doing extremely well."

Breakfast came in, followed by Emerson, who explained he had been looking for his hat.

"It is there on the table," I said. "Where I put it yesterday after I brought it back from the Valley where you had left it. Nefret, do you want to go to Luxor with us?"

As it turned out, everyone expected to go to Luxor with us. This did not please Emerson. "We may as well invite Abdullah and Carter and a few dozen of the men, and make a parade of it," he grumbled. "What about guarding the tomb?"

"What about it?" I passed him the toast. "There is nothing left to guard, Emerson. I have never seen an emptier tomb."

"It is Friday," David pointed out. "The day of —"

"Yes, yes, I know. Cursed religion," Emerson added, snapping his large white teeth on a piece of toast.

Our own religious observances were, of necessity, eclectic. David's father had been a Copt, his mother Muslim. Nefret had been priestess of Isis in a society where the old Egyptian gods were still worshipped. Her father's attempts to teach her about the Christian faith had been half-hearted at best. Emerson despised organized religion in all forms, and Ramses, through constant exposure to the faith of Islam, was more familiar with the Koran than the Bible — though what Ramses actually believed, if anything, would have been difficult to discover.

I believe I may say that I had done my best. When we were in England I always made certain the children attended services with me. In Egypt, such things were not so easy to arrange. There were Christian churches in Cairo, including the English Church of All-Saints, and upon occasion I was able to persuade my reluctant charges (excepting Emerson, of course) to accompany me. In Luxor, getting the children into proper clothes and across the river in time for the rather erratic services available there would have required considerable effort, even without the loud objections of Emerson. We had therefore become accustomed to working on Sunday, along with the men. I always say that formal observances are less important than what is in the heart.

Nefret insisted on seeing for herself how "Teti" was getting on. "Not that I don't trust your judgment, Ramses, my boy, but I am the physician in charge." She came back to report that the patient was doing well and eating everything it could get its teeth into.

"This place is turning into a confounded menagerie," Emerson grumbled. "I trust you do not expect to take it back to England with you, Nefret, because I draw the line at goats. Cats, a lion or two, yes; goats, no."

"Selim will look after her for me while we are away," Nefret said.

She was wearing a divided skirt and a wide-brimmed hat tied under her chin by a gauzy scarf and she looked very pretty. The boys . . . Well,

233

they were clean, at least. When Cyrus arrived we were ready to go. Though no one, however attired, can match Emerson's impressive appearance, Cyrus was quite the man of the world in tweed jacket, well-cut riding breeches, and polished boots. Leaving the horses at the dahabeeyah, we boarded one of the small boats, and the men pushed off.

Sitting between Cyrus and Emerson, I said briskly, "Well, gentlemen, what are your plans? We must not waste time. There is a great deal to be done."

Cyrus nodded. "I have been thinking about that poor creature lying there like a piece of discarded lumber. I would be happy to supply a decent coffin if one can be found."

"That is her husband's responsibility," Emerson said. "And his right."

"He cannot be told," I began.

"He must be told." Emerson gave me a severe look. "Peabody, I insist that you leave off trying to manage the universe and everyone in it. I am willing to give up a day of my valuable time to these distractions, but I mean to have all of them settled by this evening so that I can return to work."

He ticked off the points on his fingers. "Firstly, I will telegraph Cairo. This is not a matter for the local police or the American consular agent."

I could not but agree. Ali Murad, the agent in question, was a Turk with whom we had had several unfriendly encounters. His primary occupation was dealing in antiquities — legally or otherwise.

"Secondly," Emerson went on, "I will talk to Willoughby about Bellingham's state of health. I believe he will agree with me that Bellingham is fit to hear the news and decide on the disposition of his wife's remains. Willoughby does lose a patient occasionally; he must have access to a morgue and a coffin maker and all the rest."

"Very good, Emerson," I said when he paused to draw breath. "I see you have it all worked out. Except —"

"Thirdly," Emerson said, very loudly. "I will call on the Frasers and deal with that Mrs. Whitney-Whatever. Aha, Peabody! You thought I had forgot them, didn't you? I told you, I mean to dispose of all extraneous distractions today. That is everything, I believe."

"Not entirely, Emerson."

"What, then?"

"Even assuming you can solve the Frasers' difficulties in a single interview, which I fear is unlikely, there is the matter of Dolly Bellingham."

Emerson's eyes narrowed. This had the effect of appearing to concentrate the brilliant blue of those orbs into slits of sapphirine fire. "Dolly Bellingham," he said, forcing the words between his teeth like a stage villain, "is the silliest, vainest, most selfish, most boring female I have ever met — with the possible exception of your niece Violet. I am not a chaperon of young ladies, Peabody, nor, God be thanked, an uncle or other relation. Why you should assume . . ."

I would never have supposed Emerson could be so eloquent on the subject of vain young ladies. I made no effort to stop him, nor did Cyrus, who listened with a smile and an occasional nod. Like Cyrus, I agreed with Emerson's assessment of the girl, but I had a feeling we would not easily rid ourselves of her.

My premonitions are generally correct. Almost the first person we encountered after disembarking was Dolly. Frilled and beruffled and squeezed into stays so tight I wondered she could breathe, she was strolling back and forth along the road near the landing stage, holding the arm of the young man Ramses had treated so rudely on the terrace of Shepheard's. He was wearing what I assumed to be the latest fashion in gentleman's attire — a cream flannel suit with narrow blue stripes, and a straw boater with a black band. Cream-colored gloves, a stick, and a loosely knotted pink tie completed the ensemble. Trailing the pair at a respectful distance was one of the local dragomen, an amiably incompetent individual named Saiyid.

An encounter was not to be avoided. After greeting us, Dolly introduced her escort as Mr. Booghis Tucker Tollington. While I was trying to assimilate this remarkable appellation, the young man bowed to me and Nefret and shook hands with Cyrus, the only gentleman to offer a hand.

"I am glad to see you two have made it up," I said.

The young man looked sheepish. Dolly looked demure. "I didn't have the least idea Mr. Tollington was coming on to Luxor. You can imagine my surprise when we saw him this morning in the breakfast room."

Mr. Tollington grinned idiotically and mumbled something in which I made out the words "pleasure" and "coincidence." He then glanced curiously at Emerson, who was standing several feet away with his hands behind his back and his nose in the air.

"I am going on to the telegraph office," Emerson announced. "Are you coming, Vandergelt?"

Cyrus offered me his arm, and I said, "We must be on our way. I had expected to see you at the clinic, Miss Bellingham. I take it that your father is much improved?"

She was not so stupid as to miss the implied reproof. "Oh, yes, ma'am, he's so much better he just plain ordered me to go out for some fresh air. He doesn't like to see me looking pale and puny."

We proceeded on our way. Nefret ran ahead to walk with Emerson, and I remarked to Cyrus, "What strange names Americans have!"

"Now, Mrs. Amelia, you English are no slouches at inventing unpronounceable handles either. That unfortunate boy was probably given his mother's family name; our Southern neighbors go in for that kind of thing. I expect the

Booghises are an old distinguished Charleston family."

The boys had more or less melted into the scenery as soon as they saw Dolly and her escort. I stopped and looked back for them. They were coming, but rather slowly, and I realized that an animated discussion was in progress. Ramses was doing most of the talking, of course. When he saw I was waiting he quickened his pace.

"What were you doing?" I asked suspiciously.

"*Fahddl*ing with Saiyid," Ramses replied.

"What about?"

"I asked him," said Ramses slowly and precisely, "whether he had been hired by Colonel Bellingham, and, if so, why the Colonel had discharged Mohammed, whom we saw with the party yesterday."

"And what did he say?"

"Yes to the first question, 'Only Allah knows' to the second."

"He must have some idea," I persisted. "Had Mohammed been insolent or failed in his duties?"

Ramses considered the question and condescended to elaborate. "Mohammed claimed he had not failed in any way. That is, of course, what one would expect him to say. Perhaps Miss Bellingham took a dislike to him. She is in the habit of dismissing attendants for no particular reason."

"I cannot imagine why she would prefer Saiyid," I said with a smile. "Mohammed is a tall, upstanding fellow, and Saiyid . . . Well, the poor man cannot be blamed for his squint and his warts, but I do not suppose he would rush to Dolly's rescue if someone attacked her."

"He is one of the most notorious cowards in Luxor," Ramses agreed. "But why should any guide or dragoman risk death or injury for the magnificent wages of twenty-five piastres a day?"

Cyrus demanded to know what we were talking about, so I told him of Bellingham's fears for his daughter. "Emerson denies there is any cause for concern, of course," I said. "But we have reason to suspect otherwise."

"Ramses has reason, anyhow," said Cyrus, glancing curiously at my son, who was strolling along with his hands in his pockets, looking bored. "It's a peculiar story all right. I never heard of a foreigner being attacked in the Ezbekieh — or anyplace else in Egypt, come to think of it."

"I am glad you agree with me about the gravity of the matter, Cyrus," I said. "But I beg you won't mention it to Emerson; he is already in a considerable state of aggravation."

"With good reason, Mrs. Amelia, my dear. You folks are always getting yourselves into scrapes, but I can't recall any as complicated as this one."

We arrived at the telegraph office in time to meet Emerson and Nefret coming out. "What kept you?" he demanded, frowning horribly.

"Finished already?" Cyrus asked in surprise.

Emerson is the only individual of my acquaintance who can bully the clerks at the telegraph office into swift action. He is never able to understand why it takes other people so long.

He was persuaded to hire a carriage to take us to the clinic, since it was outside the village, in a quiet country setting. Shaded by palm and tamarisk, surrounded by gardens bright with flowers, the sprawling whitewashed house had a reposeful air designed to soothe the nerves of Dr. Willoughby's patients. He believed — as do I — that comfortable surroundings, good food, and assiduous service are essential to physical as well as mental health.

Emerson cut the civilities short — "I am a busy man, Willoughby, and so are you" — and launched at once into his tale. The good doctor had heard many a wild story, but he was visibly shaken by this one.

"Are you certain?" he exclaimed.

"Of her identity? There can be little doubt, I am afraid. Her husband is the only one who can confirm it."

"The Colonel appears to have suffered only a fainting fit," Willoughby said. "His heart is strong. But I hesitate to take the responsibility. A shock such as this —"

"He suffered the shock yesterday," I said. "The truth can be no worse than what he already suspects."

And so it proved. Leaving the others waiting in his office, the doctor escorted me and Emerson to the Colonel's room. Overstuffed chairs and low tables, vases of fresh flowers and pretty prints of kittens and puppies, made it look more like a guest chamber in someone's house than a hospital room. Bellingham was sitting by the open window. He greeted us with no appearance of surprise and rose to kiss my hand.

"So it is true," he said quietly.

"I am very sorry," I said, squeezing his hand sympathetically.

Willoughby took the Colonel's other hand and placed his fingers on his wrist. Bellingham shook his head.

"You will find my pulse perfectly steady, Doctor. I would not have exhibited such contemptible weakness yesterday if the sight had not been so sudden and unexpected. I am a soldier, sir; I will not give way again. Now, Professor and Mrs. Emerson, if you will be good enough to tell me . . ."

Emerson left it to me, knowing I would soften the terrible facts as much as was possible. Bellingham's face went a shade whiter when I asked him about the initialed undergarment, but he confirmed my assumption in a voice firm and clear.

"Her name was Lucinda. She had a dozen such garments; we selected them in Paris, together. It remains, then, only to remove her to a more fitting final resting place."

"I fear," said Emerson, "that a great deal more remains to be done. Willoughby here has offered the use of his private chapel and mortuary, and I hope those arrangements can be completed today. However, the questions of how she died and how she came to be here are equally important."

"He killed her," the Colonel said.

"He?"

"That murdering swine Dutton Scudder." For the first time emotion distorted the Colonel's dignified face. "You know the story, of course? Everyone in Cairo knew — or believed they did. They were wrong. I told the police that the vile rumors were untrue! I told them she had not deserted me, that Scudder had abducted her against her will."

"He was your secretary?" Emerson asked.

"He performed the same services as a native dragoman," Bellingham said contemptuously. "I found him through an employment agency in New York; he had lived in Egypt and knew Arabic. Had I but known . . ." The agonized lines in his face smoothed out. "She rests in peace now. Her good name will be restored and my faith in her will be vindicated."

"Er — quite," said Emerson gruffly. "It was in Cairo that she disappeared, I believe; have you any idea why he would mummify her and carry the body to Luxor?"

"He is a madman," Bellingham said.

Emerson rubbed his chin. "Hmph. No doubt he . . . Did you say 'is'?"

"He lives." Bellingham's fingers curled into his palms. "He lives — until I can find him. You doubted me, Professor Emerson, when I told you someone was trying to harm Dolly. Do you still doubt me?"

"You believe it is Scudder?" I asked.

"Who else can it be? The attacks on my little girl began after we arrived in Egypt. After abducting and murdering Lucinda, Scudder must have remained here in hiding all these years; seeing Dolly with me reawakened his homicidal mania. He followed us to Luxor and made certain I would be among the first to know what he had done to my poor wife. I told you, Mrs. Emerson, I had received an invitation yesterday. I ought to have known it was not you who sent it, though it bore your signature."

"Good Gad!" I exclaimed. "He must have been watching us too. He knew we would enter the tomb yesterday. What a diabolical plot!"

"The man is mad," Bellingham repeated. "You have seen the proof."

"Lunacy is a convenient explanation for otherwise inexplicable behavior," Emerson said dryly. "But your own behavior, Colonel, requires to be explained. Why the devil did you come back to Egypt?"

Bellingham leaned back in his chair and studied Emerson with a faint, appreciative smile. "You are a shrewd man, Professor. You must know the answer. There is only one thing that could bring me back to the scene of my tragic loss."

"Scudder wrote to you."

"Yes, a few months ago. The letter was sent

243

from Cairo. He said . . ." Bellingham hesitated, as if trying to remember the precise words. "That if I returned to Egypt, he would restore my wife to me. As you saw, he did just that."

We were well on our way to Luxor before Emerson finished telling the others about our interview with Bellingham.

"I sure am ashamed of my evil mind," Cyrus said remorsefully. "Bellingham claimed at the time his wife had not left of her own free will, but it's what a man would say, isn't it, to save his pride?"

"The police must have had other reasons for doubting him," I said. "Had they quarrelled? Had she shown any preference for the young man?"

"Not that I know of. But see here, Mrs. Amelia, it isn't as easy as your novel writers make out to abduct a lady against her will. Especially when the lady disappears out of a big hotel in a big city, with no signs of a struggle."

"It is strange," Nefret said thoughtfully. "Where was her maid when it happened?"

"In her own room, waiting for the lady to send for her. She had been a trifle unwell — the usual sort of trouble that affects visitors — and Mrs. Bellingham, who was by all accounts a kind and considerate mistress, had told the girl to rest that afternoon while she attended some kind of tea party at the American consul's house. She was seen entering the hotel round about six, but nobody saw her leave it — or ever saw her again." Cyrus shook his head. "It's still a mystery to me as to how Scudder managed it."

"My dear Cyrus, you exhibit a shocking lack of imagination," I said. "I can think of several ways in which it could have been done."

"I feel certain you can," grunted Emerson. "Spare me your melodramatic scenarios, Peabody."

"Poor man," Nefret said softly. "After all those years of suspense, never knowing what had become of her, fearing the worst — then to have his hopes raised again, only to be destroyed in such a hideous fashion! What sort of fiend is this man Scudder?"

I decided not to tell her that the Colonel had made a point of asking about her and had sent his respectful salutations.

"It is out of our hands." Emerson squared his broad shoulders. "And now for the Frasers, curse them!"

I persuaded Emerson to stop for luncheon first. It was still early, but I wanted time to consider my strategy.

I had no intention of allowing Emerson to interview Mrs. Whitney-Jones. Not that I feared he would bully her; it was the reverse, in fact. Emerson has a loud bark, but where women are concerned he is as toothless as an old hound. They can always get round him.

The Karnak Hotel, where we were lunching, is on the waterfront and offers a splendid view of the river and the West Bank. The day was unseasonably and pleasantly cool; the breeze from the water tossed Emerson's sable locks into becoming disarray.

"It is a perfect day for work," he grumbled with a longing glance at the silver-gold cliffs of his beloved Thebes.

I know a good opening when I hear one. "Go back to the Valley, then, if you cannot bear to be away from it for a single day," I said in the same grumbling voice. "I will talk with the Frasers. No, Emerson, I don't mind in the slightest. I am only too accustomed to doing the unpleasant chores you wish to avoid."

Emerson looked at me suspiciously. "What are you up to now, Peabody? I am not going to leave you on the loose in Luxor; you always get into mischief."

"I will make certain she behaves herself," said Cyrus, grinning. "We'll just have a little chat with Mrs. Whitney-Jones, and come right back. I admit I am looking forward to meeting the lady. She sounds like a smooth crook."

Emerson said he was *not* looking forward to seeing the lady and would be happy to leave her to Cyrus. I gave Cyrus an appreciative smile.

On our way back we stopped by the telegraph office and found, as we had anticipated, a reply from Cairo. Emerson scowled as he read it.

"Cromer appears to be losing his grip. He wants more information."

"You telegraphed Lord Cromer?" I exclaimed.

"Emerson, he is the most important man in Egypt!"

"Precisely," said Emerson. "It is a waste of time to deal with underlings. I cannot imagine what else he wants from me; I sent him all the relevant information."

I asked to see the original telegram and, after fumbling through his pockets, Emerson produced a crumpled piece of paper. It was certainly succinct. "Have discovered body believed that of Mrs. Bellingham, American citizen, disappeared Cairo 1897. Advise."

"You might have elaborated a little," I said while Cyrus smiled over the message.

"Why waste money?" Emerson took out his watch. "I will leave it to you, Peabody, since you are so critical. Is anyone else coming across with me? . . . Then I will see you all at teatime."

After dispatching another telegram that would give the bewildered Lord Cromer more information, I led the procession toward the Luxor Hotel.

"What are your plans?" I inquired of my son.

"I was under the impression we were to call on the Frasers," Ramses replied.

"We are not paying a social call, Ramses. I think it best if Mr. Vandergelt and I see Mrs. Whitney-Jones alone. We are, I believe, more intimidating than the rest of you."

"These two young fellows would intimidate me if they took a notion to," Cyrus said with a smile. "But I guess we won't want to resort to threats or low violence. What makes you so sure we'll find the lady at home and willing to receive us, Mrs. Amelia?"

"I have my methods, Cyrus. The rest of you run along and — er — do something harmless. We will meet you in the lobby of the hotel in an hour and a half."

"We might have a look in at some of the *antika* dealers," David suggested, adding with a laugh, "Who knows, we may find for sale some of the pieces I made for Abd el Hamed while I was his apprentice."

"Stay together," I called as they walked away. David had taken Nefret's arm; he gave me a reassuring nod over his shoulder. Ramses preceded them, his hands in his pockets.

The concierge informed us that Mrs. Whitney-Jones was indeed in the hotel, and when we sent up our names we were invited to join her in her sitting room. It was one of the most elegant suites in the hotel — paid for, I did not doubt, by Donald. Mrs. Whitney-Jones came to greet us and acknowledged my introduction of Cyrus with perfect composure, but she did not offer to shake hands. She wore an afternoon dress of silver-gray, with a yoke and boned collar of white spotted net. Her only ornaments were a locket and the gold band on her left hand.

"I rather expected you would come today, Mrs. Emerson, so I sent Mr. Fraser off to Karnak with his wife. He did not want to go, but I promised I would make it up to him."

"I hope you did not promise him a sight of the

mummy we found yesterday. It would completely destroy your illusion."

Mrs. Whitney-Jones's smile made her look more than ever like a large, friendly tabby cat. "You don't mince words, Mrs. Emerson. I too am a realist. I know when the game is up."

"So," I said, "you admit you are a charlatan? That you are exploiting Mr. Fraser's weakness for monetary gain?"

"Why deny it?" She raised her shoulders in a ladylike shrug. "I know you by reputation, Mrs. Emerson. Had I realized that the Frasers were friends of yours, I would never have let the business go so far. You need not have brought Mr. Vandergelt as an additional deterrent, though I am of course happy to make his acquaintance. I would suggest, however, that before you proceed against me we discuss the effect such a disclosure would have on Mr. Fraser."

"If that is a threat," I began angrily.

"Regard it rather as a basis for negotiation," was the smooth reply.

Cyrus had not spoken or taken his eyes off her. Perched on the edge of the straight chair he had taken, his hat in his hands, he looked as uncomfortable as a young gentleman paying his first social call. Suddenly his rigid face relaxed, and he leaned back.

"You a poker player, by any chance, Mrs. Whitney-Jones? Or is it — Mrs. Jones?"

She looked at him out of the corner of her eye, and I thought her mouth twitched a trifle. "Obviously you are, Mr. Vandergelt. You win that hand."

"I figured as much." Cyrus tossed his hat onto the sofa and crossed his legs. "Looks to me as if we're holding all the cards, ma'am. You've taken the Frasers for a tidy amount of money under false pretenses. I wouldn't be one bit surprised to learn you're not unknown to Scotland Yard. What have you got to negotiate with?"

She turned slightly to face him, folding her hands in her lap. "Mr. Fraser's sanity, Mr. Vandergelt." Then, with an abrupt change of manner, she clasped her hands tightly together. "I am to some degree culpable, I admit. But he is not the first — oh, yes, Mr. Vandergelt, you were quite right! — he is not my first client, not by any means. The gullibility of the human race is boundless; if people are stupid enough to believe in me, why not take advantage of it?

"Mr. Fraser is another matter. He is not the sort of man who would ordinarily seek out a person like myself. Not that he has sense enough to see the snares behind the illusion; he is quite uncritical, but he lacks the — the romanticism, the imagination — to desire the illusion in the first place. Do you understand what I am saying?"

"I guess so," Cyrus said slowly.

"I encountered him and Mrs. Fraser at the home of a friend. There were a good many other people there; I was a paid performer, turning tables and summoning the dead, for the amusement of the guests." Her mouth twisted. "Silly women and stupid men, looking for answers that don't exist.

"But it is unbecoming of me to mock my victims, you will say. Let me go on. I often acquire private clients from such performances. Mr. Fraser came to see me next day. One of my controls — you know the word? — is an Egyptian princess. Not very original, is it, Mrs. Emerson? But they are popular with believers, and it was Princess Tasherit with whom Mr. Fraser wanted to communicate, not his grandmother or his deceased father.

"From that time on . . ." Another shrug. "You won't believe this, but it is true. He directed me. He did not ask, he demanded, and when I gave him what he wanted, he demanded more. It was he who insisted we travel together to Egypt. What drove him to this I do not know, but he has not yet found what he seeks, and he will not stop seeking it. In short, Mrs. Emerson, your friend is on the verge of mania and I — I am out of my depth. Tell me what to do and I will do it. Give me your orders and I will obey them. Necessity has forced me to abandon many of the principles that were once mine, but I do not want a man's death on my conscience."

CHAPTER SEVEN

*Love has a corrosive effect on the brain
and the organs of moral responsibility.*

After we had left Mrs. Jones we stood in the hall waiting for the lift, and Cyrus said solemnly, "Mrs. Amelia, I am eternally indebted to you for that experience."

"You did not believe her protestations, I hope."

"Well, I don't know whether I do or not," Cyrus said, stroking his goatee. "And I tell you, Mrs. Amelia, that's not something that happens to me every day. Usually I'm pretty good at spotting a liar, but that lady . . . Consarn it, she wasn't anything like I expected. You think she was lying?"

"She left us no choice but to believe her until we can prove her false," I said bitterly. "If she is right, Donald is in a dangerous state of mind. How infuriating! I never thought when we came here that we would find ourselves in league with a confidence woman. I shudder to think what Emerson will say. Where is that confounded lift?"

"The operator's probably taking a nap. She

came clean with us about her real name, you know. And she was brutally honest about her methods."

"That, my dear Cyrus, is how a skillful liar operates. She told us all the facts we could have learned for ourselves, and very little else."

The lift did not come — it was always breaking down — so in the end we descended the stairs. The interview had taken longer than I had expected, for we had discussed various methods of convincing Donald that his dream princess did not exist. Cyrus had further prolonged the proceedings by engaging in a good-humored verbal duel with the lady — or perhaps he would have described it as a verbal poker game. In the end, Cyrus declared that such a delicate matter required further deliberation. He wanted to meet Donald and make his own assessment of the latter's mental condition.

"Here is your chance," I said as we entered the lobby.

"I beg your pardon?" Cyrus had been deep in thought.

"There is Donald now, with Enid — and David and Nefret as well. They were waiting for us, I suppose, when the Frasers came in. Curse it, I hope they didn't tell him . . . Where has Ramses got to, I wonder?"

Donald had seen me. Rising and smiling, he beckoned us to join them at their table. As he and Cyrus shook hands, I could see that Cyrus found this beaming, hearty, young gentleman a far cry from the wan neurasthenic he had pictured. It was Enid who looked ill. Her wide waist belt was unfashionably loose, though it had been buckled in to the last hole, and her eyes were shadowed.

I declined her invitation to take tea with them, explaining we were engaged to meet Emerson, but I allowed Donald to help me into a chair. "We will have to wait for Ramses, I suppose," I said. "Why isn't he here?"

David looked guilty — but then he usually did, poor lad. Before he could answer, supposing he had intended to, Nefret said, "We misplaced him. You know Ramses, he is always wandering off to gossip with some tomb robber or forger."

Donald said cheerfully, "He always was a handful. Did you know, Miss Forth, that I was once young Ramses's tutor? Can't say I taught him much; it was the other way round. Never knew such a talker as that boy."

Cyrus gave me a questioning look, to which I replied with a shrug. Maniacs, as we all know, are unpredictable. Some insane persons I have known behaved quite rationally on all subjects but one. Cyrus had not seen Donald look heavenward in an ecstasy of worship or heard his wild cry of recognition. I knew it was only a matter of time before he broke out again.

Even so, I was taken aback when Donald continued, without the slightest alteration of tone or expression, "Miss Forth tells me, Mrs. Emerson, that the mummy you found yesterday was not that of Princess Tasherit. I could have sworn I recognized her."

I said, "Er . . . no, Mr. Fraser, you were mistaken."

"You are certain?" He might have been inquiring about a mutual acquaintance. "We will have to continue looking, then. She was unable to give precise directions, since the terrain has changed a great deal in the past three thousand years, but once Mrs. Whitney-Jones has familiarized herself with the geography —"

Her face darkly flushed, Enid pushed her chair back and got to her feet. "Donald! For the love of heaven, stop it! You sound like . . ."

Fortunately her voice failed at that point, and she did not finish the sentence. I felt certain that whatever procedure might improve Donald's state of mind, this was not it. Rising in my turn, I took Enid firmly by the shoulders and was about to give her a little shake when her eyes widened and her rigid form relaxed.

"Oh," she said.

"I apologize for my tardiness," said Ramses. "I hope you have not been waiting long."

Dolly was with him, clinging to his arm. I did not doubt she was well aware of what a pretty picture she made, the brim of her flowery hat brushing his shoulder and her little gloved hand resting on his sleeve. Ramses detached her with, I thought, some difficulty and deposited her in a chair.

"Where is Mr. Tollington?" I asked. "Ramses! You didn't —"

"I sent him away," Dolly said, smoothing her gloves. "He was rude to Mr. Emerson."

I looked at Ramses, who had remained standing, hands behind his back and eyes downcast — avoiding mine, I assumed. I did not doubt he had been rude back to Mr. Tollington.

"It is time we went away," said Nefret. "Aunt Amelia?"

"Yes, we are late," I said, somewhat distractedly, for there was Dolly on my hands again, unchaperoned and unescorted and hopelessly undisciplined. I could not in conscience leave the girl alone after her father's disclosures. "Miss Bellingham, have you met our friends? Mrs. Fraser, Miss —"

"We have met," Enid said with a brusque nod. "Good afternoon, Miss Bellingham. I trust you did not take a chill?"

I had the oddest impression that several people had stopped breathing. Dolly was not one of them. With the sweetest smile imaginable she replied, "You were the one without a shawl, Mrs. Fraser. A lady your age ought to be more careful; the garden gets real chilly around midnight."

David clapped his hand over his mouth and turned away.

"Something caught in your throat?" I inquired. "Ramses, you might just give him a little pat on the back."

"Gladly," said Ramses, and did so, with such hearty goodwill that David staggered.

I presented the gentlemen to Dolly, and Cyrus,

demonstrating the shrewd American acumen I had counted upon, relieved me of my difficulty. "I reckon I'll just join my new friends in a cup of tea," he declared with a meaningful look at me. "And make sure this young lady gets safe home to her daddy afterwards. I am acquainted with your father, Miss Bellingham, and as Mrs. Emerson can testify, you will be in good hands with me."

"I'm sure," said Dolly unenthusiastically.

Enid drew me aside. "Well?" she demanded. "Did you see her?"

"Yes. I must speak with you privately, Enid; this is not the time nor the place for a long conversation. Can you come to the house tomorrow afternoon, without Donald?"

Enid wrung her hands. "Why not tonight? I cannot endure this much longer, Amelia."

"I promise you I have matters under control," I said, hoping it was so. "One word of advice, Enid. Don't challenge him or berate him. Remain calm, do nothing to excite him, and all will be well."

Her eyes moved from me to the children, who were waiting for me by the door. "Will . . . the Professor be there?"

"Yes, and Cyrus, and, if you do not object, the children. They are quite sensible for their age. We will have a little council of war."

"I do not object. Thank you, Amelia, I will be there."

When we arrived at the house we found Emerson on the verandah, his feet on a stool and Sekhmet draped across his knees.

"Finally," he said. "What kept you so long? Never mind, I do not want to hear about it. Ramses, I took the liberty of borrowing Risha this afternoon, so he will not be in need of exercise. Nefret, those photographs need to be developed. David —"

"Please go and tell Ali we are ready for tea," I interrupted, nodding at David.

"I don't want any cursed tea," said Emerson.

"Yes, you do." I seated myself and removed my hat. "So the darkroom is now . . . unoccupied?"

Emerson laid his book aside. "Willoughby's people took her away this afternoon. Cromer is sending someone down from Cairo to take charge, but he cannot be here before tomorrow evening."

"At least in this case there is no need for haste."

"No. She should keep indefinitely."

Ramses and Nefret had followed David into the house, so I did not object to the unseemly manner in which he had stated this undeniable fact. Emerson is the most sensitive of men, but he sometimes conceals his feelings under a shell of callousness.

"Cyrus and I had a most interesting conversation with Mrs. Jones," I said. "Do you want me to —"

"No," said Emerson. "Where are the children? Where is my tea?"

His irritable, clearly audible questions brought prompt responses from the persons concerned. We settled ourselves comfortably, and Sekhmet crawled from Emerson's lap onto that of Ramses, who immediately handed her over to David.

"So what have you been doing all afternoon?" Nefret asked, perching on the arm of Emerson's chair and depositing a kiss on the top of his head. She had seen he was a trifle out of sorts, and her affectionate ways seldom failed to improve his state of mind.

"A sensible question at last," he grumbled. "Do you mean there is someone in this family who is interested in Egyptology?"

"We all are, sir," David assured him earnestly. "I am sorry if I —"

"Never mind, David," said Emerson in a more affable voice. "You apologize too cursed often, my boy. My activities this afternoon — in striking contrast with those of certain other individuals — produced useful results. We have not finished with tomb Twenty-A. Not by a damned sight," he added happily.

"Why, Emerson, what do you mean?" I asked — for I knew the hint had been directed at me.

Emerson took out his pipe and tobacco pouch. "That single chamber is not all there is to the tomb. It continues for some distance."

"What!" I cried. "Why, Emerson, how did you discover that?"

Emerson gave me a critical look. "You are overdoing it, Peabody."

259

"And you, my dear Emerson, are deliberately prolonging the suspense. How did you know there was more to the tomb?"

"You ought to have known it too, Peabody. If you had not been so preoccupied with the body — an understandable distraction, I admit — you might have observed that the dimensions and shape of the space did not resemble those of a tomb chamber. It was barely six feet wide and the ceiling sloped sharply down. I suspected at once that the floor had been artificially levelled, and that the original rock floor sloped down at the same angle as the ceiling — that, in short, what we saw was not a chamber, but the first section of a descending passageway."

"How exciting!" Nefret exclaimed.

Emerson did not accuse *her* of overdoing it. He gave her a fond smile and patted her hand. Then he looked questioningly at Ramses.

Ramses had not exclaimed aloud or given any evidence of surprise. A few years earlier he would have claimed, truthfully or not, that he had observed the same clues. Now he said, "Well done, Father."

"I removed enough of the rubble on the floor yesterday to prove my theory was correct," Emerson said in a pleased voice. "How far the passage extends I cannot tell, but the tomb is obviously much more extensive than we realized."

"A royal tomb," Nefret exclaimed, her eyes shining.

"An unjustified assumption," said Ramses,

running his forefinger along his mustache. "Several of the private tombs have corridors and multiple chambers. We can hardly hope to find another tomb as rich as Tetisheri's. Two such discoveries —"

"Oh, you are always throwing cold water," Nefret said in exasperation. "Does nothing excite you? And stop playing with that silly mustache!"

David and I spoke at once. I said, "Now, children," and David said, in a feeble attempt at distraction, "Would anyone like another cup of tea?"

Emerson's forceful tones dominated ours. "Speculation of any kind is a waste of time. We will see how we get on tomorrow."

Unnoticed by any of us, including Ramses, Sekhmet had oozed (the word was, I had to admit, accurate) back onto his lap. He picked the poor creature up and returned her to David, unmoved by her plaintive protest.

"If you do not need me tomorrow, Father, I will get on with my copying. Mr. Carter has given me permission to work at Deir el Bahri."

"Don't sulk, Ramses," said Nefret, smiling at him. "I am sorry I was rude about your mustache."

"I never sulk," Ramses said. "Father?"

"Yes, of course, my boy. Just as you like."

It was agreed we would all have an early night. Ramses and David returned to the dahabeeyah, and Nefret declared she had a dozen things to do — washing her hair, catching up on her reading, mending her stockings. She was no more fond of sewing than I and her stockings were always in a shocking state of holiness, so I commended her diligence and bade her good night with all the more approval because I was anxious to have a long private conversation with Emerson.

To my pleased surprise, he was just as anxious to talk with me about matters he had profanely refused to consider heretofore.

"Please do me the favor of refraining from gloating, Peabody," he remarked after we had made ourselves comfortable in our own room. "Because I won't stand for it, do you hear?"

"Of course not, my dear. What particular event has caused you to change your mind?"

"No single event, but the relentless accumulation of evidence. Bellingham's disclosures today put the lid on it," Emerson admitted, scowling. "We were goaded into finding that tomb, with its grisly contents. The murdering bastard went so far as to mark the exact spot for us, curse him! It must have been he who attacked the girl in the Ezbekieh — for I flatly refuse, Peabody, to postulate two villains when one will serve. He sent the Colonel a message that brought him to the Valley yesterday in time to see us carry the body away."

"It makes excellent sense, Emerson."

"No, by heaven, it does not!" Emerson exploded. "There are too many unanswered questions. Why does this fellow continue to bear such a grudge against Bellingham? Why didn't he bury the body in the desert and leave it there? Why did he select us as the instrument of his disclosure? And don't so much as breathe the word 'madman,' Peabody. This fellow cannot be a raving lunatic; there is purpose and method behind his actions."

"I am in complete agreement, Emerson. It remains only to discover that purpose."

"Only?" Emerson laughed and, turning, gathered me into his arms. "One of the things I love about you, Peabody, is the directness of your mind. It will not be as easy as you suggest, but curse it! I suppose we will have to take a hand in this business after all. I will not be used as a cat's-paw by a murderer. Let us leave the children out of it, though. Especially Nefret."

"We can try," I said doubtfully.

"Oh, come, Peabody, it should not be so difficult as all that. They have their own work to do. If you refrain from discussing your eccentric theories with them, they will soon forget all about the Bellingham business."

From Manuscript H:

It seemed to David that he had been arguing for hours, to no avail, but he went on trying. "This is a very bad idea, Ramses. I wish you would not do it."

Ramses went on collecting the things he would need. He tied them into a neat bundle and glanced at the window, where the first stars of evening shone in the darkening sky. "Did you hear something?"

" 'Only the night wind, blowing through the branches.' " David had been familiarizing himself with English lyric poetry. "Are you trying to change the subject? Change your mind, rather. Please!"

Ramses rummaged around in a drawer and produced a tin of cigarettes. David groaned feelingly. "If Aunt Amelia finds out you have those, she will —"

Words failed him, but he accepted a cigarette. Ramses lit his and his own. "My mother will not be pleased at any of this," he said, cupping his hands round the cigarette Arab fashion. "David, I am not asking you to come with me, or to lie if she asks you a direct question. Just don't go haring off to the house and unburden your conscience."

"As if I would! It is for your safety I am concerned, my brother," he added in Arabic. "The man carries a knife. He has wounded you once."

"He caught me off guard," Ramses said curtly.

David sat down on the edge of the bed. "No one is better in a knife fight than you, but if he attacks, it will not be a fair fight. It will be from behind, and in darkness. Why should you take such risks for a woman who is a stranger? Do you love her?"

"Do you?" said a voice from the window.

Ramses had both hands round her throat before she finished the brief sentence. She stood perfectly still, smiling up into his horrified face.

"Nicely done, my boy. You have been busy this past summer!"

Ramses removed his hands, finger by finger. "Did I hurt you?"

"A little. I deserved it," she added, rubbing her throat.

"Damn it, Nefret!" For once, emotion robbed him of speech. He pulled her into the room and deposited her on the bed with such force that she and David both bounced.

Nefret laughed. "You didn't hear me until I spoke," she said with satisfaction. "You ought to have practiced woodcraft as well as knife fighting. Really, Ramses! Knife fighting! And smoking! What will Aunt Amelia say?"

She was wearing trousers and a flannel shirt, and her hair hung down her back, the shining waves confined only by a loose scarf. Ramses swallowed. "Are you going to tell her?"

"As if I would! May I have one of those cigarettes?"

David began to laugh. He threw his arm round Nefret. "Give her one. By Sitt Miriam and all the saints, this is a wonderful woman."

"All for one and one for all," Nefret said, hugging him back. "Except that you always try to cheat. Now give me a cigarette and we will have a council of war, as we used to do."

Wordlessly Ramses offered her the tin. She took a cigarette and looked up, waiting for him to light it. "Why, Ramses, you are rather pale. Did I frighten you, poor boy?"

"There are several ways of dealing with an uninvited visitor," Ramses said. "It was by sheer chance that I chose the least lethal. For God's sake, Nefret, promise me you won't do that again."

"Not to you, at any rate." She took his hand and guided the match to the tip of the cigarette.

"How did you get away from Aunt Amelia?" David asked.

Nefret blew out a great cloud of smoke. "It tastes quite nasty," she said. "But I suppose one becomes used to it. How did I get away? I did not tell a lie. I darned two stockings and washed my hair, just as I said I would. Then I climbed out my window and saddled one of the horses the Professor had hired. I must have him back soon, so start talking. Are you in love with that little ninny, Ramses?"

"No."

"I thought you had better sense, but I am relieved to hear it." Nefret nodded approvingly. "I understand your motives. They do you credit, I suppose, but I cannot believe you can carry on your plan for very long, even with David and me backing you up."

"It should not take long," Ramses said. "Only a day or two."

"I thought so. You won't be content with guarding her. You mean to flush him out and force a confrontation."

Ramses bit his lip in order to hold back an angry response. She could not have overheard that; he had not admitted it even to David. Sometimes she seemed to read his mind.

Only sometimes, he hoped.

"It is the most sensible course of action," he in-

266

sisted. "As you say, I cannot follow Dolly around Luxor for long, and this fellow is dangerously unpredictable. He may take a notion to attack one of us next, especially if Mother goes on in her customary fashion."

He did not have to elaborate. David looked grave and Nefret, no longer smiling, nodded. "She does have a habit of getting in the way of murderers, bless her. What you intend, in short, is to use Miss Dolly as a decoy. That is rather cold-blooded of you, Ramses."

She gave him an approving smile. Ramses decided he would never understand women.

He had some difficulty dissuading her from accompanying them, and it was only after he had promised to keep her abreast of ensuing developments — and had handed over the remainder of the cigarettes — that she consented to go back to the house. He lifted her onto the horse and stood watching until she had disappeared into the darkness.

"If you are going, we should go now," said David at his elbow.

"Oh. Yes, of course."

After they were under way, David said softly, "I did not know there was a woman like her. She has the heart of a man."

"You had better not let her hear you say that."

David laughed. "And you, my friend, had better not let her find out about the other thing. I shudder to think what she would do."

"What other thing? Oh, Tollington's challenge. It was only a bit of boyish braggadocio."

"It would serve him right if you accepted it," David said with a certain relish.

"Pistols at forty paces?" Ramses made the soft sound that was as near as he ever came to a laugh — a sound few others than David had heard. *"They don't do that sort of thing anymore, even in the Old Dominion. Or is that Virginia? I can never keep those American counties straight in my mind. He was only trying to impress Dolly."*

"Did it impress her?"

"Oh, yes. She would like nothing better than to watch two men fighting over her. She is," said Ramses judicially, *"a bloodthirsty little creature. Rather like a kitten — soft and purring and conscienceless and cruel."*

When we met at breakfast next morning Nefret pushed one trouser leg up to her knee and proudly exhibited a stocking that had been darned in two places. The darns were very lumpy. I decided not to mention this, nor did I point out that some persons might consider it improper to display a lower limb, even a stockinged limb, to three male persons. None of them appeared particularly interested, except for Emerson, who said approvingly, "Very neat, my dear."

I added my commendation and suggested she put on her boots, which she did. Ramses announced he would have a quick look at the tomb before beginning his own project. The sun had just lifted over the cliffs of the East Bank when we set out; the air was fresh and the long shadows were cool and gray.

A dozen of our men were there before us, removing the rocks Emerson had rolled against the door to hold it in place. "There is no sign of a disturbance," Abdullah reported.

Emerson nodded. "It would take even our ambitious neighbors from Gurneh some time to remove the debris in the passage. If we come across anything interesting today or tomorrow, we will take additional precautions."

We followed him down the steps. Abdullah was looking much more cheerful. Exploring an unknown tomb was his idea of what archaeology should be about. It was a viewpoint shared by most archaeologists, including, I confess, myself.

Emerson's strength and energy were superhuman, but even he had been able to remove only a small part of the rubble. It was enough, however, to show that he had been correct. A narrow section of the original stone floor was now visible beyond the doorway, and it did indeed slope down at the same angle as the ceiling. Little more could be seen; darkness filled the far end of the area where the ceiling met the rubble of the floor.

Candle in hand, head bent, Ramses edged past me. "Hmmm," he said.

Since this was not a particularly informative remark, I went back up the steps. Abdullah had preceded me; one quick look was all he had needed, and he had already given the men their instructions.

"What do you think, Abdullah?" I asked.

"Hmph," said Abdullah.

I thought I knew why he was so gruff with me; it had nothing to do with the difficulty of the task that might lie ahead. No, it was the strange mummy we had found that worried him. I debated as to whether I should tell him what we had discovered and then realized he probably knew at least part of the truth — one way or another — and that it was foolish and unkind not to take him wholly into my confidence.

"You did not know about this tomb," I said, stating it as a fact.

"If I had known, I would have told you, Sitt."

"Na'am — of course. But someone knew, Abdullah. The poor lady whose body we found yesterday was placed here not long ago."

"Within three seasons."

"How do you know?" I asked respectfully.

The old man's stern face relaxed. We had been partners before, Abdullah and I; no man had ever served me better. My reticence and my failure to ask his advice had hurt his feelings.

"There has been water in the tomb," he said. "It left a line along the wall. The last great rain was three years ago. Water had not touched the wrappings or the loose fill on the floor."

"I did not notice that," I admitted. "You are a keen observer and a shrewd man, Abdullah. Can you question the Gurnawis, and find out whether any of them knew about this tomb?"

"You think it was a man of Gurneh who killed the lady and put her here?"

Abdullah had a number of friends and relations in the village. He disapproved, but understood, their inveterate habit of tomb robbing. Murder was something else again — a sin against God and a crime that would bring down the full wrath of the authorities upon men who preferred to avoid such attention.

"I doubt that," I said truthfully. "It seems likely that the murderer was a foreigner. But the men of Gurneh know these cliffs as other men know the rooms of their houses. A foreigner, a stranger in Egypt, could not find this place without help. That help might have been given in all innocence, Abdullah."

"Aywa." Visibly relieved, Abdullah nodded. "I will find out, Sitt. Shall I tell only you, not the Father of Curses?"

I smiled at him. "It might be better not, Abdullah. Of course you must not lie to him if he asks you directly."

"One cannot lie to the Father of Curses," Abdullah said as if he were quoting. His left eyelid quivered, and I realized the dear old fellow was trying to wink. "But I will try, Sitt Hakim."

I winked back at him.

Ramses took himself off shortly thereafter, and work commenced in earnest. I wished that, like Ramses, I had thought of an excuse to absent myself, for progress was slow and very dull. It was sheer brute labor, filling baskets with loosened stone and carrying them up the steps to the dump Emerson had established some feet away

271

from the entrance. There was not much for me to do except watch. The fill the men removed was clean, without so much as a potsherd or a scrap of bone.

However, an active mind like mine can never be bored. Deprived of archaeological activity, it turned to thoughts of crime. The lunatic Scudder must have cleared that section of the passage and then levelled it to provide a platform on which the body would rest. Why had he gone to such enormous effort? The man was undoubtedly mad, but as Emerson had pointed out, madness has its methods. And how had he discovered a tomb that had been unknown before?

I congratulated myself for having had the idea of consulting with Abdullah. It only goes to prove what Scripture tells us — that kindness to others benefits oneself. In pleasing my old friend, I had served my own ends — or rather the ends of justice, for it is the duty of every citizen to investigate crime. Even Emerson had been forced to admit we were obliged to take a hand in this one.

How better to proceed than along the lines I (and Abdullah) had proposed? The man we sought must have spent some time in Luxor. He could not have discovered the tomb without the passive cooperation at least of one or more Gurnawis. He must be known to them, not as Dutton Scudder, but in another identity, the one he had assumed after abducting and murdering Mrs. Bellingham. Once the authorities in Cairo learned of recent developments they would surely resume the hunt for Scudder, but it was unlikely they would learn anything from the men of Gurneh, who were not in the habit of cooperating with the police.

A fond smile curved my lips as I thought of Abdullah trying to wink. We were co-conspirators again, he and I; why had I not realized how much he enjoyed that role? There was no need to spoil his innocent pleasure by telling him Emerson was fully cognizant of the matter.

At half-past one I extracted Emerson from the interior of the tomb, sat him down on a convenient rock, and handed him a cup of cold tea. "It is time to stop, Emerson. Except for a brief pause at midday the men have been hard at it since seven this morning."

Emerson said, "The fill beyond the first section is packed hard as cement from repeated floods. We will have to use pickaxes and —"

"Emerson!"

Emerson jumped. "You needn't shout, Peabody, I can hear you quite well. The angle of descent appears to be the same. It will take —"

"I am going back to the house, Emerson."

Emerson stared blankly at me. "Why?"

"Drink your tea, Emerson." I took his hand and brought it, and the cup it held, to his lips. While he drank I continued, "Nefret and David may as well come with me, you don't need photographs of bare walls, and since you are not making rapid progress David's plan of the tomb can wait."

"Are you bored, Peabody?"

"Yes, my dear. Very."

Emerson's bronzed brow furrowed in a frown, not of annoyance but of puzzlement.

I have said that most excavators yearn for treasure and artifacts. Emerson is one of the few exceptions. Not that he minds discovering a tomb like that of Tetisheri, but excavation for its own sake is his passion. He was genuinely enthralled by his boring tunnel packed with fill as hard as cement. Seeing his scraped hands, I realized he had been wielding a pickax along with the men.

"Well, my dear, do as you like," he said absently, rising from the rock.

"Please don't work any longer, Emerson. It is hot and dusty in there, and the air must be getting close."

"Yes, yes, Peabody." He was already halfway down the stairs. "I will follow you home shortly. I only want to see . . ."

I heard no more.

Under ordinary circumstances I would never have abandoned my dear bullheaded spouse, but since I expected Enid at four, it was necessary to leave at once. I explained the situation to Nefret and David as we crossed the *gebel* on our homeward path.

"Do you want us there?" David asked.

"You needn't be present if you prefer not to, but I see no reason why you should not both join in the discussion. And Ramses, if he has the common courtesy to be on time for tea. You may have a useful suggestion."

"I appreciate your confidence, Aunt Amelia," David said seriously.

Nefret, who had taken it for granted that she would be allowed to participate, only nodded.

I had time to bathe and change before Enid arrived. She was on horseback, and she looked considerably better than she had the day before. Though I consider riding sidesaddle both awkward and dangerous, I must confess that the costume is extremely becoming to a lady of trim figure and elegant posture. Enid was an excellent horsewoman; her dark green riding habit became her well and her cheeks were flushed with fresh air and healthful exercise.

I directed her attendant — an old acquaintance, like most of the guides and, like at least half of them, named Mohammed — to take the horses round to the stable and led Enid to a chair on the verandah. Cyrus was the next to appear. He had scarcely finished greeting us when David and Nefret joined us.

"Now then," I said, "we can get down to business. Cyrus, you might begin by telling Enid and the children about our interview with Mrs. Jones."

"Should we not wait for Ramses?" Enid asked. "And the Professor?"

"Emerson's suggestions are not likely to be helpful," I said. "He is too — er — forthright to comprehend the complexities of the matter. As for Ramses, he went off to Deir el Bahri this morning, and I suppose he has lost track of the time, as he is inclined to do. We will not wait for them. Proceed, Cyrus."

Cyrus cleared his throat. Before he could utter the first word, Enid, whose gaze had wandered to the desert path, exclaimed, "There he is! He is coming."

It was Ramses, mounted on Risha and looking remarkably neat and clean. I realized he must have taken the time to freshen himself, for a long day perched on a ladder propped against a sun-flooded temple wall does not leave an individual looking his best. After dismounting without the flamboyance to which he was prone, he handed the reins to the stableboy and joined us on the verandah.

"We will take the courtesies for granted this time, Ramses," I said before he could begin his formal litany of "good afternoon's." "Mr. Vandergelt was about to open the meeting."

But Enid had offered him her hand, and good manners compelled him to take it. He was still holding it — or the other way round — when I motioned Cyrus to begin.

His picturesque American vocabulary gave the narrative a quaint charm, but it was as succinct and accurate as I could have produced myself. Nevertheless Enid's face showed signs of increasing impatience, and when Cyrus described Mrs. Jones's offer to assist us in restoring Donald to his senses, she burst out.

"Lies! She lured him into this; does a spider

free the fly caught in its web?"

Hugging her raised knees, Nefret said, "I think *you* believed her, though, Mr. Vandergelt. Why?"

Ramses anticipated him. "Pure self-interest would explain her offer. She may have been in trouble with the law before, but if she is as clever as she sounds, she has doubtless managed to avoid any serious charge. Should Mr. Fraser suffer grievous mental or physical harm, she might be liable to arrest. At the very least, adverse publicity would have a destructive effect on her career."

"Just what I was about to say, my young friend," remarked Cyrus with a decidedly unfriendly glance at Ramses. "Now see here, folks, I'm a practical man and what we want here is a practical solution, not a lot of fancy theories. We could go after Mrs. Jones and maybe find grounds for an arrest warrant. But that might not do Mr. Fraser any good. What is more important, helping him back to his right mind or putting the lady in a cell?"

Enid stiffened. "I cannot believe I understand your meaning, Mr. Vandergelt. I want that woman punished for what she has done! It is all her doing; Donald would never have believed in this fantasy if she had not poisoned his mind."

Cyrus was not the man to contradict a lady, though I saw the muscles around his mouth tighten. In his soft American drawl he said soothingly, "I reckon it's your decision, Mrs. Fraser."

Enid's hand came to rest on the furry object

that had insinuated itself onto her lap. Not until Sekhmet began to purr did she observe the creature; with a faint smile, she went on stroking the cat and when she replied her voice was once more calm and well-bred.

"Perhaps, Mr. Vandergelt; but since I consulted you — all of you" — her eyes moved round the circle of attentive faces — "and since you have been good enough to give up your time to my affairs, I ought at the very least heed your advice. What do you propose?"

Except for David, who preserved his customary modest silence, everyone had a suggestion. "Compel Mrs. Jones to confess to Mr. Fraser," was Nefret's idea.

"With all of us present," I added. "Surely our combined, rational arguments must bring him round to a correct way of thinking."

Ramses pursed his lips and shook his head. "It would surely be futile, if not actually dangerous, to mount a direct attack against Mr. Fraser. I fear that not even Father could convince him he is mistaken."

Enid looked as if she would have objected to this, but she said nothing; and Ramses went on in his most pedantic manner, "If you are correct in your assessment of the lady, Mr. Vandergelt, which I have no reason to doubt, the key to the problem lies with her. She is now the only individual to whom he will listen. She is an expert at inventing implausible fantasies; she ought to be able to think of a story that would destroy this one. Would it be possible for you, sir, to spend some time with Mrs. Jones, exploring various possibilities?"

Cyrus's lined face broke into a broad smile. "Now that is a smart idea, young fella. I guess maybe I could do that."

Time was getting on, and I did not want my dear Emerson to find Enid there. In the voice hostesses use to indicate it is time for their guests to leave, I said, "In the meantime, Enid, you must behave civilly to Mrs. Jones and treat Donald with greater understanding. I know it won't be easy, but force yourself, my dear. Above all, don't challenge Donald's beliefs. Ramses is correct; he is far beyond reason now, and cannot be helped in that way."

Enid took the hint. Rising, she handed Sekhmet to me and said with a smile, "You are right as always, Amelia. I will do my best. Thank you — all of you."

"I will ride to the ferry with Mrs. Fraser, Mother." Ramses got to his feet. "I am on my way to the dahabeeyah in any case; I want to go over the corrections I made this afternoon while they are still fresh in my mind, so I won't be back for dinner."

After they had gone Cyrus took out one of his cheroots, and after asking permission to smoke, he leaned back in his chair and crossed his legs. "That boy of yours is getting to be as sly and cunning as you, Mrs. Amelia," he said with a smile that turned the words into a compliment.

"I'd have felt obliged to escort the lady myself if he hadn't offered, and he saw we wanted more time to talk."

Privately I doubted that had been Ramses's real motive for behaving in a gentlemanly manner. What his true motive might have been I could not imagine, but Nefret was frowning and David had an even guiltier look than usual.

"What did you think of Enid's behavior?" I asked.

"The same thing you thought, I reckon. The lady protested too much. But why?"

In fact I was beginning to think I knew why, but even if I had been certain, the subject was not one I could properly discuss with Cyrus. "Women are overly conscientious creatures," I said. "They — I do not include myself, of course — they have been trained to accept the blame for everything that goes wrong in a marriage."

"I will leave Mrs. Fraser to you, then," said Cyrus, extinguishing his cigar. "If anyone can convince a lady she is not at fault, it is you, Mrs. Amelia. Young Ramses has the right of it, though. Mrs. Jones is the most likely person to find a way out of this. I believe I will give myself the pleasure of a conference with that lady."

"How are you going to manage it?" I asked.

"Why, I will just go on over to Luxor this evening and ask her to have dinner with me," Cyrus said blandly. "No sense in sneaking around behind Fraser's back; what's the harm in a well-behaved bachelor asking a widow lady to dine with him in a public place?"

"That is clever, Cyrus," I said. "How kind of you to spend so much time on this affair."

"Not at all." Cyrus rose and picked up his hat. "I will let you know what transpires. You haven't forgotten about my little soiree tomorrow, I hope."

I had forgot, though his invitation had been among the messages awaiting us. Foreign residents and visitors to Egypt observed the Christian Sabbath as their day of rest and religious observance, but it was not kept as strictly as it had been in my youth; there was no objection to respectable social engagements, and Cyrus's were always respectable. I assured him we would be there. Emerson would roar, of course, but I did not doubt I could persuade him.

We had finished tea before Emerson appeared. I let out an exclamation of dismay.

"Good heavens, my dear, how dirty you are!"

"The place gets hotter and dirtier the farther we go," Emerson said happily.

"Any artifacts as yet?"

"A few bits of miscellaneous mummies and their wrappings." He began unbuttoning his shirt as he headed for the house. "I will be with you in a short while, my dears; never mind tea, Peabody, I will join you in a whiskey and soda as soon as I have bathed."

He was so excited about his tedious tomb, he would talk of nothing else for a time. "The passage is not completely choked up in all sections.

Selim was able to crawl along on top of the fill for another ten meters; he was unable to proceed farther, but the passage continues. . . ."

Not until he had wound down did he notice Ramses was not there. In response to his question, I explained that Ramses meant to spend the evening working on his texts. Emerson nodded approvingly.

"That was a wise decision of his, to stay on the dahabeeyah, where there are fewer distractions. The task he has undertaken will be a major contribution to the field, and I am glad to see him taking his work so seriously. I told you he would settle down, Peabody."

"Did you?"

A reminiscent smile curved Emerson's well-shaped lips. "Well, there were times when I never expected I would live to see it. Do you remember the night he stole the lion? And the time in London when he disguised himself as a beggar lad and bit the constable who told him to move on?"

"I would rather not remember, Emerson."

"He led you a merry dance, my dear," Emerson said affectionately. "But you can be proud of the results of your tireless efforts. He has become a responsible, serious young man and a first-rate Egyptologist."

David jumped up. "Excuse me. I promised Ramses I would come —"

"No, no, my boy," Emerson said, pleasantly but firmly. "Ramses will accomplish more if he is left alone. I want you to help Nefret develop those plates this evening."

"Yes, sir."

David glanced at Nefret. She leaned forward, her eyes sparkling. "Tell me about the lion."

It is said that the passage of time heals all wounds and renders painful memories endurable. Such proved to be the case with my memories of Ramses's boyhood. Nefret had heard about a few of his adventures, but not all; Emerson's stories, which he narrated with considerable gusto, kept her laughing all through dinner. Some of them struck me now as rather funny, though they certainly had not had that effect at the time.

After the young people had gone to the darkroom we settled down in the sitting room and Emerson took out his pipe.

"Now we can talk freely," I said.

"What about?"

"Oh, Emerson, don't be so aggravating. You said last night we were duty-bound to investigate Mrs. Bellingham's death."

"And you," said Emerson, giving me a severe look, "promised you would keep the children out of it. What is this I hear about Enid Fraser being here today?"

"That is another matter altogether."

"Is it?" Emerson struck a match.

Pipes appear to be very difficult to operate. It always takes him some time to get his started. By the time he had it lit I had rapidly considered the implications of his enigmatic question and determined on a reply.

"So that occurred to you, did it?"

"I would claim," said Emerson, puffing, "that it had not occurred to you until this moment were I not well acquainted with the fertility of your imagination. It is a farfetched, fantastic idea, Peabody."

"Once one has eliminated the probables, what remains, however impossible —"

"Yes, yes, I know," Emerson said impatiently. "But this really is impossible. Mrs. Jones could not have been involved with the mummification and removal of Mrs. Bellingham's body. She had not been in Egypt before this."

"We have only her word for that."

"The European community, especially here in Luxor, is small and close-knit. Someone would remember having met her."

"I have not explored that angle as thoroughly as I ought to have done," I said thoughtfully. "I will do so. Most of the members of that community will be at Cyrus's soiree tomorrow evening."

Emerson's protests about attending the soiree were less noisy than usual; he acknowledged the necessity of investigation and recognized this would be a useful opportunity for pursuing it. "It is only a matter of form, though," he said. "Consider the other difficulties. Preparing the body and placing it in the tomb required specialized knowledge, nor could she have anticipated five years ago that she would want a mummy at this time."

"Don't be so cursed pedantic and methodical, Emerson. I don't believe for a moment Mrs. Jones had anything to do with Mrs. Bellingham's death. The discovery of the body is quite another matter. Let us suppose . . ."

"By all means," Emerson said gravely. "Supposition is the basis of criminal investigation."

"Let us theorize, then. Mrs. Jones has been in the spiritualist business for some time, and one of her controls is an Egyptian princess. Unlike some of her colleagues, she has taken the trouble to learn something about Egyptology; her conversation with us in Cairo proved that. Supposing she ran across the real killer . . . Emerson, please stop grinning in that annoying fashion. Coincidences do occur and people have been known to make unwise admissions, especially under circumstances of emotional stress such as prevail during a séance. Just allow me, for a moment, to hypothesize that Mrs. Jones knew that there was a likely mummy available. Producing it would be the final proof to Donald that her talents were genuine. You see what this means, don't you? If the clues we received directing us to the tomb came from Mrs. Jones, the killer need not be in Egypt. He may have fled to darkest Antarctica or the wilds of the Rocky Mountains."

Emerson removed his pipe from his mouth. "You have progressed from 'suppose' to 'may have been' to a flat-out statement of fact, Peabody. I still believe it is a lunatic idea. However, it does raise a valid point. The killer need not be the same person who directed us to the tomb."

"You have overlooked something, though. I overlooked it too," I admitted. "The attacks on Dolly Bellingham."

"We only know for certain of one," Emerson pointed out. "I admit it is unusual, almost unheard of, for a foreign tourist to be attacked, but it could happen. The defections of her attendants might be due to purely natural causes."

"We ought to find out more about those defections."

"I will leave that in your hands, Peabody. I can't stand the girl. She is a giggler. You know how I feel about gigglers."

"Very well. I will also question Colonel Bellingham. We need a description of Scudder — his background, his physical appearance, his habits. And Abdullah . . ."

I caught myself. Emerson gave me another of those annoying grins. "Yes, Abdullah. That was a good notion of yours, Peabody. I had the same idea myself."

"You always say that."

"So do you."

"So Abdullah confessed all."

"Certainly. No doubt he will confess to you tomorrow that I bullied him into betraying your confidence. I believe the old rascal enjoys playing us off one against the other."

"Let him enjoy his game, then. He can be a great help."

"Certainly." Emerson rose and stretched. "Let us get the children out of the darkroom and send them to bed. We are fortunate parents, Peabody; David and Nefret diligent in the darkroom, Ramses laboring on the dahabeeyah. I hope the poor lad won't stay up too late straining his eyes over those texts."

CHAPTER EIGHT

It was not a sporting thing to do,
but the alternative would have been less acceptable.

My suggestion that we attend church services next morning was received with a massive display of disinclination. In his bluff fashion Emerson summed up the general consensus by remarking, "Don't be absurd, Peabody," and demanded another egg. His callused brown hands were marked by innumerable scrapes and bruises; I reminded myself to apply a few bits of sticking plaster, though I did not suppose he would leave them in place for long.

Ramses's eye sockets had the bruised look they got from lack of sleep, and when I taxed him with sitting up late over his texts he admitted he had not gone to bed until after two in the morning. My motherly lecture was interrupted by the appearance of Nefret, whose manners, as well as her appearance, showed signs of fatigue. Instead of greeting us with sunny smiles and affectionate embraces she dropped heavily into her chair and reached for the toast rack.

"You don't appear to have slept well either,"

I remarked. "Was it another of your bad dreams?"

"Yes," Nefret said shortly.

The dreams were infrequent, but disturbing enough to make it difficult for her to get back to sleep. I assumed they were prompted by childhood memories; heaven knows the poor girl's experiences in her Nubian oasis had been painful enough to provide material for a lifetime of nightmares. She claimed she could never remember the substance of them when she woke, though I had tried, tactfully and gently, to get her to recall them. I felt certain that if she could, they would stop.

"Oh, dear," I said sympathetically. "I had hoped you were getting over them."

"I doubt I ever will," Nefret said. "Ramses, will you come to the verandah with me?"

He rose obediently. She picked up the piece of bread he had left on his plate and thrust it at him. "Eat it," she snapped, and led him out.

David immediately rose and followed them. I did not ask what they were about, for I feel that children are entitled to their little secrets. The three of them were such good chums, they were always putting their heads together over some scheme or other.

Emerson was impatient to get to the Valley since, as he remarked sourly, he would be forced to stop early in order to attend a cursed party. In fact, as I believe I have said, many archaeologists left off work shortly after midday, not only because of the heat but because other tasks demanded their time. Keeping proper field notes was, by Emerson's own standards, as important as the excavation itself. Furthermore, the "cursed" parties were, in my opinion, not an unnecessary frivolity. It is necessary for great minds to enjoy periods of relaxation, and professional conversations at such social events could be illuminating. I had told Emerson this hundreds of times, so I did not bother repeating it on this occasion.

We left the house shortly after six.

The work went on even more slowly than it had the day before. The men were forced to use pickaxes to cut through the blockage, and in some sections only a skilled eye could distinguish between the hardened fill and the rock wall. Ramses went down to have a look. What he saw obviously did not inspire him to remain. He left us, and I found the opportunity for a chat with Abdullah.

He had nothing as yet to report. "One proceeds slowly with these matters, Sitt. It is known that I am in the confidence of you and the Father of Curses; a thief does not confess a robbery to the Mudir. But I have had another thought."

"Yes, Abdullah?"

"Last season the inspector [as he called Howard Carter] explored this wadi looking for tombs for the rich American. His men cleared to ground level on that side." His gesture indicated the opposite cliff and the open entrance of tomb Nineteen. "It was there in the courtyard of the prince's tomb that he found the small tomb with the two mummies. Could it have been one of the men who worked for him who discovered our tomb?"

Suddenly I remembered the workman we had met coming out of the wadi the day we located the tomb — thanks in large part to a marker someone had left for us. The basket he carried had concealed the fellow's face, and Nefret had innocently commented on his uncharacteristic haste.

"Good Gad," I exclaimed. "Abdullah, my friend, I think you have it! The murderer of Mrs. Bellingham must have lived all these years disguised as an Egyptian. He would need to work in order to earn his livelihood; what is more likely than that he should seek employment with one of the archaeologists here in Luxor? The discovery of the tomb may have been his alone, and the men of Gurneh would know nothing of it."

"It may be so, Sitt." A shout from Emerson summoned him. He heaved himself to his feet. "I will go on asking in Gurneh."

The more I thought about it, the more convinced I became that Abdullah had hit on a productive line of inquiry, and I berated myself for having overlooked the significance of the shy workman. But, to do myself justice, I had had a great many other things on my mind — and still did.

Rapidly I ran down the list of things to be done.

Delegating tasks is the mark of a good administrator. I had hoped I could safely leave Mrs. Jones to Cyrus, but I was beginning to have second thoughts. Beneath Cyrus's rough-hewn features and stalwart frame lay the heart of a romantic boy, insofar as women were concerned. He appeared to be quite fascinated by Mrs. Jones. Could I trust him to resist her female machinations?

I was not at all certain I could.

Clearly Emerson was the proper person to deal with the authorities concerning Mrs. Bellingham. His reputation and his formidable presence could induce answers from even a pompous British official. But would Emerson ask the right questions? Would he become bored or impatient with the inquiry and abandon it? Most important — would he tell me what he had learned, discuss it with me, accept my suggestions as to what he should do next?

I was fairly certain he would not.

So, as usual, it was all left to me.

I had, as was my habit, caused a little shelter of sailcloth to be erected so that we would have a shady place in which to rest and take refreshment. I always made certain we were well supplied with cold tea and water for washing; copious consumption of liquid is not a luxury in that climate, it is a necessity. Seated cross-legged on a blanket under this shelter, Nefret was writing busily in a notebook. I suspected she kept a diary — in emulation of me — but I had never asked her or looked for the book itself. (It had a distinctive dark red leather cover, so I certainly would have observed it if she had left it lying about.) Not that I would have dreamed of reading it, even if I had happened, by accident, to come across it.

Seeing her happily occupied, I took out my archaeological notebook and began a neat little list of "Questions to Be Answered" and "What to Do about Them." I have tried various methods of organizing my ideas for the purpose of criminal investigation and have found this the most useful. The list was discouragingly long, but there was one hopeful aspect. Many of the individuals I wanted to question would be at Cyrus's soiree.

Fate was on my side that morning. Scarcely had I finished my list than I heard the crunch of approaching footsteps and looked up to see several people approaching. Two were Egyptians, in the usual galabeeyahs and turbans. The third was wearing a flannel suit and a straw hat, which latter object of apparel he whipped off upon seeing me.

"Mrs. Emerson? My name is Gordon, from the American consulate in Cairo. I was told your husband would be here."

"How do you do." I introduced Nefret, who nodded politely and then returned to her writing. "I presume, Mr. Gordon, that you have come about Mrs. Bellingham?"

"Yes, ma'am. If I could speak with Professor Emerson . . ."

"I will send someone to tell him you are here. Take a seat, Mr. Gordon, and have a cup of tea."

"Thank you, ma'am, but I am in something of a hurry, and the Professor —"

"You may as well sit down. Emerson will not come out until he is good and ready."

"He is down there?" Mr. Gordon took out a handkerchief and mopped his flushed, perspiring face. He was rather stout and no longer in his first youth; a fringe of sandy hair framed his balding head.

"Yes. Put your hat back on, Mr. Gordon, or you will have a terrible sunburn. The top of the head is very sensitive."

Clapping his hat back on his head, Mr. Gordon took the seat I had indicated. "I'm new in town, Mrs. Emerson, but I have heard about you. May I say you live up to your reputation? That is meant as a compliment, ma'am."

"Thank you," I said. "Why did Lord Cromer send you instead of a police officer?"

"I expect the Professor will have the same questions, ma'am. Why don't we wait till he is here so I don't have to repeat myself?"

Mr. Gordon's round pink face looked rather like that of a friendly piglet. Pigs are proverbially stubborn animals, and the gentleman's small, deep-set eyes held a glint that told me it would be a waste of time to argue with him.

"That is sensible," I conceded. "I will call him."

I descended the steps and shouted into the

tunnel. "There is a gentleman from Cairo to see you, Emerson."

His voice came booming back. "Send him down."

"Don't be absurd, Emerson. Come out at once."

The only answer was a reverberating oath. I returned to Mr. Gordon. "I apologize for my husband, Mr. Gordon. He does not like to interrupt his work."

"So I was told in Luxor. That is why I came here, instead of asking him to call on me at my hotel, but I never expected I would have to interview him inside a tomb. Do I have to go down there?"

"That would be inadvisable," I said, eyeing Mr. Gordon's nice neat flannel suit and flushed face. "He will be along shortly."

A few minutes later Emerson came bounding up the stairs. Mr. Gordon shied back as the strange figure strode toward him. Emerson had stripped to the waist, and his bare skin was the same color as his boots and trousers — mud-colored, to be precise. His hair, gray with muddy dust, clung to his head in damp waves. He was accompanied by an unpleasant smell. I recognized it as that of bat. Mr. Gordon probably did not recognize it, but he did not like it. The wrinkling of his nose further increased the porcine resemblance.

Seizing the jar of water I offered him, Emerson poured it over his head, shook himself like a large dog, sat down on the ground, and stared fixedly at Mr. Gordon.

"My attention was first drawn to the tomb when . . . Come, come, man, get out your notebook and write this down. I will not go over it more than once. I have work to do."

"Mind your manners, Emerson," I said. "This is Mr. Gordon, the American vice-consul. He has come all this way as a courtesy to you, and — No! Don't shake hands!"

Mr. Gordon having located a writing implement and paper, Emerson proceeded with his narrative, ending the account with a description of that grisly ceremony of unwrapping. "We ceased as soon as we were certain of the identification," he said virtuously. "You know the rest. Have you any questions?"

Mr. Gordon had recovered his aplomb, which had been considerably shaken by Emerson's initial appearance. "I believe not, sir," he said slowly. "I have spoken with the bereaved husband and with Dr. Willoughby."

"If that is all, I will get back to work," said Emerson, rising.

"Certainly, Professor. I have to thank you for a well-organized account. Mrs. Emerson, have you anything to add?"

"Only a few questions, if I may."

Emerson abruptly sat down again.

I repeated the question I had first asked, and Mr. Gordon explained that since the persons involved were all of them Americans, Lord

Cromer had felt it best for an American official to take charge of the case. My next question — "What steps have you initiated in order to apprehend the murderer?" — received a less satisfactory response.

"The investigation is proceeding, Mrs. Emerson."

I recognized the usual close-minded official attitude. Almost all of the police officers and investigators I have encountered take the position that women should not be encouraged to assist them.

I said, "You would do well to consult me, Mr. Gordon."

"No, you would not," said Emerson, galvanized into speech.

"Have you seen the body?" I inquired.

A shudder rippled along Mr. Gordon's jowls. "Yes, ma'am. I have run across a few unpleasant sights in the course of my duties, but none has affected me like that one. I felt obliged to have a look, though, since I must return to Cairo this evening and Colonel Bellingham wishes to hold the funeral on Tuesday."

"What!" I cried. "So soon? But surely there has not been time for an autopsy."

"The Colonel refused to consider it. He said the poor lady had been — er — violated was the word he used — enough already. He wants to lay her to rest as soon as possible."

I glanced at Emerson. He had stopped sputtering and glaring at me; now he said, stroking his chin, "Do you think that wise, Mr. Gorgon?"

"Gordon," the American said stiffly. "I see no reason for exacerbating the Colonel's distress by unnecessary delay, Professor. We have learned all we can from the poor lady's remains."

"Nonsense," I exclaimed. "Have you probed the wound to discover its depth and angle? Did you remove a section of skin so that tests could be made to determine what substance was used to preserve the body?"

"Mrs. Emerson, please!" Mr. Gordon heaved himself to his feet. His face was no longer pink but pale puce. "I guess I should not be surprised at hearing questions like that from you, but have you no consideration for that young lady?"

He gestured at Nefret. Her blue eyes wide and innocent, she smiled at him. "I was present during the examination of the body, Mr. Gordon. You should also examine the fingernails. They are somewhat loose, but —"

Mr. Gordon did not stop, even to thank us properly. Muttering incoherently, he fled.

"Hmph," said Emerson.

"Hmph indeed," I agreed. "His failure to carry out proper procedures is unconscionable. We must have another look at the body, Emerson."

Emerson groaned. "Peabody, I cannot discuss the matter now. The passage has taken a turn to the north, it is still descending, and the air is getting foul. How the devil the devilish bats got into the place I do not know, since we had to cut through ten feet of hardened rock to do so, but at some time or other they obviously did because they left not only a thick layer of guano, but a few hundred skeletons."

After luncheon Emerson condescended to dismiss me and the children, since we were not doing anything useful anyhow. I made him put on his gloves, knowing full well he would take them off as soon as he was out of my sight. Then I asked Abdullah if he had brought his watch with him. Nodding, he pulled it from somewhere in the folds of his robe. It was a large gold watch with his name inscribed in both English and Arabic. We had presented him with it the previous year, and he was extremely proud of it.

"Good," I said. "Make certain Emerson stops work at three and bring him back to the house."

Abdullah looked doubtful. "I will try, Sitt Hakim."

"I know you will." I patted him on the shoulder. In fact I was not at all certain Abdullah could tell time by his watch; I had never wished to offend his dignity by inquiring. He could read the passage of the sun almost as accurately, however.

When we reached the house David asked — he always asked instead of announcing his intentions, as Ramses would have done — if he might go for a ride. Nefret declared that if he would wait until she had paid Teti a visit, she would go with him. Since this suited my own plans quite nicely I agreed, warning them to be back in plenty of time to change for the soiree.

"You might go round by Deir el Bahri and

bring Ramses back with you," I added. "Otherwise he will go on working till nightfall."

Nefret said that finding Ramses was precisely what she intended to do.

Once they had taken their departure I went to the boys' rooms to collect their soiled clothing. Monday was washday, and if I left the job to them, they never did it until the last minute.

I will admit in the pages of this private journal that my motives might not have been as innocent and aboveboard as that statement suggests. I had agreed to let Emerson deal with Ramses and David, even though I strongly suspected his notions of proper conduct for young men were not identical with mine. It was not a conscious violation of that agreement that led me to inspect the boys' quarters. I am a firm believer in the subconscious, however, and I do not doubt that an underlying uneasiness prompted my action — nothing so strong as suspicion, only a sense that someone was up to something.

The sight of David's room brought a smile to my lips. One would have expected him to be the neater of the two, but he had a happy masculine habit of leaving everything where he had dropped it — clothing, books, newspapers. His drawing materials covered every flat surface except the top of the bureau. On it, neatly displayed, were a number of photographs, some framed, some fastened with drawing pins to the frame of the mirror. The faces were those I knew and loved, and I gave myself up to a few minutes of fond contemplation.

The cabinet photograph of Evelyn was enclosed in a frame made by David himself. Flowers and vines, carved with infinite delicacy, twined round it. She looked very lovely but a little stiff, as one does in such posed photographs. The images taken by Nefret the previous summer with her little Kodak were more to my taste. Raddie, Evelyn's eldest and Emerson's namesake, was a fine-looking young fellow, with his father's mild features and Evelyn's sweet smile. He had gone up to Oxford this year. The twins, Johnny and Davie, were natural clowns and as close as twins often are. They always struck some comical pose when being photographed — in this case a living Hindu idol with one body, eight limbs, and two heads, both grinning.

There was an especially pretty photograph of Evelyn's oldest girl, who had been named after me. 'Melia was — I had to stop and calculate — fourteen. Fortunately for her, she did not resemble me in the slightest! (Of course there was no reason why she should; this was just one of my little jokes, which always made 'Melia laugh and protest that she would happily have exchanged her fair curls and blue eyes for my coarse black hair and rather too prominent chin. It was a falsehood, but a kindly one.)

The sight of those dear faces, so dear to David as well, made me feel — just a little — ashamed of my intrusion. Leaving the wrinkled garments lying on floor, bed, and table, I went out and gently closed the door.

Ramses's room was as bare as a monk's cell and almost as uninformative. He had left most of his personal possessions on board the boat. The single folder on his desk contained photographs of a hieratic manuscript, together with his transliteration and partial translation. It appeared to have something to do with dreams, and I remembered what Ramses had said about the significance of dreaming of a cat. I did not pause to read the translation, however, since I did not want to disturb the order of the pages.

The books he had brought with him were an interestingly eclectic collection, ranging from a ponderous study of Egyptian verb forms to a recently published thriller. I knew Ramses had a weakness for this form of fiction, but I was somewhat taken aback to discover several slim volumes of poetry hidden behind Wilkinson's *Manners and Customs of the Ancient Egyptians.*

I have always considered poetry too sensational for young minds. These poems were worse, for they were *in French,* a language Ramses read as fluently as he did most other languages. After considering the matter, I returned them to their hiding place. There were, I supposed, more shocking writers than Baudelaire and Rostand.

Those volumes were probably under the mattress. I did not look for them, nor did I open the drawers of his dresser. There were no photographs on its top.

The children were gone quite a long time. Emerson was bathing and I was on the verandah, pacing impatiently, before I saw them coming.

"What took you so long?" I demanded.

"I apologize, Mother," said Ramses, helping Nefret to dismount. "The delay was my fault."

"I assumed as much. Well, hurry and change. We are dining with Cyrus, so he can tell us about his talk with Mrs. Jones before the others arrive."

Cyrus sent his barouche for us, so Nefret and I were able to dress for the occasion. Since I sympathized with her dislike of stiff, confining garments for females, I allowed most of her frocks to be made without stays and tight-fitting bodices, though I had had the devil of a time finding a dressmaker who had enough imagination to depart from the current patterns. Nefret's slim, athletic form did not require or appreciate the confinement of corsets, and after she had ripped the sleeve seams out of two blouses by gesturing too emphatically, it became apparent she needed more room in that area too. Her second-best evening dress was of pale yellow mousseline de soie with a modest décolletage. I wore crimson, as I prefer to do, since it is Emerson's favorite; and he unbent so far as to tell me it became me well. At his own insistence Ramses mounted the seat next to the coachman, and off we went in fine style behind Cyrus's pair of matched grays.

I was as familiar with the Castle as with the rooms of my own house, for we had stayed with

Cyrus on innumerable occasions. It was a good deal grander than our humble establishment, walled like a fortress and supplied with all modern inconveniences, as Emerson called them. It is true that the electricity Cyrus had installed the year before was not very dependable, but there were oil lamps in each room and Cyrus preferred candlelight for dining anyhow.

When we were seated at the table, with the soft glow of the candles reflecting off crystal and silver, Cyrus began his account.

"Mr. Fraser wasn't well pleased at my kidnapping the lady. He wanted to know why we wouldn't dine with him and his missus; asked where we were going and when we would be back. I expected every minute to have him demand whether my intentions were honorable."

"I am sure you don't mean to give a false impression, Cyrus," I said, "but you surely are not implying that Mr. Fraser was — well — jealous."

"No, ma'am," Cyrus said just as quickly. "At least not — er — not that way. But he sure wants to keep her talents to himself. He believes nobody else can lead him to his princess."

"What the devil does he think he is going to do with her when he finds her?" demanded Emerson.

"Emerson, you have such a — a coarse way of putting things," I protested.

"The question was perfectly innocent, my dear. If you choose to interpret it —"

"Never mind, Emerson!" Grinning, Emerson returned to his soup, and I continued, "I doubt Donald has thought so far ahead."

"He has, though," Cyrus said soberly. "He's going to reanimate her."

"What?" I cried.

"Lord only knows where he got the notion, Mrs. Amelia. Katherine — uh — Mrs. Jones — swears she never suggested any such thing. Now, folks, just quit asking me questions and let me tell you what she said; it will save time in the long run.

"She talked openly and freely about her methods, and believe me, ladies and gents, they are carefully designed to keep her out of trouble with the law. She doesn't charge for her services; there's a pretty copper bowl on the table in her sitting room, and if people want to drop money into it, that's their affair. She isn't stupid enough to make promises she can't keep, neither. It's the usual vague twaddle about how happy Uncle Henry is on the Other Side, and how Granny hopes everybody loves everybody and treats 'em nice.

"The Egyptian connection is her stock in trade. Like I said, she took the trouble to study the subject, so her clients can't catch her making stupid mistakes like inventing names no Egyptian would have had, or getting her dynasties mixed up. The reincarnation stuff is very popular. Who wouldn't want to hear she was a pharaoh's favorite in another life? Or, in the case of the men, pharaoh himself? Once the victims have heard a few fancy stories about their fatal beauty or their prowess in war, they go home feeling more content with their present boring lives. She's got a great talent for fiction, has the lady. I told her she ought to write thrillers for a living."

Cyrus's soft-footed, well-trained staff had removed the soup plates and served the main course. He paused to take a sip of wine, and I said, "So that is how it began with Donald? Who did she tell him he had been?"

"Ramses the Great, naturally." Cyrus shook his head. "They all want to be Ramses the Great. She gave him the usual yarn, about what a mighty warrior he was and how many wives he had, and then — she can't remember exactly how the subject came up — he was talking about the princess he had loved and lost. You wouldn't think so to look at him, but the poor devil is a romantic. He took it into his head that her control is his lost love, and that she wants him to find her. The reanimation thing just came up recently. She says she never would have agreed to this trip if he had given any indication of being that far gone."

"The trip to Egypt was Donald's idea?" I asked skeptically.

"Yep. She says we can ask Mrs. Fraser if we don't believe her. She gave in because she figured she could string him along and keep him out of harm's way until he lost interest. She always wanted to see Egypt anyhow.

"Well, instead of losing interest, he got worse. She's at her wits' end now as to what to do with him, and she's plumb wore out from being dragged all over the cliffs of the West Bank looking for Tasherit's tomb. She showed me her —"

Cyrus broke off, looking a trifle flustered, and reached for his wineglass.

"Buy her a steamship ticket and send her back to England," Emerson growled.

"She's got her ticket," Cyrus said. "You think a lady as shrewd as that is going to take the chance of finding herself marooned a thousand miles from home? She says she won't abandon Fraser while he's in this state."

"Cyrus, I think you are losing your detachment," I declared. "You speak of that — that woman almost with admiration."

"Well, I do admire her, kind of. She's smart and she's made her own way in the world, with no help from anybody. Got quite a sense of humor, too." Cyrus's thin lips relaxed in a reminiscent smile. "Some of the stories she told me about her clients would have made a cat laugh. She can laugh at herself, too, which is pretty rare. When she showed me —"

"I am removing you from the case, Cyrus," I said, only half in jest.

"Too late for that, Mrs. Amelia, my dear. I am sticking. I think maybe Katherine — she said I could call her that — I think she's come up with a good idea. What we've got to do is convince Fraser his ancient lady friend doesn't want

307

to come back to life. She needs his blessing so she can move on to Amenti and wait for him there."

"What bloody nonsense," Emerson grunted.

"No, Professor darling, I think it is a brilliant idea," Nefret exclaimed. "I can be Princess Tasherit. A black wig and the proper makeup, and a great deal of cheesecloth to waft round me —"

"You are getting a bit ahead of yourself, Nefret," said Ramses. Elbows on the table, chin in his hands, he was watching Nefret closely, and the candle flames reflected in his black eyes flickered like lighted laughter. "No one mentioned an actual appearance by the princess. It is not a bad idea, though. You would have to remind him that suicide is a deadly sin and that he must wait out the course of his natural life, doing good deeds and behaving like an English gentleman, before he can hope to join her."

"Good Gad," I exclaimed. "What are you thinking of, Ramses? Nefret will do no such thing. It is too dangerous. What if Donald, overcome with passion, attempted to seize her in his arms?"

"He would not succeed in the attempt," said Ramses. David, who had not spoken, nodded vigorously.

"You're right, though, Mrs. Amelia," Cyrus declared. "We couldn't let a nice young lady like Miss Nefret take part in such an underhanded scheme. We could easily find some pretty little

Egyptian girl to play the part. You think it would work?"

"It might," I admitted. "We will have to give it some thought. I must consult Enid first."

That ended the discussion; the first guests would be arriving soon, and since Cyrus had neither wife nor sister nor daughter, I was pleased to act as his hostess. However, I could tell by Nefret's expressive face that she had no intention of giving up the star role to a "pretty little Egyptian girl." Not without a struggle.

Cyrus's evening parties were always the height of elegance and good taste. The electric lights burned bright that evening, reflecting off the surfaces of polished brass vessels and silver vases. Through the open French doors of the principal reception rooms wafted the scent of roses and jasmine. Lanterns illumined Cyrus's famous gardens.

Everyone who was anyone in Luxor was there. The only exception was the Fraser party. I supposed Enid had not been willing to risk having Donald make an exhibition of himself by buttonholing archaeologists and demanding information about the princess.

Dr. Willoughby, engaged in conversation with a visiting German Baron and his Frau, nodded to me across the room. Mr. Theodore Davis, looking like a very small mustachioed penguin in white tie and tails, glowered at me through his eyeglasses and left me to his "cousin," Mrs. Andrews, who was tastefully attired in purple satin and diamonds. I rather liked Mrs. Andrews. She was a cheerful soul with a genuine, if superficial, interest in Egyptology. We were soon joined by Howard Carter, who had just returned from Kom Ombo and who was dying to ask about the mummy.

It was, as I ought to have expected, the chief topic of conversation. Mrs. Andrews was delighted to get a firsthand account, and since I saw no reason why I should not, I answered her eager questions readily. Before long we were the center of a fascinated group. I managed to ask as many questions as I answered, filing the information away in my capacious memory for future consideration.

It was Mrs. Andrews who saw the newcomers first. "Good heavens," she exclaimed. "The Bellinghams have just come in. I would not have expected him to attend a social function so soon after . . ."

In fact I was not certain what social rules applied to the delayed discovery of one's wife's mummified body. The Colonel was suitably attired in black, but then he always was. The circlet of white bandage around his brow was a new addition.

"What happened to him?" I asked, too surprised to phrase the question more tactfully.

"My dear! Hadn't you heard?" Mrs. Andrews lowered her voice. "He was attacked — violently attacked — last night in Luxor. It has made us all very uneasy. Of course I would never dream of going out alone after dark, but Theo is so brave and daring —"

I did not want to hear her praise her Theo's bravery, so I took the liberty of interrupting. "What time of evening was it?"

"Quite late, I believe. Why he should be abroad at such an hour, and with his daughter, I cannot imagine; but perhaps he finds it difficult to sleep these days. And she has him wound around her little finger. Only look at that frock!"

Dolly was not wearing black. Again, the social conventions were difficult to define, and the dead woman had been — very briefly! — her step-mother. However, she might have chosen a more decorous gown than the azure silk trimmed with silk rosebuds, with a shockingly low neckline. I exchanged meaningful glances with Mrs. Andrews.

Recalling my duties, I moved through the room, making sure the glasses were kept filled and the hors d'oeuvres served. Since I had not greeted the Colonel I made haste to approach him. He was, I thought, equally anxious to talk with me, for he excused himself to his companion and stepped aside.

"Since you know it is not idle curiosity that prompts my inquiry, I will not hesitate to pursue it," I said. "You were not reckless enough, I hope, to leave the safety of the hotel in the hope that your enemy would try to kill you?"

"He has no such intention," was the grim reply. "He wants me to live and suffer. It was Dolly he was after. She . . ." He hesitated, but briefly. "She is young and high-spirited, Mrs. Emerson; that last is a quality we Southerners admire in our ladies. I do not condone her behavior, but I understand it. What drew her out was a note purporting to come from your son."

"Ramses?" I gasped.

"She has taken a girlish fancy to him," the Colonel said with a tolerance I certainly would not have displayed. "After seeing him that day on the terrace of the hotel, in those picturesque garments . . . Please, Mrs. Emerson, do not distress yourself. I asked him a few minutes ago whether he had written her. He denied it, and I believe him."

"Ramses does not lie," I said, more or less accurately.

"It is clear that the message was sent by my enemy. Fortunately I was not asleep when she crept out of her room, and the dragoman I had hired saw her."

"Saiyid? What was he doing on duty at that hour?"

"Carrying out the duties for which I had hired him. Surprising, for an Egyptian," the Colonel added. "The majority of them are not so loyal or so courageous. He had followed Dolly and was trying to persuade her to return when I caught up with them, and had it not been for him I might have gotten more than a bump on the head. He jumped the rascal and held him off until I could draw my knife." Seeing my expression, he smiled grimly. "Yes, Mrs. Emerson, I too have taken to carrying a knife. Scudder was always a cowardly weakling; so long as we meet on equal terms I do not doubt I can deal with him."

"A pity you weren't able to catch him, then."

Bellingham seemed to take this as criticism. He replied coolly, "I was briefly disoriented from the blow on my head."

"Saiyid did not pursue him?"

"Self-preservation is stronger than courage among the lesser breeds, Mrs. Emerson. He had gotten a slight cut across the ribs, but it was not serious."

"You examined the injury?" I inquired sarcastically. I was beginning to take a dislike to the Colonel.

"I? I sent him to the servants' quarters to have it looked after. With a generous pourboire, of course." He looked around. "Where is Dolly?"

"Gone into the garden, I expect," I said, following his gaze and failing, as he had done, to find the girl. "There is no cause for concern here. The garden is walled, and my young people must be with her, for I don't see them either."

Nevertheless I felt a faint stirring of uneasiness — my well-honed sixth sense at work. I decided a breath of fresh air would be just the thing.

Cyrus was justly proud of his little garden, where he grew the hollyhocks and petunias and roses that reminded him of his native heath as well as more exotic blooms permitted by the salubrious climate. In one corner of the enclosure he had constructed a kind of bower surrounded by trellised vines and hibiscus, with a pretty stone bench carved like an ancient sarcophagus. Hearing voices, I made my way thither and was just in time to see Mr. Booghis Tucker Tollington remove his gloves and strike my son across the face with them.

Before I could react, a large hand covered my mouth and a large arm went round my waist and drew me into concealment behind an hibiscus. "Hush, Peabody," Emerson hissed into my ear — half deafening me. "Remain motionless and silent. I would not want to miss a moment of this melodrama."

Young Mr. Tollington was doing his best to create one, but the only person willing to play her role was Dolly. I could not see her face clearly, for the only light, a pretty hanging lantern, shone directly down on the young men and left the others in partial shadow; but the hands clasped at her breast and her little squeaks of alarm were in the best traditions of theatrical heroines. Nefret, seated on the bench, appeared unconcerned, as did David, who was standing behind her.

Ramses had not moved, except for the reflexive jerk of his head. Now he said, in tones of deep disgust, "Oh, for God's sake!"

"Is that all you can say?" Tollington demanded.

"I could say a great deal more. What you are

proposing is not only childish and stupid, it is against the law."

"The code of a gentleman supersedes the law," said Mr. Tollington, trying to sneer. "Obviously you know nothing about that. You did not reply to my first challenge, so I determined to give you a second chance. If you are afraid to fight me —"

"I am afraid of behaving like a damned fool," said Ramses. His altered tone struck a familiar note; though it was nothing at all like the soft purr that marks Emerson's angriest moods, it had the same quality. "Which I may do, if you continue in this vein. Excuse me."

He started toward the vine-enclosed entrance of the little bower, giving the other man a wide berth. Tollington stepped in front of him, barring his way, whereupon Ramses knocked him down.

Emerson had absentmindedly neglected to take his hand away from my mouth. He was laughing soundlessly; the puffs of breath tickled my ear. He drew me farther back into the shrubbery as Ramses stalked out of the bower. Ramses saw us, though; his steps halted for an instant, and then he went on until he reached the terrace, where he stopped to wait for us. His expression was a blend of sheepishness and bravado.

"Get it over with, Mother," he said.

I reached up and straightened his cravat. "Why, my dear, I don't know why you should suppose I am going to scold you. You behaved quite well under the circumstances — for a male person, that is. Men, as I have observed, react

315

quite irrationally to words like 'afraid' and 'coward,' and you are still young enough to be susceptible to foolishness of that sort. I commend you for resisting a challenge which was, as you so rightly pointed out, both illegal and silly. Had he got so far as to propose a particular weapon?"

"Pistols," Ramses said, staring wide-eyed at me. "Er — Mother, I appreciate your approbation and your interest, but all the same, my action was an error. I ought not to have antagonized the fellow."

"True," said Emerson. Studying Ramses thoughtfully, he went on, "He seems bound and determined to antagonize you, though. Well, well, this is not the time nor the place for such a discussion. Here are Nefret and David coming. I suppose Miss Bellingham is wringing her hands over the fallen warrior."

"Not at all," Nefret said. "She was the first to follow Ramses, leaving the fallen warrior to tend his own wound. I *suggested* she return to the house through another door."

Ramses vanished within. Nefret dusted off her hands and looked at me. "What that girl needs," she said, "is a good hard slap."

"You didn't administer it, I hope," I said.

"David was holding my arm."

Emerson chuckled. "Well done, David. Keep tight hold of her; take her inside, and tell Mr. Vandergelt we will be leaving shortly."

Instead of following the children, Emerson said to me, "Ramses was right, you know. Tollington will now be all the more determined to force him to fight."

I said, "You are taking this too seriously, Emerson. Ramses will not be fool enough to allow such a thing. I confess I was surprised to see him lose his temper, though. He has always been as calculating and cool and unemotional as an old philosopher."

"Hmm, well, yes, that was a hopeful sign," Emerson said. "I have always suspected Ramses's feelings run deeper than you suppose. It is high time he began letting them out."

Farewells and thanks took some little time. Having completed my own, I looked round the room for my family. Emerson was waiting for me by the door, rolling his eyes and tapping his foot. Colonel Bellingham was talking to Nefret, his handsome head bent attentively; as I started toward them Ramses appeared, took Nefret's arm, and drew her firmly away.

A number of hired carriages were waiting outside; the drivers and attendants had gathered in a convivial circle, smoking and gossiping as they awaited the return of their employers. Among other familiar faces I recognized that of Saiyid, and an impulse for which I could not then account made me address him.

"*Salaam aleikhum*, Saiyid. I have heard of your loyalty to your master. Well done."

He sprang to his feet and returned my greeting. "I was very brave, Sitt Hakim. The man tried to kill me. If I had not fought like a lion —"

"Yes, you are a hero," Emerson broke in. He knew Saiyid would go on bragging indefinitely if he were not interrupted. Modesty is not a quality admired by Egyptians. (There are times when I find myself in some sympathy with their point of view.)

"I am glad to see your wound does not trouble you," Emerson went on.

Saiyid doubled up and clutched his side. "It burns like fire, Father of Curses. I lost much blood, it poured down my body and ruined my best galabeeyah —"

"For which I am sure the Hawadji reimbursed you," I said with a smile, for it was impossible to take Saiyid's performance seriously. The wound must have been as negligible as Bellingham had claimed.

From Manuscript H:

"Take your shirt off at once," Nefret ordered. "Or I will cut it off."

She had him backed up against the wall, and she was brandishing a pair of long-bladed scissors. He did not doubt she would use them precisely as she had said. There was obviously no help to be got from David, who was watching with his arms folded and a broad grin on his face. Morosely Ramses began undoing the buttons.

"There is no need for this," he insisted. "You ought not be here. Mother will become suspicious if you

retire so early night after night, and I must be in Luxor by — Ouch!"

She had yanked the shirt off one shoulder and down his arm and was examining the cloth wound round his ribs.

"I thought so," she said with a sniff. "What did you use, an old galabeeyah? I suppose neither of you bothered to disinfect the wound either. Sit down in that chair."

Recognizing defeat, Ramses slid his arm out of the other sleeve and tossed the shirt onto the bed. His mother would be sure to notice if it got torn or dirty. "Did you steal that muck from Mother?" he asked, watching Nefret unpack the little bundle of medical supplies.

"I have my own. Something told me," said Nefret, advancing with the scissors, "I would be needing it. Why the devil didn't you come for me last night?"

"I tried," David began.

"That's quite all right, David. I know you did your best. Hmmm. Well, it isn't very deep, but it needs attention. Swear all you like," she added generously, uncorking the bottle of alcohol.

Because she had said he might, he managed not to swear, but the sweat was pouring down his face by the time she finished. "Hold your arms out," she ordered, and began winding bandages around his ribs.

"You are as bad as Mother," Ramses said resignedly. "Sadists, both of you. That is too tight."

"It has to be tight, to hold the pad in place. Do you want to get blood on another shirt and have

Aunt Amelia scold you? Stop breathing so hard."

Both her arms were around him and her smooth cheek rested on his chest. She tied the ends of the bandage in a neat knot, sat back on her heels, and smiled at him. "There you are, my boy. You took it like a hero."

" 'J'ai fait mieux depuis,' " said Ramses before he could stop himself.

"What did you say?" Nefret asked.

"A meaningless quotation. Thank you, my girl. Now get home before you are missed."

"Oh, no." She shook her head. "I am going with you. Obviously you cannot be trusted to take care of yourself."

"I will be with him tonight, Nefret," David said. "You can trust me, I hope. This would not have happened if the Professor had not forbade me to leave the house last night."

"It would not have happened if Bellingham hadn't interfered," Ramses snapped. "I had Scudder on the ground, sans knife, when the gallant Colonel pulled me off him and —"

"Aha," said Nefret "So it was the Colonel who wounded you."

"He claimed he could not tell which of us was which."

"In galabeeyahs and headcloths you did look alike," Nefret pointed out. "And it was dark."

"To a man like Bellingham all natives look alike," Ramses said. "Even in broad daylight. In this case I must give him the benefit of the doubt, because he did his damnedest to kill me — or Scudder, as he

320

believed me to be. He is in excellent condition for a man his age, and he knows how to use a knife — underhand and up through the —"

"Don't," Nefret said, grimacing.

Ramses shrugged. "I wasn't expecting it, at least not from him. I managed to slip aside, but by the time I had recovered my balance Scudder had vanished. Next time I will make certain Bellingham is not following me."

"Surely there won't be a next time," Nefret said. "Even that empty-headed little ninny will know, if she receives another such message, that it did not come from you."

"I made that quite clear to her this evening," Ramses said, his face hardening. "No; Scudder will have to think of something else next time."

"Not tonight; not so soon afterwards. The Colonel will watch her closely tonight." Nefret put her hand on his arm. "You need to rest. Don't go. Please."

Ramses looked down at the graceful little hand that curled confidingly around his forearm. Her skin, tanned to a golden brown, was several shades lighter than his. "Leave off, Nefret, womanly tenderness is not your style. You are more convincing when you threaten. Short of physical restraint, I can think of no way of preventing you from following me, so you win. I will stay here."

"Give me your word?"

"You have it."

"Mind you keep to it," Nefret said coolly. "If you ever broke your sworn word, I would never trust you again."

"Don't worry, Nefret," David said. "I won't let him go off alone again. I should have been with him last night. A brother does not leave a brother's back unguarded."

"I need you here to be my eyes and ears," Ramses said in rapid Arabic. "How else will I know what has happened in my absence?"

"Nefret will tell you," said that young woman in the same language. "If you admit her to your councils. In other words," she went on in English, "I will keep you abreast of what the Professor and Aunt Amelia are up to, if you keep your part of the bargain."

"What bargain?" Ramses demanded. "Curse it, Nefret —"

"To tell me everything." Nefret sat cross-legged on the bed, reached into her pocket, and pulled out the tin of cigarettes. "And don't bother spouting Arabic in the hope of confusing me, I have been talking it all summer with the Professor. Now do you want to know what the man from the American consulate told us this afternoon?"

"You are working that girl too hard, Emerson," I said after Nefret had gone off to bed, hiding her yawns prettily behind her hand.

CHAPTER NINE

High-minded individuals are more dangerous than criminals. They can always find hypocritical excuses for committing acts of violence.

"I dreamed of the cat Bastet last night," I said.

Ramses looked up from his plate of eggs and bacon but did not respond. It was Nefret who asked interestedly, "What was she doing?"

"Hunting mice — or so I supposed." Musingly I continued, "I was home at Amarna House, and I was searching for something, something I wanted very badly, though I could not tell you what it was. You know how vague dreams can be. I went from room to room, looking under sofa cushions and behind pieces of furniture, with a growing sense of urgency; and wherever I went, there was Bastet engaged in some urgent search of her own. She paid no attention to me, nor I to her, yet I sensed we were bent upon the same quest, looking for the same undefined but vitally important thing."

"Did you find it?" David asked.

"No; but Bastet found her mouse. It was not a real mouse, for it glittered and sparkled, and it was attached to a long shining chain. Bastet was bringing it to me when I woke."

Emerson was watching me with a singularly sour expression. He does not believe in the portentous nature of dreams, but on at least one occasion he had been forced to acknowledge the terrible accuracy of one of mine. This was not one of that sort; the explanation of it was ludicrously simple for a student of psychology like myself. It was truth I sought, in sleep as in waking — the truth of Mrs. Bellingham's tragic death, still hidden from me by metaphorical sofa cushions. I did not mention this because Emerson does not believe in psychology either.

"Perhaps it is a sign of good fortune," I said cheerfully. "Was it not you, Ramses, who said that to dream of a large cat meant good luck?"

"Not precisely," said my son in his most repressive voice.

"He was quoting from the dream papyrus," David explained. "It is a curious text; some of the interpretations are sensible, and others make no sense at all."

"Really," I said. "I would like to have a look at it. Do we possess a copy?"

It may have been my guilty conscience that made me see suspicion in Ramses's steady dark gaze — though I cannot imagine why I should have felt guilty. I had only gone to his room to collect clothing for the wash, and I had put everything back exactly where I found it.

"By a strange coincidence," he said, "I do. You may have it whenever you like, Mother, but it is not one of your fairy tales, you know."

"I know that. I haven't had time to begin translating a new text this year. At first I was busy helping Evelyn with the Tetisheri volumes, and then there was my article for the *PSBA*. . . ." I stopped myself. Excessive and unnecessary explanations are a sure sign of an uneasy conscience, as our great national bard Shakespeare knew.

"It is on the desk in my room," Ramses said. "And at your disposal. Excuse me for mentioning this, Mother, but you and Father appear a trifle weary this morning. It is important for you to get your rest, you know."

He was developing quite a pretty talent for sarcasm. I did not allow myself to be provoked.

"We were discussing the case," I explained calmly. "After the disclosures made to us yesterday afternoon by the American vice-consul —"

"Peabody," Emerson said warningly.

Nefret laughed. "Professor, darling, if you are trying to protect me, don't bother. I heard everything the gentleman said yesterday."

"And you have passed the information on to the boys, I suppose," I said.

"Of course. We confide fully in one another. Don't we, Ramses?"

Ramses's chair creaked as he shifted his weight. "Sir, I understand your fatherly concern for my — er — dear sister, but believe me, it is impossible to keep her out of this business. We have discussed it too. Should we not combine our ideas and information, in the hope of bringing the matter to a swift conclusion?"

"Well said, Ramses." Nefret smiled at him. "What did you and the Professor decide last night, Aunt Amelia?"

Thus appealed to, I cleared my throat and began.

"We now know where Scudder has been all these years — living in Luxor, disguised as an Egyptian."

"There you go again, Peabody," Emerson said disagreeably. "We do not know that. It is a reasonable assumption, but not a fact."

"Then let us assume it," Nefret said. "It is at least a logical starting point. What do we know about the man that might help us identify him?"

With a sheepish glance at me, Emerson admitted he had telegraphed Cairo for a description of Dutton Scudder. It had been obtained from Colonel Bellingham five years previous and was still on file, since the case had never been officially closed.

"It is not very useful, is it?" I said, frowning over the paper he grudgingly produced. " 'Medium height and build, brown hair, fair complexion.' All those features can easily be altered. What about eye color?"

"The Colonel did not know," Emerson said.

"No scars, birthmarks, or other distinctive characteristics?"

"The Colonel did not know."

"The Colonel would probably not have noticed if Scudder had had ears like a donkey's," Ramses said. "The man was only a servant, after all. I suppose his is the only description the police obtained."

"Yes. The police did have some information about Scudder's background. His story of having lived in Egypt was true; his father was a clerk at the American consulate in Cairo between 1887 and 1893. One employee remembered him, but could add nothing to Bellingham's description."

"That makes our assumption that he is disguised as an Egyptian even more likely," I argued. "Officials attempt to keep their children carefully isolated from the 'natives,' but a curious young lad, as Scudder was then, might well have picked up something of the language and customs."

"Including the ancient art of mummification?" Ramses inquired.

"You did." Ramses acknowledged the riposte with a faint smile, and I went on, "We have gone as far as we can with that approach; the rest is mere speculation. There is little hope of anyone in Luxor remembering the advent of a stranger within the past five years. We will have to deduce his present identity."

"And how do you propose to go about that?" Emerson inquired mildly.

"He must be a dragoman or a guide or a fellah."

"Oh, well done, Peabody! That cuts the number of suspects down to six or seven thousand."

"Have you anything sensible to contribute, Emerson, or are you just going to sit there smoking and being sarcastic?"

"Neither," said Emerson. "I am going to work. I presume you are off to Luxor, Peabody."

"It is absolutely necessary for one of us to reexamine the body," I said. "Stop scowling, Emerson, you know we agreed last night that it should be done. The services are tomorrow morning, and after that the body will be inaccessible."

"Hmph," said Emerson. "All right, Peabody. Perhaps you can bully Willoughby into letting you have another look, but I would not count on it. He has no business doing any such thing. Is anyone else coming with me to the Valley?"

Ramses started and glanced at Nefret, who was sitting next to him. "Er — Father — I meant to ask earlier . . . May I borrow Nefret and David for a few days? I want to get photographs of certain reliefs at Luxor Temple so I can begin working on those texts. Given the rate at which the monuments are deteriorating, and the importance of —"

"I thought you were planning to concentrate on Deir el Bahri," Emerson broke in.

"Yes, I was. I have been. But M. Naville will be starting work there shortly, and you and he do not get on, and I have finished with the photographs we took last year, and the Luxor Temple —"

"Yes, yes," Emerson said. "There is no reason

why David and Nefret cannot be spared, for a day or two. I would be the last to question your candor, Ramses, but do you really intend to photograph at Luxor Temple or is that an excuse to run off to the clinic with your mother?"

"I do intend to photograph," Ramses said firmly. "But, now that you mention it, Father, perhaps someone ought to go with her."

We were still arguing about it when one of the servants came in with a note that had just been delivered. Since I was losing the argument — it was all the rest of them against me — I was not averse to a change of subject. The note was not addressed to me, however. Assuming an expression of courteous inquiry, I passed it on to Nefret.

Like myself, Nefret immediately identified the sender. Wrinkling her nose, she remarked, "She must buy attar of roses by the quart. What the devil do you suppose she has to say to me?"

"Open it," I suggested. "And don't swear."

"I beg your pardon, Aunt Amelia," Nefret murmured. "Well, what do you think of this? It is an invitation to take luncheon with her and her father."

"You mean to decline it, of course," Ramses said at once.

Nefret raised a delicate eyebrow. "Why should I?"

Emerson tossed his serviette on the table and rose. "Because I say so. No, don't argue with me, young lady. I depend on you, Peabody, to make the children behave themselves — and on them to make you behave yourself. Good Gad, there ought to be safety in numbers, but with this family one cannot depend on anything. Mind what I say, all of you!"

Nefret went off to collect her photographic equipment and the rest of us dispersed on similar errands. Conversation was of necessity spasmodic until we reached the dahabeeyah; it is difficult to talk while riding at a quick trot. As soon as we were on board the felucca the argument resumed. One of the arguments, I should say.

"I cannot understand why the Professor made such a fuss about my lunching with the Bellinghams," Nefret grumbled. "It is a heaven-sent opportunity to ask them some important questions. If you give me permission, Aunt Amelia, he cannot object, can he?"

"Well," I began.

"Out of the question," said Ramses, glowering. "Mother will not give you permission."

I said, "Ramses, kindly allow me —"

"Why not?" Nefret glowered back. She did not glower as well as he did, since her eyebrows were not designed for it.

"Because he is —"

"Ramses!" I shouted.

Silence ensued, but the glowering did not abate.

"I will make the decision," I said. "And I have not yet decided. I will have done so by the time we reach the clinic. You can send a response from there, Nefret."

I gave myself over to reflection. I was not entirely certain of the reason behind Ramses's objections, but I had several of my own. Was I reading too much into the Colonel's admiring looks and gallant speeches? It was unlikely that Dolly would seek Nefret's company on her own account. The little note had been dispatched at what would be, for that spoiled young woman, an impossibly early hour.

However, Nefret's point was well taken. An opportunity for interrogating the Bellinghams should not be neglected.

I had, as I had promised, reached my decision by the time the carriage drew up at the door of the clinic, and I announced it in tones that allowed no debate.

"You may write to Miss Bellingham accepting her invitation, Nefret. We will go with you to the hotel. The Colonel will almost certainly ask us to join him. If Miss Dolly has something she wishes to discuss with you in private, she will unquestionably be able to find a way of doing so."

"Unquestionably," Ramses muttered.

Notepaper and pen and ink having been obtained, Nefret wrote her acceptance, and we saw it dispatched by one of the servants. We were then joined by Dr. Willoughby.

I had greater difficulty than I had anticipated persuading him to allow me to inspect the body. In fact, he flatly refused, on the grounds that

Colonel Bellingham had forbidden an autopsy and that the lady now rested in her closed coffin in his little chapel. I pointed out that I was not proposing to perform an autopsy, and that a closed coffin can be opened. Willoughby countered. . . .

But it would serve no purpose to describe the absurd arguments he presented or my logically overwhelming responses. In the end he gave in, of course.

"I must inform the Colonel you were here," he said.

"Certainly. We are lunching with him; I will tell him myself that we came by to pay our respects."

Willoughby gave me a look of mingled consternation and admiration. "Mrs. Emerson, there are times when you leave me speechless. I can deny you nothing."

"Few people can," I replied.

The chapel was a small building opening off an inner courtyard. Willoughby had tactfully avoided the religious symbols of a particular denomination; the room was furnished with a few chairs and a nicely draped table on which reposed a large leather-bound Bible. Heavy velvet hangings and dim lights added to the atmosphere of quiet reverence, but they rendered the room hot and stuffy. The scent of flowers hung heavy on the air. The coffin, covered with a linen pall, reposed on a low platform behind the table. It was a plain wooden box, with only the necessary metal fittings to ornament it, but the carpentry was quite neatly done and the brass had been polished till it shone like gold.

The solemn atmosphere of the place affected all of us, and Nefret most of all, but she resolutely refused to follow my suggestion that she take a chair and leave the business to me and the lads.

"It is for a good purpose, is it not?" she whispered. "For her sake?"

I murmured a reassurance. It would not be an easy task, however. The face was covered and a decent winding sheet enveloped the body. When I drew this aside I was shocked to discover that she still wore the flimsy silk undergarments. They seemed hideously inappropriate, but after all, it was not my place to determine what a devoted husband might consider proper. Nerving myself to proceed, I bared the sunken breast and took from my bag the probe I had brought with me.

"Just a moment, Mother," Ramses said. "There may be an easier way."

It did not take long to accomplish what we had come for. When we had put everything to rights I paused to say a little prayer. The children stood by the coffin in silence, their heads bowed, but I would not care to commit myself as to whether they were praying.

Coming out of that dusty oppressive gloom was like rising in the bark of Amon-Ra from the dark waters of the Egyptian underworld. We hastened to the waiting carriage. The sun was high and hot, but groves of tall date palms cast a pleasant shade over the dusty road. We had passed the English cemetery and were nearing the hotel before anyone spoke. The speaker was myself.

"I will mention to the Colonel that we visited the chapel this morning."

Pushing his hat to the back of his head, Ramses gave me a questioning look. "Mother, do you believe the Colonel will ask the rest of us to join him?"

"I don't see how he can do otherwise, Ramses. It would be ungentlemanly not to."

Ramses's lips compressed. "I would propose a little wager were it not for the fact that my winning it would cause David embarrassment."

"What do you mean?" I asked, genuinely puzzled.

"It doesn't matter," David said quickly.

"It does," Ramses said. "Mother, are you not aware of the fact that the Colonel would not invite David to sit down at table with him?"

Nefret gasped. "You cannot be serious, Ramses."

"I assure you I am entirely serious. From the beginning he has ignored David as he would a servant; he has never addressed him directly, nor taken his hand. He has refrained from open discourtesy — though he would not consider it such — since he has met us thus far on our terms and on our territory, but he won't proffer an invitation."

"I can't believe he would be so rude."

"I may be mistaken. Do you want to take the chance?"

"No," I said slowly, remembering the Colonel's history. "It would give me great pleasure to — er — set him straight, but not if it would mean hurting David."

"Why didn't you say something before?" Nefret demanded, her cheeks flaming. "Do you suppose I would go where David was not welcome?"

I thought for a moment David was going to cry. Egyptians see nothing unmanly about tears. His English upbringing won out, but his smile was a little tremulous. "Please don't distress yourselves. What do the opinions of men like that matter, when I have such friends as you?"

Nefret looked as if she were on the verge of tears too — tears of rage, in her case. "I shan't go."

"That would be foolish," David said earnestly. "You are condemning him without so much as a trial, and anyhow, it does not affect the reason you decided to accept in the first place. Here is your chance to get the better of him, eh?"

"David is right," I said. "Do not scruple to turn his erroneous assumptions against him, Nefret; I do not doubt he has a low opinion of women too. Gallantry is often a cloak for contempt. You can trick him into confidences a man could not win."

A calculating smile replaced Nefret's furious frown. "What do you want me to find out?"

We discussed the matter. When we got out of

the carriage there was a little scuffle over which of us was to take David's arm. It amused him a great deal, so we were all smiles when we entered the hotel.

Colonel Bellingham was waiting in the lobby. Ramses was taking no chances on seeing his friend subjected to insult; ignoring the Colonel, he led David directly to the desk of the concierge, where they meant to leave the camera equipment they had carried with them. Bellingham advanced toward us and kissed my hand and Nefret's, while she simpered at him in a way that would have roused the direst suspicions in a more intelligent man.

The Colonel took no notice of the boys, though he must have seen them, nor did he invite me to join his party. He offered Nefret his arm, and I said, "We will meet you here in two hours' time, Nefret."

The Colonel gave me an approving nod. Well, of course, I thought; a proper young lady does not go about the streets unescorted. How he could cling to the delusion that Nefret was a proper young lady after seeing her in boots and trousers I could not imagine; but social conventions are so intrinsically silly that an inconsistency or two hardly matters.

The boys and I proceeded into the dining saloon, where Nefret and the Colonel had joined Dolly at a table near the long windows. Before the maître d' could reach us, another individual hurried up.

"Mrs. Emerson!" Donald Fraser seized my hand and shook it enthusiastically. "Are you lunching? Will you do us the pleasure of joining us, or are you otherwise engaged?"

"Only to Ramses and David," I replied, observing that Enid had risen from her chair and was beckoning to me.

"I included them, of course," Donald said with a hearty laugh. "No way of telling in our mother tongue, is there? Deuced difficult language in some ways, but French and German . . ."

He continued to babble cheerfully and ignorantly about linguistics as he led us to join the others. It was flattering to be received with such universal appreciation. Enid's face shone, and even Mrs. Jones appeared pleased to see me. Though she was dressed with her usual modish neatness in a gray serge skirt and braid-trimmed Zouave jacket, her face was pink with sunburn, and one hand was bandaged.

Donald insisted we share their bottle of wine. He monopolized the conversation, teasing Ramses in a good-natured fashion about their earlier adventures. It was difficult to believe that this amiable, unimaginative man was in the grip of such a strange obsession. I tried to catch Enid's eye, but she was not looking at me. Leaning across David, who was between us, I addressed a carefully innocuous comment to Mrs. Jones.

"I hope you are not neglecting to wear your hat. The sun is very hard on fair skin such as yours."

The lady rolled her eyes expressively. "My dear Mrs. Emerson, I have taken to going about veiled like a Muslim female, but even that does not suffice. As for my poor hands . . . ! I have ruined three pair of gloves and lost a good square foot of skin from my palms. Have you any suggestions?"

"One or two," I said in a meaningful manner.

Mrs. Jones smiled her feline smile. "Your advice, Mrs. Emerson, would be greatly appreciated."

We had gone as far as we could with meaningful glances and subtle hints. I was wondering how I could get the lady to myself for a less subtle, more meaningful chat when Donald cut loose.

It was Ramses who precipitated the explosion. He may have meant only to change the subject; a young man newly conscious of his dignity does not enjoy being reminded of childish escapades. However, knowing Ramses as I do, I believe he had another motive.

The question sounded innocent enough; it was only a polite inquiry as to where they had been that morning.

"The Valley of the Queens," Donald said. "Mrs. Whitney-Jones insisted we explore the Kings' Valley first, and of course she is the expert, but I have felt all along that a princess's tomb would be in the Valley of the Queens. I mean, it does seem logical, don't it?"

"It does," Ramses agreed. He glanced at Enid,

whose wide eyes were fixed imploringly on his face, and I thought he nodded, almost imperceptibly. "The terrain is difficult, though, especially for the ladies."

"So I told Enid," Donald said. "But she would come."

Again Mrs. Jones made an expressive face, unseen by anyone but me. I almost liked the woman at that moment, but my sympathy for her suffering was tempered by the recollection that she had brought it on herself.

Ramses continued the conversation as coolly as if it made sense. "Signor Schiaparelli and his crew have recently discovered several interesting tombs in the Valley of the Queens, but there are no roads, no paths, no useful maps. Locating a particular tomb in that wilderness —"

"Ah, but that is where we have the advantage, you see! To be sure, the princess's description of the location has been vague thus far. As she says, earthquakes, floods, and the passage of time itself have changed the landscape almost beyond recognition. I feel confident, however, that —" Donald broke off as the waiter, having served the ladies, placed a platter of rare roast beef in front of him. When he attacked it with knife and fork, blood puddled the plate. "I say!" he exclaimed as if the idea had just struck him. "You could be of great assistance to us, Ramses, you and your parents. You were a bookish little chap, always ranting on about mummies and tombs and so on; I expect you know that area quite well, eh?"

"You can hardly expect him — them — to take time from their work in order to act as our guides, Donald," Enid said.

I was pleased to observe that she had taken my advice to heart. Instead of scolding him, she had uttered only a mild reproof, her features wreathed in a smile.

"No, no." Donald motioned the waiter to refill his wine glass. "Though of course I would be delighted if they would. What I was about to propose was that they join us this evening. Don't know why the idea never struck me before this. Not even you diehard diggers work at night; isn't that right, Mrs. Emerson? You could speak directly with the princess and ask her for directions!"

Mrs. Jones choked on a morsel of fish.

After the Frasers had retired to their rooms for the afternoon rest that is customary in Egypt, the boys and I retreated to a corner of the lobby. We had left Nefret and the Bellinghams still at table. Nefret was smiling and dimpling as she listened to what appeared to be a monologue delivered by the Colonel; Dolly had apparently fallen asleep sitting up.

"I don't see what else I could have done but agree," I said defensively.

"Quite," said Ramses. The confounded mustache shadowed his mouth, but if he had hoped thereby to make it more difficult for me to read his expression, the attempt had failed. The ends of the mustache twitched when the muscles at the corners of his mouth moved. This expression was unquestionably smug.

"That was what you intended," I exclaimed. "Ramses, you are becoming very devious."

"More than I used to be? If we are going to carry out the scheme we discussed with Mr. Vandergelt the other evening, a preliminary reconnaissance is essential. That fact must have occurred to you."

"It had not occurred to me," David admitted. "But it makes good sense. I admit I am curious. I have never attended that sort of performance before. Do you think you can persuade the Professor to come?"

Ramses shook his head. "We ought rather persuade him not to come. You know Father; if his temper does not get the better of him, his sense of humor will. Mrs. Jones will have a hard enough time, even with the rest of us cooperating as best we can. Mr. Fraser will expect wonders and revelations."

I thought the same, and when I looked toward the lift I was not surprised to see Mrs. Jones come hurrying toward us. "I hoped you would still be here," she exclaimed. "For heaven's sake, give me some idea of what approach you mean to take so that I can prepare for it. Unless . . . unless after all you have determined to expose me?"

I hastened to explain. Her resolute expression did not change, but she let out a little sigh, and when I went on to tell her about the princess's epiphany (without specifiying the identity of the actress who would play the part), a smile of genuine amusement curled her lips. She looked more than ever like a complacent cat.

"I must say that is an ingenious idea. I think I can arrange a suitable stage setting. Give me a day or two to collect the props. I will drop a few hints tonight, to prepare him. Leave it to me; I can manage quite well, so long as you follow my cues." Glancing toward the lift, she added ironically, "You are much in demand today. There is Mrs. Fraser, bent, I do not doubt, on an errand similar to mine. I had better go."

Enid had seen her. She stopped, looking irresolutely at us. "Oh, good Gad," I said irritably. "We have not finished making the arrangements for this evening. Go to Enid, Ramses, and try to distract her for a few minutes."

"Yes, Mother," Ramses said.

David rose as well. I could never understand how the two of them communicated; they seemed to understand one another without the need for speech.

Mrs. Jones had a mind almost as well organized and logical as my own. It did not take us long to settle on a tentative scenario for the evening — subject, as we both knew, to unexpected developments.

"Improvisation," I remarked, "is a talent essential to people in your — er — profession. Never fear, I will keep pace with you."

"I don't doubt you will." Another of those catlike smiles curved her lips. "Should you ever tire of archaeology, Mrs. Emerson, you would succeed quite well in my — er — profession."

She took her leave of me, walking toward the front entrance and the gardens in order to avoid encountering Enid, who was still deep in conversation with Ramses. David was not with them; I looked round the lobby but saw no sign of him.

Two hours had passed since we entered the hotel. I decided that Nefret had suffered long enough and was about to go and fetch her when I saw her leaving the dining salon on Colonel Bellingham's arm. Dolly had fallen a step or two behind them; as Bellingham led Nefret toward me, the girl slipped away, as smoothly as a prowling cat. Bowing gracefully, the Colonel expressed his appreciation for the pleasure of my ward's company.

"I feel like a parcel that has just been delivered," Nefret said as the Colonel walked away. "Where are Ramses and David?"

"I don't know where David has got to, but Ramses has just been pounced upon," I replied. "Shall we rescue him or leave him to escape without assistance?"

"He has done nothing to deserve Dolly," Nefret said. "Avaunt and tallyho!"

Appearances are often deceiving. Had I not known better I would have supposed Ramses was the bone of contention between two foolish females. Standing close on either side of him, they were exchanging fixed smiles and frosty courtesies while Ramses looked straight ahead with a particularly petrified expression. Seeing us, he found the excuse he needed; he extricated himself with more celerity than good manners and came striding to meet us.

"Go on, run," Nefret urged. "We will be the rear guard."

"Very amusing," said Ramses. He did not slow his steps, however.

"Did you explain matters to Enid?" I asked, trotting to keep up with Ramses.

"Yes."

"Wait, we have forgot the cameras," Nefret said, trying to catch his arm.

"David has them. He will meet us at the temple."

He hailed one of the waiting carriages and bundled us in. Not until the vehicle was in motion did he address Nefret. "What did you learn from Bellingham?"

"That he is the most pompous bore in creation." Nefret took off her hat and ran both hands through her hair. "He talks like an etiquette book. One can't help feeling sorry for him, though. I mentioned that we had stopped by the chapel this morning to pay our respects, and he was so pleased and grateful, I felt guilty."

"Hmph," said Ramses. "What did he say about —"

"First," Nefret said firmly, "tell me what went on at your luncheon party. I saw you with the

Frasers and that woman, and I was dying of curiosity. Have you set a date for my performance as Princess Tasherit?"

"No," I said, giving Ramses a little nudge to keep him from challenging her assumption, as he was obviously about to do. "But we are engaged to them this evening, in order to be introduced to the princess."

"Excellent!" Nefret cried. "We need to know how it is done before we can make our final plans. It was clever of you to think of that, Aunt Amelia."

"It was Ramses's idea," I said.

"Then it was clever of you, my boy." She took his hand and gave it a little squeeze.

The carriage had come to a halt in front of the temple. Under M. Maspero's vigorous leadership the Department of Antiquities had swept away the clutter of medieval and modern buildings that had once disfigured the magnificent ruin, leaving only the small picturesque mosque of Abu'l Haggag. Before us rose the colonnade of the Amenhotep III court, its papyrus columns and architraves almost intact; the slanting afternoon sunlight warmed the limestone to pale gold and outlined the deep-cut, elegantly shaped hieroglyphs in shadow. Ramses pulled his hand from Nefret's and jumped out, directing the driver in Arabic to take the ladies on to the landing.

"*Ukaf*, driver!" Nefret said sharply. "What are you up to now, Ramses? I thought you wanted me to take photographs."

"David can manage the photographs," Ramses said. "You and Mother go —"

"David is not here yet." Lifting her skirts, she scrambled agilely out of the carriage and stood beside him.

"Really, Ramses, you are becoming very high-handed," I said. "Nefret and I will both help you with the photography. The light is perfect at this time of day. But where is David? I thought he had come on ahead."

Ramses admitted defeat with a shrug and a hand extended to assist me from the carriage. "He must be waiting inside."

The main entrance to the temple, by the great pylon, had been closed, so we entered from the road and went directly to the court of Amen-hotep. This part of the temple was the oldest, dating from the Eighteenth Dynasty, later additions having been made by that ubiquitous pharaoh Ramses II. I presumed that his modern namesake meant to begin with the older (and, in the opinion of myself and other experts, more beautiful) reliefs and hieroglyphic texts, which he admitted was the case.

"The colonnade south of the court has particularly interesting reliefs, depicting the procession of the sacred barks of the gods from Karnak to Luxor Temple," he explained in his pedantic manner. "They ought to be copied as soon as possible; the upper portion has already perished and the rest is deteriorating daily. It will be necessary to photograph at various times of day, since different portions of the wall are in shadow at different times."

Her head tipped back, Nefret walked slowly along between the row of massive columns. There were fourteen of them, each over forty feet high. We were alone except for a few of the barefoot, turbanned "guides" who infest the ruins; Luxor Temple is less popular with tourists than the monumental ruins of Karnak, though to my mind it is far more beautiful and harmonious. Except for murmured greetings and nods, the fellows did not approach us. They knew who we were.

We had been there for some time before David appeared, hurrying into the colonnade from the direction of the court. He had obviously not expected to see me and Nefret, for he checked his advance momentarily before coming on and beginning to apologize.

"I stopped to talk with — er — one of my cousins," he explained, unstrapping the bag he carried.

I would have thought nothing of it had he simply mentioned a name. David had relations all over the area, from Gurneh to Karnak. Those who were not in our employ worked at various trades, some as guides and dragomen, some at less socially acceptable occupations. David's reticence and the haste with which he and Ramses began setting up the photographic equipment roused my suspicions, and this time I observed the silent exchange of glances and nods that betokened a question asked and an answer received.

The shadows were lengthening, so we made haste to take as many exposures as possible. The same views would be taken again at other times of day, for each shift in the light brought out slightly different details. With a flexible rule the precise location of the camera was measured and recorded, so that it could be duplicated on another occasion. It was a slow, painstaking process, and rather tedious. We had been at work less than two hours when I turned my ankle jumping down from a statue base. It did not inconvenience me in the slightest, but I felt obliged to point out that time was getting on and that we were due back in Luxor by half-past eight.

I believe Ramses would not scruple to take advantage of my imminent demise for his own purposes. "I say, Mother, you look a bit done in," he said solicitously. "Nefret, will you help her back to the carriage? I told the driver to wait. David and I will pack up and join you shortly."

Nefret gave me a long look and solemnly offered me the support of her arm. I took it and limped away with her. Once we were out of sight in the adjoining court, we turned to one another in mutual suspicion.

"Wait here," Nefret said in a low voice.

"My limp was exaggerated," I explained in the same soft tones. "Proceed. I will follow."

The place might have been designed for spies. Each rounded column was large enough to conceal not one but two or more individuals of slender girth, and the shadows under the architraves were darkening. When we peered round the pylonned entrance we saw that the camera bags, packed with more haste than care, lay abandoned behind a pillar. There was no one in sight, not even a squatting custodian.

"Curse it," said Nefret. "Where have they gone?"

"The other way, obviously, into the court of Ramses II. Perhaps they only want to have a look. There is an interesting little chapel built by Thutmose III —"

"Ha," Nefret said.

She proceeded slowly, gliding from the shelter of one pillar to that of the next. But before we reached the end of the colonnade a cry and the sound of a shuddering crash made the need for caution unnecessary and — to anxious hearts — impossible. Nefret began to run. She was fleeter than I — because of my twisted ankle — and by the time I caught her up she was on her knees beside David, who was sitting on the ground, rubbing his shoulder and looking dazed. Next to him lay several good-sized fragments of red granite. The largest was approximately a foot long. It was part of a statue's head; one carved eye appeared to be staring accusingly at Ramses, who stood beside David.

"Damnation!" said Ramses. "He's broken it!"

The stone head had not struck David; he had fallen rather heavily, landing on his left shoulder, when Ramses pushed him out of the way. He insisted it was only bruised, and the agility with which he moved bore out his claim. Ramses insisted on carrying the camera cases, however. He hustled us out of the temple and into the carriage without giving us a chance to ask questions.

Nefret was obviously biding her time. Lips pinched and brow furrowed, she waited until we were on board the felucca before she burst out, "Ramses, you —"

"Please. Not in front of Mother," Ramses said.

"You lied to me! You promised —"

"Not," Ramses repeated with even greater emphasis, "in front of Mother. Look here, I fully intended to tell you — both of you — Father too — all about it. Matters did not quite work out as I had hoped."

"Now, children, don't quarrel," I said. "I take it, Ramses, that you had made an assignation with someone, through David — that is why he was so late, he had been delivering your message. Was it Colonel Bellingham you wanted to see, or that young man with the unfortunate name?"

"I told you it was a waste of time trying to deceive Aunt Amelia," David said. "She always knows everything."

"Not knowledge, but logical deduction," I corrected. "The stone head — it is a pity it was broken, I remember it as a fine example of Eighteenth Dynasty sculpture — was dropped or thrown from above, possibly from the top of the little shrine. None of the women with whom we are acquainted could have managed it, so your attacker must have been male. You must have had some reason to assume the meeting would not be cordial or you would not have been sufficiently alert to observe the missile in time to avoid it. The only persons —"

"Yes, Mother," said Ramses in the same tone Emerson sometimes employs when I get the better of him in a discussion. He went on, "You need not elaborate, I follow your reasoning. It is, of course, absolutely correct — so far as it goes. I did send a message to Mr. Tollington, suggesting that we meet and try to resolve our differences. I proposed an out-of-the-way place, since I did not want to risk being interrupted by Miss Bellingham; her presence seems to destroy what few brains the poor chap possesses. But —" Seeing I was about to speak, he raised his voice. "But that does not mean Tollington was our attacker. He may not even have received my letter; he was not at the hotel when David left it there."

"Dropping rocks on people's heads is not the sort of thing one expects of a gentleman," I agreed. "The obvious suspect, I suppose, is Dutton Scudder. He may bear a grudge because you prevented him from carrying Dolly off that night in Cairo. Really, Ramses, you are collecting enemies almost as rapidly as your father. Can you think of anyone else who might want to damage you?"

"I can," said Nefret.

That put a damper, so to speak, upon the conversation. No one spoke again until the boat reached the landing, where Ahmet was waiting with the horses. Nefret went at once to greet them, and I gave Ramses a little nudge.

"Go and make your peace with your sister. You are getting too old for this sort of nonsense, and," I added with a severe look at him, "for these secretive habits of yours."

"Yes, Mother," said Ramses.

Like his father, Ramses has the habit of leaving bits of his clothing strewn around the landscape. He had removed his coat and tie as soon as we left the hotel. As he started off his tie fell from the pocket of his coat, which he had tossed over one shoulder. I picked it up.

"How is your ankle?" David asked.

"Aching a bit. We could both do with a splash of arnica."

The sun had begun its final descent and the lovely rich light, a light I have seen only in Egypt, cast a glamour over the scene and the faces of my son and daughter.

It was almost like a miming play, for they were far enough distant so that I could not hear what they were saying. They stood close together. Ramses was doing the talking; arms folded and face averted, Nefret tapped her little foot and did not respond at first. Then she looked up at him and spoke rapidly, her hands moving in graceful gestures. He broke in; she interrupted him.

It did not appear they were getting on at all well. I had started toward them when another actor made his appearance on the scene. Risha had become impatient; he had been waiting for some hours and felt a dignified reminder would not be out of place. He came with his delicate catlike walk and pushed his head between them.

Nefret burst out laughing. She threw her arm over the stallion's arched neck and I heard her say, "He has better manners than either of us! Pax, Ramses?"

He did not reply in words. Picking her up, he lifted her into the saddle and then turned to me; but David had already assisted me to mount. We made quite a merry little party as we rode off together, for Nefret's nature was as naturally sunny as it was quick to anger.

I was pleased not to have to deal with the children's bad tempers. Emerson's temper was worse than all of theirs combined, and I knew he was not going to like what I had to tell him. Any of it!

Emerson is constantly surprising me. (That is an excellent quality in a husband, if I may be permitted a slight digression. A man who is absolutely predictable is predictably boring.) The first surprise of the afternoon was that he was already at the house, bathed, changed, and waiting, when we got there. He did not chastise us for being late; he did not reproach us for failing to assist him in his excavation; he did not even tell us, in exquisitely tedious detail, all about the day's work. So extraordinary was this forbearance that once we had settled ourselves comfortably none of us knew what to say.

A gleam of amusement warmed Emerson's brilliant blue eyes as he studied each of us in turn. "It must be even worse than I had anticipated," he said mildly. "You had better begin, Peabody; what, of all the things you have to tell me about, will I dislike most?"

"The séance, I expect," I said.

Emerson took out his pipe. "When?"

"This evening."

"Ah." Emerson proceeded to fill and light his pipe. Then he said, "Next?"

"Very well, Emerson," I said, unable to repress a smile, "you win this point. I thought you would shout."

"I had braced myself for that particular piece of news, since I expected you would want to preview the performance, and sooner rather than later. What next?"

"The examination of the body, I suppose."

"Oh, you succeeded in bullying Willoughby, did you? Well?"

"The wound went straight through the chest," I said. "The exit wound was almost as large as the entry wound. It must have been a very long, heavy knife, Emerson."

"In the hand of a man beside himself with rage

and passion," Emerson muttered. "To be able to strike with such force . . . The knives the Beduin use are of that sort. Did you observe anything else of significance?"

I hesitated for a moment, searching for the proper phraseology. "There was something I did *not* observe that was highly significant."

The blood rushed into Emerson's lean cheeks. "Curse it, Peabody," he shouted. "You have been reading those damnable detective stories again!"

"You did not observe it either," I said, pleased to have aroused him. Emerson is particularly handsome when he is in a rage, teeth bared and eyes blazing. "Or to put it another way, you ought to have observed that it was not there."

"You are not going to tell me what it was — wasn't? Damnation!" Emerson exclaimed. "All right, Peabody, I accept the challenge. Would you like to place a small wager?"

"We will discuss it later, my dear," I said, giving him a meaningful look. "Now, as to the next subject —"

"My lunch with the Bellinghams?" Nefret suggested.

"Not yet, Nefret," Emerson said. "Your aunt Amelia got me off the track with her confounded detectival digression. Let us finish with the Frasers before we deal with the other nuisances."

So I described the conversation with Enid and Donald, and my agreement with Mrs. Jones. "We must take pains to avoid a showdown. The primary purpose of this evening's performance is to set the stage for the final act, which will persuade Donald to abandon his fantasy."

"You have that all worked out, have you?" Emerson inquired.

"Mrs. Jones believes she can arrange a convincing setting. I don't doubt she has had ample practice; we can leave the ectoplasm and the spirit voices and the musical background to her. She knows, surely, that the Egyptians did not play tambourines or banjoes? The only remaining question —"

I ought to have known better. The argument flared up so quickly and became so heated, I was unable to get a word in. Clearly both of them had been primed and ready.

"There is no one else to play the part!" Nefret insisted.

"You are mistaken," said Ramses.

"No 'pretty little Egyptian girl' could do it! She would giggle or miss her cue or —"

"I am not thinking of a pretty little Egyptian —"

"Not Aunt Amelia, either. She must be one of the participants; her absence would be noted. You can tell them I am indisposed or —"

"No, not Mother. I."

I could have made myself heard then, but I was as incapable of speech as Nefret. Ramses had at least succeeded in silencing her; her mouth remained open, but for several seconds the only sounds that emerged were a series of gurgles. I was afraid she was going to laugh — the temptation to do so was strong — but she chose another, even more devastating form of mockery. After looking him up and down, she said, "You will have to shave off your mustache."

"Believe it or not, I had thought of that," Ramses said.

"And you would be willing to make the sacrifice? How touching! No, Ramses, dear, you must not. It is a nice mustache and it must have taken you a long time to grow it."

"Now, Nefret," I began.

"But, Aunt Amelia!" Nefret turned to me. "There is no way on earth anyone could mistake Ramses for a girl, even heavily veiled, sans mustache, and in deep shadow. He is — er —" She let out a choked laugh. "He is the wrong shape!"

The shadows of night had crept across the eastern sky, and a few shy stars shone in the deepening blue. Ramses was sitting on the parapet in his favorite position, his back against one of the columns and his long legs stretched out. The dusk blurred his shape, but the truth of Nefret's objection was apparent. Until . . .

I do not know what he did, but as I had learned to my sorrow, Ramses's skill at the art of disguise was not limited to false beards and other obvious items. The change was so slight as to be indefinable, but all at once his form seemed to soften and his long straight limbs took on a curving outline. "I intended to be seen reclining," said Ramses. "Voluptuously."

Nefret said with grudging admiration, "You

might pull it off at that. But why go to all that bother when I —"

"Enough," I broke in. "Neither of you is going to play the princess. I have thought of the perfect person to do it."

It had come to me in a flash, as such inspirations do — though I suppose a student of psychology would say they are the result of unconscious cogitation rising suddenly to the surface of the mind. Since I wanted time to think about it before I committed myself, I refused to answer the curious inquiries the children showered upon me.

"I will explain at a later time," I assured them. "It grows late and Nefret has not had a chance to tell us of her conversation with the Colonel."

Ali came then to call us to dinner. A beautiful bouquet of roses, mignonette, and other flowers adorned the table. I assumed one of our friends had sent it; attentions of that sort were often paid me.

After all, as Nefret admitted, she had very little to tell us. The most interesting piece of news was that the Bellinghams were no longer staying at the hotel. Cyrus had offered them the use of his dahabeeyah, the *Valley of the Kings*.

There was nothing unusual in that. It was the sort of generous, openhearted gesture Cyrus frequently made. He was always inviting people to stay with him at the Castle, for he was the most hospitable of men and enjoyed company. The dahabeeyah lay empty a good deal of the time and — as was typical of Cyrus — the crew and staff were kept on and generously paid.

Still, it was not news I wanted to hear. The *Valley of the Kings* was moored on the West Bank. The location was not as safe as Luxor, with its bright lights and flocks of tourists.

Nefret was forced to admit she had learned very little about the tragic events of five years past. "One can hardly interrogate a bereaved husband about the death of his wife — especially when he is engaged in the process of acquiring another one."

Emerson dropped his knife. "What did you say?"

"I know the signs," Nefret said coolly. "Don't think me vain; he was more concerned with finding out about my ancestry and background than with paying me compliments — though he did that too. He asked about my grandfather, and my mother's connections, and he was full of questions about those imaginary missionaries who were, as he believed, in charge of my upbringing during my youth."

She paused to take a bite of chicken. Ramses said, "It would appear that he had already investigated your history."

Nefret swallowed. "Clearly he had. Everyone in Luxor knows the story, so it would not be difficult for him to find out."

"No one has ever questioned our little fiction about the kindly missionaries," I said uneasily — for the true history of Nefret's first thirteen years was one I had taken pains to conceal.

"He did not question it. He only wanted to make certain I was still a virgin."

David caught his breath. Ramses blinked. My glass fell from my hand, spilling its contents across the tablecloth. Nefret gave me a rueful smile. "Oh, dear, I forgot. That is one of the words I am not supposed to use, except in church. He put it much more delicately, I assure you."

The only person whose countenance had not altered in the slightest was Emerson. It had been rigid as a mummy mask ever since Nefret started speaking. Only his lips moved now. "Delicately," he repeated.

"Emerson, control yourself," I said in alarm. "I feel certain the man has done nothing to justify your paternal wrath. Such unwarranted egotism is not uncommon in your sex. He is not the first; you remember the Honorable Mr. Dillinghurst and Lord Sinclair and the Comte de la Chiffonier and —"

"I cannot imagine," said Emerson, "why you should suppose I am about to lose my temper."

He rose. He leaned forward. He lifted the flowers from the vase and carried them to the open window. Slowly and methodically he wrenched the poor pretty blossoms from the dripping stems and pitched them out into the night.

"Oh," I said.

"Quite," said Emerson. "Now then, my dears, we had better get ready to leave. I presume you and Nefret will want to change, Peabody."

"And you."

"I am fully clothed and relatively clean," said Emerson, resuming his seat. "Go ahead, my dears. If you require any assistance with buttons, give me a hail, Peabody. Ramses, I would like a word with you and David."

When Emerson bellows all of us ignore him. When he speaks in that tone it is wise to do as he suggests. Meekly and in silence Nefret left the room. I followed; and the boys, obeying Emerson's gesture, moved their chairs closer to his.

They had left their serviettes at their places. As I passed I saw one of them bore a small crimson stain. Ramses had done more than blink. His nails or one of the table implements had dug deep enough to pierce his palm.

CHAPTER TEN

*I hope I number patience among my virtues,
but shilly-shallying, when nothing is to be
gained by delay, is not a virtue.*

I had finished with the buttons by the time Emerson joined me, slamming the door of our room behind him. I did not like the look of him at all. He was altogether too calm.

"What did you talk about with Ramses?" I demanded.

"I wanted to know why David is favoring his left arm."

I had not expected that. "Oh. No one was trying to keep it secret from you, Emerson. There was so much to discuss we didn't get to that."

"And yet," said Emerson, "one might reasonably suppose that a murderous attack on our son and his friend would be of interest to me."

"You are right," I admitted. "I meant to give David a good brisk arnica rub before he retired, but perhaps I should do it now."

"The boy is all right." Emerson took me by the shoulders. "Sit down for a moment, Peabody. Curse it, there are too damned many things going on at once. We must talk."

He sounded like his old self, profane and annoyed — which relieved my mind considerably. "What bothers you most, Emerson? Colonel Bellingham's intentions with regard to Nefret?"

"They can wait. I was a trifle put out at the idea initially," Emerson admitted in one of the great understatements of the year. "But I suppose that by his standards he has done nothing amiss. If he has the effrontery to come round and ask for my permission to court Nefret, I will pitch him out the window as I did his flowers, and that will take care of that."

"It should," I agreed, smiling. "The murder of Mrs. Bellingham —"

"That can wait too. Let us get the Fraser nonsense settled so we can concentrate on more serious matters. What is this latest inspiration of yours, Peabody? If you want me to play the princess, I must flatly refuse."

"Your — er — shape is even less convincing than that of Ramses," I said with a laugh, and went on to tell him what I had in mind.

Emerson nodded. "Hmmm, yes. That is really quite clever, Peabody. For it must be apparent to you, as it has been to me, that the trouble originated with her."

"That is just like a man! He was certainly the one at fault initially."

"Let us say they are both essential to a proper resolution," said Emerson, and interrupted the discussion long enough to demonstrate the truth of his remark. "Will she do it?"

"Leave it to me."

"I would much prefer to." He helped me on with my shawl and escorted me to the door. Before he opened it he said gravely, "And you, my dear, can leave the lads to me. I don't know what the incident at Luxor Temple has to do with the other matters that are interfering with my work, but I mean to find out. It would be a pity to lose Ramses now, after all the time and effort we have spent raising him."

Propelled by the strong arms of our devoted men, the little boat glided across the river. The lights of the hotels on the East Bank made a brilliant display. Even more beautiful was the play of moonlight on the dark water. The lunar orb was almost at the full; accompanied by its glittering entourage of stars, it rose serenely into the sky. We sat in silence, each occupied with his or her own thoughts, but mine, at least, were not of the beauty of the night. Even the warm clasp of Emerson's hand, holding mine under the cover of my full skirts, did not comfort me.

It was not that I blamed myself for neglecting to give full weight to the incident at Luxor Temple. I had become accustomed to people throwing things at, or dropping them on, Ramses; they usually had some reason for it, though, and I had not given sufficient thought to that question. What was Ramses up to this time? Was I allowing my obligation to an old friend to distract me from my duties as a parent? I had obligations to David as well, and he was always at Ramses's side, aiding and abetting him in all his underhanded schemes and just as vulnerable to attack.

After serious consideration of the matter I concluded that I had not been at fault — yet. The Fraser case must take precedence, and at this point in time it was impossible to know for certain whether it was unrelated to the other mysteries that surrounded us. Mrs. Jones was an enigma. She might be precisely what she had appeared to be — an unscrupulous practitioner of dubious arts who had got herself in over her head and desired only to extricate herself without unpleasant repercussions. Her claim of concern for Donald's physical and mental health had impressed Cyrus, but he was notoriously susceptible to female blandishments. She had not convinced *me*.

Was she secretly involved in the Bellingham business? Emerson had jeered at my theory, but he had produced no argument that proved me wrong. Donald had been on the spot when we removed the mummy — that was a fact. Mrs. Jones might have attempted to dissuade him, as she had claimed, or she might have subtly insinuated the idea into his head.

Another (possible) motive for her (hypothetical) actions had occurred to me. What if she were connected in some way with Dutton Scudder? What if she were his mother, aunt, older sister, cousin, mistress . . . Well, that did seem unlikely. However, stranger things have happened. We knew nothing about Mrs. Jones's background except what she had told us.

I could not imagine why she would want to disable Ramses, but then the motive behind the incident at Luxor Temple was still unclear. Why would any one of the people involved want to disable him? I had been too quick to assume that only a man could have handled the heavy granite head. Mrs. Jones was a sturdy, healthy woman; she would not have been able to keep up with Donald during his hegira through the western valleys if she were not. A clever woman would complain about sunburn and scraped hands in order to mislead me.

It was therefore with renewed interest that I studied the lady when she admitted us to her sitting room. Her initial appearance *had* misled me. She was younger than her gray-streaked hair had suggested. (Not Scudder's mother, then? She might have married young — to an American, of course.)

With some difficulty I turned my attention from these fascinating theories to the arrangements for the séance. They suited her purpose, and mine, admirably. The room was large and lofty, with long windows opening onto a small balcony, and a door that connected with her sleeping chamber. A table had been moved into the middle of the room, and chairs arranged around it. Heavy dark draperies had been drawn across the windows, and the inconveniently brilliant electric lights had been replaced by the softer glow of shaded lamps.

It would tax my patience and yours, dear

Reader, if I were to describe in detail what transpired. It was similar to other performances of the sort — the dim lights, the clasped hands, the trance, the questions and murmured replies — except that Mrs. Jones did it better than most of her fellow practitioners. She was an excellent mimic. The princess's voice was quite unlike hers; it sounded younger and lighter, with an engaging, if improbable, little accent. (Though I admit it would be difficult to know how an ancient Egyptian would sound speaking English.) She even uttered a few words of the ancient language. Here she was on safer ground, since the ancients did not write the vowels and no one knows precisely how the language was pronounced. She had the consonants right, though, and I saw Emerson's eyebrows lift in surprise when she rattled off a formula of greeting.

Donald was a bit of a nuisance. Our presence had raised his hopes and increased his impatience; his demands for information became more importunate, his frustration at the necessarily indeterminate answers more apparent. He was holding my left hand, and at times he squeezed it so hard I wanted to swear, at him and at Mrs. Jones for delaying her announcement.

She was showman enough to gauge her audience's emotions with pinpoint accuracy. Donald was on the brink of a violent outburst when she deemed it advisable to break the news.

"I vill come to you," murmured the sweet, soft voice. "Do not seek me in ze dry valleys, I am not dere. I vill come to you here and you vill see me mit your own eyes. I vill greet you and tell you vat you must do."

Well, we had to end the proceedings. Donald broke the circle, leaping to his feet and rushing at Mrs. Jones. Emerson, who had been gasping and puffing with suppressed laughter, was quick enough to intercept him in the nick of time.

"You know the danger to the medium if the trance is broken," he said sternly, catching Donald in a firm grip and returning him to his chair. "Peabody, how is she?"

"She is coming out of it," I said, bending over Mrs. Jones, who was muttering and moaning. Unseen by the others, she opened her eyes and winked at me.

The electric lights were turned on and people began moving round the room. Donald remained slumped in his chair, his head bowed as if in silent prayer. I grasped Mrs. Jones's hand, under the pretense of taking her pulse, and whispered, "Is he all right, do you think? He appears to be in a stupor."

Suddenly Donald leaped to his feet. Mrs. Jones shied back as he approached, and I braced myself; but our concern was needless. His face shining with joy, Donald dropped reverently to one knee.

"Is it true?" he exclaimed in broken accents.

"She does not remember what she said," I said quickly. "But yes, Donald, I heard it too. We all heard it."

Mrs. Jones gave me a grateful glance. "What?"

she murmured, raising a limp hand to her brow. "What happened?"

"She is coming to me." Donald grasped her other hand and raised it to his lips. "She, herself, in the flesh! When? I can't wait much longer."

"Leave her alone, Donald," I ordered. "She needs time to recover. A glass of wine, perhaps, Mrs. Jones?"

Emerson supplied the wine and stood listening while I told Mrs. Jones of the most recent refinement of our plan. There was no fear of Donald's overhearing; radiant with happiness, he had retired to the sideboard with Ramses and David and was rhapsodizing at the top of his lungs.

"Oh, well done," murmured Mrs. Jones when I had finished explaining. "If you can persuade her, that is the obvious solution. How soon can we bring it off? My nerves won't stand much more of this."

"Yet you seem to me quite a cool customer, as our friend Vandergelt would say," remarked Emerson.

I immediately shushed him. Emerson believes he can whisper, but he is mistaken.

"I hoped he would be here," murmured the lady.

"I expect he was engaged elsewhere," I said. "There was no reply to the note I sent. I feel sure he will wish to attend . . . tomorrow night? Or is that too soon?"

"The sooner the better," was the reply. "I am

not so cool as you think, Professor. What must I do?"

I had worked it all out during the séance, for I can easily think of two things simultaneously. Emerson listened in silence. I could not quite make out what he was thinking. At one moment amusement seemed to predominate, at another something verging on horror. When I showed Mrs. Jones the little bottle I had brought with me he broke out. "Good Gad, Amelia! You cannot —"

"Hush! It is essential, Emerson. He won't sleep a wink without it. Now come and help me."

He did not like it, but he distracted Donald while I tipped the laudanum into the glass. It turned the whiskey rather a horrid color, but I daresay Donald would not have noticed if it had been bright blue. Seeing his condition of frenetic excitement, I knew I had done the right thing.

Enid was next. I was tempted to administer a sleeping draft to her as well, for she looked ghastly. Nefret was with her, trying to persuade her to take a sip of brandy. I took the glass from the dear girl and dismissed her with a reassuring nod.

"Drink it," I said firmly. "And take heart. I have matters under control."

Enid did as I had ordered, with regard to the brandy, at least; a little color returned to her face, but her horrified expression did not alter.

"What have you done?" she whispered. "This is madness! In heaven's name, Amelia —"

"I am surprised you have so little confidence in me, Enid. Listen and I will explain."

The explanation was necessarily brief. Too brief, perhaps; she looked even more appalled. "Impossible, Amelia. How can you expect me to do such a thing?"

"Enid," I said, taking her limp hand. "I understand. But you must make your choice. Either you leave Donald, or you become a wife to him again. Men are rather pitiable creatures, my dear, and Donald is — well —"

"Stupid," she said bitterly. "Clumsy, unimaginative —"

"Unromantic? Quite the contrary, Enid. I don't doubt he erred in — er — a number of important ways, but it is his yearning for romance that has led him to this pass. You, my dear, can teach him — encourage him — er — need I say more?"

A wry smile touched her lips. "It is easy for you to say, Amelia. You would never need to — er — encourage your husband."

"My dear girl, I do it all the time! That is what a happy marriage is all about. I would be the first to admit, however, that Emerson is an extraordinary man."

"He is." There was a wistful light in her eyes as she watched Emerson, who had collared Ramses and appeared to be lecturing him about something.

"Are we agreed, then?"

"Oh, Amelia, I don't know. I do not see how I can —"

"It is the simplest thing in the world, my dear. I will arrange for a costume, and give you your final instructions tomorrow. Or — wait, I have a better idea. Ramses, will you come here for a moment?" He joined us, and I explained, "I have been telling Mrs. Fraser that she is the one to play the role of the princess. She will need a proper costume and a certain amount of coaching; you are the obvious one to acquire the former and do the latter."

"That would be very kind of you, Ramses," Enid said.

Ramses said in a rather odd voice, "I would be happy to advise Mrs. Fraser, but perhaps —"

"But me no buts, Ramses. I have never approved of your interest in and practice of the art of disguise; here is an opportunity to apply it to a useful end. That is settled, then. Enid, Ramses will come round — let me think — just after luncheon. We must attend the funeral services tomorrow morning. Can you get rid of Donald for the afternoon, Enid?"

"Yes, certainly," Enid said. "All afternoon, if you like."

She looked much brighter. I had sprung it on her rather abruptly; I ought to have realized it would take a little time for her to accustom herself to the idea. I gave her an approving smile. "I must take my little family home. Donald is half-asleep already."

"Mother," Ramses began.

"Say good night to Mrs. Fraser, Ramses."

"Good night, Mrs. Fraser," Ramses said.

"Good night, Ramses. I look forward to seeing you tomorrow."

We left the boys to spend the night on the dahabeeyah. Neither of them had had much to say during the trip back to the West Bank. David was never very loquacious, but it was almost unheard of for Ramses to remain silent so long. I assumed he must be tired, and before the rest of us mounted our donkeys I told him to go straight to bed and not sit up late working on his photographs.

"Very well, Mother. I will not work on the photographs."

"Good. Remember, we are attending the service for Mrs. Bellingham tomorrow, so wear your good suit."

I had been somewhat surprised to learn from Dr. Willoughby that there was not to be what I would call a proper funeral. The Colonel had told him he feared that a church service would attract the curious; there had been enough sensation already, and he wished only to see his wife laid quietly to rest. We were among the few who had been invited to attend the brief ceremony at the gravesite.

I had expected Emerson would complain. All he said was, "It cannot be avoided, I suppose. But don't get your hopes up, Peabody. He will not be there."

"Who?" I asked.

"The murderer. Don't deny it, Peabody, I know the way your mind works; you believe he will be lurking in the background, and that you will know him by his gloating expression."

"Oh, Emerson, what nonsense. I don't believe anything of the sort."

However, when we left the house I selected one of my sturdier parasols instead of the one that matched my lavender frock. It is well to be prepared for any eventuality, and over the years my trusty parasol had proved to be my most effective weapon. And it is, of course, very useful in shading one's face from the sun's rays.

The small British cemetery was outside the village, on the road to Karnak, and it contained the burials not only of Englishmen and -women, but of other Christians who had breathed their last in Luxor. I felt a pang of shame when I saw how neglected it was, the graves untended, the weedy ground showing the tracks of goat and donkey, jackal and pariah dog. I made a mental note to do something about it.

We had been told to be there at ten. When we arrived I saw that the Colonel's party had arrived before us and were waiting by the open grave. They made a somber group, for Dolly was wearing a black gown and the Colonel's garments were of the same funereal hue. With them was the only other mourner, aside from Dr. Willoughby and ourselves. Mr. Booghis Tucker Tollington was attired in the same striped flannel suit and straw boater, but he had replaced his pink tie with a black one, and his expression was suitably grave.

After murmured greetings had been exchanged, the Colonel indicated that we were ready to begin. The clergyman, a dark-haired, middle-aged gentleman suffering from a severe case of sunburn, was a stranger to me; when he opened his book and began to read the beautiful old Anglican service, I realized the Colonel must have requested the assistance of a visiting vicar. Evidently his religious views were too strict to allow a Baptist or Roman Catholic to preside.

Since I am familiar with the words of the service, it was not necessary for me to give my full attention to the proceedings. A little shiver ran through me as my eyes wandered (when my head was not bent in prayer) over the cemetery. What a sad, neglected place it was! Bright sunlight and waving palm fronds notwithstanding, I would not have wanted one I loved to lie there, and the ceremony was painfully brief. I could not blame the clergyman for curtailing his own prayer; he had not known the dead lady, and it was difficult to know what to say about the circumstances that had brought her here.

At least our little party lent dignity to the proceedings. My lavender frock and Nefret's afternoon dress, with its high net collar and long sleeves, could not have been more appropriate, and the masculine members of the group were, for once, dressed like the gentlemen they were. Emerson was even wearing a proper dark cravat.

As my eyes moved on, I saw a few other watchers in galabeeyahs and turbans, at a discreet distance from the grave. One of them was Saiyid. It had been good of him to come, I thought — though I wondered how he had found out the time and place. The Colonel would certainly not have invited his dragoman to be present.

When the time came to lower the coffin into the grave I understood the presence of the Egyptians. At a gesture from Dr. Willoughby they sidled up and took hold of the ropes. They must be the ones who had dug the grave and who would fill it in when all was over. Once the plain wooden box rested on the bottom of the grave the Colonel bent and picked up a handful of dirt, which he tossed into the hole. Of all the sounds on earth, I think, that is one of the most terrible. It is such a small, dry sound to signal the end of a life.

We repeated the gesture — Dolly with her fingertips, lips pursed and nose wrinkled — except for Emerson, who refuses to participate actively in any sort of religious ceremony. Then it was over, and we moved away from the place where the two men in turbans waited, shovels in their hands.

"In our part of the world," the Colonel said, "it is customary for us to invite a few friends to gather with us after the sad ceremonies. May I look forward to seeing you on Mr. Vandergelt's dahabeeyah, which he has been kind enough to place at my disposal?"

His glance included us all and did not linger any longer on Nefret than would have been proper for a man who has just buried his wife. I accepted with thanks, but added, "I am not certain my husband will be able —"

"He will not," said Emerson. "Apologies and all that sort of thing."

"And I regret to say that I have a previous engagement," said Ramses. "You remember, Mother?"

"Oh, yes," I said. He was not engaged to Enid until after midday, but I supposed it would take him a while to collect the necessary bits of the costume.

"I look forward to seeing you ladies shortly, then," said the Colonel with a polite bow. Dolly looked back at us, her steps dragging as her father led her away, but he gave her no opportunity to linger.

The gravediggers had begun their work; it gave me a cauld grue to hear their cheerful conversation and laughter mingling with the thud of falling earth. Emerson took my arm and David took Nefret's in a grip almost as firm; as we started toward our hired carriage, I saw that Ramses had intercepted Mr. Tollington and was speaking to him.

I stopped. "Let us wait for Ramses, Emerson. If he starts to fight with Mr. Tollington —"

"He didn't start the last one," Emerson said. "Er — not precisely."

He stopped, though.

The discussion did not last long. It ended with Ramses holding out his hand. The other young man took it and they exchanged a hearty handshake. Then Tollington hurried after the Bellinghams and Ramses joined us. He was looking rather pensive.

"So you made it up, did you?" I asked. "That was well done, Ramses."

"Thank you, Mother," said Ramses.

"What did he say?" Nefret asked curiously.

"The usual sort of thing." Ramses shrugged. "The rituals of manliness in Western culture are as formalized as those of primitive tribes. It was a foolish but necessary ceremony."

The carriage started up. Emerson loosened his cravat and took out his pipe. "I presume, Ramses, that when you told Bellingham you had another engagement it was only an excuse. Are you and David photographing this morning?"

"Not exactly. Mother has asked me to put together a costume for Mrs. Fraser and coach her in her role."

"I will go with you," Nefret said. "A man cannot —"

"No, you will not," Emerson said firmly. "I refuse to have this entire family wasting time away from the dig. I need you this afternoon. We will go first to call on Bellingham — oh, yes, Peabody, I am going; since Ramses and David won't be with you, *I* will. We will stay precisely fifteen minutes and then we will leave — together."

"Yes, my dear," I murmured.

I tried to give Ramses some suggestions as to costuming, but he cut me short. "I know the sort of thing, Mother. You can safely leave it to me."

We left Ramses and David at the Grand Hotel, where there were several shops selling tourist goods. Both boys knew their way around Luxor; they assured me again that my assistance was not needed.

Our men took us back across the river and landed us at the dock which Cyrus had caused to be built and which he graciously shared with us. The *Valley of the Kings* and the *Amelia* were the only dahabeeyahs moored on the West Bank; the other wealthy owners or hirers of these vessels preferred to be nearer the conveniences of Luxor.

I had not realized that Americans made such a festive occasion of funerals. The Colonel's "few friends" included Cyrus, Howard Carter, M. Legrain, several other archaeologists, and a few people who must have been tourists. Not the common Cook's tour visitors, however; all were dressed with an elegance that spoke of wealth, and the Colonel's introductions were sprinkled with "Lord's" and "Sir's." Mr. Tollington was there, glowering darkly at a sandy-haired, narrow-shouldered young man who was devoting himself to Dolly. From his accent, his tailoring, and his title — he was one of the "Sir's" — I took him to be English.

We accepted a glass of sherry and a biscuit, and while Emerson talked with Howard about tombs Cyrus drew me aside.

"I got your message too late last night to reply to it," he said in a low voice. "What happened?"

I told him of what had transpired and of our plans for that evening. "I assume you will want to be present," I added. "Mrs. Jones asked about you."

"Did she?" Cyrus's face split into a pleased smile. "She's a corker, isn't she?"

"She is a clever woman," I corrected. "I think it will work out, Cyrus, if Enid does her part."

Cyrus nodded. "That was a good idea, Mrs. Amelia. I am sorry, though, that I won't get to see Ramses playing the role of a languorous Egyptian maiden."

Emerson had lost track of the time, as he does when he gets to talking about tombs, but I noticed he kept a close eye on Nefret. She and Dolly were seated side by side on the divan. Whose idea that had been I did not know, but I supposed it had been the Colonel's. What fools these men are, I thought to myself; his daughter and the young woman he presumably (and vainly) hoped to marry were approximately the same age, so he may have thought it would be "nice" if they learned to know one another. The two girls certainly made a pretty picture: one in stark black that set off her silvery curls, the other in pure white with hair of red-gold. Their expressions were not so pretty. I wondered what they were talking about to bring such a sour look to Dolly's face and make Nefret's blue eyes flash.

Finally Emerson tore himself away and announced we must go. "Carter is taking luncheon with us," he informed me. "He has promised to come round and have a look at my tomb afterwards."

"Oh, you are going to allow him to have luncheon first?" I inquired.

"We must go back to the house to change in any case," said Emerson, now cravat- and coatless. "Nefret cannot climb in long skirts and frou-frou."

I asked Cyrus to make one of the party, and we set off in his carriage. We left the gentlemen to their tobacco on the verandah. I accompanied Nefret to her room to help her with hooks and buttons and to ask how she and Dolly had got on.

"Like a mongoose and a snake," said Nefret. "We are natural antagonists."

"And why is that?" I inquired.

"The only things she can talk about are flirting and fashions. I cannot determine whether she is naturally stupid or whether her brain was constricted from birth, like the bound feet of Chinese ladies."

"The latter, I believe," I said, unhooking the boned collar. "Men prefer women to be brainless."

"Not all men," Nefret said. "Whew! Thank you, Aunt Amelia, that is much better."

"Not all," I agreed. "But men like Emerson are rare."

"That makes them all the more worth pursuing," Nefret said with a fond smile. "I do Dolly an injustice, however. She can also talk about other women — spitefully and maliciously."

"Including the late Mrs. Bellingham?"

"I thought I might as well see what I could get out of her," Nefret admitted. "It wasn't a great deal, and none of it was favorable. She is still furious because Daddy would not take her with them on their bridal trip." Her face sobered. "It was rather unpleasant to hear the way she talked about the poor dead woman, Aunt Amelia; it was as if Lucinda were still alive, and her rival."

Since I knew Emerson would be fretting about the time, I did not pursue the topic, but Nefret had given me a great deal to think about. She had — I hoped! — been too innocent to understand that a Mrs. Bellingham of childbearing age was indeed a formidable rival to Dolly.

Most men prefer sons to daughters. It has something to do with their peculiar definition of masculinity, I believe. The social class to which the Colonel belonged put great emphasis on lineage and the transmission of a family name from father to son. I did not doubt he shared this absurd obsession; he was that sort of man. Four marriages had produced no sons, only a girl who would not carry on the family name. It would never have occurred to the Colonel that the fault, if fault it is, might be his, and I felt sure he had not given up hope even yet. Dolly was shrewd enough to know that a baby brother would probably replace her in the affection of her father.

Young girls make excellent murderers. (And, let me be fair — young boys as well.) The young are naturally selfish. Moral values are not innate, they are pounded into children, often with great difficulty and sometimes without success, as the history of crime sadly demonstrates.

However, Dolly had not been with her father and his bride in Cairo. Regretfully I abandoned this theory.

Over luncheon Cyrus and I discussed arrangements for the séance that evening. He was mightily intrigued by the business, and discretion was unnecessary since Howard, like most of the residents of Luxor, had heard rumors about Donald's quest. It would have been hard to keep it a secret, since he talked freely about it and quizzed every Egyptologist he encountered.

When we had eaten all Emerson deemed sufficient, he bundled us out of the house and up the path. The sun beat down and the air was as hot and dry as a furnace, but I had got my "Egypt wind" by that time and had no difficulty. When we reached the tomb, we found Abdullah and the other men sprawled on the ground in various positions of exhaustion. They started to scramble to their feet when they saw us, but Emerson waved them back.

"Not going too well?" Emerson inquired of Abdullah, who, stubborn old man that he was, had come rigidly to attention.

Abdullah shook his head. His once immaculate

robe and turban were now gray instead of white. "The debris is packed solid, Emerson, and it fills the corridor from top to bottom. We had to stop for a time because the candles were melting."

"No wonder you all look so tired," I said sympathetically.

Abdullah stiffened. "We are accustomed to the heat, Sitt Hakim, but we could not see. Because of the candles melting."

"How far have you got?" Howard asked.

"Forty meters," said Abdullah, who was accustomed to using the standard archaeological measurements. "Now we have rested. We will go back —"

"Sit down, you old fool," said Emerson irritably. Abdullah obeyed, with a sidelong glance at me; he knew Emerson well enough to recognize this as a demonstration of concern and approbation. Emerson fingered the cleft in his chin. "I am going to have a look. Coming, Peabody?"

"Of course," I said, laying my parasol aside.

"I wish you wouldn't," Howard said sincerely.

"Now, Howard, you ought to know by now that I am not deterred by heat or difficulty."

"I am well aware of that. But if you go, I will have to follow, and to be honest, I would rather not. Confound it, Mrs. E., the place is full of bat guano."

It was a reasonable deduction, to judge by the appearance of our men and the unmistakable odor that wafted from them. I smiled at Howard and straightened my belt of tools. "It is not necessary for you to prove your fortitude, Howard, it is well-known. As for Cyrus —"

"Oh, I'm going along," Cyrus declared calmly. "And I'm not going to waste my breath trying to dissuade you, Mrs. Amelia."

"At least remove your coat, Peabody," Emerson ordered, stripping off his own. "I cannot fathom why you insist on retaining it; your trousers are very becoming to you and I am sure neither Carter nor Vandergelt would be ill-bred enough to remark upon — er — them."

The gentlemen hastened to assure me that they had no intention even of glancing at that part of my anatomy. They removed their extraneous garments — and so did Nefret, in silence and with her chin stubbornly set.

Emerson sighed. "No, my dear."

"But, sir —"

"Not this time."

Nefret's chin quivered.

"Stop that," Emerson shouted. "You may not go, that is final. Stay here and — and look after Abdullah."

Abdullah started to protest. Then he caught my eye and sat down with a loud groan. Nefret went to him at once, offering tea and biscuits.

I had not been in the tomb for several days. Although Abdullah had denigrated the amount of work accomplished, I knew enough of the difficulties to appreciate the effort it had taken to get so far. Every basketful of rubble had to be carried up and out of the tomb. The slope was quite steep — close to thirty degrees. Steps had been cut along one side of the passage, but they were so rough and worn, they were as treacherous as the slope itself. Howard and Cyrus did not scruple to hold on to the rope Emerson had caused to be fastened at the mouth of the tomb, but the muscular frame of my spouse was all the support I needed. I rested one hand against his broad shoulder, and when I slipped the instantaneous hardening of those formidable muscles supported and reassured me.

Archaeological fever, too long suppressed, stirred in my breast. Most individuals, I daresay, would have found the place unprepossessing — dark, filthy, odorous, without so much as a hieroglyphic inscription or a fragment of relief to distinguish this passage from an ordinary cave. But I now understood Emerson's enthusiasm. The dimensions of this tomb already exceeded those of the pit tombs designed for commoners. The design, too, was unusual, for the passage curved as it descended. Could this have been intended for a royal sepulchre? Some of the debris the men had removed might have been washed into the tomb by floodwater, but surely not all. If the passage had been deliberately filled, there must be something at its end that warranted protection.

So absorbed was I in professional speculation, I scarcely noticed the increasing heat and stifling darkness. The flames of the candles held by

Cyrus and Emerson burned dim. When Emerson stopped, with a low-voiced warning to me and the men who followed me, the candles gave so little light that it was difficult to see what lay ahead. There was not, in fact, much to see — only a seeming wall of rock that closed the passage like a door. I could barely make out the marks of the pickaxes the men had used.

Cyrus had not uttered a word of complaint, though the descent had been harder for him than any of us. He was Emerson's height, or a little taller; both of them had to proceed with bowed heads, since the passage was barely two meters high and the ceiling was uneven. Now that we had stopped moving, I could hear his hard breathing.

"Start back, Cyrus," I said. "We will follow. Emerson?"

"Hmph," said Emerson. He had turned to examine the side walls.

"Emerson," I said more emphatically. "I want to get out of here."

"Oh?" Emerson glanced at the sagging candle. Wax covered his fingers and dripped from them; the temperature was so high, even that thin skin had not hardened. "Oh. Yes, I suppose we may as well."

I will admit, in the pages of my private journal, that I might have had some little difficulty ascending that hellish slope if Emerson had not maintained a constant pressure on me from behind. Howard, younger and in better condition than Cyrus, gave the latter a helpful push now and then. We had to stop several times to catch our breath, or try to.

When we emerged, Abdullah and Selim were waiting. The lad's strong arms pulled a wheezing Cyrus up the final stairs and deposited him solicitously on a convenient rock. Nefret hurried to him with water and cold tea. As for me, I was not too proud to take Abdullah's outstretched hand.

We presented an unsightly spectacle, coated with the gray slime resulting from a mixture of perspiration and guano-filled dust. It had not been as difficult for us as for the men, though, and I nodded appreciatively at Abdullah.

"Well!" said Howard between gasps. "You have something quite interesting there, Professor. It is beginning to bear a certain resemblance to Hatshepsut's tomb, though of course we have gone a good deal farther than you. Have you looked for foundation deposits?"

"Not yet." Emerson wiped his sweating face on his sleeve. "Does your tomb have —"

"For pity's sake, Emerson, don't smear that stuff into your eyes," I interrupted. "Here, let me —"

"Wipe your own face," Emerson said, pushing my hand away and reaching for one of the water jars. "Carter, how far along was the first —"

He interrupted himself this time, pouring water over his dishevelled head and grimy face and spitting out a mouthful of mud.

"I observed one difference," said Howard, still short of breath, but as enthusiastic as Emerson. "There is a smoothed section, probably the slide for a sarcophagus, along one side of the passage in Hatshepsut's tomb."

"Ah," said Emerson. "Interesting. I had better go and have a look."

He would have done it too, then and there, had not Howard managed to distract him.

"We had the same difficulty with the candles melting, Professor, so we installed hand wires for electric lamps. I can arrange that, if you like."

Emerson nodded. "Yes, good. I foresee another problem. The passage is now below the limestone stratum and entering the *tafl*. You know how bad the rock is there; we may need to brace the walls and roof as we go on."

Cyrus had recovered enough to join in the discussion. It was he who answered Nefret's question. "*Tafl?* It is a layer of softer rock like shale, underlying the limestone in which most of the tombs are cut. The stone in this area is not as good as the limestone around Giza and Sakkara. . . ."

They went on talking for some little time; Howard and Emerson discussed the possibility of an exhaust motor to freshen the air, while Nefret continued to ask questions of all and sundry. Finally I managed to interrupt long enough to point out that we might as well continue the discussion in more comfortable surroundings. It was late, and I was beginning to find even my own company unpleasantly odorous.

Emerson nodded. "Yes, the men may as well go home, Abdullah. It has been tiring work, and I don't want to proceed until we have braced that left wall."

Emerson drives his men hard, but no harder than himself, and he never allows them to take unnecessary risks.

Scarcely had we got our gear together, however, than we saw Ramses and David coming toward us. I deduced that they had stopped by the house to change, since they were wearing riding costumes.

"Goodness, is it so late as that?" I exclaimed. "I trust you are satisfied that Enid is ready for this evening, Ramses?"

"She seemed satisfied," said Ramses. "We brought the horses, Mother; would you and Nefret care to ride back to the house instead of walking?"

Nefret declined the offer — I supposed she had taken it as a misplaced concession to female frailty — but she urged me to ride. "I did not make that exhausting descent into the tomb, Aunt Amelia, so I am feeling quite fresh, and you are still favoring the ankle you hurt yesterday. Do you go on with David."

I had been anxious to try Risha. I accepted, therefore, and after the stirrups had been adjusted Emerson lifted me into the saddle and the others set out along the path to the plateau. Ramses began questioning Emerson about the tomb, and before they passed out of earshot I heard Nefret demand that she be allowed to enter it next day.

As soon as the lovely animal started forward, I understood his name. Risha means "feather," and that was how he moved — as lightly as if he walked on air. I let him pick his own way across the uneven floor of the Valley, and many were the admiring glances and comments that followed our progress.

"He is a wonder, isn't he?" said David. "Your English style of riding, with bit and spur, is quite unnecessary; he seems to sense your wishes and respond to them instantly."

"Your Asfur goes as easily. The name means 'flying bird,' I believe. I hope you and Ramses appreciate how fortunate you are to enjoy the sheikh's friendship. We must think of some way of repaying him for his hospitality and for his generous gifts."

David assured me that he and Ramses had already discussed the subject.

"How did you get on with Mrs. Fraser?" was my next question.

"I only stayed for a moment," David replied. "After all, Aunt Amelia, she scarcely knows me; she would have felt uncomfortable — er —"

"Rehearsing," I said helpfully. "Yes, of course. You have the instincts of a gentleman, David. She has known Ramses since he was a child, and is perfectly at ease with him."

We had traversed the narrow entrance to the

Valley and reached the open desert. "Shall we let them out now?" David suggested.

As a rule I prefer not to ride at a full gallop unless I am pursuing criminals or being pursued by them. But this was unlike anything I had ever experienced. So smooth was our progress, so even the fine creature's gait, that I felt as if I were flying. I laughed aloud from sheer delight.

We had not gone far, however, when David called to me — or more probably, since he spoke in Arabic, to Risha — to stop. He too halted and bent a piercing look upon the riders who were approaching us, and whom, in my exuberance, I had not observed until then. One was female; the skirts of her long habit hung down to the stirrup, and she was bouncing up and down in approved style.

"Dolly," I said. "Aha. Is that why Ramses was so generous in lending me Risha?"

David smiled and frowned at the same time. "We saw them when we were on our way, yes. But at that time —"

He broke off, for Dolly and her escort had reached us. The latter was the young man I had met at the postfuneral gathering. He was wearing a preposterously large pith helmet with a veil hanging down in back to protect his neck. He removed this article of apparel and bowed.

I had forgot his name, but before I could ask him to repeat it in order that I might introduce my companion, David spoke.

"Where is Saiyid?"

He had addressed Dolly. It was the first time, I believe, he had spoken to her directly, and the abruptness of the question surprised her into an answer. "I sent him back to the dahabeeyah."

"That was very foolish," I said. "He was hired to look after you."

"He was a nuisance," said the young lady with a pretty shrug. "Sir Arthur is looking after me very nicely."

Sir Arthur blushed and looked foolish. Poor Mr. Tollington, it appeared, had been supplanted. He had not struck me as an effective guard, but this fellow looked even more ineffectual.

However, it was broad daylight and there were other people abroad — tourists on their way to and from the monuments, fellahin working in the fields. I was about to direct the young man to take Dolly back to her father when David spoke again.

"Perhaps Miss Bellingham and Sir Arthur should come to the house with us, Aunt Amelia. One of the men can escort them back to the *Valley of the Kings*."

Clearly he shared my forebodings, or he would not have welcomed the company of an individual who treated him so rudely. I therefore repeated the invitation, and if my manner was less than gracious, I doubt Dolly noticed. She was, of course, delighted to agree. Sir Arthur's sputtering protestations, to the effect that they needed no escort, were coolly ignored.

The delay and the slower pace we were forced to set resulted in our finding that the others had arrived before us. Cyrus had gone back to the Castle and Howard had left the party to proceed to his own house near Deir el Medina; the only ones waiting on the terrace were Nefret and Ramses. They informed me that Emerson was changing, and I announced I would do the same.

"We met Miss Bellingham and Sir Arthur on our way," I explained. "I believe you have not met my son, Sir Arthur, and I apologize for neglecting earlier to present my — er — adopted nephew, Mr. Todros. Nefret, will you ask Ali to bring tea?"

I did not like abandoning Ramses to the tender mercies of Dolly, but I did not suppose she could do more than annoy him while David and the other young man were present. Nefret followed me into the house.

"Why did you bring her here?" she demanded.

"She was gadding about without a guard," I replied. "She said she had sent Saiyid away because he was a nuisance. That young man would be of no use at all if Scudder attacked her."

"Ah, I see." Nefret's smooth brow resumed its untroubled look. "Take all the time you like, Aunt Amelia, I will make certain everyone behaves himself. Or, more likely, herself."

My dear thoughtful Emerson had ordered the tin bath to be filled for me. Nothing less than total immersion would have sufficed; even my undergarments were stickily gray. I completed my ablutions as hastily as possible and slipped into a loose tea gown since Emerson was not in our room to assist me with buttons.

The social temperature on the terrace was far from comfortable, though it would have been hard to say whether it was chilly or heated. A little of both, I thought. Dolly must have been flirting outrageously with Ramses, since her new admirer was glaring at my son and Nefret's cheeks were prettily flushed — whether with suppressed laughter or the need to repress a sarcastic remark, I was not sure. Ramses was in his favorite position atop the wall, which prevented Dolly from sitting next to him, and Emerson was watching them all with a bland smile.

My attempts to carry on a courteous conversation met with failure. I did not suppose Dolly would linger long; she had come for only one purpose, and having failed to achieve it in that ambience, she sought another that might be more successful.

"We mustn't keep you folks," she announced, rising. "And Daddy will be wondering what has become of his little girl. Won't you ride along with us, Mr. Emerson?"

Ramses unfolded himself with less reluctance than I had expected. "David and I will both ride with you," he said, and looking at me, he added politely, "If it meets with your approval, Mother, we will remain at the *Amelia* and meet you and Father and Nefret there later."

If the proposal had come from anyone but

Ramses, I would not have thought twice about it. We would have to leave by seven in order to keep our appointment with Mrs. Jones, and there was no point in their returning to the house beforehand. I studied Ramses's bland countenance closely, but found nothing there to confirm my instinctive suspicions. Dallying with Dolly was surely not his aim, and there was not time enough for him and David to get into worse trouble.

"Very well," I said.

Dolly maneuvered Ramses into helping her to mount her horse, pushing poor Sir Arthur quite forcibly out of the way. Somehow or other her foot slipped from the stirrup, and she managed to get both arms round his neck when he caught her. Her pleased smile vanished, however, when Ramses took a firmer grip and tossed her onto her saddle with an audible thud.

After the party had ridden off Emerson burst out laughing. "She is quite a predator, isn't she? I cannot recall ever encountering a female so terrifyingly direct in her methods."

"Those silly sidesaddles are awkward things," I said fairly. "Perhaps her foot really did slip."

"Ha!" said Nefret.

"Ha indeed," said Emerson, still chuckling. "Never mind; it will be useful experience for Ramses. I remember one time in Athens . . ." Catching my eye, he stopped chuckling and reached for his pipe. "Er — as I was about to say, you did right in bringing her here, Peabody.

Do you suppose her father has not sufficiently emphasized the danger? Hang it all, the girl is practically asking to be attacked."

"So," said Nefret, "you noticed that too, Professor?"

I said, "So did I."

Emerson grinned broadly. "Of course you did, Peabody. Have we time for a whiskey and soda before dinner?"

We did.

CHAPTER ELEVEN

A fondness for martyrdom, especially of the verbal variety, is common to the young.

Donald had asked us to dine with him and Enid, but I had felt it best to decline. Mrs. Jones had explained that she always "fasted and meditated in solitude before calling upon the spirits"; that interlude would give us the opportunity we needed for a final, private conference with the lady. We had an early dinner, and as soon as Cyrus arrived we set out for the dahabeeyah, where we were to meet the boys.

Cyrus was as smartly dressed as I had ever seen him, his linen suit of snowy freshness, his gloves immaculate. The diamond in his stickpin, though tastefully modest in size, was of the finest water. I complimented him on his appearance, adding, "I am afraid the rest of us do not do you justice, my friend. We are wearing our working costumes, as you see; I felt it advisable to be prepared for any contingency, since we cannot predict what may transpire."

"You and Miss Nefret look lovely in anything you choose to wear," Cyrus said gallantly. "And

I see you have your parasol; that should prove a sufficient defense against any danger. You must have some notion of what is going to happen, though."

"Some notion, yes, but I need to talk to Ramses. He got away from me this afternoon before I could find out what plans he and Enid agreed upon."

We had to wait for him, of course. David was there to greet us when we arrived; when I expressed impatience, he said Ramses was almost ready and offered to go and hurry him up. I informed him I would take care of that matter, but as soon as I knocked on the door and announced myself, Ramses emerged, and we were soon on our way across the river.

"Now then," I said, adjusting my shawl, "tell us what went on this afternoon."

His head to one side, Ramses appeared to consider the question, and I said impatiently, "I don't want one of your long-winded, detailed descriptions of every word that was spoken and every thought that passed through your mind, Ramses. Just the pertinent facts."

"Ah," said Ramses. "Very well, Mother. First, as to the costume. I was able to acquire some rather pleasant imitations of ancient jewelry from Mustafa Kamel — a beaded collar, bracelets, earrings, and the like. The basic garment, as you know, is quite simple. A bedsheet, properly draped, sufficed, and I purchased as well a long fringed scarf to tie round her waist. The major difficulty was her hair — not its color, but its style. Copies of elaborate ancient Egyptian wigs are not obtainable in the *sûks*."

"Curse it, I knew I ought to have gone with you," Nefret exclaimed. "I could have arranged it to look authentic."

"That was not the problem," Ramses said. "What was required was a coiffure that could be quickly changed."

"Quite right," I agreed. "She will have to slip out of the sitting room into the corridor, and then into Mrs. Jones's bedchamber, from which she will emerge as Tasherit. Can she assume the costume hurriedly and without assistance, Ramses?"

"After considering various alternatives," said Ramses, "we concluded it would be best for her to wear it under a loose garment — a tea gown, I believe she called it. She will change into it and the costume after dinner."

"What about her hair?" Nefret asked.

"She will let it down. It is very thick and long," Ramses said. "It reaches almost to her waist."

"Good," I said. "Donald will be satisfied with that romantic image; he is not an authority on ancient Egyptian hairstyles. We will have to make certain the room is almost dark, even darker than it was the other evening, and create some sort of diversion so that Enid can creep out unobserved by Donald."

Emerson offered to create a diversion. After a brief, extremely apprehensive silence, I said tactfully, "We will discuss it with Mrs. Jones. She probably has some good ideas."

The question of how we were to reach Mrs. Jones's sitting room unobserved was easily resolved. I always familiarize myself with the service areas of hotels and other establishments, since one never knows when one may want to enter them surreptitiously. It was I, therefore, who led our party, skirting the Luxor's pretty gardens and entering into a narrow way that led to a small courtyard next to the kitchen. I was glad I had worn sturdy shoes instead of evening slippers. M. Pagnon, the manager of the hotel, did his best to maintain proper standards of hygiene, but trash of all varieties littered the ground.

Two of the kitchen boys stood smoking outside the back door. Our appearance startled them a good deal; they were so busy staring, they did not even return my friendly greeting. A similar state of startlement seized the inhabitants of the kitchen when we entered it. One of the waiters dropped a bowl of soup, but that was the only major accident. It was lentil soup, I believe.

The back stairs were uncarpeted and extremely dirty. We met no one, and when I opened the door giving on to the first floor corridor, I found it deserted. Most of the guests had gone down to dinner. The Frasers' rooms were at the front of the hotel, overlooking the garden. I tapped softly at the door of Mrs. Jones's sitting room. It opened almost at once, but only enough to allow a single wary eye to be seen. Recognizing me, she threw the door open.

"Come in, quickly," she whispered. "Mr. Fraser is in a state of nervous excitement, and I don't know that she can keep him occupied until the designated time."

Cyrus made rather a point of shaking hands with her, and while they exchanged greetings I examined her mauve silk crepe gown with considerable interest. It was one of the new "reform" dresses, loose fitting and suggesting a medieval robe. A long tabard of embroidered velvet fell from her shoulders to her feet. The ensemble lent dignity to her small, sturdy figure, and it had a suggestion of the exotic that suited the present occasion. It also appeared to be very comfortable. I reminded myself to ask her afterward where she had got it. Liberty's, perhaps? That establishment had become known for such garments.

After we had all entered, Mrs. Jones bolted the door. She had not been fasting; a half-eaten platter of mixed biscuits and a glass of wine stood on the table. She saw my reaction and returned my sardonic look with an amused, unabashed smile before she carried the evidence into her bedroom.

"Now then," she said briskly. "Mrs. Fraser appears to know what she is to do. We were able to talk briefly this afternoon. I promised her we would arrange a screen before the door so the light from the corridor won't be seen when she slips out. Can one of you gentlemen . . . ?"

"It would be simpler to break the light bulbs

in the corridor," said Emerson, who was taking a rather alarming interest in the proceedings.

We dissuaded him from that impractical notion, and Ramses explained that he had found a means of dealing with the problem. Taking a hammer and a handful of nails from his pocket, he requested the temporary loan of a blanket or coverlet from Mrs. Jones's bed.

"Won't Mr. Fraser wonder why the room is so much darker this time?" Nefret asked.

Ramses, standing on a chair, was busily hammering. "It must be dark if Mrs. Fraser is to steal away unseen," he said. "Our excuse will be that, as all students of the occult know, the greater strain of materialization requires total darkness."

"*He* will believe it, at any rate," said the lady cynically. "You must keep tight hold of his hands, Professor and Mr. Vandergelt, and not let him get away from you. The most dangerous moment will be at the end, when she bids him an eternal farewell. He may not be willing to let her go. Mrs. Fraser is prepared for that possibility, I hope?"

"She knows her lines," said Ramses without turning.

"She will need time to resume her normal attire and slip back into the room," Emerson said. "If we had a little tussle, Fraser and I, and I wrestled him to the floor —"

"No, Emerson," I said.

"Not unless it is necessary," amended Mrs. Jones.

She had seated herself on the sofa and was

sipping the glass of mineral water Cyrus had poured for her. I said, "You appear quite without apprehension, Mrs. Jones. Last night you talked of stretched nerves."

The lady raised her slippered feet onto a hassock and leaned back, the very picture of confidence and calm. "I am accustomed to working alone, Mrs. Emerson, with the entire burden on my shoulders. This is a new experience for me, and I relish it. I daresay no charlatan has ever had a staff of such able, willing assistants!"

Cyrus chuckled. "Nerves of steel," he said admiringly.

She turned to look at him. Voice and face were deadly serious. "Not entirely, Mr. Vandergelt. We are taking a desperate chance tonight. If our performance is not successful, it could leave Mr. Fraser worse off than before, or with his determination unchanged. And," she added with a smile, "if he goes on searching for the tomb, I will have to go with him, up the cliffs and down the wadis. My abused feet won't hold up much longer."

As she had predicted, Donald was ten minutes early. A tentative knock heralded his arrival, and when she heard it, Mrs. Jones let out a long sigh.

"Places, ladies and gentlemen," she said, and flung herself down on the sofa, closed her eyes, and clasped her hands on her breast. I went to the door.

Donald was alone. His face was not as ruddy as usual, and his eyes passed over me as if I were a parlor maid. In a soft, tremulous voice he said, "Is she ready?"

"She is still resting," I said, moving back so he could enter. "Be very quiet. You ought not to have come early, Donald."

Donald tiptoed in. He did not tiptoe any better than Emerson. With a ghost of his old smile he said, "You could not wait either."

His naive statement was a reminder of our greatest advantage. So strong was his need to believe that he would accept without question anything that suited his belief. A more suspicious man seeing all of us assembled might have wondered what the devil we were doing there beforehand. Donald only greeted the others in hushed tones and took a chair.

Mrs. Jones came out of her "meditative state" and was sitting up by the time Enid joined us. Her tea gown of pink crepe de chine might have been designed for the purpose it served that night; it had long full sleeves and a high neckline, and it buttoned conveniently down the front. There was enough fabric in its voluminous folds to cover two women of her size — which in one sense it did!

We had agreed upon the seating arrangements — Enid between me and Ramses, at the end of the table nearest the door; Donald between Emerson and Cyrus at the far end. Donald did not question that or anything else, not even the bedspread nailed to the door. I began to wonder why we had gone to so much trouble to create an illusion; Donald probably would not have objected if Mrs. Jones had demanded he lie face-down under the table while the princess took her own time about materializing.

It was no laughing matter, though. My last sight of Donald, before the lights were extinguished, was of a face engorged and eyes that were fairly popping out of his head. I wished, now that it was too late, that I had examined him to make certain his heart was sound. His strenuous physical activities over the past weeks had had no ill effect, which was encouraging. One could only hope for the best.

Mrs. Jones outdid herself. She groaned, gasped, and babbled. Ramses had not explained in detail what cues he and Enid had arranged (to be fair, I had ordered him not to), so I was as startled as Donald when my son's voice suddenly cut into the lady's moans.

"Look! What is that at the window?"

So pervasive was the eerie atmosphere that I imagined for a moment I saw an amorphous pale shape against the dark draperies. (As I learned later, I did see it — a long white cloth held at arm's length by David, whose chair was nearest the window.) Then Enid withdrew her hand from mine and I heard the soft rustle of fabric as she slipped behind the bedcover.

"It is nothing." The voice was David's. He sounded as if he were reciting a memorized speech, which was in fact the case.

Mrs. Jones picked up her cue, letting out a

piercing scream that brought Donald's attention back to her. She began to speak in broken phrases interspersed with heartrending groans and harsh gasps. "Too hard . . . the pain . . . O Gods of the Underworld . . ."

Donald began struggling to free himself. I heard Emerson admonish him, softly but savagely, reminding him of the dangers to the medium and the princess if the materialization were interrupted.

Enid must have had some difficulty with her buttons or combs; Mrs. Jones's appeals to the gods of the underworld had become somewhat repetitious before the door behind her swung open to reveal . . . Enid, wrapped in a bedsheet and decked with cheap jewelry, illumined by a single lamp behind her.

But that was not what Donald saw, and for a brief instant I saw it too — the slender woman's form outlined in light through the translucent robes, the glitter of bright metal at her throat and on her wrists, the raven locks that fell over her white shoulders.

For a few seconds the silence was so profound one could hear the hiss of flame on the wick of the lamp. I held my breath. This was the crucial moment. Would Enid remember her speech and deliver it convincingly? Would Donald accept this vision? Her face was shadowed by the dimness of the light and by a thin white veil (a good idea, that; I made a mental note to commend Ramses for thinking of it). Yet could a man fail to recognize the features of his own wife? She must not linger. How was she to get away unseen?

All this flashed through my mind in an instantaneous jumble of thought. Then Donald's pent breath came out in a sob. He tried to speak her name — the name of Tasherit — but could only pronounce the first syllable.

Enid cleared her throat. "I greet you, my lord and long-lost love," she began. "It has been a weary journey through the darkness of Amenti. . . ."

Oh, dear, I thought. She sounds like a schoolgirl trying to sound like a tragic heroine. It must have been Ramses who had composed that dreadful speech. What *had* he been reading?

It was comical and embarrassing — and pitiable. Donald was weeping. Enid's prim, self-conscious voice rambled on about the gods of the underworld and the pain of returning to the flesh and similar twaddle. I began to think I could not stand Donald's tears or the banality of Ramses's prose much longer. It was high time Enid stopped talking and dematerialized. What was she waiting for?

Since I dared not speak aloud, I groped along the table for Ramses's hand, intending to press it rhythmically in order to spell out a message. The only thing I could think of was SOS, which seemed appropriate. I found his hand; before I could signal, his fingers clasped mine and squeezed them hard. I understood that message. It ordered silence and stillness.

Then I saw that Enid had glided farther into the room. With a sudden movement she flung the veil back from her face and stretched out her arms. "Through the mercy of God I have returned to you. We are one again, she and I, and we will be with you through this cycle of . . . ermp!"

Passion lent Donald strength enough to break the grasp of the men who held him. He rushed to Enid and caught her in an embrace that cut off her breath and — thank goodness! — brought the speech to an abrupt end.

I tried to free my hand from the grasp of Ramses, but he hung on. "Lights," he said.

The chandelier overhead lit up in a blaze of brilliance, and we blinked at one another, too dazzled to move, as Donald lifted Enid into his arms, staggered, recovered, and walked toward the door. He was looking so deeply into her eyes, he would have run headlong into the bedspread and the door if Ramses had not got there first. Deftly as a well-trained butler, he held the curtain aside and flung the panel wide. Without so much as a glance at him Donald passed through and vanished.

"Well!" I exclaimed, and for once could think of nothing more to say.

Ramses closed the door. Grasping the bedspread, he gave it a sharp tug, pulling the nails from the frame, and tossed the spread onto an armchair. Then he returned to his place at the table.

"I think," said Mrs. Jones faintly, "that I could do with a glass of wine."

We all had one. Then everyone began to talk at once — all of us except David, who had obviously been in Ramses's confidence all along.

"Why didn't you warn me?" I demanded.

Emerson said, "Of all the cursed surprises! Good Gad, Ramses —"

"It appears to have worked," Nefret said grudgingly. "But you might have —"

Cyrus kept shaking his head and uttering peculiar American ejaculations, and Mrs. Jones remarked, "Young man, you are one of the most —"

As courtesy demanded, Ramses answered me first. "You told me not to go into long-winded detail."

"Oh, good Gad!" I exclaimed.

"It seemed to me," my son explained, "that this scenario solved many of the dilemmas we faced — the possibility that Mr. Fraser might recognize his wife, the difficulty of getting her back into the room unseen by him, and the greatest peril of all — that he might break down, or fall into a fit when she left him forever."

"So it was your idea?" I inquired.

"We worked it out together, Mrs. Fraser and I."

"Hmph," said Emerson, giving Ramses a piercing look. "Well. Let us hope that matter is settled. Shall we leave Mrs. Jones to her bottle and her biscuits?"

"What are your plans?" I inquired of the lady.

She met my eyes with cool defiance. "I should rather ask you, Mrs. Emerson, what your plans are for me. I will leave Egypt as soon as possible — alone or in custody, as you decide."

"There's no particular hurry about that," Cyrus said coolly. "Why don't you folks run along? After that experience Mrs. Jones requires more than a few crackers for sustenance; if it is agreeable to her, we will have a little late supper and a nice long talk."

After that experience, and the other exhausting activities of the day, I was in no fit state to fence with a woman like Mrs. Jones, so I was happy to leave her to Cyrus. As Emerson led me from the room I saw that Cyrus was slumped comfortably in the armchair, his long legs stretched out, and that Mrs. Jones was watching him like a duellist en garde.

"Lean on me, my dear," said Emerson, his arm encircling my waist. "Is that ankle bothering you?"

"Not at all," I said stoutly. "To tell you the truth, Emerson, I am still stupefied by the unexpected denouement. It is so like Ramses to spring it on us that way! Will he ever get over those secretive habits of his?"

The young people had preceded us and were already some distance ahead. "Hmph," said Emerson ambiguously. "Admit it, Peabody, it was an ingenious idea."

"I expect it was Enid who thought of it. Yes,

411

it must have been she; I gave her a little lecture the other day and she obviously took it to heart."

Emerson's arm tightened, and he said fondly, "Good for you, Peabody. But can she maintain the mystique?"

"You are talking like a man again," I retorted. "It doesn't depend entirely on her; Donald will have to do his part. Hmmm, yes. I believe I will have a little talk with him too."

Emerson laughed. An echoing peal of silvery laughter came floating back to me; Nefret was between the two lads, and as they started down the stairs arm in arm, I could see that she was chatting animatedly, though I could not make out the words. They looked well together, the three of them; I was pleased to see them so friendly.

From Manuscript H:

"You contemptible liar," Nefret exclaimed.

Ramses, who was stretched out on his bed reading, glanced up. She looked like a young, outraged goddess as she stood framed in the open window. It gave on to the deck and the night sky; moonlight outlined her straight, slim body and aureoled her hair. A Norse or Celtic goddess, Ramses thought — not Egyptian, despite the cat she held cradled in her left arm. Not with that red-gold hair.

"The window again?" he said. "You could just come up the gangplank and through the door in the ordinary way. And why did you bring the damned cat?"

"She came screaming after me. I had to bring her or she would have waked the whole household." Nefret shoved his legs out of the way and sat down on the bed. Sekhmet crawled onto Ramses, and Nefret added, "She has fallen in love with Risha, I think; she spends most of her time in the stable admiring him."

"So you rode Risha tonight."

"You don't mind, do you?"

"Would it matter if I did? No, of course I don't mind. If you insist on roaming the countryside alone at night, you are safer on his back than anywhere else."

"Where is David?" Nefret asked, ignoring the implied criticism.

"On deck, keeping an eye on the Valley of the Kings. Had you come the other way you would have seen him."

"Do you expect something will happen tonight?"

"If it does, we will be prepared for it," Ramses said evasively.

Nefret's eyes narrowed. "How fortunate that I came. I will stand my watch too, and you and David can get some sleep."

"You can't stay here all night!"

"Why not? There is plenty of room."

Ramses's hand had come to rest on the cat. He stroked it automatically, too disturbed to notice what he was doing. "Because Mother will skin us alive if she finds out."

"She will not find out." A look of maternal tenderness spread over Nefret's face. "Poor darling, she

413

was absolutely exhausted this evening, and her ankle was very painful. You know how she is; she will not admit weakness even to herself. So I — er — I just made sure she would get a good night's sleep."

Ramses sat bolt upright. "Good Lord! You drugged her?"

"Just a little laudanum in her coffee. I did it for her own good."

Ramses collapsed against the piled-up pillows and Sekhmet moved happily from his knees to his chest. "You are beginning to sound just like her," Ramses muttered. "It was inevitable, I suppose, but the prospects are somewhat alarming. Two of you. . . . I only hope the same idea did not occur to Father."

If he had been looking at Nefret, he might have observed the fleeting expression that crossed her face, but he had become aware of the weight on his diaphragm and was trying to pry Sekhmet off him.

"Now then," Nefret said firmly. "Tell me the truth for a change."

"I did not lie to you."

"Well, perhaps not directly, but there is such a thing as lying by omission. You and David know something you have not told me. What do you expect will happen tonight?"

Ramses sighed and abandoned his attempt to detach the cat. All twenty of her claws were hooked into his shirt. "It may not happen tonight. There is a good chance he will try soon again, though. He is not likely to abandon his purpose, and the more often he is thwarted the more impatient he will become."

"Scudder?" Nefret asked. Ramses nodded, and she went on dryly, "You have thwarted him a bit, haven't you? Has it occurred to you, my boy, that he may be after you now? He would find his task easier if you were out of the way."

"It occurred to me, yes."

"Does he know you were Saiyid?"

"I am still Saiyid, when the occasion requires it. Tonight is one of those occasions. I was about to make the transformation when you popped in. Would you mind popping out again while I change?"

"Yes, I would mind. I want to watch how you do it."

"I wonder Father has kept his sanity all these years," Ramses murmured. "All right, my girl, don't swear. You can watch if you like, and you can listen, for a change, while I explain what David and I are going to do, and if you are a very, very good girl, I will allow you to help."

He got rid of Sekhmet by tickling her stomach until she loosened her grip and rolled over. Leaving her indignant and forlorn on the bed, he moved to a chair and began to unlace his boots. Hands clasped around her raised knees, Nefret watched interestedly while he removed shirt, boots, and stockings and rolled his trouser legs up.

"Aren't you going to take off your trousers?" she inquired as he slipped on a worn galabeeyah.

"Not with you looking on." Quickly and expertly he wound the long cloth of his turban round his head and then turned to the mirror.

"There are only three men on board," he explained

415

as he worked. "The others live in Luxor or on the West Bank, and they go home at night. The three will be snoring by midnight; I don't anticipate any activity before then. Saiyid is waiting for me on shore, where Bellingham stationed him."

"That is not very sensible," Nefret exclaimed. "Scudder can avoid Saiyid by the simple expedient of approaching by water — swimming, or in a small boat. What was the Colonel thinking of?"

"The Colonel knows quite well what he is doing, Nefret."

Ramses turned from the mirror, and she gasped. "Good Lord! What did you . . . Stand still, I want a look at you."

"The wrinkles are drawn on," Ramses said as she inspected his face at uncomfortably close quarters. "Sethos, the man I told you of, had developed several varieties of greasepaint; I am using a water-soluble type, since the other kind is devilish hard to remove, and Mother has eyes like a hawk. The warts are constructed of another substance Sethos invented; it adheres like glue unless subjected to prolonged immersion in water."

"What do you do, put your head in a bucket?" Nefret asked, running an inquiring finger along one of his eyebrows.

"Or a washbasin. And no, you may not watch me do it. I have lightened my eyebrows and mustache with another sort of paint; Saiyid is beginning to go gray, and a lighter color along the edges of the brows makes them appear less heavy. My face is longer and thinner than Saiyid's, so I use pads to round

416

out my cheeks." He obligingly opened his mouth in response to her probing finger. "The stain on my teeth has to be removed with alcohol. It is not such an exact resemblance, you see; Bellingham never looks at the face of a servant, and the real trick is in imitating Saiyid's posture and mannerisms."

He crooked his elbow and scratched his side with clawed fingers.

"That is just how he does it," Nefret admitted. "Can you show me how to —"

"If you like," Ramses said. He turned quickly away from the lovely, eager face that looked up at him.

However, as he retreated to a safe distance he remembered to walk with Saiyid's loose-kneed shuffle, and Nefret laughed appreciatively.

"Excellent," she said. "Wait for me; I need to get something from my room."

"What?"

"My other knife. I left it in the cupboard."

"Must you?"

"Decidedly. I will join you in a moment."

"Not me, I am going to meet Saiyid. Go to David. Perhaps you can persuade him to snatch a few hours' sleep, though I doubt it."

"Thank you, my boy." She smiled at him and started for her room. Ramses slammed his door in Sekhmet's face and went out, followed by her mournful howls.

When Nefret crept on deck she saw David as a dark, motionless silhouette against the moonlight. She coughed gently to warn him of her approach; a startled outcry would have resounded through the still night.

"Ramses told me you were here," David said without turning.

"Are you going to scold me too?" She spoke in the same semi-whisper and went to stand next to him.

"What would be the use? But I am not going to go to bed and leave you here alone."

"I would not be alone. Hassan and Mustafa and several of the others are below. My eyes are as keen as yours."

"The moonlight is bright." As was his habit, David avoided an argument. "Even a swimmer's head would be visible from here."

Nefret nodded. "When — if — you see him, what will you do? Call out?"

He turned his head to look down at her and she saw the flash of white teeth. "Mew," he said.

"What?"

"Mew. Or is it me-ow? Everyone in Luxor knows about the cats; a sound from one of them will alert Ramses without frightening our visitor away."

"Oh, dear," said Nefret.

"What is wrong?"

"Back in a minute."

She could hear Sekhmet quite clearly even through the closed door. She is stupid, Nefret thought with rueful amusement; the window is wide open. Anubis or Bastet would have been out it long since. They would not have howled, either.

The howls stopped as soon as she opened the door. Sekhmet fell fondly at Nefret's feet, and the girl stooped to pick her up. "What am I going to do with you?" she demanded. "If I shut you in a cupboard, you will yell loud enough to be heard a mile away."

Carrying the cat, she went back to David, who was not at all pleased to see them. "You will have to take the creature away," he insisted. "Ramses will kill her if she spoils his plan."

"He would never do such a thing. She will be quiet as long as one of us holds her."

"Inshallah," David said dourly.

The night wore on. There was no sign of movement on the deck of the other dahabeeyah, and the smooth silvery pathway of light across the water remained undisturbed. The stillness was broken only by an occasional stamp or snort from Risha, waiting un-hobbled and untied on the bank, and by the distant howls of jackals and pariah dogs. Sekhmet's raucous purr faded into silence; David was holding her in the crook of his arm and she had fallen asleep. Nefret stifled a yawn. David put his free arm around her, and she leaned against him, grateful for the strength and warmth and affectionate support of his arm. Her eyes were getting heavy and the night air was cool.

He is much more demonstrative than Ramses, she thought drowsily. I suppose Ramses cannot help being reserved, poor boy; Englishmen don't hug one an-other, and Aunt Amelia hardly ever puts her arms around him or kisses him. She is not demonstrative either — except, I suppose, with the Professor. They are all dear to me, though, in their different ways. Perhaps if I were friendlier with Ramses . . .

She was half-asleep, her head against David's

shoulder, when she felt him stiffen. There was no break in the smooth ripple of the moonlit waters. David was looking at the bank. Something moved there, pale in the shadows. Ramses? Indistinct as the form was, it did not appear to be wearing skirts.

"Now?" she whispered.

"Wait." Tensed and watching, David removed his arm.

"He hasn't seen him," Nefret said, softly but urgently. "Where is he?"

Her pronouns were confused, but David understood. "I don't know. Hang on."

He thrust the cat into her arms and started toward the gangplank.

The pale form slipped through the trees, avoiding the moonlit open spaces. It was not Ramses; she could not have said how she knew, but she was as certain as if she had seen his face. Had David forgot the signal? Should she give it?

Sekhmet spared her the decision. Annoyed at being rudely awakened and finding Nefret's grasp uncomfortable, she opened her mouth and complained.

Not until later did Nefret understand the sequence of events. It all happened so fast, she had no time to think or react. The sharp crack of a rifle broke the silence, and a man burst out of the shadows and darted across the moonlit ground. Reaching the bank, he flung himself into the water.

Ramses was close on his heels, but not close enough. He had pulled the robe over his head and tossed it aside. As he dived in after the fugitive, several more shots rang out.

"Damn, damn, damn!" said Nefret.

When she reached David he was standing on the bank. He had taken off his coat. She started to reach for him and then realized she was still holding Sekhmet. With another, more emphatic "Damn!" she put the cat down and took hold of David's arm. "What happened? Who fired those shots?"

"I did." She turned to see Bellingham coming toward them. He was formally dressed, even to his white stock. The rifle was still in his hand. He took a handful of shells out of his pocket and began to reload. "I apologize for alarming you, Miss Forth. I did not know you were there."

The moonlight was so bright she could see every line on his face. It was courteously impassive, but he looked from her to David to the Amelia in a way that brought the blood flooding into her cheeks. She said hotly, "I had good reason to be alarmed. You might have hit Ramses."

"Ramses?" Bellingham's eyebrows rose. "What are you talking about? I fired at Dutton Scudder. It could only have been he. I knew he would come after Dolly, I waited for him —"

"Oh, do be quiet," Nefret exclaimed. She turned her back on him. "Do you see him, David?"

"No. I'm going in after him."

Again she caught hold of him, resisting his attempt to pull away. "The current will have drawn them downstream. They would come ashore farther down."

"Yes, right." He began running along the bank. Nefret stumbled over Sekhmet but managed to stay on her feet. As she followed David she heard a startled exclamation, a thud, and a yowl from Sekhmet. Bellingham must have tripped over the cat too.

Before they had gone more than a few yards she saw two dripping figures coming toward them. David jolted to a stop. "Thank God," he exclaimed breathlessly. "But who — how — is it — how did he get —"

One of the men was Ramses. The other was not the fugitive.

"I forgot to tell you," Nefret said. "I told the Professor everything."

"A damned good thing, too," said Emerson. "Can you make it back to the dahabeeyah, my boy?"

"Yes, sir, certainly." But he leaned gratefully against the strong arm that braced his shoulders and did not draw away when they started back along the bank. Bellingham had gone; a lighted window on the Valley of the Kings indicated activity of some kind. *He is probably cleaning his gun,* Nefret thought angrily.

Not far from the spot where Scudder had jumped into the water she saw the cat. Sekhmet was playing with something, batting it with her paw, trying to toss it into the air. David bent and took it from her. It was a straw hat with a black band round the crown.

"I cannot decide whether you are careless or just unlucky," Nefret remarked, slapping a square of sticking plaster over the furrow that had creased Ramses's scalp.

"Foolhardy, rather," Emerson grunted. He looked

disconsolately at his waterlogged pipe and returned it to his pocket. "You ought to have realized that Bellingham is so bent on killing Scudder that he would mow down anyone who got in his way."

"If it had not done so earlier, that fact would have dawned on me tonight," said Ramses.

He flinched back as Nefret thrust her face close to his. "The wrinkles and the warts washed off in the water," she said, inspecting him. "But your teeth need to be cleaned. You had better do it now before you forget. Here is the alcohol."

They had given the hat back to Sekhmet. Her claws hooked possessively in it, she was chewing the brim in a thoughtful manner.

"You saw no sign of Scudder?" David asked. "He may have drowned, you know."

"Unlikely," Ramses said, deciding not to shake his head. He was still a little dizzy. "He is a strong swimmer. I might have got him, though, if I had been unimpaired."

"I wasn't trying to get him," Emerson said placidly. "Not after I realized you were in difficulty."

"Thank heaven you were there," David said. "I failed to realize Ramses was hurt or I would have —"

"Don't call yourself names," Nefret interrupted. "I held you back. I would have let you go — and gone with you! — if I had not known the Professor was on the job."

She beamed admiringly at Emerson, who beamed back at her.

"Father was in your room," Ramses said. "When

you went there, ostensibly to get your knife —"

"I told him what you were planning," Nefret said calmly.

"And I," said Emerson, "went up to the top deck, where I had an excellent view of the proceedings. I was in the water almost as soon as Ramses, but since I was some distance away it took a while to reach him."

"I am very grateful, Father," said Ramses formally.

"Hmph," said Emerson, giving him a sharp look. "We are a step farther along, even though Scudder got away from us. We know who he was."

"Was?" Nefret repeated. "You believe he is dead, then?"

"No. He will not appear as Tollington again; that is why I used the past tense. But it is clear, surely, that he has another persona. He cannot have spent the past five years as an American tourist."

"And we are no nearer to knowing his other identity," David murmured. "Unless my grandfather . . ."

"Yes, we will certainly have to discuss this with Abdullah," Emerson agreed. "But no more talk tonight. You young people need your rest. Go to bed at once, boys, and I will take Nefret home. Sleep as late as you like tomorrow."

"Mother will ask questions if we are not there for breakfast," Ramses said.

Emerson had risen. He gave his son a look of surprised reproach. "I intend to tell your mother everything, Ramses. A happy marriage depends on complete honesty between husband and wife."

"But, sir," Nefret said in alarm.

"Well, perhaps not the laudanum," Emerson conceded. *"And I suppose there is no harm in allowing her to believe that this was your first unauthorized visit here. There's no keeping the rest of it from her, though. She knows a bullet wound when she sees one, and she'll insist on having a look at Ramses, you can be sure of it. And,"* he added, *"she will undoubtedly claim she knew about Tollington all along!"*

"I began to suspect Mr. Tollington some time ago," I said.

We were having a late breakfast; I had overslept, which I seldom do, but Emerson's narrative — together with the cup of strong tea he brought to my bedside — had blown away the last shreds of drowsiness. I did not miss the glances the others exchanged when I made that claim, and in justice to myself I elaborated on it.

"It was the clue that was not there. You remember, Emerson? What was missing was the lady's jewelry."

"Obviously," Emerson began, scowling. "He took it to —"

"My dear, it is not obvious at all. Just follow my reasoning, all of you. Whether she eloped with him or was carried off, she had with her her finest garments, including a ball gown. That sort of toilette demands elegant jewelry, and a good deal of it. Remembering the jewels Bellingham

425

gave his young daughter, we can assume he show-ered even finer things on his young wife. They were with her when she left him, and they were not on her body. After Dutton had murdered her in a fit of passion, he was seized with remorse. He buried her in those elegant garments, even replacing her — er — underclothing, but not her jewels. Not even her wedding ring.

"If sold through illicit channels, as it would have to have been, even a parure of precious stones would bring a relatively modest sum — not enough to support Scudder in European style for five years, even in Egypt. Our initial assump-tion still stands. He must have spent at least part of that time as an Egyptian. I think he kept the money he got from the jewels in reserve, awaiting the return of his enemy. Though not sufficient to maintain him for the entire period, it would be enough to enable him to live in the luxurious style of a wealthy tourist for a few weeks or months — long enough to strike up an acquain-tance with the Bellinghams and follow them wherever they went. When I first met Mr. 'Tollington' I believed him to be an old friend of the Bellinghams, but certain casual statements of Miss Dolly's made it clear he was not travelling with them. I was not certain it was he," I con-cluded modestly. "But as soon as I realized Scud-der might be playing the role of a tourist, Tollington became a prime suspect."

"The name was a stroke of genius," Ramses said. "Who would suspect a man named Booghis

Tucker Tollington?"

"I did," I said. "And so, I gather, did you. Ramses, I am extremely put out with you. I feel sure you were the ringleader in last night's affair, but David and Nefret must bear their share of the blame as well. I want your solemn word that you will never again —"

"Now, now, Peabody," Emerson said, rising. "I have already reprimanded the culprits, and I feel certain we can depend on them to — er — behave sensibly in the future. Hmph. Perhaps, my dear, you ought not accompany us to the Valley. Give that ankle another day of rest, eh?"

I pushed my chair back. The children were already on their feet, ready to bolt. "Naturally I intend to accompany you, Emerson. There is nothing at all wrong with me. We will leave as soon as I have had a look at Ramses."

Ramses's face fell. "I assure you, Mother, there is no need for —"

I led him to our room and made him sit down near the window. Nefret had done a neat job, but I disinfected the wound again and wound a few strips of cloth around his head to hold the cottonwool in place. He objected, of course.

"Sticking plaster does not adhere well to hair," I explained.

"It adheres only too well," said my son. "As I observed when you removed it."

"Ramses." I put my hand on his cheek and forced him to look up at me. "It is not a serious injury, but if the bullet had come an inch closer

427

. . . Must you take such chances? Promise me you will be more prudent."

After a moment of silence Ramses said, "Prudence does not appear to be a prominent characteristic of this family. I am sorry to have worried you, Mother. May I go now?"

"I suppose so," I said with a sigh. I knew that was all I was likely to get out of him. Even a promise would be worthless; Ramses's definition of "prudence" would certainly not agree with mine.

"It was the dream, wasn't it?" he said suddenly.

"What?"

"You dreamed of a large cat carrying a diamond necklace," Ramses said. "That was what made you think of Mrs. Bellingham's jewelry."

"Perhaps," I said cautiously. He held the door for me, and as we left the room I felt obliged to add, "Such dreams are not portents or omens, you know, only the subconscious mind at work."

Ramses looked thoughtful.

The others were waiting. Nefret inspected Ramses and said with a laugh, "How very romantic you look, my boy! You had better avoid Miss Dolly; the bandage and the mustache make a devastating combination."

"Stop teasing him, Nefret," I said, seeing Ramses's cheekbones darken. "The bandage was necessary, and the mustache is — er — quite a nice mustache."

Ramses's jaw dropped. "But, Mother! I thought you —"

"It was something of a shock initially," I admitted. "But I have become accustomed to it. Just make sure you keep it clean and tidy, my dear. I believe that is a crumb . . . ?"

I removed the crumb and gave him a kindly smile.

"If we are going," Emerson said in a loud voice, "let us go."

As we were leaving the house a man whom I recognized as one of Cyrus's servants approached and handed me a letter.

"Cyrus has asked us to dine," I said after reading the brief missive.

"Damned if I will," said Emerson.

"Then I will ask him to dine with us." Taking a pencil from my pocket, I scribbled a note on the back of the paper and handed it to the servant. "There are a few loose ends to be tied up in the Fraser affair," I continued as Emerson took my hand and led me away. "Aren't you curious to know what transpired last night between Cyrus and Mrs. Jones?"

"I have a fairly good idea," said Emerson.

It was his tone of voice rather than the words themselves that brought understanding. "Emerson! Are you suggesting that Cyrus . . . that Mrs. Jones . . . You cannot be serious!"

"He made no attempt to conceal his interest in the lady," Emerson said calmly. "And she is in a difficult position. She needs his goodwill."

"Cyrus would never take advantage of a woman in that fashion," I insisted.

"There's that lurid imagination of yours again, Peabody. Are you picturing Vandergelt twirling his mustache — stroking his goatee, rather — and hissing threats like a stage villain, while Mrs. Jones pleads with him to respect her honor?" Emerson chuckled. "You are quite right, he would not stoop to threats or blackmail; but they are two mature individuals, and I fancy she is not entirely indifferent to him."

"Nonsense, Emerson. His message said . . . Hmmm. It said nothing except that he looks forward to seeing us this evening. Hmmmm."

"Save your breath, Peabody, this stretch is a bit steep." He helped me up it and then continued, "I have a few loose ends to tie up myself. You don't suppose, do you, that I will allow Bellingham to use my son as a target without registering a complaint?"

We had reached the top of the *gebel*. The children were some distance ahead; they stopped and looked back, to see if we were coming, and I observed that Ramses was fingering his mustache.

"The main thing," Emerson continued, "is to find Scudder, curse him. That will put an end to this nonsense. Besides, the damned fellow is interfering with my work."

"How are you planning to go about it?" I inquired.

"I have given it some thought. Using Miss Dolly as a decoy does not appear to have been very effective, and although she is a singularly silly young woman one would not want to see her injured."

"One would not want to see anyone injured," I said with considerable emphasis. "Including you, my dear."

"If I could think how to transfer his attentions to me, without putting you and the children at risk, I would do it," Emerson admitted. "At the moment I cannot."

"Thank heaven for that." We began the descent into the valley and Emerson fell silent. I knew what he was thinking. My mind was bent on the same thing, but I was equally at a loss for a solution. Inviting Dolly to stay with us might lure Scudder into our hands, but there was risk to all of us in that scheme, and there was an equal risk that sheer exasperation would inspire someone, possibly me, to murder Dolly before Scudder got to her.

As in the past, I began to pin my hopes on Abdullah. I had asked him to make inquiries about strangers in Luxor, and about tomb Twenty-A, but I had not had the opportunity to talk with him since. A council of war was what we needed. It was too late to keep the children out of it. They were already in, deeper than I would have liked.

But when we reached the tomb we found Abdullah lying unconscious on the ground and two of the other men being tended by their companions. The ceiling of the passage had collapsed.

CHAPTER TWELVE

These hired thugs are never reliable.

"Is anyone else down there?" was Emerson's first question.

"No, Father of Curses." Selim, Abdullah's youngest and most beloved son, knelt by his father. He had removed his galabeeyah and folded it under the old man's head.

"How long has he been unconscious?" Nefret asked, taking Abdullah's hand.

"It happened just before you came." Selim gave me a look of appeal. He adored Nefret, as did all the men — but I was the Sitt Hakim, and I had tended their hurts for many years. Though I knew she was as capable as I, I felt I must respond to that appeal.

She understood. "His pulse is steady," she reported, moving aside to let me take her place.

"He was only knocked unconscious," I said confidently. Abdullah was beginning to stir, and I know that the patient's own belief can do more for him than any physician. "Turbans are very useful articles of attire; his has saved him from more serious injury."

Emerson had gone to have a look at Ali and Yussuf. He came trotting back. "How is he?" he asked anxiously.

"Just a knock on the head," I said even more firmly.

Abdullah's eyes had opened. He let out a sigh when he saw me, and then he looked up at Emerson.

"My head," he said faintly. "It is only my head, Father of Curses."

Emerson's worried face smoothed out and then creased again into a hideous scowl. "It is the hardest part of you. I told you the ceiling needed to be braced. What the devil happened?"

"It was my fault," said Abdullah.

"No," said Emerson. "It was mine. I ought to have been here." His voice deepened into a growl. "Lie still, you stubborn old fool, or I will have Selim hold you down. Peabody?"

In fact, the damage was not much worse than I had stated. He would have a number of painful bruises on his back and shoulders, but the turban had probably saved him from a severe concussion. He had a large bump on his cranium, however, so I said, "I would rather he did not move for a while. David, can you and Selim lift him, very gently, and carry him into the shade?"

We got him settled comfortably on a blanket, and I left David and Nefret to keep him company — and, as I instructed David, to sit on his head if he did not obey orders. Emerson and Ramses had already gone down into the tomb with Selim; I inspected our other wounded with my ears pricked for the dread sound of another rockfall. Ali and Yussuf were not much hurt. Abdullah must have been the first into the dangerous section, and the last to leave. It was what I would have expected of him.

Before long the three returned. I was waiting for them at the entrance.

"Well?" I said. "How bad is it?"

"Could be worse," Emerson grunted. "How is Abdullah?"

We went to join the others. Nefret was holding a wet cloth to Abdullah's head. Hands folded on his chest, face set in the too familiar expression of a man enduring female foolishness only because he must, Abdullah said irritably, "I will go back to work now, Father of Curses. Tell Nur Misur to let me up."

"No one is going back to work for a while," Emerson said, sitting down and crossing his legs. "I have sent Selim to bring beams to brace the ceiling."

"But after a few more feet the *tafl* ends," Abdullah protested. "I was careless, yes, but it was because I could see good stone and open space ahead. The passage is only half-filled with rubble, there is room to get through."

"Oh?" Emerson caught himself. "Well. We will see it tomorrow, after we have built supports for the rotten section. Stop squirming, Abdullah, there is no use fighting the ladies."

"Quite right," I said. "I don't think you have concussion, Abdullah, but I want to be certain — and I am sure you must have the devil of a headache. I have been wanting to talk with you anyhow. It is time we had a council of war!"

"Ah," said Abdullah. He rolled his eyes toward Ramses, who had seated himself on the ground next to David. "What happened to you, my son?"

It was Ramses who replied, accepting the affectionate form of address and responding in kind. "It is part of the story I promised to tell you, my father."

"When did you do that?" I demanded in surprise.

Ramses glanced at me. He had spoken Arabic to Abdullah, and he continued in the same language. "Though he was too courteous to say so, Abdullah had wondered why he had seen so little of David. I told him we were on the trail of the man who had killed the dead lady, and that I needed David to — er — protect me."

"That is as it should be," Abdullah said.

"Hmph," I said. "Well, Abdullah, now we need *you*. We have discovered that the murderer was for a time disguised as a tourist, but he cannot play that part any longer. He must have been here in Luxor for some years —"

"Yes, Sitt Hakim, we talked of that before," Abdullah said.

"You also discussed it with the Father of Curses, I believe."

"I have discussed it with many people," said

Abdullah. If a wrinkled, dignified old man could look demure, that was how he looked.

"Ramses and David too?" I exclaimed.

"And Nur Misur." Abdullah's lips parted in a broad smile. "All of you came to me. All of you said, 'Do not tell the others.' "

"Oh, dear," I said, unable to keep my face straight. "How absurdly we have behaved! Well, Abdullah, the need for your well-known discretion is at an end. Cards on the table, as Mr. Vandergelt would say! What have you found out?"

Abdullah was enjoying himself so much, I believe he had forgot about his headache. His narrative was somewhat long and literary, but I had not the heart to interrupt him. He had every right to be pleased with himself.

He had narrowed the suspects down to four. All had come to Luxor approximately five years earlier; all had worked as guides or *gaffirs* or diggers in the Valley; all lived in Gurneh or one of the nearby villages; and all, said Abdullah with a significant glance at me, lived alone.

I had not thought of that as a criterion. It was true, though; if Dutton had taken an Egyptian wife and raised a brood of Egyptian children, it would have made concealment of his identity virtually impossible.

"Good work, Abdullah," I declared. "Now we must interview these men."

"That is not so easy, Sitt," Abdullah replied. "They are not settled persons. They do not stay in the same place or work at the same job for long. They have no friends, no wives, no — er —"

"Of course," Emerson said thoughtfully. "That is precisely why they are suspects — because they are men of a certain type. Too lazy or too undependable to keep a position, solitary by nature, unable or unwilling to make friends."

"And," Ramses added, stroking his mustache, "though Abdullah's criteria were logical, they do not exclude all other possibilities. Scudder may have moved away from the Gurneh area after he finished interring the lady. We don't know how well he speaks Arabic; if he has gained native fluency, he might risk making friends or acquiring — er —"

"Hmph," I said. "That is true, Ramses, but it is deuced discouraging."

"There was another thing you asked me to find out," said Abdullah. "None of those I questioned admitted to knowing of this tomb. I do not think they were lying."

"No reason why they should," Emerson said. "What about the men who worked for Loret in ninety-eight?"

"Ah." Abdullah nodded. "I wondered if you had thought of that, Emerson."

"The former director of the Antiquities Service?" Nefret asked. "Why did you think of him?"

Ramses got in ahead of his father. "His methods were careless in the extreme. He had his people digging random pits looking for tomb

437

entrances, and often he was absent from the excavations. Even at the time there were rumors that the men had found a number of tombs they never reported to him."

"The stories were true," Abdullah said. "Those tombs were looted of what little they contained, and filled in again while Loret Effendi was away from the Valley. But there is no secret about those tombs among the men of Gurneh; they would have told me of this one if they had known of it."

"Still, one of Loret's workmen might have found it," I said. "And not told the others."

"Only if that workman was Dutton Scudder," Ramses said.

"Why not?" Nefret demanded. "We agreed he must — oh, very well, Professor, *might* —have lived as an Egyptian during those years; why not as one of M. Loret's workers?"

Emerson shook his head. "That line of inquiry is not likely to be very productive. Over the years in question Loret employed dozens of men, and if he kept pay records, which I doubt, they will have long since vanished. Ah well, the questions had to be asked. Abdullah, you have done well. Go home and rest now. I will find a carriage —"

Abdullah set up such an outcry at this that we were forced to let him have his way. He was persuaded to return to Gurneh when Emerson pointed out he could continue his detectival inquiries there, but he insisted indignantly that he *could* walk and *would* walk. None of the symptoms

I feared were apparent, so we let him go, with Mustafa and Daoud to accompany him. Daoud, Abdullah's nephew, was the largest and strongest of the men. He was also in considerable awe of me and my magical powers; after I had taken him aside and told him he must send someone for me at once if there was any change in Abdullah's condition, I knew I could depend on him to watch the old man closely.

"Now then," said Emerson after the little party had gone, "back to work, eh?"

"For pity's sake, Emerson!" I exclaimed. "You said no one was going back in there until you —"

"Made certain it was safe," Emerson interrupted. "That is what I intend to do now." He looked at Ibrahim, our most experienced carpenter, who grinned cheerfully back at him. "I wanted Abdullah away from here before we began," Emerson continued. "Someone *would* have to sit on his head to keep him from going back inside, and he was not fit. Leave off grumbling at me, Peabody, I will take care."

"At least put on your pith helmet," I said, handing it to him.

"Oh. Yes, certainly." Emerson clapped it on his head. I took it off, adjusted the chin strap, and fixed the hat firmly in place.

Naturally I felt obliged to assess the situation for myself, and Emerson overruled my objections when Nefret demanded to go along.

"I would rather neither of you came," he said. "But what is sauce for the goose is sauce for —

er — another goose."

The descent confirmed my initial impression that this was not going to be one of my favorite tombs. We had already been forced to brace the ceiling in one place, and by the time we reached the place where the passage levelled off, I was soaked with perspiration. The candles burned low; we were within a few feet of the rockfall before I saw it, a sharp slope of rotten gray shale, splintered and tumbled. One of the pickaxes lay on the floor where Ali or Yussuf had dropped it as they fled.

"What a horrid place!" said Nefret. She sounded quite cheerful, though, and the candle she carried illumined a face bright with satisfaction under the dust that smeared it. Ramses, shoulders hunched and head drawn in like a turtle's, moved up to stand beside her. I had not seen him follow Nefret, but I ought to have expected he would be unable to stay out of the place.

Emerson was conferring with Ibrahim. With a murmured apology Ramses slipped past me, and Emerson turned to include him in the discussion. Finally Emerson said, "Yes, that should do it. Go back up, Ibrahim, and get started."

Then, to my horror and alarm, he picked up the ax and began prying at a slab of rock atop the slope.

"Emerson!" I cried — softly, however, since I did not like the echo in that gloomy place.

Slowly and cautiously Emerson slid the piece

of rock out. Its removal dislodged a number of smaller bits that rolled onto the floor and the boots of my husband and son, but nothing fell from the ceiling. As yet.

"Keep quiet, Peabody," said Emerson irritably. He began pulling away more rubble. "There is often a faint scraping sound when the rock is about to give, and I cannot hear when you moan that way."

Nefret was standing beside me now. She put a hot, sticky, filthy hand on my shoulder. In the dusty mask of her face her eyes shone bright as stars. "He knows what he is doing," she whispered.

Emerson usually does know what he is doing — with regard to excavation, at least — and my fears for him lessened a trifle as I observed the delicacy of his touch and the caution he exhibited. He was doing what the men would have to do; it was noblesse oblige that moved him to take on that dangerous task. It was also curiosity. When he had opened a sufficient space between the sagging ceiling and the top of the rubble, he thrust the candle, and his head, through.

"Hmph," he said.

I bit my lip till I tasted blood. I wanted to scream at him, but I knew that would not be wise. When he drew back and handed Ramses the candle, inviting him with a gesture to have a look for himself, I did not want to scream at him. I wanted to murder him.

Luckily I did not scream or moan. I do not

know what Emerson heard; the sound was too faint for my ears to catch. With a shout of "Watch out, Peabody!" he caught hold of Ramses and with a heave of his mighty arms sent him staggering backward.

With an answering shout that was drowned out by the crash of falling rock, I dashed forward. Ramses's candle had gone out. I had dropped mine. I could see nothing but darkness. I collided with Ramses, who tried to hold on to me; pulling away, I plummeted into a hard, warm, familiar surface.

"Ah," said Emerson. "I thought I might run into you just about here. Light another candle, will you, Nefret? Ramses — all right, are you?"

"Damn you, Emerson," I gasped, running frantic hands over the parts of him I could reach.

"Tsk, tsk, such language! We may as well get out of here. I have learned what I wanted to know."

I had to save my breath for climbing. The speech I composed along the way was never delivered, however, for the first person I saw when I emerged into the soi-disant "burial chamber" was Colonel Bellingham.

He stood at the bottom of the stairs, his stick in one hand and his hat in the other, and even his well-bred countenance showed evidence of astonishment when he saw us.

I cut his attempt at a greeting short. "As you see, Colonel, we are not in a fit state to entertain guests. Will you excuse us?"

"I beg your pardon." He stood aside as I started for the stairs. "I wanted to speak to you. And . . . to see this place."

If I had been a little less exhausted, dirty, and out of breath, I would have felt sorry for him. It did not improve my temper to find Dolly primly seated on a stool someone must have brought for her. The look on her face when she saw Ramses was some compensation, however. He was quite an unpleasant sight, though not much worse than the rest of us.

By the time I finished cleaning my face and hands, I had got my breath back, and my composure. The same was not true of Emerson. Tossing his grimy towel aside, he whirled round and glared at the Colonel.

"Inconvenient as your presence is, sir, you have saved me the trouble of calling on you. What the devil — no, curse it, Peabody, I will not apologize for my language! What the devil are you up to, Bellingham? If you are such a poor marksman you cannot hit your target, you ought not use a firearm."

The Colonel flushed angrily, but he kept his temper. "I came to express my regrets for that unfortunate incident, Professor Emerson. I did not recognize your son. I took him for a native."

"Ah, well, that makes all the difference," Emerson said.

Dolly had recovered from her shock at seeing the grubby, dripping dishevellment of Ramses. Rising, she shook out her skirts and swayed toward him. Proffering a dainty lace-trimmed handkerchief, she cooed, "I cried all night after Daddy told me you had been hurt, Mr. Emerson. You are so gallant! I don't know what would have happened if you had not been there watching over me."

Ramses looked at the minuscule square of cambric and then at his hands, dripping with water and covered with bleeding scratches. "I am afraid, Miss Bellingham, that your handkerchief is inadequate for the purpose, though I thank you for offering it. You had better not come any closer."

"Sit down, Dolly, or go back with Saiyid to the carriage," her father said brusquely. Dolly glanced at Saiyid, who had remained at a discreet distance, and lifted her shoulders disdainfully. She returned to her stool and arranged her skirts.

Ibrahim started down the stairs, accompanied by several other men carrying large pieces of wood. Emerson gave them a longing glance, and Ramses said, "I will go with them, Father."

"Yes, yes," Emerson said. "Tell Ibrahim I will be along shortly. No, Nefret, stay here, you will only be in the way. Colonel, I have only one more thing to say to you, and that is this. Apparently you have decided to take the law into your own hands instead of asking for the assistance to which you are entitled from your government and mine. If your own safety means nothing to you, think of your daughter, whom your reckless behavior endangers."

He was turning away when the Colonel spoke. "You will allow me a statement of my own, sir?"

"Well?"

"I am not unappreciative of your concern and that of your son, Professor. The fact is, however, that if he had not interfered last night, I would have put an end to this business, and to Mr. Tollington." Emerson's surprised reaction brought a grim smile to his lips. "Oh, yes, Professor, I saw him clearly in the moonlight and recognized him. I could have hit him if my aim had not been spoiled by the abrupt appearance of his pursuer. Now he has made good his escape. If you know where he may have gone, you owe it to me to tell me."

"Wrong," Emerson said calmly. "You have every right to defend yourself and your daughter, Colonel, but you do not have the right to track Scudder down in order to kill him. You have other options. You know what they are as well as I do."

"I see." The Colonel's cold gray eyes measured my husband, from his resolute face to his broad shoulders and folded arms. "Well, Professor, I admire your principles. And I admire you, sir; you are a man after my own heart, even if we do not agree. May I ask one more favor?"

"Ask," was the curt reply.

"I want to go down there with you. Only once," he added quickly, for he could see Emerson was about to object. "I must see the place. I have thought about it, dreamed about it . . . Do you understand why I must go?"

"Not entirely," Emerson said dryly. "But I admit your right to do so. Come, then, if you are determined. You will not find it easy or pleasant."

"It cannot be worse than Shiloh," the Colonel replied with a smile.

"Some battlefield of his war, perhaps?" I said to Nefret after he had followed Emerson down the steps.

"Perhaps." She lowered her voice to a whisper and gestured at Dolly. "I should speak to her, I suppose. She looks rather forlorn sitting there alone."

"Bored would be more accurate," I said. "Do so if you like. I wonder if your true motive is not courtesy but the desire to offend. You smell rather strongly of bat, my dear."

She laughed and left me. They made quite a funny picture, Nefret cross-legged on the ground, Dolly on the edge of the stool, as far from Nefret as she could get without standing up.

They were still talking — at least Nefret was — when the Colonel returned, accompanied by Ramses. I offered the Colonel a damp cloth, which he accepted with a bow whose formality contrasted ironically with his bedraggled appearance.

"Thank you, Mrs. Emerson," he said, returning it after removing the worst of the dust from his face. "We will not linger. I have seen what I came to see." An involuntary shudder ran through him.

"She was never down there, you know," I said gently. "You saw where . . ."

"Yes, your husband indicated the spot and described its original appearance. I have come away with a greater respect for archaeologists," he added as we strolled toward the two girls. "I did not realize their work was carried on in places so unpleasant and so dangerous."

He had changed the subject, neatly and courteously, and I accepted it. "It is not often as bad as that," I said. "Have you changed your mind, then, about taking up Egyptology as a hobby?"

"I shall not return to Egypt again. Well, Dolly, are you ready to go?"

Realizing there was no hope of capturing Ramses, who had immediately retreated into the tomb, Dolly stood up. "Yes, Daddy."

"Run along with Saiyid, then. I will soon catch up; I want to say a few words to Miss Forth."

"Oh?" She gave Nefret a look of pure, solid dislike, but obeyed.

The Colonel was as brief as he had promised. "I fear I may have inadvertently offended you last evening, Miss Forth. If anything I said or did conveyed a false impression, I apologize profoundly."

"It is forgotten," Nefret said.

She was unkempt and sweat-stained, but she held herself in a way that reminded me she had once been High Priestess of Isis, and she met his gaze with unsmiling dignity.

The Colonel bowed. "You are most gracious. Good day to you, ladies."

"What was that about?" I asked curiously.

"He has decided my fortune is large enough to compensate for behavior unbecoming a lady." Her voice was as hard as her set face. She hesitated for a moment and then shrugged. "I will tell you if you promise not to lose your temper — or tell the Professor. All he actually said was that he had not known I was there; it was the way he looked when he said it, at me and then at David and at the *Amelia,* as if he thought we had been . . . The apology only made it worse. How can people have such evil minds?"

I suppose I ought to have pointed out that most people do have evil minds, and that it was precisely this sort of unpleasantness I had wanted to spare her when I forbade her to stay with the boys on the dahabeeyah. I could not bear to do it, though. She was such a strange mixture of worldly wisdom and innocence! As Emerson had so pithily put it, she walked in two worlds and always would, for the beliefs and values of that strange society in which she had lived so long would never be entirely eradicated. The degree of her distress made me wish I had not been so polite to Colonel Bellingham. Her cynical assessment was probably correct, though I thought it was not only her fortune that he wanted. He had, I remembered, expressed approval of "spirited young ladies."

I determined on the instant that I would put an end to the Colonel's insane expectations. Old-fashioned gentleman that he was, he would probably ask Emerson's permission before paying his addresses to Nefret, and then Emerson would toss him out the window, which would be quite satisfactory. There was no need for Emerson to take so much trouble, however, or for Nefret's being affronted by further contacts. I would speak to Bellingham myself.

My dear Emerson was in excellent spirits when we stopped for the day. Nothing cheers him so much as burrowing around in tombs. The results of the afternoon's labor had been encouraging. Beyond the broken stretch the passage entered a stratum of more stable rock. Emerson could talk of nothing else during the walk back to the house. "For once the ancient excavators displayed good sense," he declared enthusiastically. "In Carter's tomb the passageway continues to descend through the *tafl;* they must have been hoping to strike another layer of limestone or chalk farther down. Our builders decided to go up, and that has had another fortunate result. Most of the debris we removed with such effort was carried into the tomb by floodwater and packed hard by succeeding rains. But as we all know, water flows only downhill! The continuation of the passage is relatively clear. The plan itself is . . ." And so on.

After we had changed our disgusting attire and

cleansed our persons, the children decided to run over to Gurneh to visit Abdullah. They must have agreed to "take turns" with the horses; this time Nefret rode Asfur and David one of the hired mounts. That left my dear Emerson and me to take tea à deux, and it was a rare pleasure to have him all to myself.

My first act was to read the messages that were waiting. Most were the usual thing — cards from newcomers to Luxor, invitations to a tennis party, and a dinner party on board Mr. Davis's dahabeeyah, the *Bedawin*. I could not but share Emerson's view that Luxor was becoming a microcosm of the most boring aspects of English society. The only message of import was from Cyrus; he begged us again to come to him, since he had invited another guest. He added that he would send his carriage and that we need not dress, since this was to be a "business meeting."

Under those circumstances Emerson was graciously pleased to agree, and in return I allowed him to ramble on about his tomb. We had a happy hour together before the young people returned with the good news that Abdullah's recovery was proceeding as I had hoped.

"I suppose Daoud smeared that loathsome green salve of his all over Abdullah," I said.

Nefret chuckled. "How do you know these things, Aunt Amelia? Daoud asked us not to tell you about the salve. Now he will believe you can read his mind at a distance."

"He suspects me of darker talents than that,

my dear," I said with a smile. "I expect the horrid stuff cannot do Abdullah any harm so long as he doesn't eat it. Now you had better run along and change. Cyrus is sending his carriage for us."

"I was under the impression . . . ," Ramses began.

"You need not put yourself through the torture of wearing a suit," I said. "Just tidy yourself, you are very dusty and hot. We are dining with Cyrus because he has invited another guest."

Ramses raised his eyebrows. "Ah," he said, and went inside.

"I wonder what he meant by that," I said to Emerson.

"You ought by now to be able to interpret Ramses's enigmatic remarks," replied my husband. "He suspects who the other guest is. As do I."

Emerson's hints had prepared me. The fact that Cyrus did not meet us at the door as he usually did was another clue. When we entered the drawing room we found him deep in conversation with no other than Mrs. Jones.

The warmth of Cyrus's welcome made up for any earlier failure of hospitality. He pressed us to take seats and refreshment. It was all very pleasant and conventional, but I have never seen any advantage in shilly-shallying, so when we were settled in Cyrus's comfortable armchairs, with glasses in our hands, I began the conversation.

"Perhaps you can tell me, Mrs. Jones, how the

Frasers are getting on? I had hoped to hear from Enid today, but have received no communication."

"That is because she designated me as her messenger," was the suave reply. Reaching into her handbag, the lady removed an envelope, which she passed to me.

It was addressed, not to me, but to all of us, including "Miss Forth" and "Mr. Todros," so I did not hesitate to read it aloud.

My dearest friends,

The cure has begun, I believe. He is still rather in awe of "Princess Tasherit," but no woman, I suppose, should complain of being worshipped! I have taken your words to heart, dear Amelia, and I hope — I believe — that we will do well enough in future.

We leave for Cairo tomorrow on our way back to England. I felt it best I should not see you again, for parting would be more painful than I could easily bear. Rest assured that when I call you "dearest" the word comes from my heart; you have done for me what no one else in the world could have done at this juncture of my life. I will never forget you.

    Believe me,
    I am your most devoted,
    Enid.

A long silence followed my reading of this

touching epistle (which I am able to reproduce verbatim since I have treasured it among my papers ever since). They were all moved, I believe. Emerson cleared his throat noisily, David looked away, and Nefret's eyes shone with even greater luster. As usual, it was impossible to know what Ramses was thinking.

"Well, that's just fine," Cyrus said cheerfully. "It makes it easier for me to propose a little scheme I have worked out."

It was necessary for me to clear my own throat before I spoke. Enid's affectionate thanks had touched me deeply. "Does this scheme involve Mrs. Jones?" I inquired.

"You are always right on top of things, Mrs. Amelia," Cyrus declared. "Yes, ma'am, it does. You see, it occurred to me that Mrs. Jones would be without employment if matters worked out as we hoped, and that she might be willing to do us a little favor in return for — er —"

"Not sending me to prison," said Mrs. Jones calmly. "Mr. Vandergelt has discussed the matter with me, Mrs. Emerson. It is the least I can do in return for your help in rescuing me from an awkward situation, but the final decision is up to you and the Professor, of course."

"What is this favor?" I asked.

"Taking charge of Miss Bellingham," Cyrus said. "I believe the Colonel is having considerable trouble finding a chaperone for that young woman. He'd jump at the chance of getting a lady like Kath— like Mrs. Jones here."

"How much does she know about the situation?" I asked.

Cyrus looked self-conscious. "I guess you could say she knows as much as I do. Everybody in Luxor is talking about the business, of course, and if you remember, Mrs. Jones was there when you folks brought the mummy out. She asked me about it and we got to chatting, as you might say, and so — well — er."

"Quite natural," said Emerson, nodding. He appeared amused, though I could not think why.

"I have seen Miss Bellingham at the hotel," Mrs. Jones said in her cool, well-bred voice. "She is a shockingly spoiled young woman who certainly needs a firm hand."

"And you are the woman who could do it?" inquired Emerson, even more visibly amused.

"I have been employed in a number of situations, Professor, including that of governess. I believe I can deal with Miss Dolly. What the girl really needs, of course, is a husband."

The statement in itself was one any unenlightened female might utter. I detected another, less conventional meaning, however; and when I met Mrs. Jones's ironical green eyes she gave a little nod, as if to say, "You understand me, Mrs. Emerson."

And of course I did.

"However," Mrs. Jones continued as smoothly as if no unspoken message had passed between us, "if I understand Mr. Vandergelt correctly, a more important consideration at this time is to keep her out of harm's way long enough to acquire one. I am willing to take that job on too, but in fairness to me and Miss Dolly I ought to know how great the danger is and from what direction it may come."

Dinner was announced just then, and we took our places at the table. The interval allowed me time to consider Mrs. Jones's surprising offer — to wonder what had prompted it — and to admit that, whatever her motives, her request for information was justified.

I therefore gave her a brief résumé of the Bellingham case. Some of what I told her was new to Cyrus as well. He had a habit of stroking his goatee when he was agitated or profoundly interested in something. In this case it was increasing agitation that prompted him to tug at the appendage, and when I mentioned Ramses's unfortunate adventure of the past night, he went so far as to interrupt me in midsentence.

"Holy Jehosaphat! Now see here, folks, I plumb refuse to send a lady into the middle of a shooting war. If I had known that piece of sticking plaster covered a bullet hole, I would never have proposed the idea. I figured young Ramses had just had another one of his accidents."

The sticking plaster had replaced my bandage. I had observed this flagrant violation of my orders, but Ramses had not given me time to do anything about it, delaying till the last possible moment before joining us in the carriage; and when I got a good look at him I saw something else that distracted me from the sticking plaster.

The mustache was gone.

A sharp dig in the ribs from Emerson had prevented me from remarking on this. Ramses's expression did not invite commentary; arms folded and brows lowering, he looked like a youthful sultan hoping for an excuse to order someone beheaded. Even Nefret had refrained from speaking, though she gurgled a bit.

Now Ramses said, "It is not a bullet hole, Mr. Vandergelt, only a slight crease. In my opinion Mrs. Jones would be in no danger of being shot at."

"In your opinion," Cyrus repeated sarcastically. "On what do you base that opinion, if I may ask?"

"I am glad you asked me that, sir."

He looked questioningly at me and I said with a sigh, "Very well, Ramses, you may explain. Only be succinct, if you are able."

"Yes, Mother. I base my assumption on the simple fact that Colonel Bellingham is the only one of the two who has employed a firearm. He wants to kill Dutton and will use any means at his disposal. Dutton's intentions toward the Colonel may be no less lethal, but his only weapon appears to be a knife. He could easily acquire a rifle or a pistol, and he has had innumerable opportunities to fire at the Colonel. We may reasonably assume, therefore, that Scudder wants to come to close grips with Bellingham."

"Good Gad," I exclaimed. "In order to make him suffer — to torture him, even. How diabolical!"

"That is one possible interpretation," said Ramses. "The corollary is that Scudder has no murderous intentions toward Miss Dolly. Killing her would not suit his purpose. He has attempted to use her only as a means of getting her father into his hands."

"I agree," Nefret said in her soft, sweet voice. "Your greatest danger, Mrs. Jones, is from Dolly herself. Watch what you eat and drink, and take care not to be alone with her at the top of a cliff or on a busy street."

The only one of the male persons present whose face did not express shocked surprise was — of course — Ramses. He gave his sister a sidelong look, to which she responded with an amused flash of blue eyes.

"Half the trouble she has got into is of her own making," Nefret continued. "She is impatient of supervision —"

"Decidedly," said Mrs. Jones dryly, "if she has rid herself of her attendants by such drastic means."

"She hasn't actually killed anyone," Nefret admitted. "Just made them dreadfully ill or crippled them a bit."

"Good Gad," said Emerson. "My dear girl, do you really believe she would do such things? You have no proof."

"I could probably get it if I wanted to take the

trouble," Nefret said coolly. "But why bother? Professor darling, you are too kindhearted to understand women like little Miss Dolly. She wants her own way and will get it by one means or another. She would not go so far as murder, I daresay, but she is too stupid to anticipate the consequences of her acts and too indifferent to the feelings of others to care about those consequences."

Emerson's face was a study. No one cares to be accused of naiveté — especially men, who think of themselves as less sentimental and more worldly than women. Nefret was absolutely correct, however. Emerson is hopelessly naive about women. And I had an uneasy feeling that Nefret, like Mrs. Jones and me, knew exactly why Dolly Bellingham was so determined to get away from watchful guardians who would prevent her from . . . doing what she wanted to do.

Nefret turned abruptly to her brother. "Ramses knows what I am talking about."

Ramses started. For once he was unable to get out more than an incoherent, "Er — uh — what?"

"I am referring to the time she ran away from you, into the Ezbekieh," Nefret explained.

Cyrus, who had been even more thunderstruck than Emerson by Nefret's accusations, had recovered himself. Shaking his head, he said, "I guess you may be right, Miss Nefret. No well-brought-up young lady would do such a foolish thing, even if she didn't know she was in danger.

Consarn it — excuse my language, ladies, but I am now all the more opposed to this scheme."

"And I," said Mrs. Jones, who had listened with interest, "am all the more intrigued. Never fear; now that I am forewarned I can deal with Miss Dolly. All you expect of me, I take it, is to prevent her from going out alone, by day or by night."

"Our future activities would certainly be easier if we could count on that," said Ramses. "It might relieve your mind, and that of Mr. Vandergelt, to know that David and I will be on the *Amelia* only a short distance away. We can work out a system of signals so that you can summon us in the unlikely event that you need assistance."

They went on to discuss it while Nefret made suggestions and Cyrus listened in gloomy silence. What his precise relationship with Mrs. Jones might be was none of my affair; it was clear to me that he had sufficient interest in her to be concerned for her safety, but not sufficient authority over her to command her actions. Mrs. Jones interested me too. She was the sort of woman for whom I would have felt considerable sympathy if her past had not been so shady, for we had a number of characteristics in common. Modesty prevents me from listing those characteristics, but they should be apparent to anyone who is familiar with my activities.

I determined to find the opportunity for a private talk with the lady and found it when we retired to the drawing room for coffee. After we had got our pianoforte, Cyrus decided he must have one too — the largest grand piano obtainable. It had arrived in pieces, along with the German expert who put it back together. Cyrus asked Nefret to play and prevailed upon the others to join him in song; and while he and Emerson bellowed out a rousing sea chanty I took my coffee cup and Mrs. Jones to a cozy corner.

"I cannot make out why you are willing to do this," I began.

The lady's cheeks plumped up in the expression that made her look so like a smiling cat. "One of the things I admire about you, Mrs. Emerson, is your directness. Alas, I cannot respond in kind. My motives are not clear even to me. However, curiosity is certainly one of them. I could not creep tamely away without finding out how this peculiar business will be resolved — if it can be."

"Oh, I have every expectation that it will. We have encountered other cases as difficult."

"So Mr. Vandergelt tells me. You enjoy a challenge, I believe? So do I. That is another motive, I suppose; I have dealt with several difficult young women, but none I ached to slap as much as I do Dolly Bellingham."

I could not help laughing. "You were right about her, of course. She wants, not only a husband, but one who will beat her when she needs it."

The change in her expression made me regret my frivolous comment. "I ought not to have said that. Violence against women is too common and too terrible to be spoken of lightly. I did not mean it literally, I only meant —"

"I understand." After a moment she went on, "Did I give myself away? Well, why deny it? My late, unlamented husband was a wife beater, or aspired to be one. I did not take it lightly, Mrs. Emerson. I fought back when and as I could. I would have left him, but like so many women, I had nowhere to go and no way of supporting myself and my children."

"You have children?"

She lifted the gold locket that rested among the laces at her breast and opened it. "A boy and a girl. Bertie is twelve, Anna ten. Both are at school."

The faces had been cut from cheap photographs and the features were not easy to make out in the soft lamplight. There was a resemblance, I thought, between the lad's features and those of his mother; the thing that struck me most forcibly was the warmth of their smiles.

Before I could think what to say Mrs. Jones closed the locket. "To make a long story short, Mrs. Emerson, my husband was thrown from his horse while returning one night from a friend's house. He had drunk to excess, as he often did, and a December night on the Yorkshire moors finished him off — which may have saved me the trouble of doing so. Through mismanagement and indifference he had wasted most of his estate. I was determined to preserve what little he left for the education of the children, so I had to seek employment. I was a governess, a companion, and a teacher in a girls' school. I had neither the time nor the money to train myself for a more remunerative occupation, even if any were available to women. I fell into my present way of life by accident. The only thing I regret about it is that it does not pay better. If I could find something that did, I would probably do it."

I spoke without premeditation or even conscious thought. "Are you by chance acquainted with a woman named Bertha, Mrs. Jones?"

"Bertha who?"

The question was one I could not answer, and I regretted having asked it. "Never mind," I said. "It is just that she would agree with your point of view."*

She put her cup down on the nearby table. "I apologize for boring you with the story of my life, Mrs. Emerson. I will say no more; I had not meant to say as much. Shall we join the musicians and finish the evening with an appropriate chorus?"

Cyrus, who had a fine tenor voice, was rendering "Kathleen Mavourneen" with an unfortunate attempt at an Irish brogue. We all applauded when he finished, and then — it was Mrs. Jones's suggestion — we joined in a rousing chorus of "Bonnie Dundee" while Ramses, who had declined the invitation to participate, watched us from half-closed eyes like an elderly owl.

*Mrs. Emerson's encounters with the woman called Bertha are described in Volumes 7 and 8 of her memoirs: *The Snake, The Crocodile and the Dog* and *The Hippopotamus Pool.*

"It is settled, then," Mrs. Jones said as we prepared to depart. "I will offer my services to Colonel Bellingham tomorrow morning."

"I think it would be best if I accompanied you," I said. "If you would care to join us for breakfast, Mrs. Jones, we will call on the Colonel together."

She approved the scheme, and we left them waving from the doorway like any host and hostess bidding guests good night. Fearing, from Emerson's pursed lips and raised eyebrows, that he might be moved to indulge in irrelevant speculation on this matter, I deemed it advisable to head him off by introducing another subject.

"Ramses, I expect you and David to stay at the house tonight."

"Yes, Mother."

I studied him suspiciously. "In the house. All night."

"Yes, Mother."

"In your rooms. Until —"

"Leave it, Peabody," said Emerson, his voice slightly blurred by what might have been laughter. Or again, it might not. When he went on he was entirely serious. "Scudder will not go to the *Valley of the Kings* tonight. He knows Bellingham will be armed and watching for him. He will try another approach next time."

"What would you do, if you were in his position?" I asked.

"I am not in his position, curse it," said Emerson irritably. "That is to say, I do not know what he hopes to accomplish. It would not be difficult for him to acquire a rifle from one of the so-called sportsmen who hunt in the hills and marshes around Luxor. But if I hated a man as much as Scudder hates Bellingham, I would want to see his face when I killed him; give him time to know he was about to die, and by whose hand."

From Manuscript H:

They met, at her invitation, in Nefret's room. "It would not be proper, I suppose, for me to go to yours," she remarked, sitting bolt upright in her chair and folding her arms.

Ramses looked at her curiously. "In conventional terms it is just as improper for us to be here. I hope you don't think Mother and Father would object. They are neither of them so conventional or — or mistrustful."

"I know."

Her eyes were downcast and her mouth was compressed. "Something has upset you," Ramses said quietly. "What is it?"

"Something the Colonel said last night. Then he made matters worse by apologizing! Disgusting old man! I won't let him spoil it," she added angrily and somewhat incoherently.

"I should hope not." She was not looking at him, which was probably just as well. The reference might have been obscure to someone else, but not to him — not when Nefret was concerned. He went on, in a voice more controlled than his face had been. "One way or another the Colonel and his daughter will be

out of our lives shortly. I need your advice, Nefret. If I had had the sense to confide fully in you some days ago, we might not be in our present dilemma."

"What do you mean?" She looked up, her face brightening.

"I suspected before last night that Tollington was the man we were after. Not," he added with one of his rare smiles, "by following the same interesting train of deduction Mother employed. It was well reasoned, but not particularly helpful. What made me suspicious of him was an increasing sense of familiarity. I had come to grips with Dutton twice; though his face was hidden, I had observed the way he moved and certain other physical mannerisms — the way he held a knife, for example. When he struck me in Vandergelt's garden the other evening —"

"He moved in the same way?" Nefret asked.

"Not exactly. But really, it was a bloody stupid thing to do, wasn't it? No one except German university students fights duels these days. I had to ask myself what he really hoped to accomplish. The most innocent explanation was that he was trying to impress Dolly —"

"He was going about it entirely the wrong way," Nefret interrupted. "As you ought to know."

His attempt at distraction had succeeded. Her blue eyes were clear, her face unshadowed.

"What do you mean?" he asked.

"My dear boy! Don't you realize that Dolly is hot on your trail because you are indifferent to her? Not that you aren't tall and handsome and frightfully attractive to women and all the rest," she added amiably. "But it is the challenge that spurs her on. If you could bring yourself to appear attracted to her —"

"No," said Ramses without hesitation.

"Well, never mind. We will rid ourselves of her and her father, and in the meantime David and I will protect you."

"Thank you. Do you mind if we get back to the subject of Tollington?"

"Not at all, my boy. Since Tollington was Dutton, his aim could not have been to impress Dolly. What he wanted," said Nefret with assurance, "was to get you off by yourself in some isolated spot. A duel does require an isolated spot, I assume."

"Quite," said Ramses.

"He would not have been alone." David spoke for the first time.

"Poor David, you can hardly get a word in when we are both talking." Nefret smiled at him. "No, you would have been with him, of course. A proper duel requires seconds. I wonder who he would have . . . Oh, but I am being silly. He would have come alone."

"You see, that explanation makes no sense either," Ramses said. "He could not hope to overpower both of us, and we would be on the alert for an ambush."

"As you were at Luxor Temple?"

"As we were at Luxor Temple. I had written Tollington asking for that meeting. I made a point of shaking hands with him next day, after which my suspicions of him were strengthened. His was not the hand of an idle man about town; it was hard and callused."

"Then why the devil didn't you tell someone?" Nefret demanded.

"I am telling you now," Ramses said meekly. "Remember, Nefret, that then I had no proof. A vague sense of recognition is not admissible as evidence, and he might have acquired the calluses from playing polo or some other gentlemanly sport. All this leaves the primary question unanswered. What does he want with me?"

"Hmm." Nefret moved to the bed and settled herself more comfortably on a pile of cushions. "The obvious answer is that he wants you out of his way so he can get to Dolly."

"You don't believe that any more than I do," Ramses said. "Except for the first incident in the Ezbekieh, Scudder doesn't know it was I who got in his way. On the second and third occasions I was Saiyid, and if you tell me he recognized me despite my disguise, I will be extremely hurt and offended."

Nefret grinned at him. "I would never want to hurt or offend you, dear boy. I believe you are right; and if you are, it means that Scudder has no motive for wanting to injure you."

"It means," Ramses corrected, "that if he has a motive for wishing to injure me, we have yet to ascertain what it is. The incident at Luxor Temple still puzzles me. I said nothing in my letter to indicate I was suspicious of him; I only suggested a private meeting. It may have been an accident. The confounded place is falling apart, like most of *the other temples in Egypt.*"

"*If he still wants to see you, he will try to get in touch with you,*" Nefret said.

"*How? We have made it virtually impossible for him to do so. He would not risk coming here, there are too many people in and around the house. Approaching the dahabeeyah would be almost as dangerous, with Bellingham watching for him.*"

"*It is a good thing you finally got round to asking my advice,*" Nefret said. "*You seem to have forgot something.*"

"*I seem to have forgot a good many things.*"

"*Good Gad, how Aunt Amelia would stare to hear you admit it!*" She leaned forward, her smile fading, and said seriously, "*What you have forgot is that Dutton has communicated with us on several occasions by writing to us. If he wants to see you, he will send a written message — and you, my boy, will have to wait for it since you don't know his current address.*

"*You have overlooked something else, I believe. His primary target is still Colonel Bellingham. The Colonel also received a written message from him, remember?*"

"*Good Lord!*" Ramses stared at her. "*The one purporting to come from Mother, summoning Bellingham to the tomb? Confound it, I had forgot. He may write again. If he does, and Bellingham responds . . . Curse it, I should be watching the Colonel. I should be on watch now!*"

"*You can't do that.*"

"*Why not?*"

"Because," said Nefret smugly, "you promised your mother you would not leave the house tonight."

"Yes, of course," Ramses said. He turned his chair and himself and seated himself with his arms folded across the back. "How could I have overlooked that little detail?"

"I, on the other hand . . ."

Ramses stiffened like a cobra rising to strike. "Do you suppose I will allow you to do that?"

"Allow?" She gave him back stare for cold stare. "Try asking me, Ramses. Say 'please.'"

"Please. Please, Nefret, stay in the house."

"All right."

He relaxed with a long exhalation of breath, and Nefret smiled. "Do you see how easy it is? Now listen to me, Ramses — and you too, David. I have several ideas about Mr. Dutton Scudder that I believe you will find interesting, but I am not going to say a cursed word until you agree to stop treating me like a brainless, helpless child."

"Nefret!" David protested. "I never —"

"You aren't as bad as Ramses," Nefret admitted. "But both of you do it. Look here —" She leaned forward, her face softening. "I understand that you care about me and you don't want me to be hurt. Well, how the devil do you suppose I feel about you two? Do you suppose I enjoy sitting with folded hands, worrying myself sick when you are in danger? Aunt Amelia doesn't put up with that sort of nonsense from the Professor. I will not put up with it either."

"That sounds like an ultimatum," said Ramses. "What happens if we refuse to agree?"

"*I make life very, very unpleasant for you,*" said Nefret.

Ramses lowered his head onto his folded arms.

"*How dare you laugh at me?*" Nefret demanded. "*Curse you, Ramses —*"

"*I apologize.*" He raised his head. His face was flushed. "*I couldn't help it, you sounded so fierce and looked so . . . All right, Nefret. Your arguments are incontrovertible and your threats too terrifying to contemplate. I cannot promise to exhibit the fortitude Father displays with regard to Mother; he has had a good many years of practice. But I will do my best.*"

"*Shake hands on it.*" She offered a hand to each of them.

"*All for one and one for all,*" David said, smiling.

"*Now,*" said Ramses, "*what about Dutton Scudder?*"

CHAPTER THIRTEEN

*There are occasions upon which a candid
expression of opinion may be not only rude,
but counterproductive.*

Cyrus's carriage delivered Mrs. Jones to our door
early the following morning. I observed she was
wearing a sensible tweed costume and stout walking shoes instead of the ecru lace frock of the
previous evening. I drew no conclusions from
this. Cyrus might have caused her to be met at
the ferry landing. At dawn.

I was the first one dressed, as I usually am;
and since I am fond of watching the sun rise over
the eastern cliffs, I was seated on the verandah
when the lady arrived. She looked a trifle out of
spirits. I asked her if she had had second
thoughts. She replied without hesitation that she
had not; but she said no more and sat looking
out across the river while she sipped the tea
Ahmet had brought.

As the light strengthened, the landscape
seemed to spring into existence, fresh and new
born. The red, rising sun glinted on the water.
Across the river the distant cliffs of the high
desert turned from gray to violet to pale rose.

The broad brim of her hat cast a shadow across the upper half of her face so that the firmness of her tight-closed lips and prominent chin was even more pronounced. After a time she said quietly, as if to herself, "One would never tire of this."

"That depends on one's point of view," I replied.

"Practical as always, Mrs. Emerson." She turned to face me. The hint of melancholy I had observed — or fancied I had observed — had been replaced by her feline smile.

"I am not immune to poetic fancies, Mrs. Jones, but there is a time and a place for them. I hear the others, and I believe breakfast is on the table. Shall we go in?"

The ones I had heard were Nefret and Emerson. He was helping her into her chair when we entered the room, and he acknowledged Mrs. Jones with a genial if banal greeting.

"Bright and early, I see. Very commendable."

We had finished our porridge before the boys appeared, in tandem as always. I gave Ramses a suspicious look. In my opinion the removal of the mustache had improved his appearance, for it made his resemblance to his father more apparent, and Emerson is the handsomest of men. It had not made his countenance any easier to read, but the signs of sleeplessness were evident to the fond eye of a mother.

"Did you go out last night?" I asked.

"I promised you I would not, Mother."

"That does not answer my question."

"I did not leave the house last night." He tossed a sheaf of papers onto the table and seated himself. "I was working. You asked about the dream papyrus, I believe? There is my translation if you would care to read it."

I picked up the papers, and Mrs. Jones said curiously, "A dream papyrus? I was not aware of such a thing."

"It is a rather obscure text," Ramses said, politely passing her the marmalade. "Uncle Walter obtained photographs of it last year from the British Museum, and was kind enough to lend them to me."

I had been puzzling over Ramses's handwriting, which bore a distressing resemblance to the hieratic of the original text. Down the left margin of the pages ran the repeated words "If a man sees himself in a dream." This introductory phrase was followed in each case by a brief description: "killing an ox," "writing on a palette," "drinking blood," and "capturing a female slave" were some of them. The interpretation consisted of the words "good" or "bad," followed by a short explanation.

"Some of it is straightforward enough," I said. "Capturing a female slave is good. 'It means something from which he will have satisfaction.' One might reasonably suppose so. But why 'eating excrement' should be good . . . Oh. 'It means eating his possessions in his house.' "

"Fascinating," said Mrs. Jones. "If you will allow me, Mrs. Emerson, I would like to take a copy. It would add a certain cachet to my work if I were able to interpret dreams according to ancient Egyptian dogma."

"You will have to be selective," I said dryly. "There is one about uncovering . . . Dear me! Why would anyone dream of doing that with a pig?"

"Is it good or bad?" Nefret inquired innocently.

"Bad. It means being deprived of possessions."

I read out some of the others — omitting the vulgar ones — to the amusement, if not the edification, of my companions. Nefret seemed especially intrigued, and when I read out the one about seeing oneself veiled, she exclaimed, "How odd! I dreamed last night that I was playing the role of Princess Tasherit, draped in muslin and cheesecloth. What does it signify, Aunt Amelia?"

"Obviously," said Emerson, who had listened with the tolerant smile of a man superior to idle fancies, "you are still smarting over being deprived of the part."

In my opinion — and that of Professor Freud, whose works I had read with interest — it signified that she was trying to conceal something. Since I did not want to embarrass her, I read out the Egyptian interpretation. "It means removing enemies from your presence."

"Good," Nefret said, laughing.

"Enough of this nonsense," Emerson said. He tossed his serviette onto the table. "I am off to the tomb. Is anyone coming with me?"

"I will join you later, Emerson," I replied.

"You know Mrs. Jones and I intend to call on Colonel Bellingham this morning."

Ramses indicated that, with his father's permission, he would take David and Nefret across to Luxor Temple to get on with the photography.

"So long as that is your real purpose," said Emerson, giving his son a sharp look. "Try not to let anyone drop a rock on you."

"I will do my best, sir," said Ramses.

"Or on Nefret."

"I will do my best," Ramses repeated, glancing at his sister.

As courtesy demanded I dispatched a messenger to the Colonel, announcing our intention of calling on him at what might seem to some an outrageously early hour. I had pleaded the urgency of the matter as an excuse, but the truth is, I wanted to get the business over and done with. I had another errand to do that morning, and I was anxious to get back to Emerson and the tomb. After observing the dangerous condition of the passageway I did not like him working there without me. Another excavator might have left the dirty work to the men, but that was not Emerson's way.

I was uneasy in my mind. The sensation was familiar to me; always in the past it had presaged danger. What made it worse this time was that my hostages to fortune were scattered. How could I watch over all of them when they kept wandering off in different directions, doing different things, and — I strongly suspected — not telling me what they were thinking and planning?

At least the children would be together. I thought I could count on Ramses to keep Nefret out of trouble; his old-fashioned notions of chivalry annoyed her a great deal, but if they kept her safe, I was prepared to condone them.

After Emerson had gone off we had to wait for at least another hour, since it was only a little past six A.M. I occupied the time by showing Mrs. Jones round the house and waiting for the children to go away. They were all annoyingly polite that morning. Nefret accompanied us, chatting cheerfully about domestic arrangements, and Ramses offered to introduce Mrs. Jones to the horses. While we were in the stable I managed to draw Ramses aside.

"Watch over Nefret today," I said in a low voice. "Tell David."

"Is something wrong?" His eyes narrowed.

"No. At least I hope not."

"Ah. One of your famous premonitions." He touched my hand, which rested on the rail. It was only the briefest brush of his fingertips, but from that source it was equivalent to a comforting pat. "Try not to worry, Mother. She thinks she is watching over me and David, you know."

"Perhaps she is right."

"No doubt she is," Ramses said, and turned away.

At last they got off, and since Mrs. Jones was not dressed for riding horseback I commandeered two of the little donkeys. As we trotted off side by side, I decided it was time to propose another idea to her. I had hesitated about doing so, but had concluded that a woman who earned her living communicating with the dead would not balk at a spot of spying.

"Read his letters?" She stared at me in surprise.

"Not all of them. Only the suspicious ones."

"But my dear Mrs. Emerson —" A sudden jolt (for the pace of a donkey is extremely uneven, especially when it does not want to be ridden) made her clutch at her hat. "How am I to know what is suspicious and what is not? You can hardly suppose he will leave his private correspondence lying about where I can get at it."

"Especially the suspicious messages," I admitted. "Perhaps I ought to be more specific."

"Pray do," said Mrs. Jones, looking amused.

"What I expect is that Scudder will communicate with him by letter, as he has done once before. He may sign his own name or a false one. The object of the message, whomever it purports to be from, will be to lure the Colonel into an ambush. I don't really suppose you will get the chance to read any such message. Only watch him; observe any unusual behavior. If, for example, he suddenly announces he must go out —"

"I see what you are getting at. Frankly, Mrs. Emerson, I think it is a farfetched idea, but supposing I should observe something of the sort, what do you want me to do? Follow him?"

"Good Gad, no. That would be impractical as well as dangerous. Several of our crewmen are always on board the *Amelia*; I will warn them to be on the lookout for a signal from you. If you see anything that rouses your suspicions, wave. . . ." I looked her over. "I commend your taste in fashion, Mrs. Jones, but I could wish you went in for brighter colors. Take my scarf."

It was a vivid crimson — Emerson's favorite color. I untied it from round my throat and handed it to her. "Wave this from the deck, and one of the men will find me. I doubt anything interesting will happen before late afternoon. Dutton will want darkness for his evil purposes."

"Of course." She smiled. One could almost see the whiskers.

The Colonel was expecting us. He and Dolly were at breakfast when the servant showed us into the saloon. Sunlight sparkled on crystal glasses and silver tableware. Cyrus's taste in such matters was irreproachable, but I observed that the mahogany sideboard badly wanted polishing and that the gold damask draperies were in need of repair. What the place needed was a woman's hand.

Dolly had not been long out of her bed; her curls were in disarray and her eyes were heavy. She was wearing a peignoir, a fluffy mass of pale blue chiffon. The Colonel, impeccably garbed in his usual black, rose to greet us and offered us breakfast.

"We breakfasted several hours ago," I replied. "Again I apologize, Colonel Bellingham, for disturbing you, but I felt you would want to be

478

apprised of the situation at the earliest possible moment. You have not, I believe, found a lady to watch over your daughter? Mrs. Jones is at liberty and is, I can confidently state, eminently qualified for the position."

As I have said, I was in something of a hurry that morning, and I have never seen any point in wasting time. The Colonel was visibly disconcerted. Many persons react to me in that way, so I waited politely for his slower wits to catch up, and accepted, with a smile and a murmured, *"Shoukran,"* the cup of coffee offered me by Cyrus's steward.

After a brief interval the Colonel said, "I was momentarily struck dumb by your thoughtfulness, Mrs. Emerson. I am acquainted with Mrs. Jones, but I was under the impression that she was travelling with friends."

Sitting bolt upright in her chair, gloved hands folded in her lap, Mrs. Jones squinted amiably at him. She conveyed the impression of requiring spectacles she was too vain to wear, and her neat tweed costume and dowdy hat absolutely exuded respectability. In a soft voice she explained that her companions had decided to return home and that she was desirous of remaining in Egypt for a few more weeks. With a deprecating little cough, she added, "Mr. and Mrs. Fraser would, of course, have assisted me financially, but I could not accept favors from friends. I have always made my own way in the world, Colonel Bellingham, sir, and my religious beliefs demand that I be of use to my fellow creatures."

I wanted very badly to laugh, but of course dared not. The matter was soon settled. Mrs. Jones explained that she had been a governess and a teacher, but that she had not, naturally, brought references with her; the Colonel replied, as he had no choice but to reply, that my recommendation was enough. I had to suppress another chuckle when Mrs. Jones haggled, genteelly but firmly, over her salary, and got the Colonel to agree to ten pounds more than he had originally offered. Her performance was perfect. The Colonel was completely taken in and visibly relieved.

Miss Dolly was taken in and not at all pleased. She studied the neat little figure of Mrs. Jones through narrowed eyes, and I could almost read her thoughts. She would not be able to bully this woman as she had some of the others, and Mrs. Jones's air of pseudo-respectability augured poorly for the chance of any escapades.

My opinion of Mrs. Jones went up again when she set about extracting information. "You will be leaving Egypt in two weeks, then?" she inquired — a reasonable question, since that had been the term of her engagement.

"It may be sooner," was the reply. "You may depend on the full amount being paid you in any case. How soon can you begin?"

"This very moment, if you like. With your permission I will send one of your servants to fetch my luggage, and then Miss Bellingham and

I will think of something jolly to do today!"

I made haste to excuse myself. The expression on Dolly's face as she contemplated a day of jolly activities with Mrs. Jones was too much for my sobriety.

I had to contain my laughter a little longer, for the Colonel escorted me to the gangplank. It was not until I found myself alone with him that I recollected my primary reason for coming. Mrs. Jones's performance had been so enjoyable, I had almost forgot.

I was in greater haste than ever now, so I cut his thanks short. "There is one more thing I feel obliged to say to you, Colonel, and I hope you will excuse me for being blunt. I am in a hurry, and the subject is not one that lends itself to tact. It has to do with my ward, Miss Forth. Should you contemplate paying her attentions of a romantic nature, dismiss the idea at once. Such attentions would not be welcomed."

"I cannot believe I understand you, Mrs. Emerson."

The Colonel's face was as pale and hard as marble. He drew himself up to his full height. Since I am of relatively small stature physically, I am accustomed to being towered over, so I was not at all intimidated. I found myself becoming angry, however — not at *his* anger, but at the blind, uncomprehending conceit of the man. I never lose my temper, but on this occasion I allowed it to get just a little away from me.

"I believe you do, Colonel. Come now! Can you honestly suppose that a girl like Nefret would consent to become the fourth — or is it the fifth? — wife of a man who is old enough to be her grandfather? Especially when several of your former spouses have met premature ends?"

His face was no longer pale, it was livid. His breath hissed through his teeth; his hands clenched tightly on the ferrule of his stick. He was not taking it at all well. I tried again to make him see the situation sensibly.

"I am telling you this for your own good, Colonel Bellingham, to spare you the embarrassment of being rejected by Nefret or thrown out of the window by my husband. A word to the wise, eh? Good-bye. Thank you for the coffee."

I went directly to the *Amelia* and had a few words with Reis Hassan. He was accustomed to my ways, so he did not question the orders I gave him. Two of the men got out the smaller rowboat in order to take me across, and as I clambered in I was surprised to see Colonel Bellingham standing in the exact same position in which I had left him, on the deck of the *Valley of the Kings.* He appeared to be looking in my direction, so I waved my parasol. He did not respond. Ah well, I thought, if he is going to bear a grudge, so be it. I have done my duty. It had not, perhaps, been in the best possible taste to refer to the deaths of two of his wives in childbirth, but it was too late to worry about that now.

My mission in Luxor was soon accomplished.

Since it has no bearing on this part of my narrative I will not describe it here. After leaving the hotel, I hesitated, wondering if I ought to spare the time for an additional errand. I did not hesitate long; indecisiveness is a bad habit I do not allow myself to fall into. After purchasing a nosegay from one of the flower vendors, I got into a carriage and directed the driver to take me to the English cemetery.

It looked even more desolate and lonely that morning. Burials were infrequent, and the usual residents of the place had resumed their occupancy. A lean cat slunk into the brush when I approached, and a few mangy dogs growled at me from the weedy grave on which they had established residence. I paused long enough to look at one of the flat stones, and an odd little chill ran through me when I saw the inscription. It was pathetically brief: "Alan Armadale. Died Luxor 1889. Requiescat in Pace."

What strange coincidence had prompted me to examine that particular marker? Armadale had been a victim of one of the most ruthless murderers I have ever encountered.* I had not known him in life, but by all accounts he had been a worthy young man who had not deserved his sad fate. It had been I who had discovered his body and arranged for him to be buried here — and forgot him. Though I was in haste I spent a few minutes pulling weeds and blowing away

*The Curse of the Pharoahs

483

the sandy dust that blurred the inscription. Plans began to form in my head. A committee of ladies — subscriptions from visitors — Dr. Willoughby consulting . . .

Mrs. Bellingham's grave would have been easy to find even if I had not been there the previous day. The bare sandy earth had been strewn with flowers.

They were simple, homely blossoms that might have been culled from the gardens and hedges of Luxor — marigolds and roses, bougainvillea and cornflowers and scarlet geraniums. They must have been left early that morning, or even the previous night; the pretty things were wilting in the morning sun.

I placed my own nosegay among them and said a little prayer, just as the Colonel must have done. It was not the sort of gentle, sentimental gesture I would have expected from such a man. Had I misjudged him? I am seldom guilty of that error, but it does happen occasionally, with individuals who are accustomed to exercise unhealthy control over their emotions.

After brushing the sand from my skirt, I retraced my steps, seeing not another human soul until I reached my waiting carriage. I directed the driver to take me to the Luxor Temple. It was not out of my way. It would take only a few minutes. Since I was in the neighborhood, so to speak, it would be rude not to stop by and see how the children were getting on.

They were there! They were where they had said they would be, in the court of Amenhotep III, taking photographs!

Not that I had had the slightest doubt they would be.

I was glad I had come when I saw how happy they were to see me. "Don't let me interrupt," I said as Nefret gave me a quick hug and David, always the *preux chevalier,* relieved me of my heavy handbag.

"Not at all," said my son, doing neither. "We were about to stop in any case. There are too many cursed tourists at this time of day."

"What happened with Colonel Bellingham this morning?" Nefret asked. "Did he agree to employ Mrs. Jones?"

"It is all settled," I replied. "She is with them now."

Nefret's smooth brow furrowed. "I do hope she will be all right. That wretched girl —"

"Don't worry about Mrs. Jones," I said, smiling affectionately at Nefret. "If you had seen the performance she put on this morning, you would be reassured as to her ability to deal with Miss Dolly. The young lady was not at all pleased to have her as a watchdog."

"What else have you been doing?" David asked. "I didn't know you meant to come over to Luxor this morning."

I saw no reason to mention my first errand, so I told them of my visit to the cemetery. "Something must be done about it," I declared. "A committee of ladies —"

"An excellent idea," said Ramses. "So someone had been there before you? To leave flowers, you said."

"Yes. It was a touching sight."

"Quite," Ramses said.

No one spoke for a moment. David looked at Ramses, Ramses looked at Nefret, and Nefret stared intently at a headless statue of the goddess Mut.

"I must get back," I said. "Are you coming with me, or shall I send the boat to fetch you later?"

"Later, I think," Ramses said after another brief pause. "Er — Nefret?"

She turned to him with a particularly affectionate smile. "I agree. We will just finish this lot of plates, Aunt Amelia."

I offered to help, but they insisted they did not need me; they could see I was anxious to return to Emerson.

There was no sign of life on Cyrus's dahabeeyah when I reached the other side. Hassan said the ladies and the gentleman had left an hour ago on donkeyback. They had not condescended to inform him of their destination, but they had ridden off in the direction of the Valley.

So far, so good, I thought. After mounting my own donkey, I returned to the house, changed into trousers and boots, and made my way to the Valley by our usual route, accompanied by Mahmud carrying a picnic basket. Emerson would not stop to eat unless I made him, and the sun was high.

I had expected I would have to extract him from the depths of the tomb, but I found him outside it, conferring with Howard Carter. Howard was smoking a cigarette and waving it at a strange-looking piece of apparatus that stood between him and Emerson. The men had gathered round to watch, and Abdullah (whom I had ordered to stay at home until I could pay him another visit) was giving them the benefit of his advice. I have had occasion to observe that men love machinery. It does not seem to matter what the machine actually does, so long as it makes loud noises and has parts that whirl round.

They were so absorbed that I had to poke Emerson with my parasol before he noticed me. "Hallo, Peabody," he said. "I believe it needs a new piston."

Howard scratched his head. "Good day, Mrs. Emerson. The piston is working all right; in my opinion the difficulty is in the motor."

Emerson's blue eyes sparkled. "We had better take it apart."

"What is it?" I asked. "Emerson, don't touch that apparatus! You remember what happened when you tried to repair Lady Carrington's motorcar."

Emerson whirled to face me. "That was quite another matter," he said indignantly. "I —"

All at once the machine began to make loud noises and several parts started to whirl.

"What did you do?" Emerson demanded, staring at Selim.

The young man straightened. "I put this" — he pointed — "in that."

"Ah," said Emerson. "Just what I was about to propose."

With the enthusiastic assistance of Selim and several of the others, he and Howard began to attach sections of pipe to the apparatus. I turned to Abdullah.

"What are you doing here? You ought to be at home, resting."

"I do not need to rest, Sitt. I am well."

"Let me see your head."

The green paste had turned his white hair the color of rotting vegetation. It did not smell very nice either. However, the bump had subsided. I told him he could put his turban on again.

"What is that thing?" I asked, indicating the machine.

"It takes the bad air out of the tomb," Abdullah explained in the condescending tone men use to women when they talk about machines. "Emerson ordered Mr. Carter to give it to him, and the wires that make it go."

I remembered having heard Emerson mention something called an air pump. Presumably it required electricity? We seemed to have that too, which meant that it would be possible to use electric bulbs instead of candles. For once, Emerson was being sensible instead of forcing himself and the men to work under conditions that verged on the unbearable. I hoped he had not bullied Howard into handing over the pump he had acquired for his own tomb. Perhaps there were two of the things.

Having taken the pieces of pipe down into the tomb and (I presumed) fastened them together, Howard and Emerson came back up the stairs, looking extremely pleased with themselves. Selim followed them, looking demure. He was a hand-some young man, only a few years older than Ramses, who had spent one horrendous summer acting as Ramses's guard and companion before I realized he was unable to prevent Ramses from doing anything at all. It had all been Ramses's fault, of course, but they had become very close — the natural result, I suppose, of being partners in crime. Selim was Abdullah's last-born son and thus David's uncle. There was a strong physical resemblance between the two young fellows — and, I was beginning to believe, another kind of resemblance as well.

Feeling my eyes upon him, Selim smiled at me like a sun-browned Botticelli angel.

"So," I said as the men joined me. "How long does that infernal thing have to work before all the foul air is removed?"

"It is not so simple as that," Howard said patronizingly.

"You mean you don't know."

"We had some trouble with it," Howard ad-mitted. "The motor — or perhaps it was one of the chains —"

"You see, Peabody," said Emerson, "the way it works is —"

"I don't want to know how it works, Emerson. So long as it does. Have a sandwich."

Howard declined to join us; his men had already stopped work for the day and he was about to return to his house to do some of the endless paperwork his position involved. I waited until he had gone on his way before I asked Emerson what had happened that morning.

"Nothing, curse it," said Emerson through a mouthful of bread and goat cheese. "I only had time for a quick look inside before Carter arrived with his electric wires. The generator is in the tomb of Ramses IX, you know, and we had the devil of a time getting the confounded wires —"

"It was very good of Howard to supply them, Emerson. And the air pump."

"Yes, yes. It was necessary to take advantage of his offer, I suppose. But we have come upon a chamber approximately ten feet by twelve, and half-filled with rubble. If it was originally intended for a burial chamber, the architect must have changed his mind, since the passage continues —"

"You cannot work inside today, surely."

"Why not? Oh," Emerson said. "That was another of your tactful suggestions, I suppose? Very well, Peabody, it is getting late. I will leave the air pump to run all night and see how well it performs."

He finished his bread and cheese and then,

with a visible effort, turned his attention to matters that interested him less.

"How did Mrs. Jones hit it off with the Colonel?" he asked.

I told him what had transpired. My description of Mrs. Jones's performance as a prim nearsighted governess amused him a great deal, but when I related my private conversation with the Colonel his grin vanished.

"Good Gad, Peabody, did you really say *that?* In those precise words?"

"It was the simple truth, Emerson."

"Yes, but . . ." He shook his head. "I wish you had not been quite so . . . truthful."

"I could refer to pots and kettles, Emerson. Or to people who live in glass houses."

"It is not the same thing." His face was grave. "You struck a devastating blow at his *amour-propre,* Peabody. I might have said the same sort of thing, just as bluntly; he would not have liked it, but it would have been easier for him to accept from another man than from a woman."

"Indeed?" I began packing up the remainder of the food. "Well, I must take your word for it, Emerson, since it strikes me as another of those incomprehensible male notions that make no sense to a woman. The thing is done, in any case."

"Bellingham is a dangerous man."

"I am of the same opinion, Emerson."

"Oh, are you?" Emerson's voice rose. "You always say that. This time I insist you explain, in detail and without equivocation, precisely what you mean."

"Gladly, Emerson. But not here; it is getting hot and this rock is quite hard. Shall we return to the house?"

Emerson rubbed his chin and looked wistfully at the apparatus, which was making such a racket we had both been shouting. "I had planned to stay here tonight. The confounded thing has a habit of stopping suddenly for no apparent reason."

I tried to think how to put the case in a way that would leave *his amour-propre* undamaged.

"Is there electricity at night, Emerson? Perhaps they turn it off after the tourists have gone. Its primary function, I believe, is to light the popular tombs."

Emerson appeared quite struck by this idea. "Hmph. You may be right, Peabody. I neglected to ask Carter about that. I will just see if I can catch him up. Or perhaps Reis Ahmed will know. . . ."

The last word came floating back to me as he strode briskly away.

I went to Selim, who was perched on the ledge above the stairs, swinging his feet and eating his midday meal. The other men tactfully moved away as I sat down beside him.

He answered my question without hesitation. The generator functioned only during the day — when it worked at all. I said curiously, "How did you find out about these things, Selim?"

He gave me a sidelong look from under his long lashes. "I wanted to learn how they work, Sitt. It is a kind of magic, no doubt. . . ."

"It has always seemed so to me," I agreed with a smile. "But it is a kind of magic I know nothing about. Can you work this machine as well as the Father of Curses?"

"With God's help," said Selim piously — but his black eyes twinkled.

"Yes, of course. Thank you, Selim."

I left him to finish his meal and went to meet Emerson, who had learned from the reis that his beloved apparatus would indeed stop functioning at sunset when the Valley was officially closed to tourists. He was quite put out about it and unwilling to leave the confounded thing.

"Explain to Selim what he must do if it stops between now and sunset," I suggested.

Emerson continued to look doubtful, so I applied pressure. "What is more important, Emerson, bringing a murderer to justice or playing with — that is, wasting your talents on a mechanic's job? Abdullah should get out of the sun, and he won't go while you are here. We will take him with us to the house on the pretense of consulting him about the case."

The last argument convinced him. Emerson was really not especially worried about bringing a murderer to justice — unless the murderer was after one of us — but he was devoted to Abdullah.

After Emerson had given Selim a long lecture

to which he pretended to listen intently, we left the young fellow comfortably settled, with two of his cousins to keep him company, and the rest of us set off on the homeward path. As we entered the main branch of the Valley I slowed my steps.

"What are you gaping at?" Emerson demanded.

"Reis Hassan told me Mrs. Jones and the Bellinghams had gone toward the Valley this morning. I thought they might have meant to visit us."

Emerson put an arm round my shoulders and hurried me along. "They have been and gone."

"What? Why didn't you tell me?"

"Because you did not ask."

"Curse you, Emerson —"

"I beg your pardon, my dear. I cannot resist teasing you a little when you get into one of those businesslike moods of yours. Save your breath for the climb. In fact," Emerson continued, giving me a helping hand up the slope, "I have no idea what the devil the Colonel wanted; he showed us how the zinc pipe was attached, but could not explain why the pump was not functioning at that time. One would suppose that a man who claims to have been an engineer would know —"

"Emerson, please stop talking about the cursed air pump. Was the Colonel an engineer?"

"He served in the Corps of Engineers during his war," Emerson replied.

"Hmph. I would have supposed the cavalry was more to his taste."

"It is far more romantic," Emerson agreed with a curl of his handsome lip. "However, in modern warfare a man who can build and repair bridges is more useful than a fellow who wants to gallop into battle brandishing a sword. All right now, Peabody?"

We had paused at the top of the cliff to catch our breath. I indicated I was ready to proceed.

"Was Dolly with him?" I asked.

"Yes. No doubt as to what *she* was after. As soon as I informed her Ramses was in Luxor she began complaining about the heat and the dust and the flies, and the Colonel took her away." Emerson chuckled. "I must give Ramses a little lecture on how to avoid predatory young women."

"Are you certain he wants to avoid her?"

"Let me put it this way, Peabody. I do not believe you need worry about having Dolly Bellingham as your daughter-in-law."

I had expected the children would be back from Luxor, but they were not.

"Now where do you suppose they have got to?" I demanded. "They said they would finish that lot of plates and come straight here."

"Stop fussing like a mother hen, Peabody. They are perfectly capable of taking care of themselves."

I left Emerson and Abdullah on the verandah

and went to freshen up. A hail from Emerson summoned me while I was doing so, and I hastened to return, in time to see my wandering children ride up. Before I could begin my lecture Nefret slid off Risha's back and hurried toward us. "Good, you are all here," she exclaimed. "*Salaam aleikhum*, Abdullah. Look! Look, all of you!"

I had a nasty feeling I knew what she was about to do. So did Emerson, I believe. He jumped up with a muffled oath. Before he could prevent her she returned to Risha and sprang . . .

Smack up against the horse's side. Her feet hit the ground and her forehead came into emphatic contact with the saddle.

"Curse it," said Nefret cheerfully.

The boys had both dismounted and were watching, David with a grin and Ramses with a face that might have been carved from granite. He had flinched visibly, though, when Nefret slipped.

"Nefret," Emerson began, "I wish you would not —"

"I know how, really I do!" She rubbed her forehead and gave him a wide smile. "I did it before. That is always what happens when one tries to show off! Now then, Risha . . ."

If a horse could shrug, Risha would have. He seemed to brace himself. So did Ramses.

After a moment I said, "You can open your eyes, Ramses."

Triumphantly aloft, Nefret turned to frown at her brother. "Didn't you see me? Why weren't you watching? I did it! Abdullah, did you see? Professor?"

"Yes, my dear," said Emerson faintly. "That was splendid. Would you mind not doing it again?"

"You have to spring," Nefret explained, gesticulating. "With one leg. Your hand and your other foot only steady you while Risha —"

"We saw," I said. "So you were practicing, were you? Very nice. You had better let Risha have a little rest now. Run in and bathe your face and hands, we are going to have a council of war."

They claimed they had eaten, but I suspected it was only some mess or other they had bought from a food seller in Luxor. Anyhow, young people can always eat. I told Ali to bring tomatoes and cucumbers, bread and cheese, and all of them tucked in with good appetite. Nefret's forehead was rather lumpy and she would have a scab on the end of her nose, but she was obviously unconcerned about her bumps and bruises. She is still such a child, I thought, affectionately. And why not? She had never had a childhood or a normal life until we brought her to live with us.

Some pompous individuals might have said her life since then had not been normal either. Climbing pyramids, excavating tombs, and pursuing criminals seemed to suit her, however, and who was I to deny her the rights upon which I had always insisted and of which most females in our society are unfairly deprived? Even the right to fall off a horse when she chose.

They left it to me to open the meeting, which was only proper. I chose an oblique approach.

"I suppose you all went round to the English cemetery after I left you?"

David's eyes sparkled. "I told you she would find out. She always knows."

"Yes," Abdullah agreed. "She does. What is this about the cemetery?"

"There were wildflowers scattered over Mrs. Bellingham's grave," I explained. "We know it was not the Colonel who put them there."

"We know?" Emerson repeated.

Nefret pushed her plate aside and leaned forward. "I think Aunt Amelia is right. But never mind that now. There are some things we *do* know. I have made a list."

She took a folded paper from her shirt pocket.

"An interesting approach," I said with an approving nod. "I have made a list too — not of facts, but of questions to be answered. Let us hear yours first, Nefret."

"It is a collaborative effort, in fact," Nefret said, smiling at Ramses and David. "We worked it out together."

"Excellent," said Emerson. "Proceed, my dear."

"Yes, sir." Nefret unfolded the paper. "Fact number one. Mrs. Bellingham was not abducted by Scudder. She eloped with him."

"Oh, come," Emerson exclaimed. "That may

well be the case, but how can you state it as a fact?"

"Too many petticoats," I said. Nefret grinned at me. Emerson threw up his hands.

"My dear, it is obvious," I said. "She had at least ten petticoats with her. Women do not wear more than three or four under today's skirts; a smooth line from the waist to . . ." Seeing Emerson's expression, I concluded I had better not enlarge on the subject of skirts. "Another conclusive point is that she also had with her a ball gown — the blue damask that served as the outermost shroud. She was last seen wearing an afternoon frock. She could not have changed into evening attire without the assistance of her maid or her husband, neither of whom admitted to having seen her. Ergo, she must have left the hotel shortly after she returned from the tea party at the consulate — with a trunk or suitcase. Can you picture a kidnapper waiting for her to pack her clothing and then removing it and the lady without her active cooperation?"

"Hmph," said Emerson.

"I am glad you agree, Emerson. Proceed, Nefret."

"Point two. The wound that killed her was made by a long sharp blade that went straight through her body. She was facing the killer, and on her feet at the time."

"*Bismallah!*" Abdullah exclaimed. "How could you —"

"That was Ramses's contribution," Nefret said, nodding graciously at my son. "I confess I was not cool enough to examine the body so closely."

"It was obvious from the positions and relative sizes of the entry and exit wounds," said Ramses.

"Quite right," I said. "Had she been kneeling, the blade would have penetrated her body at an angle."

Emerson began, "What if she . . . ." Then he stopped. "I think I see what you are getting at. Go on, Nefret."

"Point three. There were traces of natron on the body."

"What!" Emerson exploded. "When did you — how did you —"

"Emerson, this is going to take all day if you continue interrupting," I said. "I told Mr. Gordon from the American consulate — in your presence, if you recall — that samples of the skin ought to be taken in order to determine the substance employed to preserve the body. We took such scrapings the other morning. You tested them, Ramses?"

Ramses nodded. "I have myself experimented with natron as a preservative agent. It is much more effective than ordinary sand, which is why the ancients used it to —"

"But that is extraordinary," Emerson ejaculated. "How did Scudder get it to Luxor? He would need several hundred pounds of the stuff to cover . . . Hmmmm."

"Precisely," said Ramses. "The logical conclusion is that he did not have to transport that weight of natron because it was already available to him. They must have been at or near the Wadi Natrun when she died."

"So when they fled from Cairo they went south, instead of to Alexandria or Port Said," I said thoughtfully. "That is where the Colonel and the police would look for them, at one of the ports. Scudder must have had friends or acquaintances in one of the villages. Excellent! That should be our next —"

"I believe, Mother, that such an investigation would be a waste of time," Ramses said. "It would give us no clue to Scudder's present whereabouts. Nefret, you have one more item on your list, I believe."

"Number four. It was Scudder who wrapped the body and brought it to Luxor —"

Emerson's lips parted, and I said quickly, "Now, Emerson, don't argue. We had *assumed* it was so, but had never subjected the assumption to logical analysis. Given what we now know, it is the only possible conclusion."

"Ha," said Emerson.

"I had not quite finished, Aunt Amelia," Nefret said. "He brought it to Luxor and found a proper tomb for it, not as a ghastly joke but as an act of reverence and atonement. He loved her and he loves her still. It was he who scattered the flowers on her grave."

Abdullah inserted a finger under his turban

and delicately scratched his head. "Hmph," he said in almost Emerson's tones. "A man might kill his woman if she was unfaithful or if she tried to leave him. But why did he not bury her in the sand and leave her there?"

"Very good, Abdullah," I said. "That was one of my questions. I think we know the answer, though. Scudder is mad."

Abdullah looked pleased. "But," he said, "if the man is mad, he is under the protection of God."

Ramses stared at the old man as if he had just said something clever. Before he could comment, supposing he had intended to do so, I took my list from my pocket.

"Here are my other questions. First — why did Colonel Bellingham come back to Egypt?"

"No," Emerson said. "That is the wrong question, Peabody. We know why he returned."

"Do you believe he told us the truth?"

"Yes," said Emerson.

"Hmph. Well, so do I. Then how would you —"

"You might rather ask why he remains."

"We know that too," I said. "He wants to kill Scudder. Curse it, Emerson, will you let me get on with my questions?"

"Certainly, my dear."

I looked at my list. "Two — why did Scudder want us to find the mummy?"

"Again," said Emerson before anyone else could speak, "I must take exception to the way you have phrased the question, Peabody. Do you mean, why did Scudder want the mummy to be found, or why did he select us to find it?"

"But who else would he choose?" Abdullah asked. "Who but the wisest, the most famous, the most skilled man — uh — people — in the world?"

I smiled at the ingenuous compliment — and then I, like Ramses, stared at Abdullah. "Good Gad," I breathed.

"Quite," said Ramses. He went on in Arabic, addressing Abdullah. "My father, you are the wisest of us all. Not once, not twice, but three times you have showed us the way."

"Then," said Abdullah, going straight to the point, "you will not kill the madman? He is innocent in the eyes of God."

"We do not wish to harm him, my father," Ramses said. "We must find him to keep him from being harmed, or harming others."

"What is your next question, Peabody?" Emerson inquired.

"They have been answered, Emerson." I folded my list and returned it to my pocket.

I was sitting on the verandah, deep in thought, and the sun was low in the western sky when I saw the rider approaching. The others were with Emerson in his study, or in the darkroom, for as he had acrimoniously remarked, there was no sense in wasting the entire day on unnecessary discussion. I went at once to summon them, for

I felt sure they would want to hear what our visitor had to say. Cyrus did not ride at that speed unless urgency drove him.

"Have you been to the dahabeeyah?" I asked.

"Yes, ma'am, I have." Cyrus began tugging at his goatee in a manner that must have been quite painful. It was a sign of extreme perturbation. "Gol darn it, it is my boat, after all. I got to feeling a mite uneasy about Katherine being there. I'm even more uneasy now."

"Take a little whiskey, Cyrus, and tell us what happened," I urged.

"Thanks, Mrs. Amelia, but I won't have anything to drink just yet. I want to keep my wits about me. The Colonel has invited me to go shooting jackals with him. Now as you know, I don't take any pleasure in killing creatures that can't fight back on equal terms, not even varmints like jackals, but I decided I'd better go along and see what he was up to. I figured you folks ought to know about this right away."

"Can he have made an appointment with Scudder?" I asked. "But how? Did Mrs. Jones say anything to you about a message?"

Cyrus shook his head. "We didn't get much chance to talk. She did say he's been acting peculiar all day. Something happened to get him worked up, but she didn't mention any message."

Emerson and I exchanged glances.

"Perhaps he only wants to relieve his feelings by murdering helpless animals," said Ramses, whose views on hunting were well-known to us all. "But if Scudder has managed to communicate with him, we cannot allow Mr. Vandergelt to run the risk of accompanying him. One of us should —"

Four of us spoke in chorus. "Not you!"

Cyrus was the only one who had not spoken, but he had his own objections. "I can take care of myself, young fellow. What makes you think I'd be in danger? Bellingham doesn't bear any grudge against me."

"Bellingham will shoot anyone who gets between him and Dutton Scudder," Ramses said. "Just now he is as dangerous as a rabid dog, and as unpredictable."

"Which is precisely why you are not stirring from this house," I said. "Nor is David. Bellingham would have even fewer scruples about injuring him."

"Quite right," Nefret said coolly. "But I agree that someone ought to go with Mr. Vandergelt. I am the obvious person."

Ramses, already on his feet, went absolutely rigid. Before the words hovering on his lips could burst forth, Emerson spoke.

"This discussion has got completely out of hand," he said in the mild voice that had become a proverb in the villages of Egypt. Hardened criminals cowered when Emerson spoke in that purring tone. "Be quiet, all of you. Ramses — sit down."

"But, Father —"

"Sit down, I said. Your sister is not going anywhere. Neither are you. Vandergelt, where and at what time are you to meet the Colonel?"

"The favorite spots, as you know, are near the Ramesseum and the Valley of the Kings," Cyrus replied. "He suggested the latter. At sunset."

Emerson nodded. "Yes, that is the preferred time of day, when the creatures come out to hunt in the fading light. A perfect time of day for an assassination or an unfortunate accident. It is a popular sport with some visitors. Bellingham has not done so before, has he?"

"I don't think so," Cyrus answered. "That does not mean —"

I said, "In criminal investigation, any deviation from a suspect's established routine is significant."

"He is well armed?" Emerson asked. "Rifle and shotgun?"

"And a brace of pistols," Cyrus said grimly. "He showed me his arsenal this afternoon."

"Hmph," said Emerson. He knocked out his pipe, rose, and stretched. Muscles rippled along his arms and shoulders. It was an impressive spectacle, and it warned me of his intentions.

"Emerson, you are behaving just like a man!" I exclaimed.

"I hope so," said my husband, giving me a piercing look.

I was not to be distracted. "Flexing your muscles and issuing orders in that autocratic fashion! In this case what is wanted is not muscle but cunning and common sense. Nefret has the right of it. The Colonel might not scruple to endanger another man, but he would not shoot at her or any other woman."

Ramses jumped to his feet. "Mother, if you mean to allow Nefret to —"

"She is not referring to Nefret," said Emerson. "She is referring to herself. Peabody, you damned fool, don't you realize that at this moment Bellingham hates you more than anyone in the world except Scudder?"

This remarkable statement had the effect of capturing everyone's attention. Even Ramses, who was vibrating like the cursed air pump, sat down and stared at me.

"Somehow that doesn't surprise me," Cyrus remarked. "What have you done now, Mrs. Amelia?"

Emerson told them.

Ramses's eyes opened very wide. "You said that?"

"Dear Aunt Amelia." Nefret turned her face away. Her voice was a trifle unsteady.

"I do not understand why you are all making such a fuss," I remarked irritably.

Cyrus shook his head. "That would sure explain why Bellingham is worked up. Better keep your lady away from the fellow, Emerson, till he's had time to cool off."

The opinion was unanimous, so I was forced to give in, but I was unable to persuade Emerson to abandon his intention.

We stood in the open archway, watching as they rode off.

"Come back and sit down," I ordered, for to express my own anxiety would have been to increase theirs. "You cannot stand there like obelisks for the next two hours. Ramses, you might just get me a glass of whiskey and soda, if you would be so good."

Ramses went obediently to the table. "I don't suppose —" he began.

"No whiskey, Ramses."

"Yes, Mother."

CHAPTER FOURTEEN

A man asking for help
ought at least give directions.

The evening fusillade, as Emerson called it, was not always audible at our house; it depended on the direction of the wind and the kinds of weaponry employed by the hunters. It sounded very loud that evening. As the eastern sky darkened and dusk spread her veils across the ground, the distant echo of gunfire reached a crescendo.

"There must be dozens of hunters out this evening," David said. "It is a wonder they don't shoot one another."

He may have been trying to make polite conversation, but the subject was ill chosen. Ramses's response was not much more comforting. "There have been occasional accidents."

Gradually the frequency of firing diminished as the darkness grew. The first bright stars of night appeared in the sky over Luxor, and then, at last, we heard them coming. I ran to the doorway.

"Thank heaven you are back safely," I exclaimed. "What happened?"

"What did you expect would happen?" Emerson tossed the reins to Ramses. "I cannot imagine why I allowed all of you to hypnotize me into supposing something was going to happen! We spent most of the time lying flat behind a ridge, while a pack of nitwits blazed away at one another. The jackals must have been laughing themselves sick."

"Did you see Bellingham?" I asked.

"Yes." Emerson stumbled over a chair and swore. "What are you sitting in the dark for?"

"Watching for you. Do not curse the darkness, Emerson, light a lamp. No, let me do it, you always knock them over."

I proceeded to do so while Emerson mixed our whiskey. Cyrus scooped up Sekhmet and settled himself in a chair with the cat on his knee. The children had gone to the stable with the horses.

"Well?" I said.

"Well, bah," said Emerson. "If there was some hidden purpose behind Bellingham's expedition this evening, it eludes me. Scudder may be insane, but he is not stupid enough to wander into a melee like that one."

"Something funny is going on, though," Cyrus said slowly. "The Colonel was too darned pleased to see us. Solicitous, too. He was the one who insisted we take cover."

"He did not?" I asked.

"Not with us. Went off by himself. Didn't hear any screams, so I figure nobody got shot." Cyrus finished his whiskey and rose, depositing

Sekhmet onto his vacated chair. "Guess I'll head for home. The boys will be on the *Amelia* tonight, like Ramses promised?"

"Did he? Yes, I believe he did, now that you mention it. We ought not leave Mrs. Jones without some rescuer at hand, just in case; but —"

"Good. I might just pay them a little visit myself later on. You might mention it to them; I wouldn't want those lads to mistake me for a burglar." Hat in hand, he stood for a moment looking out into the twilight. "Supposed to be a full moon tonight," he said, as if to himself. "I always have a hard time sleeping when it's a full moon."

The moonlight is always bright in Egypt; some claim that when the moon is at the full it is possible to read a newspaper by its light. I had never done so, since I usually have other things to occupy me at that time; but as the boys rode off toward the dahabeeyah, the silvery glow allowed us to make out their retreating forms until they reached the cultivation, almost a mile away.

I had lectured them before I sent them off, reiterating my adjurations to take care until even David showed signs of restlessness and Emerson requested that I stop talking. It had been a waste of breath. How could they take care against an unknown danger? I could not forbid them to go, however. Ramses had told Mrs. Jones they would be there, and an English gentleman keeps his word.

I had extracted a promise from Nefret that she would not go out; but as I prepared for bed I heard her soft footsteps moving restlessly around the house. The smell of pipe tobacco floated in through the open window; Emerson was outside, walking back and forth. Something landed on the windowsill with a thud. I jumped and dropped my brush. I had not seen Anubis for several days. He had a habit of going off by himself, to hunt or perhaps to sulk; now he sat poised on the sill, his eyes lambent in the candlelight, his fur bristling.

"He is outside," I said. My voice sounded strange in the silence. "Good Gad, don't stare at me in that accusing way! What is wrong with you tonight?"

The cat vanished more silently than he had come. If I had had fur, mine would have been standing on end too. There was something in the air, a sense of waiting, of imminence, of . . .

"Why the devil are you sitting there staring at the mirror?" Emerson inquired.

I let out a little scream of exasperation and dropped my brush. "I wish you would not creep up on me like that, Emerson!"

"I was not creeping," said Emerson indignantly. "You were in such a brown study you failed to hear me. Why aren't you in bed?"

"I am not tired."

"Yes, you are." He turned his head sharply toward the door. "Someone *is* creeping around the house. I heard —"

"Nefret, I expect," I said. "Emerson, for heaven's sake don't leap on her! You are nervous tonight too."

"Nervous, bah," said Emerson. He opened the door. "Nefret, is that you? Go to bed at once."

"I won't sleep," Nefret said darkly.

"That is beyond my control," said Emerson. "Go to your room."

"Yes, sir," Nefret snapped. She went off, slim and indignant, still in trousers and shirt and boots. I felt certain she did not intend to change into her nightgown.

"I suppose there is no way of insuring that she will sleep," Emerson said. He gave me a hopeful look.

"No, Emerson, she is too intelligent to accept the offer of a nice hot cup of cocoa tonight."

Emerson threw himself down on the bed, fully clothed. "Come to bed, Peabody."

I did not bother to tell him to take off his boots. After a while he began to snore in an ostentatious manner.

I lay down, but I did not undress either. After a while I fell into one of those abominable states of consciousness when one is not sound asleep or fully awake. Every noise made me start. Finally, after an interminable interval, I gave it up. Surely morning could not be far off now. Emerson had stopped snoring, but I knew he was not asleep. When I spoke his name he responded instantly.

"Yes, Peabody?"

513

"I cannot sleep, Emerson."

"No more can I." He turned and put his arm around me. "Are you worried about the boys?"

"I always worry about them. It isn't that, however. We know most of the truth now; we ought to be able to anticipate what Scudder will do next."

"He wrote to us before. He may do so again."

"It would not be easy for him to deliver a message. We are overlooking something, Emerson. Scudder is doubtless a madman, but he is a romantic madman."

"I don't follow, Peabody."

"Everything he has done has been inspired by woolly-minded romanticism, like something out of a novel. The way he prepared her body, not in ancient Egyptian style but in a way that might have served as an illustration for such a novel — the enigmatic clues he sent us — the futile melodrama of bringing Bellingham to the scene to confront the body of his wife. He will play some equally futile, melodramatic game for his final confrontation. Would you care to guess what setting he will choose?"

"The tomb, of course," Emerson said, adding an emphatic swear word. "Why the devil didn't you say so before?"

"It only just now occurred to me. I was trying to think of a reason for Bellingham's unusual behavior this evening. Put the two facts together, Emerson: Bellingham was out with a shotgun, and he was near the entrance to the Valley."

"You think he received a message from Scudder?"

"Why else would he go out tonight?"

"Possible," Emerson muttered. "No, but see here, Peabody, if your — our — understanding of Scudder's motives is correct, he will want an audience, won't he? He would not have arranged to meet Bellingham alone, after dark."

"Audience, witnesses, referees," I replied. "In short, he will want *us*. I don't believe the rendezvous was set for this evening. Bellingham was merely scouting out the terrain. Scudder does not need to summon us to the performance. He will expect us to be at the tomb tomorrow. We always are."

"Then he will wait until we get there," Emerson said, pretending to yawn. "We may as well get some sleep for what is left —"

"He will wait. Will Bellingham?"

Before Emerson could answer we heard Nefret's voice.

"Someone is coming. Hurry!"

She had not been sleeping either. We reached the verandah in time to see the boys dismount. "What are you doing here so early?" Emerson demanded. "It is not —"

"Dawn will break in another hour," Ramses interrupted. "And I fear it is already too late."

The moon was setting, but there was light enough for me to see the lines of anxiety that marked his face. I started impetuously forward. Emerson caught me in an iron grip.

"If it is already too late, five more minutes will not matter," he said calmly. "Explain yourself, Ramses."

"Colonel Bellingham did not return to the *Valley of the Kings* this evening," Ramses said. "To the dahabeeyah of that name, that is; he must have gone directly . . ." He took a deep breath and started over. "It was Mrs. Jones who signalled us. She was waving a piece of cloth, I think; I could not see it clearly, but her presence on deck at that hour and the way she kept waving her arms were sufficient evidence of agitation. The Colonel had told her he would not be there for dinner, so she did not begin to worry until she woke an hour ago and realized he had not come back. Is that enough for you, Father? We must go at once. Some hunters find moonlight sufficient. Or the first light of dawn."

We took the path over the *gebel;* even the horses could not go as quickly in the dark and along the uneven surface of the Valley. The moon was down and the first streaks of dawn were pale in the sky before we started down the steep path. The glow of a fire below greeted us; the *gaffirs* who guarded the Valley were gathered round it, brewing their morning coffee. They greeted us with pleasure but without surprise. Nothing Emerson did could surprise them. When he asked if they had seen any strangers, they exchanged glances and shrugged.

"We slept, Father of Curses. There were hunters on the *gebel,* but no one came this way."

We hastened on. Ramses and Emerson outstripped the rest of us; they were standing near the entrance of the tomb when we caught them up. They were staring at something lying on the ground.

Ramses picked it up — a heavy stick with a golden handle. Grasping both ends of the stick, he twisted and pulled. Steel glimmered in the pale light.

"A sword stick," I said. "We ought to have known, oughtn't we? He was here. How did he get here unobserved?"

Ramses gestured. "The goat path. We showed him how! The rope is probably still there. He was here before dawn, waiting. He may not be dead. Yet . . ."

Then he was gone, plunging down the steps and into the tomb at breakneck speed.

"Stay here," Emerson snapped, and followed after him.

He could not possibly have supposed that any of us would. There was nowhere else the two men we sought could have gone. I too had observed the disturbance of the fine sandy dust on the steps, as if something large and heavy had been dragged down them.

As I entered the hot, dark passageway I was pleased to see that Emerson had had the good sense to stop long enough to light a candle. It glimmered like a will-o'-the-wisp, ahead and below. I stumbled over the pipe and fell forward against Emerson.

"Curse it, Peabody," he remarked.

"Never mind that," I gasped. "Where is Ramses?"

"Bring the light." It was my son's voice. I could just make him out, crouched on the sloping floor. Behind him was a dark opening — that of the chamber Emerson had found the day before. Above and beside him were the dim shapes of the beams that supported the ceiling; next to him was another shape, like a bundle of rags.

Emerson advanced, holding the candle high. Ramses did not look up. Taking hold of the amorphous thing beside him, he pulled at it until it lay flat — as flat as it could get on that slanted surface. The light reflected off eyeballs opaque as frosted glass. The mouth gaped open and the crooked nose cast a grotesque shadow across one cheek. Dutton Scudder had come to his final resting place in the tomb he had prepared for the woman he loved.

Ramses took the candle from his father and drew the torn galabeeyah aside. The feeble light left the lower part of the torso in merciful shadow; flesh and fabric, bone and muscle, had been smashed into a dark and dreadful mass. Ramses's forefinger touched an old scar, approximately an inch long, just below the collarbone.

"If he had aimed a few inches higher, he would have obliterated this," Ramses said. "It was not bad shooting in that light, though."

"Thank you." The Colonel stepped forward from the darkness of the chamber. His tweed hunting suit was stained and ripped, but his face was the usual courteous mask. He held a double-barrelled shotgun in the crook of his arm.

Ramses straightened, and Bellingham said pleasantly, "What a pity you were early this morning. Had you come at your usual time, you would have found me gone and the evidence buried under several tons of fallen stone. No, Professor, stay where you are. I have nothing to lose now, and few compunctions about harming those who have brought me to this. Except . . . Go back, Miss Forth. I have no desire to injure you."

Naturally Nefret did not go back; only Emerson's outstretched arm kept her from advancing farther. "Please, Colonel, there is no need for anyone to be injured," she said in a gentle, soothing voice. "Let us all go back — you, too. Come with me. Take my hand."

Bellingham laughed. "Very pretty, Miss Forth, but it is too late for your feminine wiles. I knew yesterday that Mrs. Emerson had succeeded in poisoning your mind against me. She accused me then of killing Lucinda —"

"Oh, dear," I said. "How true it is that the guilty flee where no man pursueth. You misunderstood my meaning, Colonel."

"There is no longer any doubt in your mind, is there? But perhaps there are a few points about which you are still uncertain. That must vex you. Come here to me, and I will answer your questions."

"Peabody," Emerson exclaimed. "If you move one step —"

"Now, Emerson, calm yourself," I said. The shotgun was aimed at his chest, and Nefret was beside him.

"Come here, Mrs. Emerson," the Colonel repeated.

I could not see that I had much choice. As soon as I was close enough he caught hold of me with his left arm. I had hoped I might be able to wrest the weapon away from him, but I realized at once there was no chance of that. His finger was firm on the triggers, and in that confined space even a random shot would strike someone. My only hope, and a frail hope it was, lay in persuading him to talk and go on talking. Murderers, I have observed, like to boast of their cleverness. And one never knew — something to our advantage might yet turn up!

"So," I said encouragingly. "How were you able to track Scudder and Lucinda down, when the police failed to do so?"

"I made certain the police would not find them, Mrs. Emerson. It was a private matter, a matter of honor. I knew her maid must have been involved; without her assistance Lucinda could not have left the hotel unobserved. When I questioned the wretched creature she confessed all. Lucinda had worn one of her dresses and gone out the servants' entrance, where she met Scudder, who had disguised himself as an Egyptian. With that information it was not difficult to track them, especially when the Negress told me he had mentioned a village near the Wadi Natrun."

"Very clever," I said. My eyes remained fixed on his right hand. The finger had not moved.

"It was clever of *you*," Bellingham said with a horrible travesty of politeness, "to notice, as I suppose you did, that the wound that killed her was not made by a knife, but by something longer and not so heavy. I still carry that stick. It is a memento, one might say.

"I thought I had killed Scudder too, but I could not stay to make certain; Lucinda's screams had attracted attention, and I could hear people approaching. A few shots from my pistol dispersed the crowd, and I got away in the dark without being recognized."

"Even if they had seen you clearly, the villagers would not have dared go to the police," Ramses said. "They have more to fear than to hope from our so-called justice."

The muzzle of the shotgun swung toward him. "That is close enough, young man," Bellingham said sharply. "I have been watching you; don't move again."

"The message from Scudder that brought you back to Egypt threatened you with exposure," I said, trying to distract his attention from Ramses. "You feared —"

"Feared?" Bellingham's grip tightened, squeezing my ribs in a painful fashion. "It was vengeance, not fear, that brought me back, Mrs. Emerson. I fear no man. He had informed me he intended to involve you and your husband, so I took pains to make your acquaintance —"

"And encouraged your daughter to make that of Ramses?"

"That was not planned, Mrs. Emerson, but it might have served me well if fate had not intervened. Scudder hoped to force a confession out of me by threatening Dolly, and I hoped that by following her, I could get my hands on him."

"Contemptible!" I exclaimed. "To use your own daughter —"

"Enough! I tire of this, Mrs. Emerson. Have I satisfied your curiosity? It is a dangerous trait. You know the saying: 'Curiosity killed the cat.' "

He took a step back, pulling me with him. Emerson said very quietly, "You talk of honor, while using a woman as a shield? Let her go, Bellingham. There is still a way out for you, so long as you harm no one else. You can live —"

"Live? To face scandal, disgrace, and possibly prison? I know you, sir; you would do your best to see me accused and convicted. As for your wife — women like her should not be allowed to live! Defiant of authority, demanding her own way — sooner or later she would betray you, as Lucinda did me. I have no wish to harm the rest of you," he went on, looking at the pale faces that stared at him in horror from the shadows. "Retreat, before it is too late."

He gave them little time to save themselves. Almost negligently he raised the weapon and fired both barrels at the juncture of wall and ceiling, where the bracing beams met. The roof gave way with a thunderous crash as he pulled me off my feet and drew me through a hail of stone into the darkness of the chamber beyond.

I felt fairly confident that one of two things would happen. Either I would be crushed and/or mangled by falling rock, or I would find myself entombed with an individual who could murder me at his leisure and without fear of interruption. Before I could proceed with this depressing chain of reasoning, darkness and intense pain overcame me.

The darkness was that of unconsciousness, but it did not endure long; I opened my eyes to another kind of darkness, the complete absence of light. When I tried to move, a stab of pain shot through my body. I had struck the rocky floor with considerable force, but the worst of the pain seemed to emanate from one of my lower limbs. Gritting my teeth, I dragged myself toward my right, where, if memory served, there was a wall. It is always a good idea to have a wall at one's back.

Especially at the present time. Something strange was going on. I could see nothing, but I could hear, and the sounds I heard were not the sort I had expected. They were strongly suggestive of a violent struggle — grunts, gasps, the thud of blows. Though I was still giddy with pain and confusion, my intelligence drew the logical conclusion. I was not alone with my murderer.

Someone, or some *thing,* was there too.

My first thought, of course, was of my devoted spouse. But no — impossible — I told myself. Not even Emerson could have got there in time; he had been a good ten feet distant when I was dragged through the rain of stones. Who — or what — had lurked, waiting, in the dark recesses of the tomb?

Intense curiosity gave me renewed strength. I fumbled in my pockets until I located a candle stub and a box of matches. The match flared up. I stared, struck dumb and motionless with astonishment, until the flame seared my fingers and I was forced to drop the match.

"Mother?"

If I had not seen him, I would not have known the voice was his. (Though logic would have reminded me that no one else uses that name to address me.) What I had seen was as stupefying as the mere fact of his presence — my son astride the prostrate body of Bellingham, in the act of smashing the latter's head against the floor.

"Here," I croaked, and then let out an involuntary scream as Ramses stumbled over my outstretched lower limbs.

"Thank God," Ramses gasped. "I feared . . . Are you injured?"

"I believe my leg — that is, my lower limb — is broken. What . . . How . . . ?"

I knew the answer, though. He had been closest to me of any. He must have moved at the same instant as Bellingham, diving through the rain of falling rocks.

"It could be worse." His voice was back to normal — cool, unemotional. "Can you strike another match?"

"Certainly, and I believe it would be advisable to do so at once. Perhaps you had better take the candle."

Our hands fumbled in the darkness. I confess without shame that it took me some time to get the flame of the match in contact with the wick of the candle. Ramses's hand was steady, but not even the eerie flickering light could account for the alteration of his features.

"Are you hurt?" I asked.

"Only a few bruises."

Just beyond the limited circle of light I made out a dark, motionless form. "You had better tie him up," I said. "My belt and yours —"

"No need. I think . . . I am fairly certain he is dead." After a brief pause, during which I could think of nothing to say, he went on, "You look rather ill, Mother. May I suggest a sip of that brandy you always carry?"

We both had a little nip of the brandy — for medicinal purposes.

"Now," said Ramses, wiping his mouth on the back of his hand, "tell me what I can do for you. With your verbal assistance I feel certain I could set your — er — lower limb."

"No, thank you," I said firmly. "At the moment it is not too painful, and I don't see anything that would serve as a splint. In my opinion, we would be better employed in searching for a way out of here. Is that blood on your mouth?"

"What? Oh. A cut lip, that is all." He extracted a filthy handkerchief from his pocket. Ramses's handkerchiefs are always nasty; I do not suppose he will ever grow out of that deplorable habit, since his father never has. I took it away from him and gave him mine, and my canteen.

"Your father will dig us out eventually," I continued. "But it may take him a while, and — ouch! Give me the handkerchief, Ramses, and I will wipe my own face. Do not believe I am insensible of the kindly motive behind the gesture, however. Er — are you sure . . ."

"Yes." I saw he was shivering. The air was not cool. Quite the reverse, in fact.

I said quickly, "As I was saying, your father will certainly reach us, but since we have nothing better to do anyhow, we may as well explore the tomb. There must be another way out, or Bellingham would not have retreated here."

Ramses eyed me askance. "If you will forgive me for saying so, Mother, that is a most unlikely possibility."

I was relieved that my attempt to distract him had succeeded. An Emerson who can argue is back to normal.

"Be that as it may," I began.

"Yes, quite. It will do no harm to have a look. You mean me to do so, I presume, for movement on your part would be ill advised, if not actually impossible. I don't like to leave you alone in the dark, though."

"I have another candle. But I think we ought not squander them. Go on, I am not afraid of the dark."

I gave him my candle. He hesitated for a moment, nodded without speaking, and moved away.

I then allowed myself to lean against the wall. I did not want him to see how ill I felt or how frightened I was — not for myself, or even for Ramses. Our position was by no means enviable, but we lived, and Emerson would certainly dig until he got us out.

If *he* lived. My last view of the avalanche had been far from reassuring. Would the supports he had erected hold, or would they fall like a row of dominoes under the weight of tons of stone? Had he rushed impulsively toward me instead of retreating, as prudence would dictate? Emerson was not prudent when my safety or that of Ramses was concerned.

Ramses knew this as well as I. He knew he might have lost those he loved best — his father, his sister, his best friend. He also knew, as did I, that there was no other way out. Egyptian rock-cut tombs are not constructed with back doors. But the search would keep him busy, and away from the thing lying motionless on the floor.

Since I had nothing better to do at the moment, I tried to remember how many people I had killed. After considerable cogitation I found, rather to my surprise, that the total appeared to be nil. Somehow I had had the impression there had been quite a few. Not that I hadn't tried — always, of course, in self-defense or defense of my loved ones. I consoled myself with the reminder that a parasol, useful though it is, is not really a lethal weapon, and that my little pistol had a very limited range.

The rumble of a rockfall deep in the recesses of the tomb made me start. It was followed by Ramses's voice. "All right. No harm done."

"Be careful," I called — as if that were possible.

No doubt, I reflected, one's first homicide would be something of a strain on the nerves, especially a homicide as brutally intimate as that one. It would be a long time before I could forget the sound I had heard — the crack of shattering bone and a kind of liquescent, soggy splash.

I felt sure Ramses had not intended to kill the man, only incapacitate him in order to prevent him from killing one of us. He was young and inexperienced, and he had been fighting for his life and mine against an opponent crazed by fury and despair. It is difficult to calculate the precise degree of force required under those conditions. Christian woman though I am, I could not regret the fact. We were in dire enough straits without having to worry about controlling a malevolent murderer.

They would find us eventually, even if Emerson had been . . . But no! I would not entertain that idea for an instant. He lived, and he would demolish the entire cliff if he had to, with a dozen devoted men working like fiends at his side. I did rather hope it would not take them too long. The air was not very good. In fact, it was very bad. We would run short of water before we ran short of air, however. The heat was intense.

The faint glow of Ramses's candle had vanished. I was alone in the dark.

From Manuscript H:

He knew why she had sent him away. Action, however futile — and this search was unquestionably futile — was easier than waiting in the dark. Perhaps she wanted to cry a little; she would not break down in front of him, and she was desperately worried about his father. The others too, of course, but mostly his father. He had always known they cared more for one another than for anyone else.

He stopped crawling in order to catch his breath and force his shaking hand to steadiness. Nefret must be all right; his father would have seen to that. He would have realized there was no chance he could reach his wife. He loved Nefret too. He wouldn't let her . . .

He was afraid even to think about David. David had been closer to the others than to him, but if loyalty had overcome good sense . . . No, he wouldn't think about David. Or Nefret.

He wiped the stinging sweat out of his eyes with the back of his hand and started forward.

The passage curved and climbed. The floor was almost clear; he crawled over one pile of rock that had fallen from the ceiling, but there was no rubble, no fill. That was odd, he thought, trying to concentrate on something other than the image of bodies broken and buried — of one white arm and a flood of golden-red hair protruding from under a pile of stones . . .

Odd, yes. If there was a burial chamber, the fill ought to be present throughout the passage. He had seen no artifacts, not even a piece of broken pottery, only blank walls and bare floor. That would indicate that the tomb could not have been finished or used for a burial. . . .

He wondered why he was doing this. He should not have left his mother alone. She was hurt, possibly unconscious by now. The least he could do was hold her hand and give her the little comfort he could offer.

Perhaps she could comfort him. God knew he needed it.

He had been crawling on his hands and knees, since the ceiling was just a little too low for him to walk upright, and it was hard to see the occasional protrusions in the dim light. He rose to his knees, preparatory to turning back.

Straight ahead the passage ended.

For a few seconds he remained motionless, staring bemusedly at the wall. He couldn't seem to think clearly. The end of the passage — right. Time to turn back. Past time. But it was odd, that wall. Not rubble or rough stone. Squared-off blocks, carefully mortared.

After a moment he realized the strange sound was

that of harsh laughter — his own. She'd been right after all. He ought to have known; his mother was always right. There was a back door.

One fading part of his consciousness informed him he was losing his mind. "Too much heat, not enough oxygen. There are no back doors in Egyptian tombs, you bloody fool." A burial chamber, perhaps. Not a back door.

"Delayed shock," the remnant of common sense insisted. "It wasn't pleasant, was it, hearing that crunch of bone, knowing you had killed a man? I wonder if your father felt so sick the first time he . . ."

No, he thought, not Father. Father is Zeus and Amon-Ra and all the heroes of all the sagas rolled into one. He can do anything. He fears nothing. Forget the burial chamber. Go back and hold your mother's hand, you poor little coward.

He stuck the stub of the candle onto the floor and pulled his knife from its scabbard.

It didn't seem to take long. The mortar was dry. It fell in a shower of flakes, and he began to lever one of the blocks out. He wasn't thinking at all now, just moving by instinct. He knew how to do it, he had watched his father often enough. The block slipped neatly out onto his hands. He laid it aside and put his head through the hole.

Through a fog of dusty dimness four wide terrified eyes stared back at him. The bare bulb in the lamp one of them carried half blinded him.

Even if he had been entirely in his right mind, it would not have been possible for him to resist. "Sa-

531

laam aleikhum, *friends. Will one of you tell Carter Effendi I am here?"*

"Mr. Carter was not there, of course," Ramses said, ending his surprisingly brief and boringly factual description of his discovery. "He had gone round to help Father and the others dig us out. I would have returned to you at once, Mother, had I not known you would be vexed with me if I did so without first ascertaining how the rest of the family had fared. When I reached them I discovered they were on the verge of getting through, so I remained to help."

He was perched on the wall in his favorite position, and except for his bandaged hands and the darkening bruises on his face he looked and sounded quite normal. However, the infallible instincts of a mother informed me that he was, as usual, concealing something.

The most difficult thing to believe was that I had been in that hellish place for less than an hour. It had seemed a good deal longer, even though I had fallen asleep shortly after he left me and had failed to hear the reassuring sounds of activity beyond the rockfall. It was the relatively fresher air that woke me. The first sight my eyes beheld was the face of Emerson, and when he caught me up in his arms I hardly felt the pain of my hurt leg.

Nefret made him put me down at once and supervised my removal on a litter. They were all there, David and Abdullah and Selim; Selim was crying, and Abdullah was thanking God in a loud, tremulous voice, and David kept taking my hand and then reaching for the hand of Ramses and then trying to take mine again. I had seen Ramses, of course, but because I was still a trifle sleepy I had not fully realized how he had got there until he told his story.

He had waited until we were back at the house and our more pressing needs had been attended to. Nefret and I had decided my leg was probably not broken, but it was badly bruised and swollen, so she bound it up — following my instructions — and helped me bathe, and after I had changed into a loose but becoming gown Emerson carried me out onto the verandah and settled me on the sofa. Howard and Cyrus were there too, and Abdullah and Selim and Daoud, so we made quite a jolly party. I had told the cook to prepare a very large luncheon.

"So it was Hatshepsut's tomb you broke into?" I asked. "Astonishing! You know, Ramses, when I sent you off I really did not expect you would find another way out."

"Nor did I," replied my son. "Yet I suppose that unconsciously I had been aware of the direction in which the passage was leading. You had not observed the opening, Mr. Carter?"

"It was not an opening," Howard replied somewhat snappishly. "It had been neatly plastered on the other side and we did not use the electric bulbs until after we had passed that point, and the candlelight . . . Well, never mind that. Your tomb is obviously later in date than that of Hatshepsut. When the workmen broke by accident into hers, they carefully disguised the opening and —"

"And Scudder found it," Nefret exclaimed. "While working for you last year, Mr. Carter."

Howard looked as if he wanted to laugh, but was too polite to do so. "Now, Miss Nefret, that is deuced unlikely, you know. He might have followed the passage partway, but he could not have got through to the original entrance. It took your crew days to remove the hardened fill."

"Unlikely, but not impossible," said Emerson, unable to endure the look of disappointment on Nefret's face. "He had all summer, after you ended your season's work. He might have deduced where the entrance was located and come at it from the other end."

"Never mind the dad-blamed tomb," Cyrus exclaimed. "You folks may not want to talk about it, but it's got to be faced sooner or later. Bellingham is dead — and a durned good job, too, in my opinion. He murdered Scudder in cold blood, didn't he?"

"Yes," I said. "Mr. Scudder never wanted to kill the Colonel; he wanted to expose him as the murderer of his own wife. That was why Scudder selected us as the ones to find poor Lucinda's body. He knew we had been working in Thebes, and we had acquired a certain reputation for our detectival talents. He believed we would see through Bellingham's lies and discern the truth.

Which we did — eventually."

"Too late for Scudder," Emerson said grimly.

"It was all because Mr. Scudder was a hopeless romantic," I explained. "When romanticism is not tempered by common sense, Nefret and gentlemen, it becomes a fatal weakness. All Mr. Scudder's actions were directed by untempered romanticism — the way he prepared her body, the mysterious hints he sent us — and it led inevitably to tragedy. The saddest example of this weakness was the way he lured Bellingham onto the scene when we removed Lucinda's body from the tomb. I expect he actually believed Bellingham would confess on the spot."

"No," Ramses said. "The saddest were his attempts to get me to meet with him in private. He only wanted to talk to me. I was too stupid to understand."

I assumed it had been Nefret who had bandaged his torn hands and made him wash. He must have done something to annoy her, for she was watching him intently, and when she spoke her voice was hard and unsympathetic.

"If there is blame, we all share it. Including Scudder. He might have been more direct, you know."

"I doubt anyone would have believed such a wild tale," I admitted. "No, Emerson, not even I! We would have thought him mad, especially after seeing what he had done to her body."

"He *was* mad," Ramses said. "Grief and guilt combined —"

"Why should he feel guilty?" Nefret demanded. She sounded angry, though I could not think why. "It was her husband who ran her through with that sword stick of his."

"As she tried to shield Scudder with her own body," Ramses said. "But it was he who brought her to her death. At least that is how he would have seen it."

"So now you are reading his mind?" Nefret said unpleasantly. "You are a damned romantic yourself, Ramses, and I advise you to stop it at once. I don't doubt it was Lucinda who instigated the elopement. She didn't run away *with* Scudder, she ran away *from* Bellingham. I hate to think what he did to her after they were married and she was in his power —"

Emerson and I spoke as one.

"Nefret, please!"

"Oh, very well," she snapped. "I suppose that is another of the subjects a woman is not supposed to talk about! All I am saying is that *some people* take too much on themselves. Bellingham was the only villain, no one else is at fault — not even Scudder. Of course the poor man lost his mind after seeing her murdered so viciously. Who could blame him?"

"Not I," Cyrus said heavily. "Nor any man who ever loved a woman."

"What will become of Dolly?" I asked, for I felt the atmosphere was getting a bit thick.

"Cat — I mean, Katherine — is with her," Cyrus said. "She says she'll take her back home.

I kind of — well — left it to her. Now, if you'll excuse me —"

"You musn't go just yet, Cyrus," I said. "At the risk of sounding callous, we have much to be thankful for. Poor Mr. Scudder has been vindicated and his loss avenged. Death was undoubtedly the happiest ending for him; the only possible alternative would have been an asylum. And we have survived! Stay and have luncheon."

"I'll stay for a while, I guess," Cyrus said. He sighed. "I was told to keep away."

I was beginning to have an idea as to why he seemed depressed. If I was right — and I usually am — the subject was not one to be discussed in the presence of the others. I promised myself I would deal with it as soon as I could.

My dear Emerson was the next to speak. He had kept tight hold of my hand the entire time. Now he returned it to me. Rising to his impressive height, he cleared his throat.

"Ramses."

Ramses started. "Er — yes, sir? Have I done something?"

"Yes," said Emerson. Going to Ramses, he held out his hand. "You saved your mother's life today. If you had not acted instantaneously and without regard for your own safety, she would have been another of Bellingham's victims. You acted as I would have done had I been able. I — er — I — hmph — I appreciate it."

"Oh," Ramses said. "Thank you, sir." They shook hands.

"Not at all." Emerson coughed. "Well! Have you anything to add, Peabody?"

"No, my dear, I think not. You have summed up the situation quite neatly." Emerson gave me an odd look, and I went on cheerfully, "It is early, but I think perhaps we might indulge in a whiskey and soda before luncheon. We have some justification for celebrating, after all. I shall propose a little toast."

They gathered round my couch, and Emerson served us — lemon juice and water for the others, whiskey without soda for Cyrus, and the usual for me.

"Another whiskey and soda, please, Emerson," I said, and handed mine to Ramses.

For a moment that rigidly controlled countenance relaxed into a look of boyish pleasure and surprise. Only for a moment. With a little bow he took the glass from my hand. "Thank you, Mother."

Smiling broadly, Emerson supplied me with a glass of my own. I looked round at the faces of my friends and beloved family.

"Cheers!" I said.

Life is never so simple as that, however. There were still a number of loose ends to be tied up. I had to leave some of them to Emerson, since I was confined to the house by my confounded leg, but in fact I did not particularly want to deal with the British and American authorities. They carried on quite unnecessarily and extravagantly about the arrangements for disposing of the various bodies. There was one matter I meant to attend to myself, and I found an opportunity of doing so the following day while Emerson was in Luxor telegraphing to some people and shouting at others. I had asked Mrs. Jones to come to me, which she was good enough to do. She looked quite her old self, smartly dressed and in command of herself. Only a perceptive observer like myself would have seen that her eyes looked tired.

"How is Dolly getting on?" I asked after Ali had served tea.

"As you might expect. She does nothing and says nothing."

"I hope you will express my condolences and apologies for not calling on her. There will not be time for me to see her, I suppose, before you go."

"We leave tomorrow. But I don't believe she particularly wants to see you, Mrs. Emerson."

"That is understandable. Is it true that you mean to accompany her all the way back to America?"

Mrs. Jones shrugged. "She cannot travel alone. Who else is there?"

"Mrs. Gordon," I said.

"I beg your pardon?"

"The wife of the American vice-consul. Or some other lady from that office. It is their responsibility, after all, and I expect they would be glad of an excuse to go home for a visit. You are looking for an excuse too, I think. Why are you running away?"

It was most interesting to observe the varied emotions that passed in rapid succession across her face. She did not reply, so I went on.

"I do not believe in beating around the bush, Mrs. Jones. I had thought you were of the same mind. Has Cyrus asked you — er — has he proposed —"

"He has proposed marriage," said Mrs. Jones.

"He has?" I gasped.

"Ah, that surprises you. What did you think he had proposed?"

She looked almost her old self again, cynically amused and watchful.

"I ought to have known," I admitted. "Cyrus is too well bred to suggest anything improper. When will the nuptials take place?"

"They will not. I have refused him."

That surprised me even more. "Why, in heaven's name? He is a wonderful man, and rich besides! Not in his first youth, perhaps, but you are no romantic girl."

"Not a girl, certainly, but romance, as you of all people know, does not necessarily vanish with age. I have not lost all sense of decency. How could I accept — being what I am?"

"Do you care for him?"

"I have never known a man like him," she said softly. "Kind, generous, intelligent, understanding, brave . . . He makes me laugh, Mrs. Emerson. I have not laughed a great deal."

"Then you ought to marry him."

"What?" She stared at me. "You cannot be serious."

"I am entirely serious. You are worse than romantic, you are hopelessly silly if you throw away a chance of happiness such as few women can know on such grounds. You have been unfortunate, but that is in the past. Your sins, if they can be viewed as such, are light compared with those of many others. If you will take my advice . . ."

She drew in a long, difficult breath. "Most people do, don't they?"

"Yes, and quite rightly. I have had a good deal of experience in such things. I have known Cyrus for many years, and I believe he would be happy with you. You are certainly the most — er — interesting woman he has ever proposed marriage to; you can keep him entertained. I presume there is no difficulty about . . . no reason of a personal nature why you would . . . You understand me, I believe?"

Every muscle in her face loosened, and for a moment I thought she was going to cry. Instead she threw her head back and burst into a shout of laughter. "No," she gasped. "That is — yes, Mrs. Emerson, I do understand you. There is no difficulty about . . . Quite the contrary. Oh, dear. Where is my handkerchief?"

I gave her mine. She covered her face; when she removed the handkerchief I saw her eyes were wet. Prolonged laughter does have that effect.

"Better now?" I inquired. "Good. What I propose is that you escort Dolly to Cairo and hand her over to one of the ladies from the consulate. By the time those arrangements have been completed you will have been able to consider your own feelings more rationally. Take a day or two longer if you like; visit the museum and the Pyramids, have a nice rest. You can telegraph Cyrus when you have reached your decision."

Recognizing that there was nothing more to be said at that time, she rose. "If I needed a further reason to accept, Mrs. Emerson, the possibility of improving my acquaintance with you would certainly be an inducement. You are really the most —"

"Many people have been kind enough to say so," I assured her.

I told Emerson and the children all about it when we met for dinner. Emerson had to have an additional whiskey and soda before he was calm enough to comment.

"Peabody, your incredible effrontery never ceases to amaze me! What will Vandergelt say when he learns you have interfered in his private affairs?"

"If it works out, Mr. Vandergelt will be pleased and grateful," Ramses said. I believe he was mildly amused. "Mrs. Jones is a remarkable woman. She should be an interesting addition to Luxor society."

"Quite," Nefret said, stroking Sekhmet. She was unquestionably amused (Nefret, I mean).

"Well done, Aunt Amelia. I like Mrs. Jones, and I hope she will make Mr. Vandergelt the happiest of men!"

"Hmph," said Emerson. "I hope your meddling in the Frasers' affairs will have an equally happy result. You were not able to talk with Donald Fraser —"

"You are mistaken, Emerson. I would not have neglected something so important. I spoke with Donald two days ago, that morning I went to Luxor."

"Oh, good Gad!" Emerson looked at me almost in awe. Musingly he added, "I would give a great deal to have overheard that conversation."

"I expressed myself with the utmost delicacy," I assured him. "I simply pointed out that since heaven had granted him the extraordinary favor of uniting the two women he loved in a single body — er — person — the least he could do was abandon unseemly habits that might offend an aristocratic lady. Excessive eating and drinking, insufficient exercise, and — and that sort of thing."

"Excellent advice," Emerson said. "Did you also recommend a course of selected readings?"

"Certainly." I thought it wiser to pretend I did not know what he meant. "It is necessary to exercise the mind as well as the body."

Emerson nodded gravely, but there was a gleam in his sapphirine orbs that warned me I had better change the subject. Nefret was leaning forward, lips parted, David's eyes were very wide, and Ramses . . . Well, heaven only knows what was going on behind that blank, bland face of his!

"Mens sana in corpore sano," I summarized. "As Donald strives to please his wife, so will she endeavor to please him. Eventually the fantasy will fade; he will find in Enid all the attributes of his desired princess, and she will no longer have to pretend to be Tasherit. Though she may find that she rather enjoys . . . I beg your pardon, Ramses. Did you speak?"

Ramses raised his glass in salute. "I only wanted to say: You are right as always, Mother."

From Manuscript H:

They had their own celebration that night on the dahabeeyah, sitting on the deck so the smell of the forbidden cigarettes would not linger in Ramses's room. The awning had been rolled back; the moon and stars made the night bright as day. Seated next to Ramses on the settee, Nefret reached for the whiskey she had "borrowed" and ceremoniously poured it into three glasses.

"It tastes even nastier than the cigarettes," she decided after a tentative sip.

"I don't like it very much either," Ramses admitted.

"Then why did you keep asking for it?" David inquired curiously.

"You know why. Mother understood too; it was a rather touching gesture, really."

David leaned back in his chair. "Perhaps now she will admit you are a man and will let you do what you like — even smoke cigarettes!"

Ramses smiled. "If she had not read me so many lectures about the evils of smoking, I probably would not do it."

Nefret put her glass on the table and nerved herself to speak. He looked all right and he sounded all right, but she knew he wasn't. Something had to be done about it. She couldn't bear the thought of him lying awake night after night, staring into the darkness. "Do you want to talk about it?" she demanded.

"No."

"Then I will. Did you mean to kill him?"

"Nefret!" David exclaimed.

"Be still, David. I know what I'm doing." At least I hope I do, she thought. She reached for Ramses's hand. It was like holding a bundle of sticks. "Did you, Ramses?"

"No! No, I only . . ." He tried to pull his hand away, but she hung on. There was no way he could free it without hurting her. "I don't know," he said in a ragged whisper. "Oh, God. I don't know!"

He turned blindly toward her and she moved to meet him, holding him close with his face hidden against her breast.

"You did what had to be done," she said softly. "Do you think I would not have done it if I could, or David? You have friends who love you, Ramses. Don't shut us out. Don't try to bear everything alone. You would do the same for us, my dear."

She felt his breath go out in a long sigh. He raised

his head, and she sat back, letting him draw away.

"Thank you," he said formally.

"There are times when I could cheerfully kill you, Walter Peabody Emerson," Nefret said in a choked voice.

"I know. I'm sorry. I'm not very good at this sort of thing." He caught her hand and raised it to his lips. "Some day, perhaps, you will teach me how to do it."

"Are you feeling better?" David asked anxiously. "Perhaps you ought to have another glass of whiskey."

They all had one, and after they had talked a while longer they went with Nefret to where Risha was waiting. She graciously consented to be lifted onto his back. After she had gone they went to Ramses's room, where they found the bed already occupied.

"I suppose Nefret brought her," Ramses said resignedly, trying to remove Sekhmet from the pillow. Claws extended, body flattened, she adhered like a limpet. Ramses threw himself down next to the cat and clasped his hands behind his head.

"Do you want to go to sleep?" David asked, sitting cross-legged on the floor. "I will leave if you are tired."

"I'm not tired. Is there something you want to talk about?"

"Only — I hope you are all right now. I saw you were troubled, but I did not know what to say."

"I'm all right."

"Nefret always knows the right thing to say."

"She knew that time. I still don't know the answer to her question, but it had to be asked. And now . . . now I can face it, whatever the answer is."

"She is wonderful. What a woman!"

"Yes. I hope you are not going to fall in love with her, David."

"She is my sister, my comrade. Anyhow, you will marry her one day —"

"Will I?"

"But surely it is the most suitable arrangement," David said, puzzled by his reaction. "It is how such things are done, even in your England. You like one another, and she is very wealthy as well as very beautiful. Why, don't you want to marry her?"

Even David, who knew Ramses better than anyone else, had never seen his friend look like that. It was as if the skin had been stripped from his face, baring not bone and muscle, but raw emotion. David caught his breath. "Forgive me. I did not understand."

"You still don't. Not entirely."

"No," David admitted. "I have read the stories you gave me, and the poems; there are poems in Arabic too, about the desire of a man for a woman. I understand that, but your Western talk about love confuses me a great deal. You make such a fuss about such a simple thing!"

"It really cannot be described," Ramses said, staring abstractedly at the cat, now lying across his stomach. "It must be experienced. Like being extremely drunk."

"Perhaps you would rather not talk about it."

"Why not? This has been a night for exposing

myself, I may as well finish the job. Nefret was right about that, bless her; it is a relief to unburden oneself to a friend, but I could not talk about this to her."

David made an encouraging noise. Ramses started to sit up, but Sekhmet refused to move. "Damn," he said. "Well, let me think how to explain it. Take my mother, for example. Would you call her beautiful?"

"Well —"

"No, David. She is a handsome lady, and she has many admirable qualities. But to my father she is quite simply the most beautiful, desirable, intelligent, amusing, exasperating, infuriating, wonderful woman on the face of the earth. He loves her for all those qualities, including the ones that drive him wild; and that is how I feel about Nefret. She does have a few maddening characteristics, you know."

"But she is beautiful," David said, bewildered.

"Yes. But that is not why I . . . I said it was impossible to explain."

"All right, then," David said with the air of a man trying to follow a maze blindfolded and in a thick fog. "You feel this — feeling. Why is that a difficulty? You want her, why should you not have her? Your parents would be pleased, I think, and she is very fond of you —"

Ramses groaned. "If you were starving, would a crust of bread content you?"

"It would be better than nothing. Oh," David said. "A poetic metaphor, was it?"

"Not a very good one, evidently. I know she is fond of me. She is fond of you too, and of Mother and Father, and the damned cats!" Unconsciously

he had begun stroking Sekhmet, who had the good sense, for once, not to react by sticking her claws into him. "Do you suppose I could be satisfied with that? She mustn't know how I feel about her, David, not unless — until — I can prove I am worthy of her and make her feel the same for me. Rather a tall order, that! As for my parents, it will be years before they consider me old enough to marry."

"How old must you be?" David asked.

Ramses groaned again and raised his arms to cover his face. "My father was almost thirty. Uncle Walter was twenty-six. Mr. Petrie was well over forty!"

The methodical catalogue would have sounded funny if he had not been so tragically in earnest. David found it equally discouraging. To eighteen, thirty sounds like the brink of senility.

"Your feelings may change," he suggested.

"I wish I could believe they would."

David did not know quite what to say to that. He ventured, "I must say it sounds damned uncomfortable."

Ramses laughed wryly and sat up, cradling the cat in one arm. "The most difficult part is keeping my feelings hidden. She is so sweet and so affectionate, and when she touches me I . . . What the devil, I may be lucky; I may have to control myself for only ten or eleven years instead of fifteen or twenty. What am I going to do with this damned cat?"

"Let her stay with you," David said. "You shouldn't blame her because she is not Bastet. She cannot help that."

"You are quite a philosopher, David. Why don't you point out that I should sympathize with another creature suffering the pangs of unrequited love?" He added in a gentler voice, "Thank you, my brother. It has helped me to talk of her."

"Whenever you like," David said. "Even if I do not understand."

They embraced in the Arab fashion, and Ramses clapped his friend on the back as the English do. "Perhaps you will someday."

"God forbid," David said sincerely.

By Saturday we were ready to resume work — though not on tomb Twenty-A. After mapping its position and dimensions, Emerson had ordered the entrance filled. He had gone back to his original plan, and we would begin that day on number Forty-four. My limb was still a bit stiff, so he considerately slowed his steps to mine and let the children go on ahead. Ramses had Sekhmet draped over one shoulder; he had hold of her hindquarters to keep her from slipping off and I could see her face, set in a blissful smirk.

"I am relieved he has taken to the poor thing at last," I remarked. "She was positively pining away."

"You are a hopeless sentimentalist, Peabody," Emerson said. "That cat doesn't give a curse who holds her, so long as someone does."

"She may not need Ramses, but he needs her," I said. "And now poor Anubis can return. He was jealous, you know."

"Of me? Nonsense." But he looked pleased all the same. Anubis had brought him a rat that morning, the first time in weeks he had offered that courtesy.

"We have had a good many cats around in one form or another," I said jestingly. "Mrs. Jones's name is Katherine, and she does remind one of a pleasant tabby. I think Cyrus calls her Cat when they are — er — when they are in private. He slipped once, and used that name."

"That is a commonplace and rather insulting observation," Emerson scoffed. "Men who despise women speak of them as cats or kittens; I am surprised you should countenance it."

"There are worse things one might be compared with," I replied. "Have I ever reminded you —"

"Never, my dear. A tiger, perhaps, but never anything so harmless as a domestic cat."

The sound of Nefret's laughter floated back to us and Emerson smiled. "It is good to see them so fond and friendly. You must be as proud of them as I."

"Now you are being sentimental, Emerson."

"There is nothing wrong with a little sentiment," Emerson declared, squeezing my arm against his side. "I am one of the most fortunate of men, Peabody, and I am not ashamed to say so. I could wish no more for our children than that they find the same happiness I have found with you."

A shiver ran through me.

"Now what's the matter?" Emerson demanded. "Confound it, Peabody, I thought you would appreciate my graceful little compliment. If you are having premonitions or dire forebodings, keep the damned things to yourself, curse it!"

He was his old self again, his handsome blue eyes snapping with temper. I laughed and leaned on his arm, as he likes me to do, and his good humor was restored.

It would not require extraordinary foresight to realize that even bright, confident youth may suffer sorrow and grief; but it was not one of my famous premonitions that had caused that involuntary shudder. I had forgot the dream until Emerson spoke.

I had seen the three together just as they were now, walking in the sunlight with the blue sky arching above. Slowly and inexorably the heavens darkened from azure, to gray, to a deeper gray, until the entire sky was black with stormclouds. From the north and east came a rumbling of thunder, and a long spear of lightning split the boiling clouds. It wrapped round them like a rope of living light, binding them together as the avenging serpents had entwined Laocoön and his children.

I did not need Dr. Freud or an Egyptian dream papyrus to know the meaning of that vision. When it would come I did not know. That it would come I did not doubt.